JENNY'S
MOUNTAIN

JENNY'S
MOUNTAIN

▲▲▲▲▲▲▲

ELAINE LONG

ST. MARTIN'S PRESS / *New York*

JENNY'S MOUNTAIN. Copyright © 1987 by Elaine Long.
All rights reserved.
Printed in the United States of America.
No part of this book may be used or reproduced
in any manner whatsoever without written permission
except in the case of brief quotations
embodied in critical articles or reviews.
For information, address St. Martin's Press,
175 Fifth Avenue, New York, N.Y. 10010.

Design by M. Paul

Library of Congress Cataloging in Publication Data

Long, Elaine.
  Jenny's mountain.
  I. Title.
PS3562.04937J4   1987   813'.54   87-16277
ISBN 0-312-01049-4

First Edition

10 9 8 7 6 5 4 3 2 1

To my husband Arthur.

To that old powder man, Ray Osborne.

In memory of Max Cannady.

JENNY'S
MOUNTAIN

CHAPTER

1

▲▲▲▲▲▲

When the first pain hit Jenny sharply in the small of her back, she cried out and grabbed the edge of the sink. Billy, who was scooting an empty milk carton across the floor, stopped making truck noises and looked up.

"What's the matter, Mama?"

Jenny picked up the one-legged alarm clock and made a mental note of the time. "I think our baby is ready to come and use the crib."

Billy crawled to the crib in the corner of the room, stood up, and peered through the bars. "The baby's not here," he said.

The pain eased, and Jenny laughed. "No, not yet, but I'm still glad we made you a new bed."

Billy ran to the padded bedspring that rested on the floor near the wall. He plopped onto it, stuck his feet out, and bounced up and down.

Jenny wiped off the sink, scratching in vain at the rusty streaks under the faucet. She took Billy's pants, Mike's shirt, a bra, and a pair of panties from the wire above the coal-oil stove. Pushing aside the sheet that curtained the double bed near the corner of the room, she put the pants and shirt into the labeled wooden milk crates at the foot of the bed. Mike's crate was a mess, as usual. She tossed the bra and panties onto the bed and sat down on its edge. The headboard banged against the metal stall that enclosed the sink, shower, and stool in the far corner of the room. She reached around her immense belly to the box labeled JENNY.

"Billy, come here a minute, will you?" The little boy bounced once more and then skipped over to the big bed. "Crawl under the bed and pull out that little suitcase, please."

Billy lay on his stomach to wriggle under the bed and slid back, pulling out a scuffed brown overnight bag. Jenny reached for the rope handle and lifted the suitcase. Quickly she put a hairbrush, toothbrush, and a pair of sneakers into the case; then she stood and, taking her lavender terry-cloth robe down from its nail, packed it on top of the shoes.

Billy ran across the room and dived onto the bedspring again. Jenny took a deep breath and followed slowly, picking up a paperback novel with a ragged cover from the milk crate full of similar books that stood beside the kitchen table. She packed the book on top of her robe and closed the suitcase.

"Billy, I want you to stay on your bed and play. I'll be back in a minute." She reached for her coat on the hook by the door just as another grinding pain bored into the small of her back. She gasped, bit her lip, and hung on to the coat hook until the pain receded; then she struggled into her coat and returned to the table to look at the clock. Nine minutes had passed since the first pain. She put the clock in her pocket and turned toward the door, but before she could open it, Billy was tugging at the edge of her coat. Jenny looked down, then squatted to put her arms around him.

"It's all right, honey. I'm going to try to find somebody to take us to town."

"Daddy could take us."

"Daddy's at the mine already."

"I want to go with you." Billy's eyes were wide in his pale face. He still held a fistful of coat.

Jenny put her hand on his taut knuckles. "Okay, Billy, but we both need boots. Can you help me?"

Billy ran to the corner beside the door and brought back two pairs of four-buckle overshoes. Jenny stood, lifting first one foot and then the other as Billy tugged the bulky galoshes on over her shoes. He hunkered down on the floor, sticking his tongue out and grunting with effort as he pulled the buckles over and pushed them down.

Jenny ruffled his hair and said, "Good. Now climb up on the kitchen table, and I'll do you." Billy grabbed his boots, clambered onto a kitchen chair, turned, and sat down on the table with a thump, his arms straight out, a boot dangling from each hand. He swung his feet, banging the table leg noisily, until Jenny caught one foot and said, "Whoa. I can't shoe a galloping horse."

Billy scrunched his eyes to tiny slits and giggled. Jenny put his boots on, then zipped Billy into his coat and pulled mittens over his hands. When she slipped her own hands into her gloves, her right index finger poked through the split end. She wiggled the finger at Billy and said, "How do you do, Lord William. I'm Lady Pointer." The finger bowed. Billy giggled again and jumped down from the table.

As she went out onto the wide plank flooring that stretched across the front of the small house, serving as both porch and doorstep, Jenny glanced at the sky. It had stopped snowing; the clouds were patchy. She looked up the steep embankment toward the highway. The sun was already slipping down behind the top of the mountain on the other side of the road.

Billy jumped off the porch into the partially frozen mud. "Is Daddy gonna get stuck on the mine road again?"

"I hope not." Jenny stepped down and held out her hand to Billy. "Let's go see if anybody's home."

They went around the corner of the little frame house and walked across the snowy ground to the two trailers parked on the other side of the lot near the dump fence. As they crossed the rutted drive to the Bradleys' trailer, another pain slid down Jenny's back and encircled her lower belly. She stopped, drawing a sharp breath that brought icy air into her lungs and made her cough.

"Mama, you're squeezin' me," Billy said, struggling to free his hand from her grip. She let go of his hand and took the clock from her pocket. Only eight minutes this time. She reached for the stair rail on Mom Bradley's trailer and pulled herself up the steps.

She knocked, but the trailer echoed emptily. Jenny turned. "Mom Bradley's always up at the bar this time of day, but I thought Richard might be here." She went down the steps and started around the corner of the trailer. "Maybe he's out back."

Billy said, "If Richard's not out back working on that damn old truck, he's prob'ly 'horing round in his Caddy."

Jenny whirled and stared at Billy. "And who told you that?"

"That's what Tony says."

"Yes," Jenny said, "I'm sure that's what Mr. DiAngelo says, but I'd just as soon you didn't say it." She held out her hand, and they walked behind the trailer to where a faded green Ford pickup sat, its hood raised, the engine buried under lumpy-looking mounds of snow. The truck rode high on immense wheels. Mike's Chevy had four-wheel drive, too, but Jenny could at least climb into it. She stood on tiptoe, peering into the driver's window of the Ford. The keys dangled from the ignition, but that didn't solve the problem. She'd never be able to get her pregnant bulk into that seat without help. As she looked around for something to stand on, she noticed that the right rear end of the pickup was jacked up, the wheel missing.

"Damn," she said under her breath.

"What did you say, Mama?"

"Let's go see if Mr. DiAngelo is home."

They crossed the wide muddy space at the back of the lot, the soles of their overshoes quickly gathering mud. Tony's two-story shed pushed up against the slope of the mountain. The Douglas firs at the bottom of the slope, still winter-dark although it was the end of April, were already in shadow. At the crest of the hill, the sun's watery light settled in the fringe of trees.

Jenny walked quickly toward Tony's shop. The building was sided with corrugated iron aged to a rich rust; faded black letters read ROCKY MOUNTAIN SALVAGE, DOLBY, COLORADO. A sagging pole fence extended along the far side of the shop toward the house and the highway, enclosing an acre of old trucks and crippled machinery, newly coated with snow. A rusted, long-necked crane capped with furry whiteness reminded Jenny of the snowy egret in one of the books Tony had brought her from the dump.

She opened the door to the shop and stepped inside, blinking in the darkness. The acrid smell of the grease-soaked dirt floor rose to her nostrils. Billy pressed his face against the side of her leg. It was warm in the shop. Jenny hadn't realized how cold she was until she felt the warm dark air enfold her. She leaned against the doorjamb and rubbed her icy index finger. Tony obviously wasn't here. He slept on a cot in the little room off the back of the shop, but he had probably gone directly from the dump to the bar.

"Why does Tony live in the dark, Mama? Doesn't he have a house?"

Jenny turned away from the shop, pulling the door closed behind her. "We live in Tony's house," she answered, glancing toward the front trailer. Mom Bradley had said yesterday that somebody new had rented it from Tony. Jenny thought she'd seen a light. She hurried back across the driveway to the other trailer, which rested on cinder blocks but had no skirting.

One large cinder block served as a step. The trailer door was ajar. Jenny stuck her head in and called out, "Anybody home?" There was a pile of boxes in the middle of the floor, but nobody answered. A small pain skittered through Jenny's stomach. "Let's go back to the house and get warm, Billy."

"Aren't we going to town?"

Jenny swallowed and looked up the gravel road toward Mom's Bar and Café, which had the nearest telephone. She could see the neon light at the top where the road rose out of the gulch.

"I don't think we have time to walk three miles today, honey." She wished Mike were there. "You go get warm."

Billy ran to the house and went inside, leaving the door open. Jenny followed slowly. Just as she stepped up on the porch another labor pain grabbed her insides, and she hugged her belly, bent awkwardly against herself, until the pain subsided. Then she went into the house and shut the door behind her. Tears stung her eyes, and her pulse beat hard in her throat. I can't have this baby by myself. She leaned against the door, blinking back the tears. Billy started to cry.

Jenny moved to the counter. She took crackers and peanut butter to the table and made several small sandwiches. She smiled at Billy, who had stopped crying to watch her.

"Eat these all up, Bill. We're going to go mountain climbing."

While Billy ate, Jenny took a pair of jeans from Mike's milk crate and struggled into them. They were at least six inches too long for her; they would never have fit over her boots if they hadn't been ripped at the bottom. They wouldn't zip over her enormous belly, but she jerked them on, fastening the waistband to her maternity skirt with a safety pin and stuffing the legs into the tops of her overshoes.

She extracted a khaki canvas backpack from the pile of gold pans, chains, rock hammers, pieces of iron, and chunks of rock in the tool corner. Then she opened the suitcase again, taking the clothes, brushes, and the book and putting them into the pack. She took her wallet from the table, placed it in the pack, and snapped the flap shut.

She wiped the peanut butter from Billy's face and hands and put his mittens back on. "Now, Billy, come over here to the bed and pull these straps around where I can reach them."

Billy helped her get the backpack straps over her shoulders. Jenny waited while another pain rocked through her—now they were only six minutes apart—and then stood up. The backpack pulled sharply on her shoulders. She swayed, but managed to regain her balance.

She checked the thermostat on the coal-oil stove, took Billy's hand, and went back out into the cold air. The light was fading. She looked up the steep embankment toward the highway, where she could see the tops of cars as they sped past. If she and Billy could somehow get up there . . . Glancing back toward the gravel road, she saw no lights. She turned her attention back to the embankment.

"We're going to be mountain goats, Billy. You start first. Climb up on that rock. When you get there, say 'Baa-baa,' and I'll come too."

Billy didn't giggle—he didn't even smile. He just grabbed a small bush on the slope and pulled himself up to the rock that Jenny pointed to. When he reached the top he turned and said, "Now, you come."

Jenny searched for a handhold and began to climb the bank. The bulk of her belly held her at the wrong angle, and the pack pulled her backward, but she leaned into the hill and reached Billy's rock at last.

As she scrambled up beside him the sky began to spit hard kernels of snow. Jenny tried to smile. "Up you go, Billy Goat. See that rock there? It's your next mountain."

Billy turned and went up again, his big overshoes slipping in the snow. Jenny followed his path with her eyes until he made the rock and then wiped the snow from her face and dragged herself up after him.

The slope seemed to get steeper with each rock they reached. The larger rocks were slick with the new snow, but they provided an almost level ledge where Jenny and Billy could rest.

"Mama, my front hurts," Billy said, putting his mittened hands against his chest.

"Mine, too," Jenny said. She drew him into her arms to warm him, trying to ignore the insistent pain throbbing inside her.

"Will Daddy know we're on the mountain being goats?"

She should have left a note for Mike. Jenny looked down the slope toward the white house, which seemed far away and tiny. It was too late now. She could never get Billy back up this hill.

She stood and hoisted Billy toward the crest of the bank. "Stay on the side of the road, Billy," she said as he disappeared above her head. Before she could look down she lost her footing and fell. She reached for the large rock she'd been standing on, missed it, and slid down, her fingers scrabbling for a handhold.

The thorns of a wild rosebush scraped along her bare index finger, and she grabbed for the branch. As she gripped the rough bark, thorns bit into the flesh of her hand. Then she heard the sound of air brakes and the screech of tires on the highway above her.

"Billy!" she screamed, "Oh, my God, Billy!"

CHAPTER

2

▲▲▲▲▲▲

Jenny let go of the branch with one hand and, reaching above her, found a small rock that seemed securely embedded in the mountain. She tried to drag herself upward, but the labor pains were starting again. She lay down on the slope to let them pass, straining to hear some sound from Billy. She was just about to lift herself once more when she heard a man's voice.

"What's your name, little fellow?"

A tiny, scared-sounding reply: "I'm Billy." Tears stung Jenny's eyes, and her throat ached with relief.

The deep male voice said, "Where do you live, Billy?"

"My mama's down there," Billy said.

Jenny heard footsteps in the gravel at the side of the highway. Before she could call out, the man said, "Oh, my God. Your mama really is down there. Here, Billy. You hold on to this bush and don't move. I'll go help your mother."

Jenny gripped the bush tightly and tried to pull herself up. Suddenly a pair of the biggest work boots she'd ever seen were planted in the snow beside her. The man knelt and put his arm around Jenny's waist. He grasped her left arm firmly with his free hand.

"You can let go of the rosebush," he said. His voice was matter-of-fact, almost businesslike. Jenny let go of the branch and then the rock.

The man stood up slowly, drawing Jenny up with him. As soon as she stood erect another contraction began. Jenny swayed, and the man put both arms around her. He held her close to him until the pain subsided. He was so tall that Jenny's head barely grazed his chin.

She looked up after the pain eased. The man smiled, his blue eyes crinkling at the corners, and said, "Come on, let's get you up the hill to Billy."

He turned her around in his arms and walked her up the slope in front of him, supporting her body. When they reached the top, Billy let go of the juniper he was clinging to and ran to her. She smoothed his hair as he leaned against her.

A blue and silver semitrailer was idling on the other side of the road. The tall man said to Billy, "You want to go for a ride in my truck?"

Billy looked up at Jenny; she nodded. He let go of her coat, and the truck driver swung him up into his arms. "I'll be back for you in a minute," he said to Jenny.

The sun was almost out of sight behind the mountain, and a chilly wind snaked down the canyon. Jenny shivered. Her left hand hurt. She looked at it. Thorns stuck from her glove like porcupine quills from a dog's nose. Another labor pain shook her as she looked at the truck. She could see Billy's head in the driver's window. The tall man waited near the rear of the trailer while a green pickup and a potato-chip delivery van sped past before he ran across the highway. Jenny smiled slightly. He was a lot more graceful than he should have been with feet that big.

When the truck driver reached Jenny, he bent and picked her up in his arms. "I'm too heavy," she protested.

He laughed. "What do you weigh? Ninety pounds?"

"A hundred and ten pounds most of the time," she said, putting her arm around his neck. Before there was time for another contraction she had been lifted into the warm cab, where Billy, with both hands on the big wheel, was making truck noises.

"Is there a hospital near here?" the truck driver asked her, scooting Billy across the seat and releasing the brakes.

She nodded. "It's on the other side of town, three blocks off the highway. You'll see the signs."

As the truck pulled onto the highway Jenny leaned her head against the window; the fan poured hot air on her legs and feet, which dangled awkwardly inches above the floor.

"I feel like Humpty Dumpty," she said.

The man looked over and grinned. "If you go out with me like this very often, I'll have to build you a footstool."

Jenny giggled nervously. He was nice. She'd probably screwed up his whole schedule. "I'm sorry we're such a bother," she said. "My husband is up at his mine, and I couldn't find anyone else to take me to the hospital."

"Your husband's a miner?"

Jenny bit her lip and waited for another contraction to pass. Then she said, "Only part time. He does construction part time, too, and goes up to the mine after he gets off work."

"Is he mining for gold?"

"The assays show some gold—more silver, though."

The trucker drove steadily through town. Billy sat in the middle of the seat, his head against Jenny's side, his eyes on the driver's hands. The man turned into a residential street that led to the hospital, swinging the truck around the curved drive in front of the emergency entrance. He set the brake and climbed out quickly, leaving the truck running.

He ran in through the emergency door and came back a moment later with a wheelchair. Lifting Jenny from the truck, he wheeled her to a level spot, then turned back for Billy.

Jenny looked at the side of the truck where the words TULSA TRUCKING COMPANY were painted, blue on silver.

Billy ran along beside the wheelchair as the truck driver took Jenny to the admitting window. The woman behind the counter had just asked for the name of Jenny's doctor when a security guard came in and said, "Is that your rig out there, mister?" At the same moment, an agonizing pain made Jenny gasp.

Billy started to cry. "Mama, I have to go potty," he said.

The guard said, "You'll have to move that truck; you're blocking the ambulance entrance."

The truck driver looked at Jenny and Billy and turned to the guard. "Let me take the boy to the bathroom, and then I'll move the truck."

Jenny's pain was constant now. The truck driver put his hand on her shoulder. "Don't worry about Billy. I'll look after him." Jenny looked up through the tears that suddenly clouded her eyes. Because of this big man, the baby would be all right. She touched her hand to his for a moment. Then he turned, picked Billy up, and went down the hall.

The woman behind the desk said, "Do you have insurance?"

Jenny shook her head. "No, but we can pay the bill." She didn't voice the rest: My husband says we can pay the bill as long as there aren't any complications and I can get out of here in two days.

She couldn't focus on the questions the clerk asked her; when they were asked a second time, she couldn't remember the right answers. The pain roared loudly in her ears and she shivered uncontrollably, making the wheelchair bounce on its rubber wheels.

Finally someone dressed in white rolled her away from the desk and down a long blurry hallway. Someone pulled the pack from her back, helped her out of her clothes, and lifted her into a bed. She turned from side to side as the pain scraped down the inside of her belly and tore at her back. She moaned, and a nurse arrived with a needle.

Jenny roused herself. "No," she said thickly, "no drugs. Not good for the baby." Then she tangled her hands in the bedclothes and held on as the nurse faded back from the bed.

The pain surged forward again, roaring like the wind at the top of the mountain. The trees around her bent and swayed. She stumbled along a road. The wind made her eyes tear. She huddled inside her coat collar and kept going, searching the weeds and tall grass. Hugging the pain inside herself, turning her head from side to side, she nearly stumbled over the body. It was partly hidden in the grass near the grove of aspens, but when Jenny bent to lift the head that lay face down in the matted weeds, rough hands pulled her back, lifted her up. Her body heaved and writhed as she struggled, but her feet were shoved into cold metal stirrups, her shoulders held by strong fingers.

"Bear down now," a voice said above her head. "It won't be long."

But it seemed long. The pain would not be pushed out, would not be pushed away. She heard another voice say, "I don't care what she said. Give her the shot. I want her more relaxed."

She whispered, "Mama," and then the storm rose up again. It washed over her, and she cried out loud, "Mama, Mama." Her own voice echoed in her head and then was swallowed up by the roar of the wind.

CHAPTER
3

▲▲▲▲▲▲

"Mrs. Williams."

Jenny stirred, pulling her shoulder away from the insistent hand.

"Jenny, wake up. Your daughter is hungry."

Jenny rolled over and sat up in bed. She tried to remember where she was, looking into the shadows behind the nurse. Finally she made out the shapes of other beds in the light coming from the hall. She couldn't remember being brought here.

"What time is it?" she asked.

"About nine thirty. You were tired, but you've had a good nap, and your daughter's hungry. She's been keeping the nursery in an uproar."

"My daughter . . ." Now she remembered. She had been in the woods, and then someone had said, "It's a girl."

She sat up straight. "Oh, let me see her. I want to hold her." The nurse, who carried the baby in the curve of one arm, pulled the privacy curtain around the bed and turned on the small light. She pushed a button, raising Jenny's bed to a semisitting position, and laid the blanket-swathed child in Jenny's arms. Jenny looked down into her daughter's solemn pink face. The baby sucked on her fist and blinked. Jenny glanced up at the nurse. "Can I be alone with her?"

"Do you need help getting her to nurse?"

"No. Between the two of us, I'm sure we'll manage."

The nurse left the ward, and Jenny rested the baby on her outstretched legs, rolling the blanket back so she could see her child. She counted the baby's fingers and toes, noticed the gauze around the umbilical cord, and checked the diaper. Then she lifted the baby in her arms and bent her face to the tiny head.

"Hello, daughter," she said, sniffing. "You smell good, all warm and sweet. They tell me you've been bothering the other folks in the nursery, but I don't believe that for a minute. Why, look at you: just as patient as can be."

The baby made little sucking sounds against her fist and looked up at Jenny.

"And you see more than they think you do, too. Don't you, Corinne Mary Williams?"

Jenny reached inside her nightgown and slipped her breast free. She moved the baby to the curve of her left elbow, placing her right hand, palm down, on her left breast with the first two fingers on either side of the nipple. She rubbed the nipple against the baby's cheek. Then, gently pushing the little fist aside, she guided the tip of the nipple into the baby's mouth.

"Here you go, Corey. We're safe in our tent."

Corey tightened her mouth around the nipple and began to suck. Jenny moved her hand to her daughter's head. The soft hair was so blond she looked almost bald. "My daughter," Jenny whispered. "I wonder where your daddy is and if that nice truck driver is still baby-sitting your big brother." Jenny was still aware of pain in her lower body and in her left hand, but the hurting was far off, at the edge of her senses. In the center were just Corey and Jenny. "I sure bounced you around enough getting here, didn't I?"

"Jenny?" a voice whispered. A dark head popped around the edge of the curtain.

"Mike? Oh, Mike, come look at her."

Jenny's husband came inside the curtain. He bent and kissed Jenny on the cheek. "I'm sorry I didn't get here in time," he said.

"Everything worked out," Jenny said. "Where's Billy?"

"He's at the shop with Tony now. When I first got here, though, he was having the time of his life bouncing on the biggest foot I ever saw."

Jenny laughed. "Isn't it terrible? That poor truck driver rescued me, and all I can remember are his feet; I can't remember what his face looks like. I hope he doesn't get fired for delaying his run."

"Don't worry about him. I tried to give him ten dollars, but he wouldn't take it."

"You said the first time you came here. You mean you were here earlier?"

"Yeah, but they wouldn't let me in."

"Be serious. You're the father."

"I am serious. They said I was too dirty."

"Dirty? You didn't come here in your mining clothes?"

"Yep. With a little extra mud from getting stuck."

"Oh, Mike."

"Well, what the hell. I stopped off at Mom Bradley's for a couple of beers—she didn't throw me out for being too dirty—and then when I got down to the house and found you and Billy gone, I was so goddamn scared, I didn't even think about my clothes."

"I couldn't find anybody to help me, Mike."

"Yeah, I know. I ran all over the place. Richard was gone; the new people hadn't seen you."

"Where are they from?"

"Jesus, Jenny, I don't know. I seen that empty suitcase on the bed and knew you left in a hurry. I didn't stop to ask them their life story. I was trying to find you."

"You look nice now," Jenny said.

Mike smiled. "After I found out that you and the baby were okay, I went home and cleaned up as fast as I could."

Jenny reached her free arm up, put it around her husband's neck, and pulled his head down to hers. She kissed him on the mouth. He smelled of beer and shaving cream.

"Look at Corey," Jenny said. "She's blond like me, but I think she's got your eyes."

Mike put his finger inside the baby's fist. Corey slept peacefully, her lips still holding the nipple.

"Do you think you can get out of here in two days after all this?" he asked Jenny, avoiding her eyes.

"Sure. Most of my pain came from climbing the hill to the highway." She showed him the angry red marks on her hand. "I grabbed hold of a rosebush."

The nurse came into the ward then and poked her head inside the curtains. "I'm sorry, Mr. Williams, you'll have to go now. Official visiting hours were over more than an hour ago." She turned as a buzzer rang in the hall. "I'll be back for the baby in a minute."

Mike pulled his finger from the baby's fist. "I'm glad you're not mad because I wasn't here," he said. "I'll see you tomorrow. Do you need anything?"

"No, I don't." Jenny hesitated. "But . . . do you think we could afford a box of throwaway diapers for the first day I'm home?"

"Yeah, there ought to be that much left over from the hospital bill."

As he started to leave, Jenny said, "What was that truck driver's name?"

Mike turned back, frowning. "I don't know, Jenny. I never asked him."

CHAPTER

4

▲▲▲▲▲▲

It rained steadily the first two weeks Jenny and Corey were home. Mike stayed home from the mine the first Sunday, but he went back to his job on Monday and back to working at the mine soon after that.

On the second Monday Jenny and Billy had just waved good-bye to Mike at the door and were turning back toward the warm room when a car pulled up alongside the duplex.

"Hi, Mom Bradley," Billy said, running out into the rain as the heavyset woman hoisted herself up from under the steering wheel. She had a bulging black purse in one hand and a brown paper sack in the other. Swinging her broad hip against the door of the car, she slammed it shut. Billy hopped along beside her as she lumbered toward the porch.

Jenny was laughing, and the older woman said, "What's so funny?"

"I like your third hand—the one you use to shut the car door."

"Huh," Mom Bradley grunted, stepping up onto the porch. "I hit that swinging door between the kitchen and the bar two hundred times a day with both hands full. I need some extra help from somewhere."

"Come in out of the rain," Jenny said, opening the door. "Billy, kick your shoes off. They're all muddy."

Mom Bradley waddled over to the kitchen table, set her purse and the package down, and struggled out of her denim jacket. She grasped her flowered polyester shirt at each side and gave a sharp pull, smoothing the bright material across her bosom and ample belly.

Jenny said, "You're wearing your new yellow slacks. Aren't you afraid this mud will stain them?"

"Yeah, it probably will, but what the hell. It's gloomy up there at the bar. I wanted to look like a broad band of color." She patted a chunky thigh and sat down in one of the kitchen chairs.

Jenny said, "You want some coffee? I can make a fresh pot."

"Sure," Mom Bradley said, "I always want a cup of coffee, but I really came to see that baby again."

Jenny filled the pot, scooped coffee into it from a red can, and ducked under the line of diapers drying above the stove to set the pot on the burner.

"Why in hell doesn't Mike take all that stuff to the Laundromat and dry it for you?" Mom Bradley said.

"Money's kind of tight," Jenny said, picking Corey up from the crib and going to the bed to change her. Billy climbed up beside his sister to watch.

"Poor Corey," he said. "You don't got a potty thing like me."

"Scoot," said Jenny. "The baby has everything a girl needs. Don't go calling her poor Corey."

"Did I wear pajamas on my feet when I was a baby?"

"You wore these very same pajamas," Jenny said, holding Corey against one shoulder. "Why don't you play on your bed, honey. The floor's cold."

Billy said, "I don't want to play. I want to see Mom Bradley." He went to the heavy woman's side. She put her arm around him for a minute and then reached for her purse.

"Do you want a breath mint, Billy?"

Billy nodded, popped the candy disk into his mouth, and stood sucking on it as Mom Bradley took the baby in her arms. She put her fat index finger under the baby's chin. Corey studied the woman gravely, her fist against her cheek.

"You feeling okay, Jenny?" Mom Bradley asked.

"Now that my hand has healed."

"What about the birth pains? You never mention them."

Jenny glanced at her daughter. "I forget all about them when I look at Corey."

The coffee began to perk. Jenny took a cup from the shelf above the sink, filled it, and set it on the table.

"Here, let me take the baby."

Mom Bradley relinquished Corey; Jenny put her back in her crib and sat down at the table.

"You look tired," Mom Bradley said. "You don't wait up for Mike, do you?"

"No, I go to bed when Billy does, but I have to nurse Corey in the night, and last night the new people were having a loud fight. At least, *he* was loud."

"Yeah," Mom Bradley said. "He was pretty tanked up when he left the bar."

"He talks awful to her. Is she his wife?"

"She uses his name: Karen Stocker."

"What's his name?"

"Tully. Tully Stocker, and he's a bad one in my opinion. Kind of nice-looking, if you like a bit of a beer belly, but mean-mouthed when he's drinking."

"Why do you let him get so drunk?"

"Hell, Jenny, I can't start running my customers off. With the construction company moving, business is bad enough. Half of 'em are gone already. You think you'll be moving?"

"Mike's been cut back. He says we're barely making enough for truck payments, food, and rent, but he doesn't want to leave his claim."

"He'd have more money if he'd quit fooling around with that useless claim."

Jenny felt herself flush, but she said, "Maybe it's not so useless. He says the assay reports are getting better." She refilled her neighbor's cup.

Mom Bradley stirred two spoonfuls of sugar into her coffee. "Miners always think the next one's gonna be the big one. Mike's just been bit by an old bug."

Jenny didn't answer. Mom Bradley said, "I brought a present for the baby."

Jenny looked at her. "You did?"

Mom Bradley stared down into her cup. "It's something I made for Richard a long time ago." She unrolled the top of the brown paper sack and pulled out an afghan made of yellow and orange granny squares.

Jenny drew a quick breath. "It's beautiful," she said. "It looks brand new."

"Richard never liked it," Mom Bradley said. "He had a ratty old blanket he dragged around for years. I packed this away, thinking I might have a grandkid." She was silent for a long moment and then said, "I want Corey to have it."

Jenny touched the afghan. "It's so soft—and just the right size for the crib." She looked up at the other woman through sudden tears, seeing the bright double blur of the afghan and Mom Bradley's yellow and orange shirt. She wiped the back of her hand across her eyes and said, "Thank you, Mom B., I didn't know you crocheted."

Mom Bradley put her hands on the table and heaved herself upward. "That was when I was a lady of leisure. Right now, I've got to open up Mom's Café."

Jenny smiled and said, "Yes. It's not the same without Mom." She stood up and put her arm around the broad shoulders of her neighbor. "Thank you. This is the nicest present we've ever had."

Mom Bradley opened the door. "Well, lookit here; the sun's shining," she said.

Corey began to cry. Jenny picked her up and unbuttoned her shirt. She gave her breast to the baby, who sucked greedily. Jenny went to the door with Corey. Billy ran out, jumped from the porch, and squished his way through the mud to the car with Mom Bradley. He ran back to the porch as she drove away, his bare feet leaving muddy footprints on the floorboards.

"Can I play outside, Mama?"

Jenny leaned against the doorjamb. It was pleasant in the spring sun as the last little drops of water sparkled on the edge of the eaves, the trees on the mountains above the highway looking sharp-needled and clean after the rain.

"You can mess around in the mud for a minute," she said. She shifted Corey to the curve of her other arm. Corey tried to hang on to the nipple. "It's empty, you greedy little girl," Jenny said, tucking her left breast inside her blouse and releasing the right one for Corey, who began nursing again immediately.

"You're going to be as fat as Mom Bradley," Jenny said. She closed her eyes and let the sun warm them both. She could hear the traffic swishing through the puddles on the highway above them.

▽   ▽

The next morning at breakfast Jenny said to Mike, "Mom Bradley says we ought to wash at the Laundromat." Billy was stirring his egg with his toast, making big yolky circles.

"I can't spare the truck. Besides, we can't afford it," Mike said. "Unless you want to use the money in your jar."

Jenny glanced toward the shelf where she kept her jar of pennies, dimes, and nickles. She'd been saving up for three months, whenever there was any change left from the grocery money Mike gave her. She shook her head. "You know what that's for."

"Aren't you getting kind of big for a red wagon?" Mike teased her.

"I don't care. Billy and I could have fun with it. And I could pull both kids in it."

Mike laughed. "And haul more stuff home from Jenny's Supermarket. You better be careful or Tony will start charging you."

"Tony brings me stuff from the dump himself."

"Yeah. Books. Jesus, Jenny, what are you going to do with all these books? This ain't no library." Mike drained his cup and stood up.

"I'm going to read them. There's all kinds of stuff to learn." She turned to Billy. "Eat that and stop messing with it."

"What do you need to learn? You're a good cook and a good mama, and"—Mike leaned over and kissed her—"you're pretty damn good in bed, too. I don't think I can stand another two weeks. Didn't the doc say to wait a month?"

Jenny stood up and handed him his lunch bucket. "He said six weeks."

Mike took the bucket, but he stood looking at her. "Well, you're all right aren't you? We won't have to wait that long."

"What are we waiting for, Daddy?" Billy said.

Mike grinned at Jenny and turned to his son. "We're waiting for the big strike, Bill—the bonanza." He glanced around the room and said to Jenny, "I better go. I don't know what the hell time it is. I wish you hadn't squashed the damn clock."

Jenny thought of her long climb up the bank to the highway and her abrupt slide down. The clock she had carried in her pocket had hit a rock when she fell. Before she left the hospital Jenny had thrown the broken glass away, but she had brought the springs and gears home to Billy.

"If the weather stays nice, maybe we'll go find another clock."

Mike came over and put his arm around her. "You're a funny

little thing," he said, looking down at her. "You honestly believe you can just go up to that dump and find another clock that runs."

Jenny moved away. "You make it sound like I'm simpleminded."

Mike said, "Jesus, you're a grouch these days."

Jenny bit her lip and said nothing. "Never mind," she said finally. "I've just got cabin fever. Will you be home late tonight?"

"Who can tell? The roads were pure gunk yesterday. All this damn rain—more like April than May. I put the compressor and the generator in the shop, but the rest of my supplies are still in that old cabin, and the roof leaks. I'll have to fix that."

"Won't somebody steal your supplies?"

"What somebody? Who would want to go seventeen miles—the last three on that mine road—to steal what little stuff I've got?"

"Well, I didn't know, since I've never been there."

"I keep the shop locked. It's tight."

Billy finished eating his toast and egg and climbed down from the wooden milk crate that served as his chair.

"Are you gonna go to work, Daddy?"

Mike set his lunch bucket down on the floor, picked Billy up, and tossed him into the air. "I just might go fishing instead."

Jenny watched him anxiously. Mike was probably late already. He tossed Billy a second time, then caught the squealing child and swung him to the floor. Picking up his lunch bucket again, he went over and looked into the crib. Corey lay asleep on her stomach with her bottom sticking up. Mike patted her rump. "Lucky kid. Still sacked out while your old man goes off to work."

When Mike finally left, Jenny sat back down at the table. She looked at her hands. They were rough from washing clothes every day. Her wedding ring was tight on her swollen finger. Another pile of dirty diapers had accumulated in the sink; wet clothes hung on the line and dishes littered the table. Her mother's house had looked like this toward the end, only there had been fewer dishes and more empty bottles.

Jenny shivered a little and looked down at the milk crate full of ragged books. Putting her head down on the table, she felt as if she might choke on the huge emptiness that rose up, blocking her mind. She began to cry.

She lifted her head when Billy shook her arm. "Mama, Corey's awake. Don't cry, Mama. It makes the baby cry."

The quaver in his voice caught Jenny's attention. She looked at her son. His eyes were blue like her own, and they reflected the same dark feeling she sometimes saw in the eyes that looked out at her from the mirror.

She could see the muscles jerking in his jaw, but Billy's eyes were dry. In her crib, Corey was already wailing. Jenny sniffed and got up.

"Come on, Billy," she said, picking up the baby and checking her diaper. "Let's take Corey up to see Tony."

Billy's face relaxed. He ran to the corner and picked up one of the rock sacks. "Are we gonna get a clock, Mama?"

The child never missed a thing. She and Mike ought to be more careful. She smiled and said, "I don't know, honey, but let's go shopping at Jenny's Supermarket and see what we can find."

CHAPTER

5

▲▲▲▲▲▲

Billy carried the canvas bag; Jenny carried Corey. They walked slowly up the sloping gravel road, the dump looming above them to the left and the highway to the right. Mom's Bar and Café was three miles ahead, where the dump road rose and widened out before joining the highway.

The May sun warmed the air. The rain had dissolved much of the snow, but there were a few stubborn drifts under the trees and in the shadows of the road banks. Jenny had decided not to wear the heavy overshoes; she was much more agile on the dump in tennis shoes. But Billy wore his overshoes, and he was slogging up the road, avoiding the gravel and the dry spine on the ruts by walking in the muddy puddles.

Jenny pushed her scarf back and let the sun shine directly on her head as she watched the sturdy little boy. He was only four, but he was so smart it sometimes scared her. We can't keep living down here by the dump when he starts school, she thought suddenly. Kids are mean. Let one of them call him trash and he'll be branded forever. Jenny shifted Corey to her other arm and pushed away the thought. If I'm going to be miserable, I might as well be doing the laundry, she told herself.

The rain had turned the new grass a fresh lime green. There was a friendly purple pasqueflower at the edge of the road in a tangle of old grass. Jenny stopped.

"Come back a minute, Billy, and see the flower."

The two of them squatted on the ground. Billy touched the fuzzy leaves. "Can I pick it?"

"No," Jenny said. "If we pick it, the next person won't get to enjoy it."

"Oh," said Billy, rocking back so he seemed to be sitting on top of his overshoes. He looked at the flower for a long time and then looked back at Jenny, his eyes purple-blue like the flower, his brown lashes as soft as the fuzz of its leaves. Jenny took one hand away from Corey and touched her son's face.

"I love you, Billy Bright," she said.

He giggled and said, "I'm Billy Michael Williams."

Jenny's knees began to ache from squatting. She rose and returned to the road. "Come along, then, Billy Michael Williams, and let's see what other treasures we can find while we're playing hooky."

Billy was already ahead of her, swinging his arms and seesawing his body from side to side. When they reached the dump gate, he yelled, "I see Tony," and ran toward the shack. Jenny followed more slowly with Corey, who slept intermittently, always peaceful.

Inside the high chain link fence that helped to contain the trash that was brought to the landfill, the road divided and wound around the dump. The caretaker's shack was on the right-hand spur, just inside the gate. Jenny could see Tony inside with Billy, who was bouncing up and down and talking as fast as he could. When Jenny got to the steps of the shack she heard Billy say, "And I drove that big truck all by myself."

Tony DiAngelo looked down at Jenny and grinned. Tony's grin always made Jenny feel good. The old man's face was the texture of leather, the color of walnuts. Creases and laugh lines rayed out from the corners of his dark brown eyes. His teeth were tobacco-stained; several were capped and the lower front one was missing. But Tony's grin appeared like fireworks in his dusky face.

"Hello, Mr. DiAngelo," Jenny said, taking the hand he held out to help her up the steps and into the shack.

"I thought you'd come today, Jenny," he said. "And I got a good box waiting for you. Here, let me take the little girl."

Tony was sitting on a high stool in front of a wide linoleum-covered shelf, which served as both desk and table. A coffeepot sat on a one-burner hot plate at the far end of the shelf next to an open box of doughnuts. The battered green toolbox that Tony used for dump fees rested in the middle, along with dog-eared receipt books and a coffee can filled with ballpoint pens and stubby pencils. At the end of the shelf near the door were a greasy wrench, several screwdrivers with blue and yellow plastic handles, and two large pairs of pliers.

Jenny handed Corey to Tony, and he held her in one arm, placing one gnarled finger of his free hand into her fist. Corey seemed to smile as her deep brown eyes gazed up into the old miner's eyes. He said, "You're a pretty little girl. Yes you are." He kept making little clucking sounds to the baby while Jenny was digging through the box on the floor of the shack.

Tony rescued books from the dump for Jenny before they got wet and dirty. He operated the D-8 which worked the trash into the landfill, and he always kept one eye out for salvage. Most of his cooking utensils and many of Jenny's had come from the dump. She disinfected them with Clorox before she used them. Tony often complained that Americans threw stuff away just because they got tired of it, and Jenny agreed with him.

"Oh," Jenny exclaimed, sitting down on the floor to look at an aging leather-bound copy of the Old Testament. The delicate pages were edged with gold. She could understand why people threw away paperback novels and some of the how-to manuals that Tony had brought her, but she could hardly believe that a book like this one would end up at the dump. She looked up at Tony. "It's beautiful. And I've never read it. Thank you."

"I'm glad to save it," he said, smiling. "And I have something else out in my truck. He turned to Billy. "Can you bring me the sack that's on the seat of my pickup?" Billy stuffed the last bite of a doughnut into his mouth and scrambled down the stairs and out to the red pickup.

Jenny replaced the Old Testament carefully in its box and stood up. Tony would haul all the books down to the house for her later. When Billy returned with the sack, Tony took it from him and brought out a child's picture book, which he handed to Jenny.

Jenny opened the book carefully; the cover was immaculate, the price tag was still inside—fifty-nine cents. "It's new," she exclaimed.

Tony said, "I wanted Corey to have a brand new book."

Jenny's eyes stung. She leaned over and kissed his wrinkled brown cheek. Then she took a pen from the coffee can and opened the book carefully. She wrote on the flyleaf, speaking the words aloud: "Corey's first book, a gift from Antonio . . ." She paused to ask, "What's your middle name?"

"My name is Antonio Steven Paul DiAngelo."

Jenny completed the name with a flourish and showed the inscription to Corey and Tony.

Tony beamed at her. "Now, why don't you and Billy go search for treasures while the little one and I look at these pictures of animals."

Jenny glanced back as she left the shack with Billy. The old man was actually showing the pictures in the book to Corey. Her daughter sucked on one fist, a little frown wrinkling her forehead.

Billy and Jenny moved slowly back and forth across the dump. Sunlight sparkled on discarded bottles and broken glass. "Be careful where you step, Billy. If you cut a hole in your galoshes, they'll leak." Billy nodded, but he was studying the ground and didn't answer.

Jenny picked up one white Pyrex dish that wasn't chipped or cracked. It was nearly as translucent as the broken china cup she had kept because of its painted flower design. She saw an alarm clock, but the winding knob was missing.

Jenny threw the clock back down just as Billy called out, "Mama come look." He was sitting on his haunches, tugging at something in the wet dirt.

Jenny stopped beside Billy, who held the front end of a toy truck. Jenny dug the dirt away from the back, and Billy pulled the truck free. It was a miniature tractor trailer, about seven inches long. It was a bit corroded and was missing its back wheels, but Billy was delighted. He hugged the truck to him and begged, "Can I play with it now, Mama? Can I?"

"No, Billy. You know the rules. I have to clean it first." Billy pouted. Jenny said, "We'll quit looking now and go right home. I'll clean it off for you first thing." She let him carry the truck back to the shack but made him wash his hands after he showed the toy to Tony and put it in the rock sack.

She washed her hands, too, with water from Tony's jug, and then she took the baby from him. "Thank you, Mr. DiAngelo. We all needed to get out. I love Corey's new book—and the old one you found for me."

"I'll bring them down this evening after I lock the gate," he said.

Billy skipped all the way home, his overshoes flapping up and down around his ankles. Jenny laughed as she watched him, and she was out of breath by the time she reached the house.

She changed Corey and said, "Now, if you can keep her happy for a few minutes, I'll sterilize your truck before I feed her." She put Corey on Billy's bed. Billy bent over her.

"Hi, baby," he said. "I have a new truck. We rode in a big truck to get you, but my truck's not so big."

Jenny scrubbed the toy and the Pyrex dish in hot water and Clorox. She rinsed and dried the truck before giving it to Billy, who drove it happily across the floor while she nursed Corey.

After lunch, instead of napping with the children, Jenny did the laundry and took the clothes outside to dry on the wire Mike had stretched between two wooden posts in the ground behind the house. Without the laundry over the stove the house seemed bigger. She did the dishes and put a pot of stew on for dinner.

When Billy and Corey were awake again, Jenny said, "Bring your truck outside, Billy." She picked up the milk crate that he used for a chair, placed it on the porch, and sat in the late sun with Corey in her arms, watching Billy push his new toy through the dirt. The traffic noises from the highway increased as the rush hour approached.

Suddenly the musical notes of an air horn sounded. Jenny glanced up in time to see a blur of silver and blue before it passed out of sight. She smiled and waved, hoping it had really been the truck from Tulsa and not just an impatient driver passing by.

She took Corey inside to nurse her, then put her in the crib and went out to take the clothes from the line. It was dusk by the time she had put the clothes away in the crates by their bed. She heard a pickup come down the road and went to the door, eager to greet Tony.

But it wasn't Tony's pickup. When the driver got out, Jenny recognized him as a man she'd seen once at Mom's place.

"Hello," she said. "Are you looking for someone?"

"You're Jenny Williams, aren't you?"

"Yes, I am."

"I've got something for you." The man went to the bed of his pickup and lifted out a small lady's rocking chair with a smooth wooden seat, a tall back, graceful arms, and curved wooden rockers. "Where do you want this?" he asked as he brought it up on the porch.

Jenny was so startled that she took a step back from the door letting the man past her to set the rocking chair down in the middle of the room. "There must be some mistake," she stammered. "I didn't order a rocking chair."

"No mistake," the man said, pushing his cap to the back of his head and smiling at her. "A truck driver in a big silver rig gave me five bucks to deliver this thing to you. He said he was running late, but he wanted to be sure you got it."

Jenny felt herself flush as she looked at the chair. She already owed that truck driver more than she could repay. The chair sat low to the floor. Her feet would never dangle from it like Humpty Dumpty's had in the cab of the truck. She turned back to the man and said, "Thank you."

"Hey, that's okay," he said. "Easiest five bucks I ever made." He had started out the door when Jenny stopped him.

"You don't by chance know that truck driver's name, do you?"

The man shook his head. "No, Mrs. Williams, I never seen him before—but, say, I did hear one of the other drivers call him Bigfoot."

Jenny smiled. The man went out. She turned back to the rocking chair, wiped her hand on her shirt, and reached out to touch the satiny finish. She set the empty chair to rocking slowly. Then, glancing at the two chairs and the crate at the table and back to the glowing varnish on the rocker, Jenny frowned slightly and stopped the rocking chair. Just then Billy ran into the house.

"Mama, come quick. There's a lady outside crying, and her face is all bloody."

CHAPTER

6

▲▲▲▲▲▲

"You stay here with Corey," she said to Billy, "and I mean *stay*." Jenny stepped out and looked toward the Stockers' trailer. A woman sat on the cinder-block step, her face in her hands. Jenny left the porch and walked slowly toward her.

"Can I help you?" she said and gasped as the woman looked up. Her nose had been bleeding, and her face was smeared with blood.

Her right eye was swollen; a purple bruise spread under the skin. A small cut on her cheekbone had bled and clotted. The woman's eyes seemed hazy and out of focus. She looked at Jenny but didn't speak or move until Jenny held out her hand. After a moment she took Jenny's hand and, getting up from the step, allowed herself to be led across the driveway and into the house. When Jenny dropped her hand the woman stood still in the middle of the floor.

"Outside, Billy," Jenny said. "It's still warm enough to play near the front of the house." Billy took his toy truck and went through the door slowly, looking over his shoulder as he went. Jenny set a chair near the sink. "What's your name?" she asked.

"Karen Stocker."

"Well, I'm Jenny Williams. Come sit down and let me clean you up."

Karen sat on the chair. Jenny dampened a washcloth and began to clean the woman's face. She wiped away the blood from her nose and cleaned around the swollen eye gently and slowly.

But Jenny's mind was speeding up, double-timing. A cloud of debris spun inside her head like a dust devil, catching up bits of memory and flinging them at her, only to snatch them away again before she could see them clearly. She spoke to ease her own tension. "Is he your husband?"

"Yes," Karen said, "and he's all right when he isn't drinking."

"Does he drink often?" Jenny asked, although she already knew the answer.

"Well . . . fairly often. Some times worse than others." Karen winced as Jenny washed the cut under her eye. Jenny wanted to ask, Why do you stay? but it wasn't any of her business, and the woman certainly wasn't offering information. She dropped her head each time Jenny let go of her face to rinse the cloth. But when Jenny finished and said, "There, that's the best I can do," the woman caught Jenny's hand and held it to her cheek. Jenny said, "Would you like something to drink? I can make coffee."

Karen looked up and shook her head. "No. I'd better get back."

"You can't," Jenny protested.

"I have to. He won't like it if he wakes up and I'm gone." Karen turned her eyes to the side and hunched her shoulders like a cold sparrow.

"Will you be all right?" Jenny asked.

"I think he's passed out now. He probably won't wake up until morning."

With a sense of sorrow that she felt might suffocate her, Jenny let the woman leave.

▽ ▽

The children were both asleep when Mike came in. Jenny was very much aware of the beer on his breath. Mike said, "Here, I brought you something." He took a small clock from his pocket.

"Oh," Jenny said, smiling. "A new one! Where did you get it?"

"I picked it up at the dime store."

Something in Mike's tone caught her attention. Holding the clock, she looked at him. "Picked it up? Oh, Mike, you didn't really just pick it up?"

"Yeah." He shrugged. "What the hell, Jenny. There were twenty-five clocks there. They won't miss one."

Jenny set the clock on the table. She should never have broken the old one. Before she could say anything more, Mike noticed the rocking chair.

"Where in the hell did this come from?" He gave the chair a push with his foot. "You didn't find *this* at the dump."

Jenny bit the inside of her cheek, hesitating. "It's from that truck driver."

Mike whirled toward her. "What in the hell does he think he's doing, bringing presents down here?"

"He wasn't here," she said. "He sent it with a guy in a pickup."

"Good God. Now everyone will know that some fuckin' truck driver is sending presents to my wife."

Jenny swallowed and said, "Mike, it's just a present for Corey. He probably got a good deal along the way somewhere and decided to bring it for the baby."

Mike calmed down a little. "Well, I don't want him around you and my kids again, and I'm going to tell him so. What's his name?"

Jenny said, "I don't know. And I don't think he makes this run very often. The guy who brought the chair didn't know him."

"Daddy?" Billy sat up on the mattress, blinking his eyes.

Mike turned. "Go back to sleep."

Jenny began to dish up Mike's dinner. "How's it going at the mine?"

Mike smiled at her. "Hey, I think I'm getting close to something. The look of the ore has changed. I'm gonna get another batch ready for the assayer next weekend." He sat down and pulled off his muddy boots. "But, Jesus, is that hard work."

While Mike ate, Jenny nursed Corey. Then she put Mike's boots away and wiped the mud from the floor. Mike was silent; each time she glanced his way, his eyes were on the rocking chair. Finally, pushing the table away, he rose and began to get ready for bed. When Jenny started to gather up his dirty dishes, he reached over and took hold of her wrist.

"Leave the goddamn dishes and come to bed."

Jenny undressed and turned out the light. She felt Mike's body tense and his breath quicken as she crawled into bed. No. Please. Let him go to sleep. Mike turned to Jenny and put his hands on her body. She stiffened, but he pulled her toward him. "By God, Jenny, I'll get your mind off that son-of-a-bitchin' truck driver." His hands moved downward; his breathing got faster and faster.

When he climbed on top of her she said, "No, Mike, it's too soon after the baby."

"I won't go in," he said, and he didn't. He was so hot and ready that in a moment Jenny's belly and thighs were slippery with his warm, sticky discharge. Mike rolled off of her and went to sleep.

Jenny could not lie there. She got up and washed herself in the dark, changed into her other nightgown, and sat down in Bigfoot's rocking chair. She rocked quietly in the shadowy room until Corey woke. Jenny changed her and nursed her, then after covering Billy, who had kicked his blankets off, she crawled back into bed beside Mike.

She had just started to fall asleep when a car roared down the dump road and turned the corner by their house. The squealing of brakes was followed by a crash and the sounds of splitting wood and crumpling metal.

Mike sat straight up in bed. "Jesus Christ," he said. "What was that?"

CHAPTER

7

▲▲▲▲▲▲

Jenny grabbed her robe while Mike slipped his pants on. Corey was sound asleep, but Billy sat up and whimpered. Jenny knelt by his mattress. "It's okay, honey," she said, "lie down." She tucked him in and rested her hand on his shoulder until he closed his eyes and went back to sleep. Mike had already gone out.

When Jenny went outside she heard a gabble of voices behind the house. She went around the corner. Richard's ancient Cadillac nestled against her clothesline pole, which was broken almost in half and bent over as though it had a stomachache. The clothesline sagged near Richard's car; the left front fender was crumpled. Richard stood near the car, obviously drunk. He seemed to be giving a speech.

"There has to be a Devil," Richard roared into the cold night air. "Or else we have to blame God for the evil in this stinking world, and if God is to blame"—he looked around at the group of neighbors—"then all we have left is each other." Richard raised his arms to the sky and laughed toward the stars with big whooping sounds.

Jenny felt uneasy. Richard's laughter sounded so painful, and nobody was doing anything. Tony DiAngelo stood on the far side of the pink Cadillac, clad only in long underwear and a pair of rubber overshoes. His spotlight lit the area, and Mike had moved over near him. They were talking to each other and ignoring Richard's laughter. Karen and Tully Stocker stood near the rear bumper of the damaged car, looking at Richard. Karen's face was still swollen. Tully looked pale and hung over in the harsh glare of the spotlight. He wore jeans and an undershirt, and the beer belly Mom Bradley had mentioned pushed against the undershirt, sagging over his belt.

Mom Bradley stared at Richard, too, her hair a reddish tumbleweed in the spotlight. She clutched her gray robe around her fat body and stared at her son. Richard continued to laugh, and the pain in the lonely sound was more than Jenny could bear.

She moved forward, reaching up for one of Richard's arms. She pulled it down so she could grasp his hand. She held the cold hand in both of hers and said, "Richard, don't."

At Jenny's touch, Richard stopped laughing and looked down. His eyes didn't look drunk. He's high on pain, Jenny thought, and her throat tightened. She wanted to look away, but Richard had placed his other hand on hers, and his eyes never left her face. Jenny waited, suddenly aware that the murmur of Mike's voice had stopped. There was absolute silence in the cold May night; the mountain air carved its way around them, isolating each from the other.

Then Richard said in a normal voice, "Ah, gentle Jenny, I have ruined your clothesline." He let go of her hands, and turning toward his car, got in, started it up and backed away from the post. Deprived of the supporting fender, the post broke from its own weight and nose-dived to the ground, trailing the lines like uncombed hair.

Richard drove his car across the lot to Mom Bradley's trailer, parked it, and went inside the house. Mom Bradley followed without a word, walking across the driveway and up the steps into the trailer.

"Shit," said Tully Stocker. "That bastard is crazy when he's drunk."

Jenny glanced at the Stockers, but Karen said nothing; she and Tully went back to their own trailer.

Tony said, "Let me see some of that ore, Mike. I think you may be on to something."

"I'll bring some down," Mike said over his shoulder as he joined Jenny, and they walked around to their door.

▽ ▽

The next afternoon while Billy was napping, Jenny heard a strange noise at the back and went outside with Corey in her arms. Richard was digging around the bottom section of the broken clothesline pole with a shovel. Jenny sat down and leaned against the wall of the house. Corey nestled in her lap. The sun was warm, and the steady *chung, chung, chung* of the shovel in the rocky soil was a pleasant sound.

After Richard pulled up the broken shaft, he settled a new pole in the hole and tamped the dirt firmly around it. Then he nailed the crossbar to the new pole and tightened the line. When he finished Jenny said, "Come in for a cup of coffee."

Richard sat quietly at the kitchen table as Jenny brewed a fresh pot of coffee. After filling two cups she sat down at the table and said, "Do you really believe in the Devil?"

Richard said, "Do you believe in God?"

Jenny considered his question. "I think I used to when my father was alive."

"How old were you when he died?"

"Eight."

"Then that doesn't count," Richard said. "All children believe in God."

Jenny protested, "You're saying that children don't know anything."

"They live in an unreal world. Even if they're not innocent, they're ignorant."

"Billy's not ignorant."

"I wasn't trying to insult your kid."

"I'm not insulted. It's just that Billy's not ignorant. He knows when things are serious; he knows that life is painful. He always reports to me when he sees someone's pain. He trusts me to do something about it."

"Then you are God to him."

"No, I'm not. He has another—a separate—relationship with life, or God, maybe. He burrows into his life, dealing with whatever happens to come along at the moment. I don't know anybody else like my son. He seems so united with the world."

"So what does that have to do with God?"

"I think Billy knows something I've forgotten. Something I can't find anymore because my mind is blurry."

Richard looked at Jenny for a long silent moment, and then he said, "You too, Jenny?" He shook his head. "You too?"

"What do you mean, me too?" she asked.

"We're all of us doomed then," he said, "every sorry one of us in this forgotten corner. Do you know what I heard someone say the other day about us? Someone in the bar said, 'They live below the dump.'"

"I didn't know people talked about this neighborhood at all."

Richard snorted. "People always talk. And they love to talk about us because it makes them feel like they're high up on the social ladder. They can point to us down here—below the dump."

"It's just a place to live. We won't stay here forever."

"Don't count on it, Jenny. My mom's been here forever. She's got money enough to get out, but she's afraid to spend it. She won't even admit she has any. She's paralyzed by fear and greed. We're all paralyzed by something."

"Why don't you get out?"

Richard smiled, and a wild vacant look came into his eyes. "I've been out, Jenny. Clear to Vietnam and back again."

Jenny refilled their cups. Corey was making cooing sounds in the crib. Billy slept on his bedspring, arms and legs tucked close to his body.

Jenny said, "Until you mentioned it, I never thought of the people down here as 'us.' Do you really see it that way?"

Richard said, "The whole world is 'us,' Jenny. If we're going to survive, we've got to stop dividing everything into us and them." He stood up abruptly. "But then, of course, we're not going to survive."

Leaving the cup full and without saying good-bye, Richard went out the door. Jenny poured his coffee down the sink. In a few moments, she heard Richard's old Cadillac going up the road toward town.

She hung the clean laundry on the newly repaired clothesline, fed Billy when he woke, and nursed Corey. After the children were asleep that night she rocked in Bigfoot's chair, waiting for Mike. But he didn't come, and finally she went to bed, waking early in the morning when Mike crawled into bed beside her, smelling of beer and sweat. He kissed her and ran his hands across her breasts, down her stomach, and between her legs. Then he fell asleep and snored. She waited for a while and moved out of his embrace.

▽ ▽

One Friday night at the end of May, when Corey was nearly four weeks old, Tully beat Karen again. After he passed out, Karen came to Jenny's door, bloody as before. Jenny washed her face and put a Band-Aid on a cut and then simply stood by the chair and held Karen in her arms.

Mike was late at the mine, but Karen insisted on going home. The next morning, after Tully left, Jenny went over to the trailer. Corey was asleep, and she could see Billy driving his truck in the dirt by the side of the house.

"Please have breakfast with me," Karen said, putting two yellow mats on the table and setting out shining blue stoneware and stainless tableware with roses in the design. Jenny was tempted by the lovely table.

She said, "The window's open. I can hear Corey if she wakes."

Karen poured orange juice into two glasses and filled their cups with coffee. She fried bacon, scrambled four eggs, and toasted whole wheat bread in the toaster on the counter.

"This is marvelous," Jenny said. "We haven't been able to afford bacon for ages. And your beautiful table makes it perfect." Karen said nothing.

They ate quietly. Jenny watched her new neighbor, trying to think of something to say that wouldn't have to do with Tully's violence. But the beatings hung between them, and when Karen winced as the orange juice touched the cut on her lip, Jenny said, "Why do you put up with it? Why do you stay?"

Karen set the orange juice down and looked at Jenny. She said, "Why do *you?*"

CHAPTER

8

▲▲▲▲▲▲

Jenny was too startled to respond at once. After a short silence she said, "Mike doesn't beat me."

Karen said, "He doesn't have to beat you to abuse you. Good God. At least Tully provides me with a few decent things."

Jenny swallowed. Karen's blunt attack was overwhelming. "But we can't afford to live the way you do. We don't have the money."

"*You* may not have any money, Jenny," Karen said, "but your husband has plenty."

"How do you know that?"

"I've sat in Mom's Bar many a night with Tully, Mom's and other places, and watched your husband big-dealing, buying drinks for the house, playing the horses and dogs through this bookie who comes around." Jenny wished she had never come to the trailer. But Karen wasn't finished yet. She waved her coffee cup in the air and went on. "And how many thousands of dollars has he put into that worthless mine?"

"I don't know," Jenny said, the expensive bacon sticking in her throat. "But I don't think Mike should give up his dreams just because he took me in."

"What do you mean, took you in?"

"I ran away from a foster home."

"Why?"

Jenny looked down. "The man tried to rape me."

"Jesus. How old were you?"

"Fifteen."

"What did you do?"

"I ran first, and then I hid. I got a ride away from that town and kept moving. I washed dishes in restaurants, but I never stayed more than a week at any one place; I didn't want them to find me and make me go back."

"And Mike took you in?"

"One of the truckers I hitched with dropped me off near a construction project. Mike picked me up on his way home. He offered to share his trailer with me."

"Out of the frying pan and into the fire," Karen said.

"No," Jenny said. Karen didn't even know Mike. "Mike was really good to me. All he asked was that I cook for him and keep the trailer up." She stood. "I'd better go."

Karen put her hand on Jenny's arm. "I'm sorry if I hurt your feelings. But you're so pretty and so smart; it doesn't seem like *you'd* have to be trapped."

Jenny felt trapped by Karen's presence. "I owe Mike so much. I didn't have anything at all when he married me."

Karen picked up the coffeepot. "Oh, Jesus, Jenny. And what do you have now? Mike got the best of the deal."

Jenny waved the coffeepot away. "Corey's probably awake by now," she said.

Karen filled Jenny's cup anyway and said, "Go get her and come back. I want you to look in my mirror."

▽ ▽

But Jenny didn't go back that day. She was troubled by Karen's blunt observations. She was confused—and angry.

The next morning Karen came to the house in a gentler mood. Neither of them mentioned the previous day's conversation, and after that, having coffee with Karen became part of Jenny's mid-morning routine.

Jenny was fascinated by the contradictions she found in her

friend's personality. When the two of them were alone together or with the children, Karen was loud and frank. She poked into the corners of Jenny's life, asking questions, urging Jenny to do things differently.

She stood Jenny in front of the full-length mirror in the trailer. "Look at you. You're cute and blond, and you have a fabulous figure. Any guy would be proud to have you for his wife. Why don't you make Mike buy you some decent clothes? Get him to take you out and show you off."

"I don't know how to make Mike do anything."

Karen tossed her head. "Well, you could at least get him to buy you that red wagon you've been scrimping for."

Karen always knew what Jenny should do, and she always told her in blunt language that scared Jenny as much as it fascinated her.

But the moment Tully came around, Karen grew quiet. Jenny didn't have the courage to ask again, "Why do you stay?" Karen didn't seem to know the answer herself. When she was hurt, she came to Jenny and let her wounds be washed and bound. Once, as Jenny stood by the chair with a washcloth, Karen leaned her head against Jenny's stomach and said, "Why can't I get out?"

And then Tully would stay sober for several days and bring Karen a present or take her out to dinner, and Jenny would hear them laughing late at night when they came home.

But as Karen and Jenny became closer, Tully turned meaner. He didn't want Karen to visit Jenny's house, even for coffee, and when he found out that Karen had bought Jenny a blouse, he took Karen's checkbook away from her.

"The checking account is in his name," Karen said, "and so are the truck and the trailer." She paused before adding, "I'm no better off than you."

After that, Karen didn't talk any more about how Jenny should get out. One morning she said to Jenny, "If it weren't for you, I swear to God, I'd kill myself."

"No," Jenny said. "Don't talk that way." She looked around for Billy. He had heard too many of their conversations already. Luckily, he was playing outside. She turned back to Karen. "Has Tully acted like this before?"

Karen nodded. "Every time someone else gets close to me, he acts worse." She ran her fingernail along the edge of the table. "But he's never been this bad before."

"What can I do to help you, Karen?"

Karen began to cry. "Nothing, Jenny. Not a goddamn thing. Maybe if I just stick close to home and don't provoke him, things will get better again." She rose from the table, touched Jenny's shoulder, and went out the door.

Jenny watched her go, her feeling of regret mixed with relief. Karen had stirred up her mind. The whirling storm never seemed to stop. She needed to be alone with the children. She missed the quiet hours, and she hadn't been to the dump or read a whole book since the day she'd had breakfast with Karen. Karen didn't come to the house the next morning. Jenny sat at the kitchen table for a long time, but she didn't go to the trailer.

▽   ▽

Mike was becoming more and more excited about the ore he was working. Tony liked the looks of it too. One Sunday in June he went up to the mine with Mike. When they got back, Mike said to Jenny, "That old bastard has forgotten more about mining than I'll ever know. We drilled and shot a round today and chose some good broad samples to send for assay reports."

The next week, on a night when Mike was late, Jenny asked Tony to sit with the children for a while. Looking into the blurred mirror above the sink, she combed her hair and put on some lipstick. She dressed in clean jeans and the blouse Karen had bought for her and walked up the sloping road to the highway. She opened the door under the pink neon that said MOM'S BAR AND CAFÉ.

No one noticed her as she looked around the bar. Mike sat in a booth with two men and a woman, all strangers to her. When he raised his head and waved at the waitress for another round, he saw Jenny.

He got up from the booth and came over. "What are you doing here? Is something the matter with the kids?"

"Tony's with the kids," Jenny said. "I thought I'd take the night off."

Mike gave her a sharp glance but said, "Well, sure, come on over and sit down. Do you want a Coke?"

Jenny said, "I want a Scotch and soda."

Mike said, "You're kidding."

"No I'm not," Jenny said. "I read about Scotch and soda in a book. I want to taste one."

Mike shrugged and said to the waitress, "A Scotch and soda and four more bottles of Coors."

Jenny thought the drink tasted strange; it reminded her of the way a pan smelled when she let it burn dry and scorched the potatoes. But when Mike ordered more beer for the group at the table, she asked for another Scotch and soda.

Mike was beginning to act nervous. From the corner of her eye Jenny could tell he was watching her. As soon as she turned her head he looked away.

After her second drink Jenny excused herself and stood up. She swayed a little. "I think I'll go home now," she said, but Mike wouldn't let her walk down the hill alone. He paid the bill and went outside with her. Opening the door on the passenger's side of the truck, he helped her up into the high seat.

"Thanks for baby-sitting," Jenny said to Tony when they got back to the house. Mike let Tony go without starting a mining discussion. As soon as he and Jenny were in bed, he pulled her to him. They made love for the first time since Corey's birth.

▽ ▽

At breakfast the next morning, Mike said, "Are you feeling all right?"

"Sure," Jenny said. "Why?"

"You've been acting kind of funny, lately."

"Funny how?"

"Different," Mike said. "Kind of pushy."

Jenny turned toward the stove and bit her lip to keep her sudden anger from exploding. When she didn't answer, Mike lapsed into silence.

He left for work right on time, and he came home early from the mine that night. He was early the next night, too, and the night after that.

And it was on that third night, after supper, while Jenny was washing the dishes and Mike was putting a new handle on a miner's pick, that Tully began to beat Karen again.

Mike had never been there before when it happened. The June night was warm. The door of the house was open and so were the trailer windows. Tully had roared home drunk and stumbled up the steps to the trailer. He cursed and shouted obscenities, and when he began to slap Karen she started to cry, her rough sobs painfully loud in the quiet night.

Jenny swallowed nervously. She caught Mike's eye. He said, "Jesus, what did she do to rile him up like that?"

Jenny said, "This isn't the first time he's beat her. Why do you think it's *her* fault?"

"Well, good God, he must have a reason."

"He's always drunk when he hits her, and he never needs a reason."

Mike was silent. And then Karen screamed, "No, Tully, please, no. You're going to break my arm. God, Tully. Stop."

Jenny gritted her teeth. She wiped her hands on her jeans, took the jar of coins she'd saved toward her red wagon from the counter, and said to Mike, "Give me the keys to the truck."

"What for?"

"I'm going to get her out of there."

"Jenny, you're crazy. This is none of our business."

But Jenny said again, "Give me the keys, Mike."

"God damn it, Jenny, you can't be serious. She probably deserves what she's getting. Besides, she's his wife. Why do you want to interfere?"

Karen's screams continued.

Jenny said, "If you don't give me the keys, I'll go get Tony's truck." She started for the door, but Mike grabbed her wrist.

"I won't let you get mixed up in this."

She looked at him coldly. "You don't have anything to say about it—especially if you think it's all right for Tully to beat his wife. *You* are aggravating *me*. Would it be all right for me to hit you?"

"Hell no!"

"What's the difference? Karen's his wife. You're my husband."

"I'm bigger than you are. What makes you think you could beat me?"

"Jesus, Mike," Jenny said, jerking her wrist free. "Did you hear what you just said? It's okay to beat someone if you're bigger?"

Mike flushed and reached into his pocket for the keys. "You're being a goddamn fool, Jenny. Don't expect me to back you up."

Jenny snatched the keys and ran out the door.

CHAPTER

9

▲▲▲▲▲▲

Jenny climbed up into the truck and drove down near Tony's shop, turned around, and drove back toward the Stockers' trailer. She parked the truck beside the road, facing uphill, and left the door open and the motor running.

She slid down from the seat and took a deep breath. Then she ran up to the door of the trailer and jerked it open. In the loudest voice she could command, she yelled, "Tully, you stop that." She stepped forward and grabbed Karen's arm, saying firmly, "You come with me."

Karen followed her dumbly out the door. Jenny hurried her to the truck, boosted her in, and pushed her across the seat. As she climbed up after Karen, Jenny heard Tully shout, "What the hell is going on?"

Jenny slammed the door and took off up the road toward the highway, her heart pounding against her ribs.

Karen was crying, but Jenny didn't have time to look at her. She drove into town and through it to the bus depot on the far side. She parked in a shadowed spot beside a large dumpster in back of the bus station. "Stay here," she said to Karen and went inside.

When she came back she had several wet towels, several dry towels, and a Mitchell phone book. She cleaned Karen's face and combed her hair. Then she said, "I saw a flyer at the grocery store about some kind of house in Mitchell, a place that takes care of battered women."

"Battered," Karen murmured.

Jenny was flipping through the phone book. She ran her fingers down the *H* listings. "'Hope'—'Hope'—Here it is: 'Hope House.' Come on," she said, picking up her money jar.

Karen took hold of her wrist. "But, Jenny, that's your red-wagon money. I can't use that."

"You have to," Jenny said, "or Tully is going to kill you." She tried to smile at her friend as she added, "Come on, instead of a red wagon, let's go buy a Greyhound."

Karen got out and straightened her clothes. They went inside and bought a one-way ticket to Mitchell. There was a little money left. Jenny gave most of it to Karen, but she took a handful of change to a phone booth. "I'm going to call them so they know you're coming." Karen waited by the door of the booth.

When Jenny hung up she turned to Karen. "I never heard anybody who sounded so nice. Someone will be there to meet the bus. You're going to be all right."

"Stay with me until the bus leaves," Karen said, suddenly pale and trembling. "I don't know if I have the courage to do this. What about my things?"

"Don't worry about your things," Jenny said, "worry about your life. If there's one truth I've learned while picking the dump, it's that there are always more things."

Karen reached for Jenny's hand. "I'll never forget this, Jenny. God, when my stepfather used to hit Mama, I sometimes screamed at her to run away. Now I know why she could never do it." Karen tightened her hold on Jenny's hand and said again, "I'll never forget this."

Jenny said, "I owe you a lot, too, Karen. You made me see things in a new way." She turned as the loudspeaker blared. "They're announcing your bus. We'd better go out there."

Before Karen got on the bus, they embraced. Jenny waited, making herself smile at Karen's face in the bus window and waving until the Greyhound pulled out into traffic and headed north toward Mitchell.

Jenny climbed back into Mike's truck and locked the doors. She rested her hands and her head on the steering wheel until her heart quit pounding. Even then her hand shook as she turned the key in the ignition.

When Jenny started down the road beside the dump her heart began pounding again. She shut off the lights, put the truck in neutral, and coasted quietly in toward the house, her throat tightening as she thought, If he's still awake, I'll stay in the truck and honk the horn until everyone in the whole place wakes up.

There wasn't a sound in the area, but she was glad to see a light in the house.

When Jenny came in, Mike was sitting at the table, drinking coffee. He got up and came toward her. "Are you okay?"

Jenny was suddenly terribly tired. She walked past Mike to the coffeepot and poured herself a cup of thick, bottom-of-the-pot coffee. "I'm all right," she said.

"What did you do with Karen?"

Jenny turned. "I've decided not to tell anyone, Mike. Not anyone at all. I'm surprised Tully didn't follow us, drunk as he was."

Mike grinned. "He came here first, and after that, he didn't feel like following you."

"What do you mean?"

"He came raging up onto the porch; when he found out you and Karen weren't here, he started in on me for letting you go." Mike grinned again. "He took a swing at me, and I just happened to have that pick handle I was working on in my hand."

"Oh, my Lord," Jenny said.

"Yep," Mike said, sounding quite satisfied with himself. "I hit him up alongside the head, and then I dragged him across the driveway and dumped him inside his trailer."

"You didn't kill him, did you?"

"Don't worry. He's too mean to die. He'll sleep it off and won't even remember."

Jenny said, "I wish I could be sure of that. Tully isn't going to be happy when he realizes that Karen is really gone."

"You should have thought of that before you butted in," Mike said.

Jenny didn't want to start another argument. She just said, "Anyway, thanks for keeping him here."

▽   ▽

Jenny did not see Tully for the next few days. She missed Karen, but after a week she slipped back into her old routine. One morning she took Corey and Billy up to the dump. They spoke to Tony for a moment. He reached for Corey, and Jenny and Billy went wandering. They were kneeling to look at a little bucket that had a spot where the enamel was chipped off when Billy leaned against her.

"I'm lonesome for you, Mama," he said.

Quick tears wet Jenny's eyes. She knew what Billy meant. She had immersed herself in her conversations with Karen in the last weeks and had left Billy out. She put her arm around her son. "I'm sorry, Billy. My other friend was in such trouble. She needed me most."

Billy nodded, but he said, "I need you most, too."

Something was troubling him. She put both arms around Billy and rocked him back and forth in the sunshine.

Finally Billy said in a small voice, "Why did Daddy hit that man with a stick?"

Jenny took Billy's hand, and they both stood. She bent to pick up the bucket. "Let's go find some grass to sit on, Billy, and we'll talk about it."

She thought quickly as they walked toward the side of the dump.

How can I explain this without criticizing Mike and yet without saying it's all right to hit people?

They sat down in the scraggly shade of a bush. Jenny took Billy on her lap and smoothed his hair. Finally she spoke.

"Billy, when people have problems, they ought to talk about them, like you did just now when you said you were lonesome. But not everybody's mama told them that, so some people can't talk about their problems. And that makes them feel mean. And some people are very dangerous when they feel mean."

"Was that loud man gonna hurt Daddy? He sounded mean."

"He has hurt other people. Your daddy had to stop him quickly."

Billy nodded. "I thought you liked Karen better than me." He dropped his head. "I felt mean."

"Oh, honey." Jenny hugged him tight. "I never in this whole world liked anybody better than you. Let's take our bucket and our baby and go home and have lunch."

▽   ▽

The assay report came the next day. Jenny had never seen Mike so excited. He and Tony sat at the kitchen table for hours, making plans to develop the mine. The assay report had given them hope that the mine would eventually pay its way.

Jenny listened, realizing that they would have even less money now. Tony and Mike talked of blasting, of crushing the ore, of concentrating. She remembered telling Richard that they wouldn't be here forever, and Richard had said, "Don't count on it."

A couple of days later Mike came home right after work without going to the mine. Jenny said, "Well, hi. I wasn't expecting you."

Mike kissed her and said, "I have to talk some business with you."

"Business?" Mike never talked business with her. He gave her the grocery money and that was all she ever knew about their business.

Mike took some papers out of his hip pocket and sat down at the table. "I need you to sign these."

"Me? Why?"

"I'm remortgaging the truck, but that old bastard at the bank won't loan me the money unless you sign."

"How can I sign, Mike? I couldn't repay the loan. I don't have anything—not even my red-wagon money."

Mike flushed. "You've got to sign, Jenny, or I can't work the mine. It's for both of us."

Jenny hesitated; a pulse started beating in her neck. She swallowed and said, "If it's for both of us, I want my name on the mine claim before I sign."

"Jesus," Mike said, "that's not necessary, Jenny. It would hold everything up."

Jenny turned away and thought about Karen until her lips stopped trembling, and she could make her voice sound steady. Then she said, "If you don't put my name on the papers for the mine, I won't sign my name on the loan papers." She picked Corey up from the crib and walked out the door. She crossed the driveway and went around behind Mom Bradley's trailer, where Billy was watching Richard work on the engine of the Ford pickup.

CHAPTER

10

▲▲▲▲▲▲

Richard looked up as she approached. "Hi, Jenny."

He backed away from the pickup and wiped his hands on a grease-stained red rag. He poked a finger at Corey's fist. She studied the finger, blinked, then curled her fist around it. Jenny looked down at her daughter and smiled.

Richard said, "She takes life as it comes, doesn't she? I bet she isn't a fusser."

Jenny laughed. "She doesn't have to be. As soon as Corey opens her mouth for a good holler, Billy tells me what she needs."

Billy came over to them. Leaning against Jenny, he reached out and took Corey's bare foot in his hand. For a moment everyone looked at the baby. The late afternoon sun was warm on Jenny's back. She could smell the grease from the engine on Richard, mixed with a clean smell of soap and after-shave. The baby scent of Corey floated over the other scents like dust in a sunbeam. Jenny rested in the moment. It had taken all her courage to stand up to Mike about the loan.

It was unsettling to change things, but nothing could ever be the way it was before Karen came. Karen had stirred up Jenny's mind, and strange strong feelings kept floating to the surface. They didn't join together to form a single clear thought, but the feelings couldn't be submerged. They clustered like bubbles on a stream, swirled with the current, broke apart and reformed, and Jenny felt tired from their constant motion.

She said, "The sun feels good."

Richard pulled his finger out of Corey's fist and said, "I'd better get back to work."

Jenny said, "In all the time you've been working on that pickup, I've never seen you drive it. Does it run?"

Richard looked at her and smiled. "It will, Jenny, one of these days, but I'm in no hurry. I need the therapy."

"Therapy?"

"Yeah. This pickup is cheaper than a shrink, and it tells me about the same thing."

"You're kidding."

"No, I'm not. The manual assures me that there is a logical way to make this vehicle work, if I don't screw up the wires or overlook a defective part. A psychiatrist would say the same thing about me."

"How can you live with all those thoughts whirling around in your head?" Jenny asked.

Richard frowned a little but said lightly, "I outrun them, Jenny. When that old Caddy and I get up to ninety miles an hour, there's nothing fast enough to catch us. One by one, all the pursuing demons throttle down and back off."

"There must be other ways to deal with demons."

Richard gave her a piercing glance. "Not everyone needs a hot Cadillac, Jenny, if that's what you mean. Some people have the courage to face their demons."

"I wish I had your brains," Jenny said.

Richard went to the pickup. Grasping the wrench, he said over his shoulder. "You do have brains, Jenny. What you lack is education. Why don't you go back to school?"

Billy let go of Corey and climbed up on the bumper of the Ford to watch Richard.

"Go to school?" Jenny said. She shifted Corey to her hip. "I've got a husband and two kids, and besides, I never even finished high school."

"You could study for a GED."

"What's that?"

"A general equivalency diploma. If you learn the stuff and pass the tests, it's as good as a high school diploma."

Jenny sighed. "I wouldn't know where to begin. I don't have much time."

"Well, you could at least start reading some of the right books instead of all that crap Tony brings down from the dump."

Mike came around the corner of the trailer and walked over to them. "How about some supper?" he said to Jenny.

Relieved that he didn't want to argue about the truck mortgage, she smiled and said, "Sure. You hang on to Cory for a while, and I'll go fix something." She put the baby in Mike's arms.

After dinner, Mike said, "Do you think we should take the kids into town on Thursday for the Fourth of July celebration?"

Jenny was surprised and a little suspicious. He hadn't ever taken them anywhere on the Fourth of July before. But she said, "Billy would like that."

Mike turned to Billy. "What do you say, Bill? Do you want to go see the fireworks?"

"What's fireworks, Daddy?"

Mike laughed, rose from the table, and swung his son high up toward the ceiling. "It's lights and noise and smoke, kid. All the stuff that makes life interesting."

When the children were in bed, Mike said, "Won't you change your mind and sign the papers?"

Jenny met Mike's eyes, clenched her teeth, and shook her head.

Mike said, "Well, Jesus, can't we even talk about it?"

Jenny shook her head again and began to fold diapers. If they started to talk, she'd give in. And it seemed so important not to give in. She was only asking for what was fair, even if it did make Mike angry.

When they got in bed, Mike turned his back to her and moved to the far side. They both lay tense and silent. Finally, Mike began to snore.

Jenny couldn't sleep. Her decision seemed like the right one, but how could she be sure? It seemed to upset Mike so much. It would be awful if Mike acted cold and angry all the time.

She slipped out of bed, turned on the light, and went to the book crate, but she couldn't find anything she wanted to read. Richard was right. It was all crap. Except for the Old Testament. Jenny took the leather-bound book and sat down in Bigfoot's chair. She ran her hand over the satiny finish on the arm of the chair and smiled. It seemed longer than nine weeks since she had seen that gigantic boot planted next to her on the snow.

▽   ▽

Billy loved the Fourth of July demonstration given by the Dolby Volunteer Fire Department. Mike got a little drunk on free beer, but not too drunk to intervene when Tully Stocker, who was more than a little drunk, grabbed Jenny's shoulder as they stood in the line for barbecue.

"Where in hell did you take my wife?" Tully said, gripping hard.

Mike moved forward as Jenny cried out. "Get your goddamn hands off of her," he said, knocking Tully's hand away from Jenny's shoulder.

Tully stumbled backward but caught himself and came at Mike. "It's all her fault, and I'm going to find out where she took my wife." Tully raised his arm as if to push Mike out of the way.

Mike grasped Tully's wrist and held it in midair. People were stepping back from Mike and Tully. A small space cleared around the five of them. Mike stood in front of Jenny, holding Tully's arm. Billy clung to Jenny's leg. Jenny held Corey close in her arms and shivered, although the sun was hot.

"We don't know where your wife is, so get off Jenny's case, you son of a bitch. It's your fault Karen left." Mike gripped Tully's arm tighter. Jenny could see his fingers dig into the other man's flesh.

Tully twisted his body sideways and pulled his arm free. "She wouldn't have gone off if that bitch hadn't helped her," he said, rubbing his wrist, "but she'll be back. She hasn't got a goddamn thing to her name." He turned and staggered away toward the parking lot, the crowd parting to let him pass.

Mike turned to Jenny. She smiled at him, though she felt like crying. Mike looked down at Billy, whose eyes were wide and anxious. He lifted the boy into his arms.

"Let's eat, son, and then we'll go watch the softball game until it's time for the fireworks."

Mike didn't drink any more, and he stayed near his family the rest of the day. Gradually Jenny relaxed. When she saw Billy's face as the first rocket exploded, sending red umbrellas of light across the sky, she began to feel happy. No one in the crowd seemed to remember the ugly scene with Tully. The Williams family was just like all the other families, with an excited little boy squealing each time the fireworks lit the sky above the mountain.

▽   ▽

The next day Mike left at the usual time for work, but he was back by three o'clock that afternoon. When he came in, Jenny was washing diapers at the sink. "Hi," she said, glancing around. "Are you okay? How come you're so early?"

"I didn't go to work today," Mike said.

Jenny looked directly at him then. He was grinning. She dried her hands on her jeans and said, "Where did you go?"

Mike pulled a roll of papers from his hip pocket. "Come here, Jen," he said, and went to the table.

The loan again, she thought, going slowly toward him. But it wasn't just the loan. Mike laid out three pieces of official-looking paper.

"I went into Mitchell, to the field office of the Bureau of Land Management." He pointed to a line that said *Know all men by these presents that Michael Alan Williams and Jennifer Norton Williams* . . . Jenny looked at the papers only long enough to see her name, and then she turned and put her arms around Mike. He hugged her.

When she looked up at him he said, "Now nobody can say you don't have a damn thing to *your* name."

With a sudden tightness in her throat as she thought of Karen, Jenny turned back to the table. She picked up Mike's pen and signed the new mortgage on the truck.

▽   ▽

Mike started working late hours at the mine again. Jenny, Billy, and Corey lived casually through the hot July and August days, following the children's schedule. The weeds and grass grew up around the house and the clothesline pole. Jenny pulled and chopped around the front porch and in the back area, but it rained a little each afternoon, and the weeds grew faster than she could cut them down. She worried about snakes at first, and then when the rains stopped and the weeds turned dry, she worried about fire.

She kept the house tidy and worked every day on the laundry. Billy played outside most of the day. Corey cut a tooth and cried a lot. Jenny knew the baby felt miserable; she rocked her and rubbed her gums and told her soothing little stories.

It was too hot on the dump for the children, but the three of them went up to visit Tony now and then.

Jenny went back to reading the books in the milk crate, and when she had read them all she threw them away, except for the Old Testament and a book of Shakespeare's plays, which Richard had given her. She didn't understand half the ideas in the Shakespeare book, but she liked the way the words sounded.

Mike came home late every night. His clothes were always dirty, and he was always glum.

One morning at breakfast, Jenny got up the nerve to ask about his moodiness. "Is something wrong at the mine?"

"No," he said. "Why do you ask?"

"You don't seem very happy."

Mike said, "Mining's a lot harder work than prospecting. I'd hoped to have enough concentrate by now to pay the loan payment and the insurance on the truck."

"The ore's good isn't it? The gold's there?"

"Jesus, Jenny, you sound like a tenderfoot from the East. Do you think the gold is just lying in the dirt like nickels and dimes?"

"No, of course not, but I've never been to the mine. What am I supposed to know?"

Mike ran his hand over his face. "It's too hot to fight, and I'm too goddamn tired. Would you run up to Mom's and get me a cold six-pack?"

▽   ▽

On the Saturday before Labor Day, Tony closed the dump to go fishing. He asked Billy to come along. Mike and Jenny helped load up the fishing gear and waved good-bye to Billy. He waved back until Tony's truck topped the rise near the highway.

As Mike turned toward the house he said to Jenny. "How would you like to see this mine you own half of?"

Jenny said, "Really, Mike? Will you really take me to the mountain?"

"I get kinda tired of working that tunnel alone. Put on some rough clothes; maybe you can help me."

Jenny hurried to dress and get Corey's things together. Corey was holding her left foot with her right hand. She seemed to be memorizing her toes. "Come on, baby-face," Jenny said as she picked up Corey and began to dress her. "We're going to my mountain."

CHAPTER

11

▲▲▲▲▲▲

Jenny sang a little song to Corey as Mike drove along the dump road: "Going in the pickup, going on the highway, going up the mountain, going to the mine." She bounced Corey lightly, and the baby held on to Jenny's finger and looked at her with solemn eyes.

Mike said, "You talk to that kid as if she were ten years old."

"Most of the time," Jenny said, "she acts like an old lady. She's wise and serious."

"Well, she's probably more realistic about the mine than you are," Mike said. "You wouldn't sing if you knew anything about it." He shifted his eyes to the side of the road, where Richard's pink Cadillac leaned into the shallow barrow pit. "Jesus, doesn't he ever manage to get that thing all the way home?"

Jenny could see Richard in the front seat, his head lolled back, his mouth open. Mike slowed and honked the horn as they passed. Richard woke abruptly; his head came up from the seat.

Jenny looked back. "I feel sorry for him."

"Why?"

"He's such a sad person."

"Yeah," Mike said. "He's sour on life. He'll probably kill himself in that Caddy one of these days, and the sheriff will call it an accident."

"That would be hard on Mom Bradley."

"What good is he to her?"

"He's her son, Mike."

"Hell, I'm somebody's son, too, but you'd never know it."

Jenny turned to study Mike. His face seemed thinner than usual. She could see the muscle bulge in his cheek near his ear, as if he'd clenched his teeth for a moment. She said, "Do you suppose your mother ever wonders if she's got grandchildren?"

"Hell no," Mike said. "When she took off for the East Coast she was done with kids forever." He reached down between his legs to the floor of the pickup, pulled a can of Coors from a six-pack, popped it open, and took a long swallow. He set the beer on the seat near his legs and turned to look at Jenny. "Hell of a pair we are. Your old lady was a drunk, and mine was a floozy."

Jenny turned away from Mike and looked out the window. They were passing through Dolby now, where the highway was called First Street. The Laundromat shared a low brick building with a hardware store; the post office was next, its flag hanging limply in the hot August air. Beyond that was the grocery store where Jenny shopped, but the parking lot was almost empty.

"Dolby looks like a ghost town," she said, glancing back at Mike. "Is the company going to move us too?"

"I don't know what the goddamn company is going to do," Mike said, the muscle jerking in his jaw again. He slowed as they neared the curve where First Street became Highway 86 once more and wound its way north through the hills toward Mitchell. He turned left onto a narrow street that followed Virgo Creek to the south.

To change the subject, Jenny said, "Are there many other mines like ours?"

"This isn't really mining country anymore," Mike said, picking up the beer can. "It's still a mining district, but the real estate developers keep moving closer, and they scream to the county commissioners every time a miner sets off a round of dynamite."

"Do you use dynamite?"

"Hell yes, I use dynamite. That ore is solid rock. What did you think I used?" Mike tipped the beer can, draining the rest. "For a miner's daughter, you're pretty goddamn dumb."

"My father was a *coal* miner, and he died when I was eight years old."

The pavement ended, and Corey, who had been napping in Jenny's arms, woke up as the pickup started onto the rough gravel road. Jenny opened her shirt and gave her breast to the baby. She didn't say anything else. Mike seemed determined to pick on her. She almost wished she had stayed home.

They drove down the road in silence, except for Corey's sucking and the sound of gravel spattering the truck. Mike looked over at Jenny; she looked out the window at the grass and willow trees in the low-lying meadow. The sun glinted on a small beaver pond. She could see the tangled branches of the dam.

Mike reached for the six-pack again and took out two cans. He popped the first one and held it out to Jenny. "Have a beer, Jenny, and I'll tell you about this mining life."

You don't know how to say "I'm sorry," do you? thought Jenny. But she smiled at Mike and took the beer.

"I fired a round of dynamite last night," Mike said. "The smoke will be pretty well cleared away by now, but it will still stink like hell when we go into the tunnel."

"What are we going to do in there?"

"Muck it out, Jenny. Do you think you can run a shovel?"

"You mean the kind with an engine?"

"Hell no. I mean the kind with a handle."

Jenny sipped from the beer can. "Well, I've been chopping weeds with a shovel all summer, I can try."

The road ended at a small bridge, which crossed Virgo Creek to their left. Jenny could see that the creek had been high along there some time before. The dried mud flats on the other side of the bridge showed ruts and ridges where several cars had gotten stuck. She pointed. "Is that where you got so muddy last spring?"

As Mike swung across the bridge, he laughed. "Those aren't all my ruts. At least half of them were made by Quent Lacey."

"Who's he? Another miner?"

"Shit. He's everything a miner isn't and wouldn't be caught dead being."

"Well, what does he do out here?"

"He's a real estate developer—not the top guy, but one of their promoters. Pushy as hell. They bought up a bunch of old mine claims and they've built some cracker-box houses on them. You'll see them when we get to the top of the hill."

After they crossed the bridge, and Mike shifted into four-wheel drive, they started up a rocky road that climbed the hill at a steep angle, curving back and forth through the trees, always rising. Though the road showed signs of recent bulldozing, it was still fairly narrow. Jenny took a quick breath when they rounded a curve and met a small red Datsun.

Mike crowded the right side of the road. Tree branches scratched along the side of the pickup and snapped at the edge of Jenny's open window. She slid toward the middle of the seat as the Datsun passed their truck, and through Mike's window she caught a glimpse of blond hair and a mustache. The man nodded to Mike.

"That's Quentin Lacey," Mike said. "Son of a bitch doesn't seem to know that the vehicle coming up the hill has the right-of-way."

"Why does it?" Jenny asked.

"Because it's more dangerous to back downhill to a turnout than it is to back uphill to a turnout."

The pickup crested the hill. The road narrowed and curved away to the left; to the right a broad new path had been slashed through the timber. Mike stopped the pickup and pointed to the Caterpillar that sat on one side of the road.

"They say the miners destroy the land, but the bastard who runs that D-eight has done more damage in two years than the miners did in a hundred."

Jenny looked back through the pines and firs that grew thickly on the hillside. She could see several wooden houses, some built on a slope so steep that the front half of each building had to be supported by long poles set into the ground. The houses looked raw; the varnished pine wood was a glaring yellow against the green of the mountainside.

"How awful," Jenny said. "What do they call it?"

"Craggy Claims," Mike said. "Isn't that a goddamn phony name?"

Jenny wrinkled her nose and nodded. Mike started up again, and they began the steep climb toward the left, away from the development.

"If this has always been a mining district, how can they build houses here?"

"Oh, they stay just within the law. Mining law says you can put one miner's residence on each claim. They've bought up claims all over this mountain."

Jenny was glad when they rounded another curve, crossed a bridge, and left the ugly houses behind.

"That's Simpson Creek," Mike said, "and this is Simpson Gulch."

Now the road was even narrower, but it settled beneath the trees as if it belonged there, winding around the side of the mountain, always climbing, always accompanied by the silvery stream. They drove slowly. Jenny moved back to her window and looked out. The grass on the slope was turning tan and gold. Yellow flowers bloomed here and there, and on one delicate stalk she saw a tiny bell-shaped purple flower. The sun came through the trees in hot yellow splotches; from the shade rose the cool smell of evergreens.

Jenny began to hum another little tune to Corey. They reached a fork in the road. The creek and a small spur turned off to the right. Mike took the spur. The pickup dipped down to cross the creek on a log-and-plank bridge and then rose with the steep road that curved to the right again, ending at the top of a large mine dump.

"Oh," breathed Jenny and was silent. In front of her on the left, a patchwork quilt of green and yellow meadow grass covered a small level area. At the back of the meadow, snuggled against the mountain underneath an immense pine tree, sat a weathered log cabin. It had one door and two windows in front, like a nose and two eyes. Jenny could see a few new-looking plank ends extending from the roof, but the rest of the cabin seemed as old as the mountain. The logs were chocolate brown, and beneath the right-hand window a wild rosebush reached thorny fingers toward the sill.

To the right of the cabin, about fifty feet away, was the tunnel. A heavy steel-mesh door covered the mouth of the tunnel; a huge padlock hung from the chain that held the door to the fat tree trunk that was the door post. A few feet from the door a little railcar rested its wheels on narrow tracks that extended back into the tunnel.

On the far side of the tracks was another small log structure surrounded by a fence made of slender tree trunks. And beyond the fenced area stood an outhouse.

Mike opened his door. "Welcome to the Spanish Mary."

CHAPTER
12

▲▲▲▲▲▲

Jenny started to ask a question about the name of the mine, but her mouth fell open as a figure came out the door of the smaller log building.

Mike jumped from the truck and ran yelling toward the pole fence. "Rosie, God damn you, if you busted that shop door again, I'll . . ." The rest of his words were lost as he vaulted the fence and lit beside the small gray burro, who reared back and wheeled away to the far corner of the pen.

Corey, who had fallen asleep again during the climb up the hill, slept on. "You funny little mouse," Jenny said, "you've learned to sleep through all the noises we inflict on you." Jenny looked down at the tall center hump in the floor of the pickup. It made a perfect barrier. "If I put you down here to sleep, you'll be safe. Even if you wiggle a little, you can't get to anything that will hurt you."

Jenny arranged Corey's blankets on the truck floor in front of her seat and laid Corey down. She slid to the ground from the high seat and shut the door. After going around to close Mike's door, too, she walked across the mine dump to the fence. She could hear Mike muttering curses inside the small shop as he banged on something metallic. The burro was still in the far corner of the pen, her head lowered, her ears forward like antennae. Jenny moved slowly around the pole fence. "It's all right, little donkey," she murmured. "Don't be scared. That's a good baby." The burro's ears swiveled toward Jenny, but she didn't move away as Jenny drew near. Jenny reached out slowly and quietly and finally put her hand through the poles and touched the burro's nose. The burro turned her head toward Jenny and pulled the rubbery flesh of her lips back a little.

"There, girl. You're okay." Jenny ran her hand up the bony nose to the hump between the ears. She scratched the rough hair at the base of the burro's ears.

The burro was mostly gray, but a smart black stripe ran down her spine, and like the top bar of the letter *T,* another black stripe crossed the first at right angles along the creature's shoulders.

Mike had replaced the hinge on the shop door. He closed it behind him and crossed the pen to where Jenny stood. The burro shied away from him, trotting to the other side of the pen.

"You didn't tell me you had a burro," Jenny said.

"I haven't had her very long," Mike said. "I won her off a guy in a poker game, but the damn little devil is more trouble than she's worth."

"What do you do with her?"

"Hitch her to that ore car when it's full."

Jenny began to move back around the pen toward the animal. "Did you call her Rosie?"

"Yeah," Mike said as he climbed out of the pen.

Jenny reached through the poles and touched the burro's furry side hair. She glanced down at Rosie's feet. "Oh, Mike, what happened to her hooves? They look so ragged; they're all chipped and cracked around the edges."

"The guy had her in a mine full of water. Her hooves dried out and cracked. They're some better now."

"Poor Rosie," Jenny said. The burro turned her head toward Jenny and looked at her with one eye. Jenny laughed. "She's cute."

"Cute, hell. She's a pain in the ass. She's more aggravating than any of the equipment. As soon as I can afford a tractor to pull the ore car, I'm going to get rid of her."

The burro's ears flicked toward Mike. "He doesn't mean it, Rosie," Jenny said as she reached through the poles again to rub the burro's neck. The big muscles surprised her. Rosie was so little; her head only came to Jenny's shoulder.

"Come on, Jenny," Mike said. "You came up here to help, didn't you?"

Jenny turned away from the fence. "I want to help you, but I'm worried about leaving Corey alone."

"Hell, Jenny, the two of us will fill that ore car every ten minutes. When it's full, you can play with Corey while Rosie takes it to the end of the track so I can dump it."

"What if she cries while we're still in there?"

"I'll move the truck right up beside the portal," Mike said, "and we'll leave the window open. The generator's muffled by the shop walls, and we won't be drilling. If she cries, we'll hear her."

"What if a wild animal comes around?"

Mike looked at Jenny and laughed. "Jesus, Jenny. Don't you know anything about wild animals? They won't come anywhere near this place. They're more scared of you than you are of them." Mike started toward the cabin. "Come on," he said again, "let's get started while she's still asleep."

Jenny followed Mike to the plank door of the log cabin. Mike unlocked the padlock and Jenny stepped inside. When her eyes were accustomed to the dim light she looked around. The cabin had just one room, which was smaller than their house, about fourteen by eighteen feet. The windows were boarded up on the outside; a few pieces of glass hung in the inner frames. Piled on the wooden floor were boxes she recognized, old wooden milk crates with Mike's tools in them. At one end of the cabin a small coal stove stood on three legs, with a pile of bricks serving as the fourth. Five bales of hay had been dumped near the stove.

Mike rummaged through one of the boxes and pulled out an olive drab hard hat. "Here, put this on."

Jenny settled the liner of the hat down around her ears. She giggled. "I feel like I'm wearing a soup kettle."

"You'll be glad you're wearing that thing first time you hit your head on the back."

"The back of what?"

"The back of the tunnel. I suppose you'd call it the top of the tunnel."

"Oh. Is being in the tunnel like being inside a whale?"

Mike turned around frowning. "What?"

"Well, if the back is over your head . . ." Jenny said no more; Mike had already turned back to the box. He brought out another hard hat and a flashlight.

"That's all we'll need right now. The shovels are in the tunnel. I'll bring the truck closer and get the generator started. You wanna give some hay to that donkey and get the water bucket out of the pen?"

Mike parked the truck close to the mine opening and then went to the shop. For the first time Jenny noticed the wires that ran from the shop door along the top fence pole. They angled down toward the tunnel, disappearing into it through the crack at the right-hand side of the door. As she went to the truck she heard a motor start up in the shop.

Corey was still sound asleep. Jenny picked up the big Navajo blanket Mike kept in the truck and draped it over the steering wheel and along the dash to keep the sun out of Corey's face. Before she shut the door she took an apple from the lunch sack. She stuck it into her pocket and went to get the hay.

The bales were partly broken; she pulled away a piece that was about ten inches thick and carried it to the pen. There was a gate on the near corner by the shop. She shoved the hay under the fence and opened the gate. Rosie came forward. Jenny closed the gate and took the apple from her pocket. The donkey pulled her lips back, sticking her long nose forward. Jenny could see bits of chewed grass in the cracks of her yellow teeth.

"My, what big teeth you have," she said, "but you need a tooth-brush."

Rosie fumbled for the apple with her lips and then took it into her mouth. Picking up the hay, Jenny carried it to the corner by the water bucket. As she bent to reach the wire handle Rosie nudged her gently in the rear. Laughing, Jenny stood up and turned around. The burro nibbled her pocket.

"Somebody used to spoil you, huh?" She rubbed the soft muzzle gently.

"Stop messing with that damn jackass," Mike said from the door of the shop. "You'll make her more worthless than she is already."

"She's not a jack, she's a jenny."

Mike grinned and said, "So now I've got two jennies working for me."

Jenny bit her lip and picked up the water bucket. She walked to the gate. "Where do I get the water?"

Mike flung his head back. "Down at the creek."

Jenny went down the mine road to the bridge and knelt to dip the bucket. The water was cold. She looked into the creek. In the shade, everything was dark brown and olive green, but where the sun hit the water, the rocks and sand were salmon and peach and orange and gold.

"You coming, Jenny?" Mike called.

She lugged the bucket up the slope and set it down in the corner of the pen. Rosie stuck her nose into the bucket and sucked noisily.

Jenny followed Mike to the tunnel. "You said you won Rosie in a poker game. I didn't know you'd been playing cards," she said as he bent to put the key in the padlock. "I thought you worked up here every night."

"Jesus, Jenny, you'll find out soon enough how much fun this is." He took the padlock from the hasp. "I need a night off once in a while."

Mike swung the heavy metal gate wide, lifting the front end as it sagged and dragging it across the tracks to prop it open against the dirt bank. Then he picked up the two short-handled shovels that leaned against the tunnel wall and handed one to Jenny. She took it and followed Mike into the tunnel, stepping carefully from one rough tie to the next inside the rails. At the left-hand side of the track the water flowed along in a little ditch. She could hear more water running somewhere ahead. The air in the tunnel was moist and cold, and rich with a smell like burnt sulphur matches or firecrackers. Light bulbs dangled at twenty-foot intervals from the wires that came in from the shop. Their light was dim near the mouth, but as soon as Mike and Jenny rounded a bend in the tunnel the lights seemed much brighter.

Jenny looked around. The tunnel was small. When she stretched out her arms she could almost touch the walls on either side. The roof—no, the back—was only a foot or so above Mike's head. She saw needles of stone overhead, thin as pencils, but longer, hanging down from the roof.

"Look, Mike," she said.

He stopped and glanced up. "Yeah, this place will be another Carlsbad Caverns in a thousand years. Those things are worthless though, mostly iron." He turned and went on down the tunnel.

Jenny continued to look at the stone formations. The drops of water at the ends of the long needles shimmered in the light. The water sounds were peaceful; the world seemed far away. She listened for a moment to see if she could hear Corey and then went onward into the tunnel, moving slowly on the uneven ties.

When she was more sure of her footing again Jenny looked around her. About every eight feet a section of sawed log was placed across the top, wedged tightly between the sides of the tunnel. The rock in the tunnel was pretty: patches of dark brown set off wide sections of mustard yellow, light tan, and rust. In one spot the tunnel was covered with a fine coat of sparkling white crystals—hundreds of slivers of stone, reflecting the light. Some of the silvery formation looked like a field of feathers; other parts were like tiny flowers.

Mike moved steadily into the tunnel, and Jenny hurried to catch up. They reached a wide spot where another tunnel had been started, but it ran for only a few feet. The water came from there. High up the wall a spring bubbled from the rock. The water tumbled into an old wooden trough at the bottom.

Jenny asked, "Is that good water?"

Mike stopped. "Hell no. It's full of minerals; it would probably poison you."

They moved straight down the main tunnel for another hundred feet, following the rail. The firecracker smell grew stronger, but the air was not unpleasant to Jenny.

"I didn't think you would be able to breathe very well in a mine tunnel," she said, "but this is nice."

"Yeah, there's a fresh-air shaft around here somewhere. I found signs of pack rats in the tunnel; they had plenty of air. But you'd better not breathe the gas that comes off the muck pile. It could kill you too."

The tunnel made an abrupt turn to the left. The track followed a gentler curve in the same direction.

"Why did they turn here?" Jenny asked.

"To follow the vein of ore."

"How did *you* know what to look for?"

"I've been in mines before, and Tony helps some when I can get him away from Mom's."

"I thought he wasn't supposed to go in mines anymore on account of his lungs."

"He doesn't go in when I'm shooting. Besides, we've been working in the shop. He's showing me how to concentrate my own ore."

"Do you have to do that?"

"When and if that son of a bitch at the mill accepts your ore, he takes forty percent of its value for milling it. And anyway, I don't know if he's going to start taking small lots again or not. So I'm going to cheat the bastard by doing the whole thing myself."

Just then the lights flickered and went out. "Oh, damn it to hell," Mike said.

Jenny heard him fumbling in his clothes, and then he turned on the flashlight. Its tiny beam made the darkness around them seem immense.

"I've got to take the flashlight. Will you be scared to stay here by yourself?"

"I don't know, Mike. I don't think so, but I've never been in a mine tunnel before."

"I'll be back as soon as I get the generator going."

"Check on Corey. It seems like we've been in here a long time."

"I'd take you with me, but it will be faster if I don't have to light the way for both of us, and it's not safe for you to try it in the dark."

"Are those pack rats still in here?"

"Nope, they took off with the first blast of dynamite."

Mike turned and started back down the rail. Jenny leaned her shovel against the rock wall. It was wet and muddy on both sides of the track, so she squatted to sit between the rails. She looked up at the rock in the tunnel, but Mike's light was fading quickly. When he rounded the curve, Jenny was in total darkness. She could hear Mike's steps for a while, and then all she could hear was the faraway whispering of the water.

CHAPTER
13

▲▲▲▲▲▲

Jenny held her hand in front of her face, but she couldn't see anything. The darkness was thick and soft around her. It seemed warm—warmer at least than the cold metal of the rails and the damp ties beneath her. She shifted a little and settled on her bottom to wait.

She wasn't afraid. She thought suddenly of Richard. Would Richard's demons follow him in here? Did she have demons of her own? Maybe her memories of Mama. Maybe thoughts of Karen now, too. Jenny's mind began to speed up, and the old sense of blurred vision seemed to fill her eyes, even though she was sitting in darkness. She tried, as she had before, to slow the images. *If I could stop them one time they wouldn't make me feel so sick.* She leaned her head into her hands and the full weight of the darkness moved closer to her. Silence merged with the darkness, and Jenny felt comforted.

The earth beneath her was hard-packed and solid. Nothing moved. She reached out her arms and drew them back, her palms facing her as she pulled the darkness even nearer. Her mind cleared, and she thought about Billy. *I have to find a way to get Billy away* from the dump. Maybe they'll move us soon. Mike's been acting like something's happening at work.

Jenny stretched her legs out in front of her and stopped thinking. The darkness moved gently into her mind; she felt something inside her reach up to meet it. She floated in the dark moist air, swaying with a deep slow rhythm that seemed part of the darkness, part of the rock above her and beneath her.

When the lights came on she blinked and looked around. She was sitting flat on the ties, but she was still moving gently from side to side. She slowed her movements and stopped; the peaceful feeling floated softly inside her.

Hearing a rumbling sound from the tunnel, she stood up and waited. She could hear Mike's voice and more than one set of footsteps. In a few moments Mike rounded the curve, pulling on a rope, which was fastened to Rosie's halter. Rosie, now in collar and harness, stepped gracefully along at the side of the rail, and grumbling along the track behind her came the empty ore car.

When Rosie saw Jenny she moved forward eagerly and nibbled Jenny's pocket with her rubbery lips. Jenny scratched her ears.

"No more apples, Rosie. I think us jennies have to work before we can eat." If Mike's remark about the jennies had hurt, it didn't anymore. She felt pleasant and happy.

She turned for her shovel and walked up the track as far as she could go, stopping at the dead end of the tunnel, where a pile of rock blocked the track.

Mike brought Rosie forward. He pulled a lever on the car. "Unhook the chain," he said.

"Which one?"

"The long one hanging down from the butt stick." He pointed to the bolt, covered in rubber hose, that hung behind the burro's legs.

Jenny unlatched the safety lock and lifted the hook from the metal loop on the ore car; Mike walked Rosie around to the other end of the car and hooked the chain to a loop on that end. Rosie dropped her head, shook herself slightly, and stood still.

"Will she just stand there?"

"Sure. She's been in and out of mines most of her life. Donkeys learn the routines pretty quick." Mike turned to Jenny. "Corey's still asleep, but she'll probably be hungry before long. We better start mucking." He picked up a shovel and began to pitch rock into the car.

Jenny loaded her shovel, but it was too heavy for her to lift. She dumped it out and started again with a smaller load. Lifting and dumping, filling and lifting, dumping and filling, she soon found herself back in the rhythm of the darkness. She swayed from side to side as she moved the rock.

Jenny was only vaguely aware that her back had begun to hurt when she realized that Mike was standing still, looking at her. She dumped her shovel load and leaned against the ore car.

"Well, lady, you're one helluva mucker," Mike said. "You better slow down, honey. You'll get damn tired before we're done."

Tears sprang to Jenny's eyes. Mike seldom praised her and almost never called her honey. She started shoveling again and tried to work more slowly, but soon the wonderful rhythm was in her body again. She gave in to it and moved the rock at her own pace.

The ore car was full and piled high by the time they quit. Mike moved around to Rosie's head and picked up the halter rope. He released the brake on the car and gave the rope a tug, but the donkey pulled her head to the side. When Mike stepped back and jerked the rope Rosie didn't move a hoof. She just stretched her head and then her neck, forward.

"You goddamn stubborn donkey; you do this every time. Come on."

Rosie switched her tail from side to side and tossed her head. Then she turned sideways and looked at Jenny. Jenny moved next to Mike. Rosie swung her head around and nudged Jenny gently. Jenny bent down and scratched under the burro's chin. She whispered in Rosie's ear, "Come on, honey, let's go get an apple."

Jenny pulled lightly on the halter. Rosie leaned into the collar, humped her back, and with her front legs slanting backward, gave a forward heave. The ore car full of rock trembled and began to roll forward.

"Well, I'll be damned," Mike said. "What did you say to her?"

"Oh, I just whispered a little love word that seems to work on jennies."

The rail was on a slight downward incline going out of the tunnel, and it wasn't hard for Rosie to keep the car moving along. When they reached the sunlight Mike dumped the ore into the sorting pile while Jenny got another apple for Rosie.

Corey was awake and wet, but not crying. "You're so patient," Jenny said, kissing her cheek. She changed the baby and fed her. When Corey was full and dry Jenny put her back in her cozy little hollow. Corey kicked her feet and reached for the stray sunbeam that sneaked around the edge of the Navajo blanket and angled across her corner.

Jenny and Mike loaded the ore car three more times. While Mike urged Rosie to the end of the track, unlatched the car, swung it around, and opened the end to let the ore slide out, Jenny held Corey in her arms and told her about the tunnel and the mountain. She showed her one of the tiny purple bells and a sturdy stalk full of salmon-colored blooms.

At noon she and Mike ate lunch on the tailgate of the pickup while Corey kicked and gurgled and wiggled on the blanket Mike had spread out in the back of the truck.

Jenny looked down at her clothes. "Now I know where the word *mucky* comes from," she said.

Mike was also covered with yellow-gray mud. "I have to run water in there when I'm drilling," he said. "It makes a sloppy mess for mucking."

"I don't see anything to drill with. Do you use electricity?"

"No. I've got that old compressor and a bunch of air hose in the shop. I drag the hose down there and hook it up to the jackhammer. I run a little electric pump from the trough for water."

"Where'd you get all that stuff?" Jenny asked, remembering Karen's comments about the money Mike spent at the mine.

"Bought it cheap and fixed it up, mostly. Stole the rail from an old mine up on top of the hill. It's dryer than this one, and the rail was in good shape."

"Won't somebody miss it?"

"Haven't yet. Nobody's mining up here but me."

After they ate they settled Corey inside the truck again, hooked

Rosie to the ore car, and went back into the tunnel. They filled and emptied the car three times more before the tunnel was cleared to the breast, as Mike called the dead end. Mike had to set a joint-rail on the ties he'd put down earlier so he'd be able to get the ore car close enough to the muck pile after the next shot. A joint-rail was just a temporary rail. Jenny asked Mike the names of things as he used them and tried to remember everything.

"Richard said I should go back to school," she said to Mike when they were resting.

"Richard should mind his own business," Mike said.

"This is kind of like school," she said, "with you as the teacher."

Mike gave her a funny little grin. Why, he's pleased, she thought. The day was turning out much better than it had started.

It was late afternoon by the time they dumped the last load. Jenny rinsed her hands and opened her shirt to feed Corey. When the baby was sleeping again, Jenny asked Mike, "Does anybody ever come up this road?"

"Not very often. The development's over on the other side. Why?"

"I'm so dirty. I want to go down to the creek and take a bath."

Mike turned toward her, and she saw the quick hot look that always lit his eyes when he wanted to make love.

"We'll probably freeze to death," he said, "but I'll join you."

CHAPTER

14

▲▲▲▲▲▲

Mike put his arm around Jenny's shoulders as they went down the road. When they reached the creek, Jenny took off her shirt and jeans and laid them on the bridge. She started to unhook her bra, but Mike said in a husky voice, "Let me." He dropped her bra on top of her other clothes and took her breasts in his hands. "I want to wash you," he said.

"You've never wanted to do that before," Jenny said. Mike grinned and ran his finger around her nipple. Jenny shivered and pulled away to slip out of her panties.

When she stepped into the stream, Mike leaned down from the bridge and splashed water up her legs and over her back and breasts. Her nipples stood out. Mike pulled her toward him. He kissed one nipple and then sucked it gently. He glanced up, a surprised expression on his face.

"I forgot about the milk," he said.

Jenny laughed and reached for Mike's shirt buttons, but he backed away. "No. I'll wash myself. You're getting too cold. Take the truck blanket to the cabin."

Jenny washed her face and arms and climbed onto the bridge. She put on her shirt, stuck her feet in her shoes, scooped up the rest of her clothes and ran up the road. By the time she had taken Corey and her afghan and the bigger blanket from the pickup, Mike was on the mine dump. He went into the cabin and arranged two bales of hay at right angles so that they formed a little pen with the corner walls. He took Corey from Jenny's arms and settled her inside with her orange and yellow blanket. Then he pushed his tool crates out of the way and spread the Navajo blanket on the wide, worn planks of the floor.

Jenny was still shivering, but Mike pulled her onto the blanket. "I'll warm you," he said, running his hands up and down her body. Jenny's skin tingled from the water and the mountain air. Mike's hands were warm; when he pulled her close his body felt hot against her skin.

Mike didn't hurry her. He continued to stroke her body, and Jenny's shivering turned to excitement. The floor was hard beneath the blanket, but Jenny forgot it as the rhythm of their lovemaking began. There were no sounds anywhere but the sounds they made together.

When at last they lay side by side, relaxed, Jenny said, "That was nice. You're different up here in the mountains."

Mike said, "I'm glad you're here. Sometimes that tunnel gives me the spooks."

"Oh, I liked the tunnel," Jenny said. "I'll help you again." Mike put his arm around her, and they drifted off to sleep.

It was only later, when Mike helped her into the truck and settled Corey in her lap, that Jenny realized how stiff she was going to be on Sunday. As they jolted down the rough road cut by the developer's D-8, her arms and back began to ache, and she winced when they hit a bump.

Mike glanced at her. "Sore?"

"I'll have to run that shovel every day or not at all," she said, smiling at him.

"I could damn well use your help," Mike said. "If we got some gold, I'd tell that construction company to go to hell." The muscle in his jaw made a hard line.

▽ ▽

Billy had caught an eight-inch trout. Tony said he'd only helped Billy to net it. In Mike's opinion, voiced quietly to Jenny, the fish had to be either damn stupid or damn hungry to let a four-year-old kid hook it. But he listened to Billy's excited babble and didn't scold when the boy bumped into the table on one of his wide happy swings around the room.

Jenny cooked the fish Tony had caught along with Billy's and they all ate together.

"Jenny's a helluva good mucker," Mike said to Tony.

Tony smiled and asked, "Are you going to teach her to drill and shoot?"

"Why not?" Mike joked. "If she handles the jackhammer the way she handles a shovel, I can just sit back and get rich." He smiled at Jenny and ran his hand up her arm. "I might even change the name of the mine to the American Jenny."

"In honor of Rosie and me."

"How are Rosie's feet?" Tony asked.

"Some better."

"You ought to get some pine tar on those hooves before you use her in the muck too often."

Jenny poured coffee for the three of them and sat at the table listening contentedly to the talk about the Spanish Mary and Tony's stories about other mines. Billy sat on her lap until he fell asleep; then Mike got up and took the boy from her and put him to bed.

If it could always be this way, I'd never have to think about Karen's questions, Jenny thought, as she turned Bigfoot's rocking chair around and nursed the baby. After Tony left she did the dishes and slipped into bed beside Mike.

The weather stayed warm after Labor Day, and the week began peacefully. In the shade of the porch roof, Jenny made a playpen out of milk crates to keep Corey from traveling too far. Corey didn't seem to be moving when you watched her, but Jenny always found her in the opposite crib corner from the one she started out in. "Corey concentrates," Jenny told Mike. "I swear she does things by willpower."

Mike just grunted. He had come home late, and he went to bed right after he ate.

Jenny washed clothes Monday and Tuesday and hung them outside to dry. Her muscles ached as she lifted the basket and when she reached up to the line, but the sun was warm on her back, and above her head the sky was blue for as far as she could see. After a while her muscles stopped hurting. Mike didn't mention her helping him at the mine again.

She and Billy found a little wheelbarrow and a one-eyed doll at the dump, and she let Tony bring her a new box of books. Most of them were Westerns and romance novels, but there was a tattered copy of a book about flowers. Though it had no cover, she set it alongside the Bible and the Shakespeare book. She thought about going to town and buying a better book, but she didn't have any money. She decided to read the Westerns and romances and throw them away before Richard saw them.

Mom Bradley dropped by late Tuesday afternoon and sat on the porch for a while. "I better rest while I can," she said. "My relief help will be moving out soon. The construction company's about finished up here, and my one waitress goes when her husband goes."

Jenny said, "I wish I knew what was going to happen to us. I don't think they've told Mike yet."

Mom Bradley tugged at her shirt and smoothed it across her belly. "At least I've got Richard to wash dishes—such help as he is."

"I like Richard," Jenny said.

Mom Bradley patted Jenny's arm. "You're a good girl, Jenny. You like everybody."

"I don't like Tully Stocker."

"Has that bastard been bothering you again?"

"Not so much lately. I think he's scared of Mike. But he's still mad about my taking Karen away."

Mom Bradley raised her bulk from the chair. "I'd better get back up there. Richard's tending bar, and he might go Socialist on me and start serving drinks on the house again."

Jenny laughed. She walked Mom Bradley to the car and watched her drive off; then she brought the rocking chair and her mending to the porch. Billy was fishing off the end of the porch with a dried weed stalk and a piece of string; Corey had fallen asleep in the playpen. Jenny glanced up occasionally when she heard a truck go by. She hadn't seen the blue and silver truck for a long time.

▽ ▽

On Friday evening, to Jenny's surprise, Richard parked his Cadillac by their porch and came to her door. He had been drinking but he wasn't loud. When she invited him in, he didn't mention the new crate of books, but he took a book from his pocket. "This is haiku," he said and began to read Jenny some of the short verses. The book was called *The Jade Tree,* and Jenny loved the verses.

Billy and Corey fell asleep listening to Richard read. Jenny did the dishes and then sat in her rocker and listened. Mike came in around midnight, greeted Richard gruffly and said, "Did you keep something hot for me?"

Jenny quickly served his meal. Richard closed the book, nodded his good-byes to Mike and Jenny, and went home.

"What in the hell was he doing here?" Mike asked.

"Just reading poetry," Jenny said.

Mike snorted. "Jesus. Poetry. Weird company you choose."

"There's hardly any other kind around here," Jenny said, and began to get ready for bed. Mike followed her and fell asleep immediately. As Jenny listened to his snores she thought of the tunnel. The Japanese verses had some of the darkness in them. There wasn't any harm in Richard's reading to her. Mike shifted in his sleep and flung his leg across hers. She pulled her leg out and kicked his leg with her heel until he moved over.

CHAPTER

15

▲▲▲▲▲▲

Mike woke Jenny in the gray light before dawn, his hands moving hard across her breasts and down her body. She murmured a sleepy protest, but Mike was already on top of her. Jenny let him do what he wanted, trying to remember the gentle cold water bath he had given her on the mountain. He didn't seem like the same person, and she bit her lip to keep from crying until he came and rolled off of her, panting.

She got up and washed herself. Before she could go back to bed, Corey was crying. Billy woke, too, and didn't go back to sleep. Jenny fed both the children, trying to keep them quiet so they wouldn't wake Mike. Billy stayed on his bed for an hour. Then he began to play on the floor with his truck.

Mike rolled over. "What's all the goddamn noise?" Jenny didn't reply, but Billy got back up on his bed and held the truck in his lap.

▽　▽

Mike left after breakfast, and Jenny tried to catch up on the laundry, but by four o'clock Saturday afternoon she had a headache and Billy was whiny. She left the diapers in the sink and took Billy on her lap in the rocking chair.

She read him the story from Corey's book. Then she held him

close to her and traced his nose and eyebrows, cheeks, and chin with her finger. Billy lay against her quietly.

"What are you thinking about, Billy Bright?"

He raised his eyes. "I'm glad mamas are soft." She laughed and squeezed him tightly. He sat up. "Can I go outside and play?"

"Sure, and let's put Corey on the porch."

When Corey was settled on her blankets in the milk crate playpen, Jenny went behind the house to hang the dipers. Alone with her children and her own routine, Jenny began to relax. She fixed a picnic supper and they ate on the porch. But when Tully Stocker drove down to his trailer, Jenny took the children inside and locked the door. She was relieved when his pickup went back up the dump road, but she left the door locked and stayed inside, putting the children to bed earlier than usual and dozing in the rocking chair as she waited for Mike to come home.

It was past midnight when she heard a pickup coming down the road. Hearing footsteps on the porch, Jenny started to unlock the door, then stopped uncertainly. It didn't sound like Mike.

Someone tried the door. She watched the handle turn and heard Tully Stocker say, "Let me in, you bitch. I'll teach you to mind your own business."

Jenny's heart began to beat in her throat. She switched off the light and stood silently in the center of the room. Tully rattled the knob again. "You're going to tell me where you took my wife," he said in a louder voice.

Jenny stayed still and prayed that the children wouldn't wake. Tully crashed his fist against the door panel. "Ow! Jesus Christ!" he said, and then she heard him say, "Oh, shit" and the sound of his footsteps leaving the porch.

Jenny stood in the same spot until she heard the door of Tully's trailer close. Then she went to the stove and turned the heat on under the coffeepot. Where was Mike? She felt as much anger at him as she did at Tully; he ought to be there when she needed him.

She drank the hot bitter coffee in the dark. Finally, when no more sounds came from Tully's trailer, she turned on the light. She tried to read, but she was too unsettled to concentrate.

It was two o'clock before Mike's truck came down the road. She stood instantly when his steps sounded on the porch. Mike tried the lock, but before she could reach the door to unlock it, he said, "What the hell," and kicked the door open with one blow from his booted foot.

Jenny jumped away toward the crib as Mike came roaring in. She had never seen him so drunk.

"Goddamn dirty sonsabitches. They can take their fuckin' job and shove it." Mike picked up a kitchen chair and threw it across the room. He picked up another and brought it down on the table, splintering the leg.

Billy woke and began to cry. Corey woke and wailed along with her brother. Mike whirled toward Jenny.

"Take the kids and get out of here," he said. "Get the hell out."

Jenny snatched Corey and her blankets from the crib, grabbed Billy's blanket and Billy's hand, and left the house. Oh, God, I should have taken the truck keys, she thought. But she didn't dare go back. Once outside she noticed that the light was still on in Tully's trailer. She ducked into the shadow behind the house and headed for Tony's shop.

Tony had gone fishing again, but the shop door was open. Jenny pulled Billy inside and shut it behind her.

The shop was dark. Jenny felt her way toward the back room and finally stumbled against the cot. She set Corey down on the narrow bed and held Billy close to her.

He whimpered a little and said, "What's the matter with Daddy?"

"He's upset about something," Jenny said, trying to keep her voice from shaking. "He wanted us to go away until he's not mad anymore."

"Is he mad at us?"

"I don't think so, Billy." She wrapped his blanket around him. "Lie down here beside Corey, honey."

"You lie down, too, Mama."

Jenny listened for a minute. She couldn't hear any sounds near the shop. She moved Corey slightly and lay down beside Billy, covering them all with Billy's blanket.

Billy snuggled close to her, and she rubbed his hair gently until she felt him relax. She patted Corey's bottom, feeling sorry for the poor little girl. Wakened by a raving maniac and then snatched from her crib in the middle of the night. Poor, poor baby.

When the children were asleep, Jenny lay awake in the darkness. She was tired, but her stomach was in a tight knot, and she couldn't relax. My life is worse than any of those crappy books I read. I am so ashamed, she thought.

The thought startled her, but it was true. The strongest emotion she felt was a humiliating sense of shame.

How did I ever let myself end up below the dump, living with crazy people and drunks? What am I doing to my children? She shifted her legs a little, easing a cramp. Then, remembering Karen, she thought, At least Mike didn't hit me.

The darkness was a blessing. It made her feel safer. She began to unwind a little. Billy's warm body eased the knot in her stomach, and Jenny began to cry silently in the dark. She needed someone to put her on the bus. She couldn't do it alone.

CHAPTER

16

▲▲▲▲▲▲

The door of Tony's shop swung open. Jenny was alert at once. She looked toward the door, but the bright morning light behind the figure there blinded her.

"Jenny? Oh my God, Jenny, I'm glad you're here."

Mike came forward. Jenny swung her legs over the edge of the bed and sat up, using her body to shield the children. Corey had wakened near dawn, but slept again after nursing, although Jenny had little milk for her. Billy was still asleep. Jenny's heart pounded as she said, "What do you want?" almost holding her breath to keep her voice steady.

Mike stood in front of her. When he didn't answer she repeated, "What do you want?"

Billy woke then and sat up. He looked at Mike and rubbed his eyes with the heel of his hand. He said to Jenny, "Is Daddy still mad, Mama?"

Jenny stood up slowly. She reached out and patted Billy's head. "It's okay, Billy," she said, wishing she knew for certain that it *was* okay. "It's morning, and I bet you're hungry; we'd better go eat some breakfast."

Mike said, "Don't go to the house, Jenny. I'll take you out to breakfast."

Jenny said, "I have to get diapers for Corey." She turned and picked up the baby, who stirred in her arms and woke as they stepped into the sunlight.

"Let Billy wait in the truck with me," Mike said.

Jenny turned. Mike looked miserable. His skin had a yellow cast, and there were dark shadows under his eyes. He waited for her answer.

"All right, Billy," she said. "Wait with Daddy."

"I have to go potty."

"We can go behind the shop," Mike said.

Mike and Billy walked around to the back of the shop. Jenny took Corey to the house. The broken door had been pulled partway closed. Jenny pushed it open, stepped inside, and stopped. She had seen Mike break the chairs, but even so, the shattered door and ruined furniture were shocking in the daylight. No wonder Mike hadn't wanted Billy to see the room.

She put Corey in the crib and took off the baby's nightgown, then changed her diapers and washed her. Corey gurgled. Jenny put her face against the baby's tummy and said, "Kiss, kiss, kiss." After putting clean clothes on Corey, she gathered supplies for the baby and then washed her own face and hands, smoothed her hair, and changed into clean jeans and the blouse Karen had given her.

The knot was back in her stomach. She had thought all night

about getting away, but would she be able to handle two kids and find a job? She didn't even have bus fare to Mitchell. Beside that, as she'd known all along, she couldn't leave her children with strangers. But how could she stand another night like last night?

She took Corey from the crib and stepped onto the porch, looking back as she pulled the crippled door closed. Thank God he didn't break my rocking chair, she thought. The smooth, graceful rocker sat in its space by the crib. Tears filled her eyes. She wiped them away and went out to the truck.

Mike drove past Mom's Café and took them to a little doughnut shop on a side street in Dolby. Jenny hadn't even known it was there. They sat in one of the two booths in the small shop. A man stood at a table behind the counter, rolling and thumping a mound of dough. A middle-aged woman brought them water and menus.

Mike ordered juice, milk, and doughnuts for Billy, and coffee, juice, and doughnuts for Jenny and himself. When the coffee came he held the cup in his hands as if he were cold. Jenny sipped her coffee, but she couldn't eat.

"Can I go watch the man make doughnuts, Mama?"

Jenny slid out of the booth so Billy could get out. He went to the counter, climbed onto a stool, and watched solemnly as the man began to cut doughnuts with a round metal cutter.

Jenny sat down again and took a deep breath. She said, "Mike, I want some money."

Mike set his cup down. "I don't have any money." He looked down at his hands. "I don't even have a job."

Jenny opened her mouth in shock. After a moment, she said, "What happened?"

"They fired me. They said I was stealing dynamite. They couldn't prove a thing, but the bastards just told me not to bother packing up. We're not moving with the company."

Jenny didn't know what to say. She hadn't expected this. Finally she asked, "*Were* you stealing dynamite?"

"Oh, hell. I took a few sticks, just to use in the mine. The company's so goddamn big they'll never miss it."

Jenny was silent. Apparently they *had* missed it.

Mike said, "Jenny, I'm sorry about breaking the door and the chairs." He looked down again. "I'm sorry about everything."

Jenny couldn't think of a reply. Mike's news had wiped out the careful speech she'd worked on during the long night. Even if she'd had some money, how could she walk out on Mike now? But she couldn't go back to that house.

Mike looked up again. The whites of his eyes were streaked with red. "God, Jenny, I want you to say something, but please don't tell me you're going to leave."

Jenny picked up her cup and drank the rest of the lukewarm coffee. "Mike, I *was* going to leave you," she said. "You have to know that. And I won't go back and live below the dump, but I won't leave you this way."

"What are we going to do?" He sounded as young as Billy.

"Do we have *any* money?" she asked.

"Enough to pay for breakfast, buy a few groceries, maybe pay next month's rent."

She decided not to ask where the money from the mortgaged truck had gone. It had probably all gone into the mine. The mine . . . She felt a sudden surge of excitement.

"Mike, is there really any good ore in that mine?"

He ran his hand across his face. "Well, yeah. It's fair—one or two ounces of gold to the ton. But, hell, Jenny, it's no good to us inside that tunnel."

Jenny swallowed. "Mike, maybe we could move up to the cabin and work the Spanish Mary."

Mike stared at her. "You're crazy. It takes money to run a mine. I just told you we'll be lucky to pay for breakfast." His voice rose as he spoke.

Jenny glanced around the shop. Billy had turned away from the doughnut maker; he looked as though he were about to cry.

Jenny rose. "Let's not talk about it here. Let's get some groceries and go up and see if that old cabin can be made livable."

Mike's face darkened, but he followed as Jenny held out her free hand to Billy. "Come on, honeybunch. We're going on a picnic, and you'll get to meet a long-eared lady named Rosie."

Billy giggld as he skipped along toward the truck. "I never saw a long-eared lady."

Mike was silent, but Billy chattered all the way to the mine. Jenny tried to work out some kind of plan. If they moved to the cabin, she'd at least be safe from Tully Stocker. The children would be safer there too. Mike hadn't hit her; he hadn't hurt the children. She turned to look at him. He looked so sick. He really did seem sorry. If they could get away from the dump, maybe they would have a chance. As they crossed the Simpson Creek bridge, Jenny suddenly felt very nervous. And maybe, she thought, maybe Karen would tell me I'm a fool. When Mike pulled the truck up on the mine dump, Rosie stuck her head through the corral fence, and Billy began jumping up and down in the front seat.

"Is that the long-eared Rosie, Mama? Can I go see it?"

"She's a burro, Billy—a donkey. Her name is Rosie."

Jenny turned and held Corey out to Mike. After he took her, she fished in the grocery sack for an apple, then climbed down from the truck and held her arms out to Billy. He jumped down right away and headed toward the pen.

Rosie wheeled away, then came back and put her nose down to sniff at the little boy. Billy grasped Jenny's hand but stood still and let the burro nuzzle him. Finally he reached out and touched Rosie's muzzle with one finger.

"It's got a soft nose."

Jenny held the apple out to Rosie, who took it in one bite and chewed noisily.

Mike got down from the truck with the baby and walked toward the cabin. Jenny turned, but Billy said, "Can I stay and talk to her, Mama?"

"Yes, but don't put your fingers in the pen anymore. She might think you're part of an apple."

Billy sat down on the ground outside the pen. Rosie turned her head sideways and looked at him out of one eye. Jenny watched for a moment, then followed Mike inside the cabin.

Mike looked around the place. "Do you really think you want to live here? It's just a run-down old miner's shack."

"It's no worse than our house," Jenny said and was immediately sorry. Mike's face tightened. She tried for a lighter tone. "Rosie will be a better neighbor than some of the ones we've got now." Mike didn't say anything. Jenny surveyed the cabin. To the left of the door, under the window, was a wide shelf, and there was another set of crude board shelves against the west wall behind the bales of hay, to the left of the stove. The ceiling and walls of the old cabin had been covered with cardboard. Where the roof had leaked the cardboard on the ceiling was warped and water-spotted; it sagged away from the boards to which it had been nailed.

"We could put up clean cardboard," Jenny said. She walked over to the right side of the stove. "Billy's mattress and bedspring would fit here, and Corey's crib could go against the north wall across from the door." She turned to her right again. Another set of shelves, dust-covered and showing signs of mice, leaned into the northwest corner. She turned south. "Our bed would fit under the other window."

Mike had spread the Navajo blanket on the floor for Corey. He walked over to the window. "I'd have to replace the glass."

"And you'll have to keep Rosie's hay in the shop from now on."

Billy stuck his head in the door. "Whose house is this?"

Jenny said, "It's our house. Would you like to live here for a while?"

"Is Rosie our burro?"

"Uh-huh."

"Then I want to live here."

Mike ruffled the boy's hair. Turning back to Jenny, he said, "We might stay here until I get another job."

Jenny said, "Why don't I get a job?"

"You? Where in the hell would you get a job?"

"Mom Bradley said that her waitress is leaving."

"Jesus Christ, I don't want my wife working in a bar."

"It wouldn't be for very long, Mike. You could work in the mine. The money I'd make would at least buy food and gas."

"What makes you think you know how to be a waitress?"

Jenny felt herself flush. "My mother was a waitress." She forced away the thought of her mother. "Besides, all I do now is cook and wait on you and wash dishes and clothes."

"Who'd take care of the kids?"

Jenny looked at Mike for a long moment. Then she said, "You, Mike. You're their father."

Mike's eyes watered, and he looked away. "You'd trust me with them after last night?"

Jenny said slowly, "You weren't mad at us, and you didn't hurt anything but two old chairs. It's probably my fault you had to break down the door, anyway."

"You never locked me out before."

"I wasn't locking you out last night." She told him about Tully Stocker's trying to get in.

"Jesus, Jenny. No wonder you hate the place."

"I won't go back there, Mike."

Mike came over and put his arm around her. "If you think Mom Bradley would hire you, we can give it a try. I'd hate to let the claim go just when it might start to pay off." He looked around. "We'll have to use creek water." He pointed to the wide shelf under the window. "That's probably where they sat the water bucket and wash pan. And I'll need to get some firewood cut and stacked." He turned back to Jenny. "Maybe we can do it."

CHAPTER

17

▲▲▲▲▲▲

Though Mike offered her the truck keys on Monday morning, Jenny chose to walk the three miles from their house up to Mom's Bar and Café. She said, "I need to think about what to say." She set out some applesauce and baby cereal, nursed Corey at the last moment, and kissed Billy. When she started up the hill, Billy and Mike were fitting a new lock on the door.

The walk didn't help much. Jenny's heart was pounding as she approached the crowded parking lot. Her stomach tightened and bile rose, burning her throat. She ran to the back of the lot and threw up into the weeds. Then she sat down on the log that served as a parking barrier and wiped her mouth on the tail of her blouse—on the inside hem so it wouldn't show. Her mouth tasted terrible. Rising and stepping over the log, she climbed a ways up the mountain behind the café. She pulled a cluster of pine needles from a tree and chewed them one by one, spitting often, until her mouth tasted clean. She looked across to the mountain on the other side of the highway. The aspens hadn't turned—it was too early—but they were a golden-green instead of the lime green they'd been in April when Corey was born. April seemed a very long time ago. Glancing down the dump road, Jenny thought briefly about returning to the house. "No," she said out loud, wishing she had brought Billy with her, "I'm going in there and ask for a job before I lose the last bit of nerve I've got."

She made her way down the hill and without stopping went to the front door of the building and opened it. She stood in the vestibule a moment, looking at the people. If she got the job, these people would be her customers. Three of the front booths were filled with truck drivers in billed caps, eating breakfast. In the fourth booth, sprawled against the window, Richard slept with his mouth open. Several men sat at the bar, bottles of Coors and Budweiser in front of them.

Mom Bradley was just coming through the swinging doors. She held two plates in her left hand, one on her left arm, another in her right hand. She went to one of the tables on the north side, and in an instant all the plates were placed smoothly in front of the customers. Jenny's heart sank. Mom Bradley hadn't even asked who got what. If I get nervous, I'll never be able to remember their orders, she thought.

Mom Bradley turned then and spotted Jenny. "Well, hi. What are you doing here at this time of day? Need the phone?"

"No," Jenny said, "I wanted to talk to you—but you're busy."

"The worst problem is that I'm running out of clean dishes, and that"—Mom Bradley jerked her head toward her son—"that wreck is too hung over to see straight."

"I'll wash dishes for you," Jenny said.

Mom Bradley looked at her sharply. "Where are your kids?"

"Mike's home. He's staying with the kids."

Mom Bradley opened her mouth, but at the same time the front door opened and several people came in.

"Oh, Christ," she said to Jenny. "If you really want to help, come on, and I'll show you how to run the machine."

Jenny remembered right away how to stack the dish trays, which stood on the runway in front of the large gray enamel machine. After filling the tray she slid it into the machine and pushed the On button. While the machine rumbled and hissed, she loaded another tray of dirty dishes. When the machine stopped she pulled the clean tray through a rubber curtain on the far side and left the dishes to cool a minute while she slid the dirty tray into the machine. She grabbed the hot clean dishes and stacked them quickly, her fingertips turning red from the heat. She carried the warm stacks to the nearly empty shelves by the grill and work counter, going back to take the empty tray to the other side.

The noise and the steam isolated her. She felt suspended between lives, between selves—the self she'd been before Mike kicked the door down and the Jenny who was trying to ask for a job.

As she steadily moved dishes—dirty dishes, clean dishes, dirty dishes again—she thought about money. It was stupid not to have any money. I didn't think about things like this before Karen came, Jenny thought. She made me feel uncomfortable, but she was right. I don't even have anything I could *sell* to buy food or bus tickets. My poor kids.

Just then Mom Bradley touched her arm and shouted over the noise of the dishwasher, "That's the last batch. Come sit down, and I'll fix you some breakfast."

Jenny carried the last stack to the shelves, grateful for the end of the noise. She pushed the hair back from her face. The steam had made it stringy. She hadn't brought a comb. Looking down, she said, "Darn." Catsup from somebody's plate had stained her blouse. She felt like crying.

Mom Bradley gave her a gentle shove. "Go out and sit down. I'll bring you a plate. Orange juice okay?"

Jenny nodded as she went through the door. Sitting in the first booth near the door was the big-footed truck driver. She took a step backward, but he had already seen her. He rose from the booth with a smile and held out his hand.

Jenny smoothed her blouse and tossed her hair back and went slowly forward. She had remembered his face after all. He had strong high cheekbones, a beak of a nose, and a determined-looking chin. With his dark hair and deeply tanned skin, he looked like an Indian, but he had blue eyes. His eyes were just as she remembered them, deep blue with crinkles at the corners. And he was so tall. She looked up at him as he waited for her to join him in the booth. He was at least six four. She slid into the booth and sat; she looked down at her hands. They were red from the hot water.

"I didn't know you worked here," the truck driver said. Jenny looked up. The blue eyes were kind.

"I don't. I was just helping out," she said, adding abruptly, "I got the rocking chair."

He smiled. She felt the warmth spread from her neck to her forehead. "I wanted to say thank you. It's so . . . gentle. All curves, and so smooth." She stopped and took a breath. "I should have thanked you months ago, but nobody seems to know your name. I couldn't write a letter to Bigfoot."

The driver burst out laughing. Jenny bit her lip. She hadn't meant to let him know that people noticed his feet. She slid out of the booth and walked blindly toward the rest rooms in the back corner. She pushed open the ladies' room door, stepped inside, and burst into tears.

She leaned against the door and cried until her throat hurt and her nose was stuffed up. Then she washed her face in cold water and looked in the mirror. Her hair hung down on either side of her face like old yellow string. Her eyes were rimmed with red; her nose was red, too, and her upper lip was swollen.

She looked up at the little window. Could she crawl through it? No, she'd probably get stuck, and then that truck driver would have to rescue her again. She was a fool. He would think she was completely stupid and had absolutely no manners. Billy would have done better.

Someone tried the door. Jenny unlocked it and went out slowly. The first booth was empty. She walked back to it and sat down. The paper menu was folded over. She smoothed it with her hand and noticed that a quarter of it had been torn away. Mom Bradley came out from the kitchen with a plate in her hand. She set it in front of Jenny, and turning back to the bar she picked up the glass of orange juice there.

"Here, Jenny," she said, putting the juice down and handing Jenny a piece of paper. "That big truck driver asked me to give you this."

Jenny saw that it was the corner torn from the menu. It was folded over and had her name on it, but she didn't want to open it in front of Mom Bradley. She stuck it in her jeans pocket.

Air rushed out of the blue cushion as Mom Bradley sat down across from her. "We'd better talk while you eat your breakfast. I don't have much time before the noon rush."

Jenny glanced at the clock. It was eleven thirty. "I didn't realize so much time had passed."

"You were busy, girl. You're one helluva dishwasher."

Jenny laughed. "Mike said I was one helluva mucker."

Mom Bradley said, "You've got rhythm."

It's now or never, thought Jenny, and said, "I'm glad you think I can work because I came up here to ask you for a waitress job."

Mom Bradley leaned back and regarded her. "So it's true," she said finally.

"What's true?"

"They canned Mike, didn't they?"

Jenny nodded.

"Why don't you just pack up and move on? He could find work somewhere."

"We can't afford to go, and Mike will lose the claim if he doesn't stay."

"Hell, he only has to do assessment work to keep it."

"But the ore's good. We're going to move up there and mine it. That is, if you'll let me have a job, so I can buy groceries and supplies."

Mom Bradley picked up Jenny's knife and ran her finger down the handle. "You been bit by the mining bug?"

"No, but Mike won't have anything left if he loses the mine."

"He's got you, though the stupid son of a bitch probably doesn't appreciate you. Is he the one who broke your door?" Mom looked straight into Jenny's eyes.

"Yes, Mike broke it," Jenny said, "but I locked it because Tully Stocker tried to get in."

"Oh, Jesus. Maybe you better move up to that mine." Mom Bradley put the knife down. "All right, Jenny, you can have the job—on one condition."

Jenny waited, but Mom Bradley didn't go on; her face was flushed, and she looked away as if she were embarrassed.

"What's the condition?"

"I don't want to hurt your feelings, Jenny, but you can't wait tables here without doing something about your clothes and your hair."

CHAPTER

18

▲▲▲▲▲▲

Jenny ran her hand through her hair and met Mom Bradley's eyes. "You're right. I just took a good look at myself for the first time in five years. I'm a mess." She started to rise, saying, "Thanks anyway."

Mom Bradley put a hand on her arm. "Hey, wait a minute. I need a waitress. We can figure this out." She got up and went to the cash register. Richard was leaning against the bar. Mom Bradley said, "Now that you're awake, run this place for half an hour." She took money from the drawer and slammed it shut. "Come on, Jenny."

"I should go home and nurse Corey. She's not really used to her cereal yet."

"Corey will be all right. If she's not, Mike will come hunting for you." She turned to Richard. "We'll be up at Natalie's Beauty Shop."

Jenny followed Mom Bradley out the door and to her car, but she stopped there. "I can't go with you," she said. "I don't have any money, and if I did, Mike would never let me spend it in a beauty shop."

"Mike's not here right now. Get in; we'll talk on the way."

Jenny got in the car. The day seemed to be out of her control.

"I'm going to advance you the money for a haircut, perm, and styling—and throw in a manicure." Mom Bradley glanced at Jenny's hands. "Jesus, what have you been doing besides my dishes?"

Jenny smiled. "Washing clothes on the board and mucking out a mine."

"You're going to kill yourself."

"No, I liked the mine work. It feels peaceful in the mine. And Mike said I was good at it."

"Well, we'll throw in a pair of gloves, too. If you're going to stay with that bum, you'll always be working too hard."

Jenny was offended by Mom Bradley's words. Mike wasn't as bad as Mom Bradley and Karen thought he was. She shouldn't have mentioned the money. "Mike's not a bum," she said. "He works most of the time, and he's been good to the kids and me."

"Sorry, Jenny." Mom Bradley reached over and patted her knee. "I admire you for being loyal. I didn't mean to overstep my bounds. Just mouthy. Anyway, let's talk about the job. I provide the uniforms; you keep 'em clean. And as long as you're coming in to work, why don't you bring the laundry to the Laundromat. Save your hands and keep yourself pretty. You'll make a lot more tips that way."

Jenny looked out the window. "I thought I was just serving food and drinks. I didn't think I was included in the bargain."

"Oh, Christ, Jenny. What's the matter with you all of a sudden? You know damn well these guys like a good-looking woman to wait on them. It's a truck driver's fringe benefit."

Jenny felt angry. "I know how it is. My mother was a waitress. Anyway, I don't qualify."

Mom Bradley pulled her car up alongside the curb in front of Natalie's Beauty Shop. It was just two doors away from the dough-nut shop Mike had taken them to on Sunday.

"You will," Mom Bradley said. "I can see what's underneath that stringy hair."

"I'm going to pay you back every cent," Jenny said.

"Of course you are. I don't hand out charity." Mom Bradley sounded gruff, but Jenny thought of the afghan in Corey's crib and smiled at her.

"Thank you for helping me," she said. They got out of the car, and Mom Bradley pushed open the door to the shop.

Jenny had never been in a beauty shop. Her mother had always cut her hair, and had once given her a home permanent. Jenny's nostrils twitched as she remembered the awful smelling stuff that went on the rollers.

"Hi, Nat," Mom Bradley said. "I've got a customer for you."

The trim gray-haired woman moved forward and held out her hand. "I'm Natalie Swanson."

Jenny liked her warmth. "I'm Jenny Williams."

"Well, Jenny, just sit right down here." She whirled the high-backed chair on its casters and Jenny sat down. Natalie turned her toward the mirror. "Now what did you have in mind?"

Before Jenny could reply, Mom Bradley said, "I thought you could cut it so it curls around her head. Used to be something called an Italian-boy cut. Do you know what I mean?"

Natalie nodded, her hands busy with Jenny's hair. She pulled it back from her face. Even Jenny could see the difference. She seemed suddenly to have more of a face, and though her eyes and nose were still a little red, it wasn't such a bad face.

"Okay," Mom Bradley said. "I'll be back in two hours to get her. Don't forget the manicure, Jenny."

Jenny could not remember a time when anyone had paid so much attention to her. Natalie shampooed and conditioned her hair, then cut it short and gave her a permanent wave. As Natalie rolled the curlers onto her head Jenny began to feel excited. She'd been thinking about a new Jenny, but she'd been thinking *tough,* not *pretty.*

While she was under the hair dryer, a girl named Alice came to do her nails. She gave Jenny a friendly smile as she took her hand and began to smooth the nails with a pink-handled file. Another woman entered the shop, glanced at Jenny, and smiled too. Alice lowered Jenny's hand into a bowl of warm water. The warmth and the soft touch of the manicurist's hands made Jenny feel peaceful and cherished. Now that Karen was gone, she didn't know any women in Dolby except Mom Bradley. Alice put conditioner and sealer on Jenny's nails and then two coats of pale pink polish. Surprised at the improvement, Jenny smiled at Alice and thought, Why, I have very nice hands.

When Jenny's hair was dry Natalie put her back in the swivel chair. As the hairdresser took out the curlers Jenny's stomach quivered a little, and for a moment, she felt guilty. She hadn't thought about her children for hours. She hoped Billy and Mike were getting along all right, and that Corey thought mushy oatmeal was as good as Mama. Not that Mama had been much good lately. She was almost dry. She'd have to put Corey on a bottle. Probably a good thing if she was going to start working.

Natalie began to brush Jenny's hair softly across the top, curving it around her head at her neck and ears. She stepped in front of Jenny and tipped her head back slightly so that she could feather the curls along the brow.

"Oh, I *am* pleased with myself," the woman said, holding Jenny's chin in her hand and studying Jenny's face. "You've got good skin." Still blocking Jenny's view, she turned to the counter behind her and picked up a pencil, a small plastic box, and a lipstick tube.

"Here," she said, handing Jenny the pencil. "Run this around lightly at the base of your lashes. Then we'll add some blue eye shadow to show off those gorgeous blue eyes."

Jenny laughed. "That's the first time anybody ever called anything about me gorgeous."

"But not the last, I'll bet you," Natalie said. "Shut your eyes."

Jenny did as she was told and felt a smooth brush go across her lids.

"Now, for a bit of Peppermint Spice." Natalie handed Jenny a lipstick, and Jenny colored her lips a shining pink, wishing she could see her hair in the little mirror on the tube. She started to hand the lipstick back to Natalie, but the hairdresser said, "Just keep that, and the pencil, and the eye shadow, too. You'll want to wash all that gunk off your face at night and put it on again in the morning. Are you ready to look at yourself?"

Jenny nodded, and Natalie stepped aside. A smooth cap of silvery-blond hair curled around the heart-shaped face of the girl in the mirror. Jenny smiled and the girl smiled with her; the blue eyes sparkled, seeming large in the small face.

Natalie said, "When you wash your hair, you can just blow it dry."

"I don't have a dryer."

"Well, brushing it dry works almost as well."

The door to the shop opened and Mom Bradley heaved herself inside. Jenny whirled, hopped out of the chair, ran to the woman, and hugged her. "I look so different!"

Mom Bradley held her at arm's length and surveyed her. "You look gorgeous."

Natalie said, "I told you so."

"Thank you," Jenny said. "Thank you both." She walked around the room and looked at herself in every mirror. Mom Bradley paid the bill and added a tip for the manicurist. Jenny made a mental note of the total, telling herself, I *will* pay her back.

"Now," said Mom Bradley, "the uniform, shoes to go with it, and the gloves."

"Is there time?" Jenny said. "I'm sure Corey needs me by now."

"Corey and Billy and Mike are all in fine shape. They're back at the café. Corey's slurping soft ice cream from a spoon, and Mike and Billy are eating hamburgers. I told Mike you got the job, but we had to get you ready for work."

They found a pair of low-heeled black shoes, and Mom Bradley bought stockings and two of the skimpy black dresses she called uniforms.

Jenny went into the dressing room to try one on. The neckline was low; the bodice fit her waist snugly. The skirt scarcely reached her knees. The girl in the mirror was now a total stranger to her. It made her nervous to think of showing herself to Mike. Even though the other waitress had worn a uniform like this, Mike would not be pleased to see his wife in it. Jenny was sure of that, but she wasn't sure how she felt about it. The girl in the mirror did look awfully bare. Jenny took a deep breath, which made the tops of her breasts rise into the low-cut neckline. She let the breath out slowly. I don't know what I think. I don't know how I feel. She took the dress off and picked up her jeans. The piece of torn menu fell from her jeans pocket. She bent and took it from the floor. Unfolding it, she read:

> I wasn't laughing at you. It's just that everybody in at
> least three states calls me Bigfoot. Please don't be hurt. My
> name is David Garvey.

Jenny reread the note, then glanced in the mirror. Why couldn't he have seen me this way instead of the way I looked this morning? She glanced at the note again. She wanted to keep it, but she didn't have a private place for anything of her own. And Mike was going to be jealous enough when he saw the uniform. She read the note for the fourth time and then tore it into little pieces and dropped them in the wastebasket. She sighed. She owed so much to other people—the truck driver, Mom Bradley. She felt beholden, burdened by all she had to repay.

She dressed in her jeans and the catsup-stained blouse. Maybe she shouldn't wear the uniform around Mike at first. Let him get used to her hair and to her working. She could change at Mom's. She glanced in the mirror one last time. How will I manage to do this job and still have time for the kids? she wondered. I may look brand new, but I feel like the same old Jenny. She was suddenly tired and very lonely. I wish I could talk to my mother.

CHAPTER

19

▲▲▲▲▲▲

Mike's truck was still at the café when Mom Bradley pulled in. Jenny said, "I'll wait in the truck. Will you tell Mike I'm here?" She opened the door. "I'll pay you back every penny. I owe you forty-one dollars."

"Make it thirty-five," Mom Bradley said. "You washed dishes for two hours. I pay my dishwasher three dollars an hour. I also give the waitress three dollars an hour, but of course, tips add a lot to her salary." I hope so, Jenny thought. Three dollars an hour isn't going to go very far. Mom Bradley continued, "You'll work six nights a week. You get one full meal and a late snack per shift. Come in on Friday at about five thirty, and I'll show you the ropes. The bar closes at two. If your shakers and sugars and napkin holders are done by then, you can take off when the bar closes. Richard does the heavy cleanup."

"Okay," Jenny said and got out of the car feeling overwhelmed. She climbed up into the truck.

Mike and the children came right out. Mike started to hand Corey to Jenny, but stopped with the baby in midair and said, "Jesus, Jenny. Is that you?"

Jenny giggled, raised her hand toward her hair, and then reached for Corey. She opened her blouse and put the baby to her breast. Mike hoisted Billy into the truck on the driver's side.

"Hi, Billy Bright," Jenny said.

Billy looked at her and said, "Where did your hair go?"

"Most of it went into a wastebasket," Jenny said. She turned to Mike. "Don't you like it?"

"Yeah—well . . . yeah, I like it. It just takes some getting used to."

Jenny ran her finger along the baby's face from cheekbone to chin. "Oh, you males. I bet Corey would say it was pretty."

"I didn't say you weren't pretty," Mike said, "but, shit, why now? When we're so goddamn broke?"

"I couldn't have the job unless I got my hair fixed. Mom Bradley gave me the money. I'll pay her back out of what I earn."

"You're damn sure you can handle this job, aren't you?"

Jenny snapped at him, "I'm not sure I can handle anything, Mike, and you're not helping me any."

"You don't have to yell."

Jenny bit her lip and looked out the window until they pulled up in front of the house. The door lock had been replaced. A circle of raw wood made a bright patch against the old paint.

Jenny fixed dinner quickly, fed Corey, bathed her, and put her to bed. She gave Billy his bath and rocked him for a few minutes in the chair—now David Garvey's chair.

Billy snuggled close to her. It was quiet except for the creak of the chair and the small noises Mike made as he hit the sides of the stall while he showered. Then Billy raised his hand to her cheek. "Mama?"

"Yes, honey?"

"You're too different."

"Different? Don't you think I look pretty?"

"You were pretty all the time."

Jenny hugged him tightly. "Bless you. I'm not different, Billy, any more than you are when I cut your hair. We're going to change houses and change the way we do some things, but I'll still be the same old Mama." She rocked for a moment before adding, "And we're going to have Rosie. If things aren't different, we can't have Rosie."

"But I *want* Rosie."

"Then you have to take me, too, even if I'm a different ugly old mama."

Billy giggled. "You don't talk different."

Mike looked around the edge of the curtain by the double bed. "Are you coming to bed, or are you afraid to mess up your fancy hairdo?"

Jenny rose and put Billy in bed and kissed him. Then, remembering Mike, she said, "You better go kiss Daddy good night." She waited until Billy was back and tucked him in again.

When Jenny crawled into bed, Mike put his arm around her and rested his hand on her breast. Jenny said, "Billy thinks I'm too different."

"Billy's a smart little kid," Mike said.

Jenny picked up his hand, kissed it, and placed it back on her breast. Mike moved his hand away.

"What's the matter?" Jenny said.

"Nothing," Mike said. "We'd better get some sleep. We've got a hell of a lot to do in the next three days."

▽   ▽

Tuesday they used the rent money to buy glass and nails, and they raided the trash bin behind the grocery store for cardboard boxes.

"Get something to get rid of mice," Jenny told Mike, "and some Clorox and a new scrub brush." She waited with the children in the truck until Mike came back with groceries and supplies, and then they drove to the mine.

After Mike cleaned out the stove and checked the chimney, he built a fire so Jenny could heat water for scrubbing. Jenny and Billy carried water up from the creek and lugged the rest of the hay to the shop.

While the water heated in a bucket on the stove, Corey slept in the truck. Billy kept Rosie entertained, and Mike and Jenny tore down the cardboard ceiling.

As each piece pulled away, eighty-five years of collected dirt and mouse leavings cascaded to the floor. Jenny touched the dish towel she'd tied over her hair.

"Smells like hell," Mike said. "Probably always will stink of mouse."

"Wait until I get going with the Clorox bottle," Jenny said.

After Jenny swept up the dirt, they flattened some of the new cardboard boxes and built a clean ceiling. Mike placed a tin piece four feet long and four feet wide around the chimney. "Don't want to burn the place down."

They tore the cardboard from the walls of the room, too, and replaced it. While Jenny played with Corey for a few minutes, Mike burned the old cardboard.

"Do you have to do that?" Jenny asked. "It smells terrible."

"There's not much wood down," he said. "Tomorrow I'll have to start cutting wood for winter."

Mike put the pieces of glass in the windows. Then Jenny swept up one more time and began to scrub.

She washed the three sets of shelves first and covered them with the last of the cardboard. After that she got down on her hands and knees with rags and the scrub brush, Clorox and hot soapy water, and scrubbed the plank floors. As the water got dirty Mike dumped it outside, refilling her bucket with fresh water. He and Billy went to the creek for more water to heat and to get water for Rosie.

Finally Jenny was satisfied with the floor. She scrubbed the wooden door and its frame and washed the windows inside and out. "Come here, Billy," she called. Billy came and stood beside her at the door. The sun was just starting to move behind the mountain to the west. Its slanting rays hit the corner of the window and sent a slash of light across the floor.

"It smells like us," Billy said.

Mike laughed. "Now that's a real compliment, Jenny. We smell like Clorox."

"We could smell worse," Jenny said.

Mike wrinkled his nose. "Better keep some Clorox on hand," he said. "We'll need a pot for the kid to use at night. We'll have to get a lantern, too."

"Can't we use the generator?"

Mike shook his head. "Burns too much gas. We can't afford it.

Anyhow, we need to use it in the mine, and we don't have enough wire for both places."

Jenny looked down at her hands. Her manicured nails were no longer nice. One had broken. Two others were ragged on the edges. "Darn," she said. "I'll have to fix my hands again. Mom Bradley says if I look nice, I'll make better tips."

Mike put his arm around her shoulders. "It's okay for those bastards to look at you, but by God, you tell them to keep their hands to themselves. You tell them you belong to me."

Jenny leaned against Mike's shoulder. She was too tired to worry about what he was saying.

▽　▽

On Wednesday they backed the truck up to the porch at their old house and began to fill it with their furniture. "It's surprising how much stuff we've got," Jenny said when they had loaded the crib, the beds, and the kitchen table.

"Yeah," Mike said, "we'll have to make two trips."

After they returned to the cabin on the mine dump and the furniture was set in place, Jenny arranged the canned goods, her dishes, and the cooking utensils on the shelves by the stove. She made the bed and turned to Mike. "Can I use that Navajo blanket?"

"If you want."

Jenny spread the red, gray, and black blanket across their bed. Mike had put a wire from the front wall to the back, and Jenny hung the sheets they used for curtains, but now she tied them back with a string. "It makes the room seem too small if we close them. We'll leave them open in the daytime."

On their second trip they brought the clothes crates and Jenny's book crate, the stuff from Mike's mining corner, Billy's toys, and the rocking chair. Mike borrowed a lantern from Tony. By the time they had everything put away, it was nearly dark. Mike lit the lantern and built up the fire in the stove.

Jenny made creamed hamburger and biscuits. The wood-fired oven got too hot, and she scorched the biscuits, but nobody seemed to care. Billy went with Jenny to take the burnt biscuits to Rosie and giggled with delight when she took them from his hand. Jenny rubbed the hard knot between Rosie's ears, and the burro raised her nose to nudge Jenny's shoulder, making a *huff-huff* sound.

"She says, 'Thank you for burning the biscuits,'" Billy said.

Jenny laughed, and as she turned back toward the cabin she exclaimed, "Oh, look. You can see the stars already."

Billy held her hand and gazed upward at the blue-black sky spattered with specks of light. "I like living on a mine," he said.

Jenny looked around. The pines and Douglas firs were quiet shadows on the hillside. She could see a bit of smoke at the top of the chimney before it was lost in the air. Rosie chewed steadily on a wedge of hay. There were no other sounds and no lights but the lantern-lit windows.

▽   ▽

On Thursday Jenny took Corey and went to clean the house below the dump, while Mike and Billy stayed at the cabin to cut firewood. "You might as well get used to driving the truck on that road," Mike said. "Take it real easy. Shift down instead of braking." He pushed the seat forward, strapped a crate for Corey onto the seat, and waved as Jenny started down the hill.

Jenny's muscles were taut as she inched her way down the winding trail. She had just passed the fork in the road where the big D-8 sat when she met the red Datsun. Jenny was on the downhill run and she knew she should yield, but she didn't feel like backing up the hill. She just stopped in the middle of the road and waited. The man with the mustache honked his horn, but when she stayed still he finally backed downhill to a wide spot. *He wants his way coming and going,* she thought as she drove slowly past the red car.

After Jenny cleaned the house and mopped the floors, she shut the door and locked it and stood for a moment with Corey in her arms, looking up at the highway. Then she strapped the baby back in the crate and drove to the county dump. "Here's the key," she said to Tony. "Don't forget, you promised to come for dinner on Sunday."

"I'll be there," Tony said. "I'll try to get you some books."

Jenny smiled. "I've got a bookshelf now, but I doubt that I'll have much time to read. Have you got any mining books? That's what I'll need if I'm going to help Mike."

"You gonna be the mucker or the driller?" the old man asked, his eyes sparkling.

"I guess I'm just a mucker," Jenny said. "I don't know anything about drilling."

"I'll see you at Mom's," Tony said. "You guys need something up on that claim, you let me know."

The trip home was easier. "It's not as hard to go uphill as it is to go down," Jenny said at dinner. She told Mike about making Quentin Lacey back downhill.

"Good enough," Mike said. "The son of a bitch had it coming to him."

When they were in bed and the children were asleep, Mike reached for Jenny, and she turned toward him. He was gentle and sweet. "It's better up here," she whispered to him.

"This has to last me until Sunday night," he said. "You're a working woman now."

▽ ▽

Friday afternoon Jenny fixed beef and dumplings and set the pot at the back of the stove. She combed her hair carefully, smoothed her nails on the edge of a piece of sandstone, hugged Billy, kissed Corey, and climbed into the truck. "Wish me luck," she said to Mike.

Mike looked at the children. "I may need a bit of luck myself."

Jenny said, "Take good care of them." She swallowed and started the pickup. "I'm not sure what time I'll get home."

When she got to Mom's Bar and Café, Jenny parked the truck at the back of the lot and went inside. The bar, the booths, and the tables were all crowded. She peered through the bluish air around the bar and caught Mom Bradley's eye. The older woman jerked her head toward the kitchen.

"Your uniform's hanging on the hook behind the door. Change in the john and give me a hand."

The black dress looked even skimpier than it had in the dressing room mirror. Her breasts and legs seemed so—defenseless. She turned away from the mirror. Opening the rest room door, she stepped out into the crowded room and hurried toward the kitchen.

CHAPTER
20
▲▲▲▲▲▲

Richard was washing a huge silver-colored pot in the stainless steel sink at the back of the kitchen. He turned as Jenny entered. His eyes widened slightly, but all he said was, "You look nice, Jenny. Are you ready for the Friday night mob?"

"I think so, but I want to look at the menu a minute; could I have a pad and pencil, so I can keep the orders straight?"

Richard wiped his hands on his apron and went to the shelf near the work counter by the cooler. Jenny followed, stopping to peer through the glass doors of the cooler at the large stainless steel bowls full of salad greens. Richard handed her a menu, a green order pad, and a stubby pencil.

"Choose one corner of the table," he said, "and take the orders clockwise. It helps to keep the plates in line for carrying and serving."

"Thanks," Jenny said. "If I can just find the rhythm to it, I think I'll do okay."

"Some of the bar customers will try to shake you up. Don't let them throw you."

"I don't know if I can handle that part of it."

"Just smile, Jenny, no matter what they say. If they think they can get you rattled, they'll all try. Pretend you've been waiting tables for years."

As Jenny studied the menu, Mom Bradley came through the doors, her arms loaded with dirty dishes. She put them in the dishwasher tray and turned. "All set, Jenny?"

Jenny nodded, wishing Mom Bradley would give her the instruction she'd promised.

"Okay, you're on your own. I've got to get to the stove. Stick the orders on those nails above the counter in front of it. I'll pick them off as they come in." She pointed toward the cooler. "Keep the customers happy with salad and bread and butter. And coffee. If their coffee cups are full, they never bitch about how slow I cook."

Jenny tugged at her skirt, picked up the pad and pencil again, and went out. She stood still for a moment, surveying the room. She could tell by the water glasses and coffee cups that Mom Bradley had already waited on some of the tables at the north end. Her eye rested for a moment on a family of five near the front window. The three children were on their knees backward in their chairs, bobbing up and down. The mother looked tense. Jenny took two menus and two glasses of water to that table. She smiled at the tired-looking woman as she set the water down and said, "Do you want water and menus for the children?"

The woman's face relaxed a little. "Water, yes. Menus, no."

"Would you like a cup of tea or coffee first?" Jenny asked, still looking at the woman. She was afraid to glance at the man for fear he was looking at her uniform.

The woman said, "I'd love a cup of tea." She turned toward her husband. "You want coffee, Ted?"

"No, I think I'll have a bottle of Coors."

Jenny turned and met the man's eyes. He smiled in a friendly way. She left them studying their menus and got the tea and beer and the water for the children. Then she went into the kitchen and took some packaged crackers from the work shelf. Putting them on a saucer, she went back to the table.

"These should keep the children happy," she said. "I'll be back for your orders in a moment."

She hurried to the next table, warmed by the woman's smile. She provided water, menus, and coffee to two more tables and went back to pick up the order from the first. She delivered orders to the kitchen and returned with soups and salads, never going in or out empty-handed, though her arms trembled when she tried to carry as many dishes as she had seen Mom Bradley carry.

Jenny soon found the rhythm she had mentioned to Richard. She did the whole room clockwise, taking orders, serving, and cleaning tables in a broad circle that swung her past each of the customers every few minutes.

Richard had come out to man the register and keep an eye on the bar. Jenny caught his eye once, and he gave her a thumbs-up.

The dinner hour passed swiftly. The crowd began to die down at about eight forty-five. Mom Bradley said, "You'd better eat before the boozers start, Jenny. They'll keep you busy till closing time."

Jenny took a salad and went to the first booth. It was good to sit and let someone else cook her supper. She stretched her shoulders backward; there was a sore spot between her shoulder blades from carrying dishes nonstop for three hours. Her legs were tired. Richard opened a beer and came to sit across from her.

"Who drinks in here mostly?" Jenny asked. "The miners or tourists?"

"It's mostly working guys and their women."

"Does Tully Stocker drink here a lot?"

"Not a lot, thank God. He's a mean bastard."

"I'm kinda scared of him. He's got a grudge against me."

"Yeah, I've heard him bitching about you."

"Oh well. He can't do anything in here. I guess I have to take the bad with the good." Jenny pulled her tips out of her uniform pocket and counted the money. "Fifteen dollars. That's five dollars an hour."

"You'll do better than that with the bar crowd, at least on Friday and Saturday nights."

Jenny was fascinated by the money in front of her. "I can get bottles and rubber pants for Corey and underwear for Billy."

"That'll scarcely buy beer and cigarettes for your old man," Mom Bradley said, setting a chicken-fried-steak dinner in front of Jenny.

Jenny hadn't thought about that. Mike probably would want some of this money. She gathered the coins and bills together with both hands.

After Jenny finished her dinner, she returned to her routine. The orders were different now: beer and mixed drinks, nachos, an occasional hamburger. Smoke dimmed the air; country music from the jukebox beat its way through the smoke; loud voices and laughter mingled with the music.

Jenny went from table to table, keeping the ashtrays empty, the glasses full. Richard tended bar for awhile, and then he was gone and Mom Bradley was at the bar, laughing with a loud open-mouthed bray Jenny had not heard before. When Jenny came to the bar for drinks, she picked up the conversation as it made its way up and down the bar, moved deftly along by Mom Bradley when it faltered. Jenny heard arguments about sports; she heard parts of dirty jokes and a few crude remarks about local politicians.

Jenny felt removed from it all. She was getting tired; her legs and her lower back ached. But worst of all, Jenny was aware of a dull anger that made it harder and harder to smile.

A group of young men had taken over the three tables on the north side in the shadowy corner near the rest room door. When Jenny first came to their table she said, "What would you like?"

One of the young men ran his hand swiftly up Jenny's side from thigh to breast. "You," he said.

Jenny felt her muscles contract. She stepped away from the groping hand, but remembering Richard's advice, she attempted a smile and said as lightly as she could, "Sorry. That's not on the menu."

The man wouldn't quit. "Okay, if you're not on the menu, I'll take you on the table—or on the floor."

Jenny could feel the warmth rise to her face as the other young men laughed and joined in. "Hey, Charlie, you can't have this new stuff all to yourself. It's share and share alike," said one.

"No," Charlie answered. "I laid first claim. You guys will have to make do with Mom Bradley."

That brought a whoop of laughter. Jenny thought fiercely, I *hate* them, but she set her face in a tight smile and finally got an order from the table. All evening long the group at that table tormented her. If she was across the room when they wanted more drinks, they raised their voices and yelled, "Jen-nee!" Whenever she was near enough, the smart-mouthed one managed to put his hand on her.

By one o'clock Jenny didn't care if she made another dime in tips. When Charlie reached out his hand and laid it on her waist just below her breast, she turned and said, "Remove your hand, Charlie."

"Why, baby?" he said, flexing his fingers so they brushed her breast but not moving his hand.

"Because," Jenny said, lifting the hand from her waist and holding it out over the table, "because I belong to me."

She was startled. She had meant to say, *I belong to Mike.* But she liked the sound of what she'd said. It made her feel good, and she laughed and dropped Charlie's hand. "Yes," she said again, "I belong to me."

The other young men laughed at Charlie and cheered raucously. But Jenny didn't think it was safe to let Charlie feel too put down. She didn't need to have another man get mad at her. She fished in her pocket for some money and said to Charlie with a big smile, "Now that we've got that settled, can I buy you a beer?"

The young man met her eyes. She didn't look away. Finally he laughed and said, "What the hell! Why not?"

Jenny whirled away to the bar and brought drinks back to the table. When Charlie tipped her more than the price of the beer, Jenny winked at him and went away smiling. She felt both elated and exhausted. Deciding to take a break, she went into the kitchen.

Richard was sitting on a stool, a bottle of Jim Beam near him on the sink. He looked up. "Perfect example of the hypocrisy of the human race."

Jenny was startled. "Me?"

"Out there grinning at a bunch of lewd bastards just to make a dirty dollar."

"You *told* me to smile at them."

"God damn it. Who told you you could use me as a resident expert? I'm not your psychiatrist or your lawyer. Don't blame me for your lost innocence." Richard pointed a finger at Jenny. "I did not send beauty to the beasts. Beauty went of her own accord."

"Richard, you're drunk. You always make speeches when you're drunk."

"Not drunk enough," Richard said and picked up the bottle. Jenny went back through the swinging doors and began to fill the sugars and saltshakers and napkin holders. When Mom Bradley turned off the bar sign at two o'clock, Jenny was ready to go home.

"Better have a cup of coffee to keep you awake on the road," Mom Bradley said after Jenny changed into her jeans.

"No thanks," Jenny said. "I've got to get home and see how Mike made out with the kids."

"You did a good job tonight, Jenny," Mom Bradley said. "You're the smartest new waitress I ever had. You set up a good system right off."

The praise brought tears to Jenny's eyes; she smiled at Mom Bradley and said, "Thanks. I liked the dinner hour. I'll see you tomorrow."

When she went outside, the parking lot was dark, and the truck seemed half a mile away. By the time she reached it her heart was beating against her ribs. I'm going to park right in front of the bar tomorrow, she thought as she locked her door.

The road up the mountain was dark, too, and narrow. Once the truck lights caught a pair of eyes in the black depths at the side of the road, but the only other spark of light she saw was the lantern in the cabin window. Grateful to Mike for leaving it lit, Jenny brought the truck up onto the mine dump and turned off the engine.

Mike's figure was silhouetted in the open cabin door before she was out of the truck. Jenny went inside. Billy was sprawled on his bed, asleep.

Mike said, "I wore him out. We cut wood until dark. He carried kindling."

"How about Corey? Is she doing all right with the formula?"

"She seems to like the taste, but she fights that rubber nipple. I had to rock her and talk to her to get her to suck."

Jenny smiled at the thought of Mike in the little rocking chair. She patted the sleeping baby's bottom gently and turned toward the table. "Come see how much money I made."

She dumped all her tips on the table and they counted up the total. She had earned thirty-seven dollars and ten cents.

"We're going to have to build up a fund for the truck bill," Mike said.

"How much?"

"We need three hundred and eighty-six dollars a month. Part for the bank, part for the insurance company."

"Oh," Jenny said, making a slight movement toward the money. But Mike put his hand on the stack.

"Let me keep track of the truck money," he said.

"Why can't we do it together?"

Mike looked at Jenny. In the dim light of the lantern, his eyes looked deep and shadowy. "God, Jenny. It's bad enough you're supporting me. I'll look like a bum if I don't go in and pay my bills like I always have."

Jenny was torn. Her first tips were special to her, yet Mike seemed so wounded. She picked up twelve dollars.

"I need to get some things for the children," she said. Mike swept the rest of the money from the table.

Jenny got up and put the twelve dollars in the Pyrex dish she'd found at the dump. "I'm beat," she said, beginning to undress. "And I have to start all over again tomorrow." Turning toward the bed, she noticed a rifle in the corner of the cabin by the window. "Where did that gun come from?"

"I brought it in from the shop." Mike said.

"Where did you get it in the first place?"

"Bought it off a guy who was broke."

"I don't like it there. It's dangerous for Billy. What are you going to do with it?"

Mike grinned. "As soon as the weather cools, I'm going to get us some venison."

"It's not hunting season, Mike."

"Ah, that don't matter for us locals. The game warden won't be around this way."

Jenny was too tired to argue, but she said, "Hang it up high where Billy can't reach it. I don't like guns."

Mike turned the lantern out and crawled into bed beside her. "You'll be damn glad I've got that twenty-two when there's a hundred pounds of free meat hanging in the tunnel."

"I won't be glad if you go to jail for poaching deer."

Mike put his arm around her and pulled her in toward the curve of his body. "Are you going to start a bail-money jar like you used to have a jar for the red wagon?" he joked.

"I wonder where Karen is now," Jenny said.

"Did that bastard Tully show up at Mom's tonight?"

"No," Jenny said, "but he's not the only bastard in town."

"Did they hassle you?"

"Some."

"Oh Jesus, Jenny. Can you handle it?"

Jenny thought for a moment about Charlie and his rowdy friends. It could have gone either way. "I'll just take one bastard at a time," she said, "and let you know."

CHAPTER

21

▲▲▲▲▲▲

Jenny's legs and back still ached when Corey woke her at five. She changed the baby and took her back to bed with the bottle, but she had to hold it while she coaxed the baby to suck, and she couldn't doze as she had when she nursed Corey in bed. She felt cross at the baby and ashamed of her mood. "It's not your fault the grown-ups' world turned upside down, is it?" she whispered, petting the silky head with one finger. "If I keep working, I won't get to watch you grow up."

The cabin was cold; the stove had gone out. By six the first light turned the room from black to gray. Jenny looked around. Her three books were on the shelf. What happened to Mama's books? she wondered. I suppose they sold them, too. I wish they had asked me if I wanted anything. She wandered mentally through her mother's house, trying to remember. I'd have taken the books and the blue vase and some pictures of Mama and Daddy. They wouldn't have sold those. Jenny felt bewildered. I can't remember what they did with Mama's things.

The baby was asleep. Jenny bunched the covers up around her shoulders and tried to go back to sleep, but before she shut her eyes Billy said, "Mama, I'm cold. Can I get in with you?"

Jenny turned and looked over her shoulder. Billy stood by the bed, shivering. "Sure, honey, but you'll have to crawl up from the foot and lie close to Daddy."

By the time Billy got settled in the bed, Mike was awake. "Jesus, what's this?" he grumbled. "A convention?" He sat up on the bed and ran his hand through his hair. "God, I'm tired. I don't think I'll wait up for you every night."

Jenny thought of all the nights she'd kept dinner hot—the nights Mike hadn't come home until dawn. She looked down at the baby, but not before Billy had seen the tears in her eyes. He reached for her left eye and put one finger on her lower lashes. She caught his hand and held it to her cheek.

Mike got up and stretched. Pulling on his pants, he stepped outside, leaving the door open behind him. Jenny could hear the splatter as he peed on the mine dump. Then he came back in, went to the stove, and began a fire.

After the cabin warmed up, Jenny rose and brewed a pot of coffee. While it heated, she dressed and made the bed.

Mike said, "I need some gas for the chain saw. I think I'll take the truck to town."

"I have to go, too," Jenny said, piling dirty clothes near the door.

"Can't you wash those here?" he said. "I wasn't planning to take the whole goddamn family."

"I'm washing at the Laundromat from now on," Jenny said. She jerked open the door and went out to dump the pile of clothes into the truck.

▽   ▽

Jenny found bottles for Corey at Safeway. She picked plastic baby panties and a package of boy's underwear from a rack. After counting her money, she bought a package of emery boards. The Laundromat had been expensive. She had hoped to have lunch in town, but she bought bread and apples and salami, and they ate on the way back to the mine.

"Did you do any work in the tunnel yesterday?" Jenny asked.

Mike looked across the pickup and frowned. "I didn't have time to do anything. If the baby wasn't screaming, Billy needed something. When I finally got Corey to sleep, we spent the rest of the time coaxing that burro to pull a few logs to the dump so I could cut them up." Mike looked down at Billy who was nodding off against Jenny's arm. "It's funny, but the kid can make that jackass move better than I can. I finally just let him lead her."

"What did you do after you put the kids to bed last night?"

"I sharpened the chain-saw blade, oiled the gun, kept the fire going."

"Do you think you could work in the tunnel while they're asleep?"

"I can't worry about the goddamn mining until I get us enough wood to last the winter."

Jenny was too tired to continue the conversation. She stayed quiet until they reached the cabin. In the afternoon she heated water and washed her hair. Thinking of the way the hairdresser had curled it around her face, she went outside to brush it dry in the sunshine. Billy came to sit beside her.

"Did you miss me yesterday?" she asked.

"I was working with Daddy," Billy said. "I made Rosie go." He jumped up and ran to the corral fence but turned back to ask, "Where's Rosie?"

"While you were taking your nap, Daddy put her on the picket rope."

"Oh," Billy said and started up the hill. "I'm gonna go see her."

"Watch her teeth and her feet," Jenny said.

"I know that," Billy said. "Daddy told me yesterday."

Mike came out of the shop and watched Billy. Jenny went to the corral fence. "He seems to have grown up overnight."

Mike laughed. "He's just trying out a few things in a man's world. He's probably sick of picking the dump with his mama."

Jenny turned toward the house. She went into the cabin and took the sleeping baby from the crib. Sitting down in the rocking chair, she held Corey close. I chose this, she thought. I can't quit after one day. I don't believe Billy hated going to the dump. He liked finding treasures.

Mike came into the cabin. "You gonna fix our supper before you go to work?"

Jenny stood and put Corey back in the crib; she looked at her for a moment. "I'm going to teach her to *do* something," she said.

"Like what?" Mike asked, stretching out on the bed.

"Like—like the lady who came in the restaurant last night. Mom Bradley says she's a geologist. She gets paid a lot because she's a mineral expert."

"Things have changed," Mike said. "Used to be they wouldn't let a woman in a mine. The miners would flat walk off the job if they did."

Jenny set the table. "That Mrs. Marsh is a nice lady. If I ever get the chance, I want to talk to her more. They left a big tip, too."

Mike got up, pulled a crate away from the table, and sat on it. "Wish I hadn't busted up the goddamn chairs," he said.

Billy poked his head in the door. "Rosie kissed me," he said. He came in, dragged his crate to the table, and climbed on it. "I'm hungry. Rosie's teeth are dirty. Know that, Mama?"

Jenny laughed. "Yes. Rosie has icky teeth."

She set their dinner on the table. Then, taking the makeup Natalie had given her, she went outside to look in the pickup mirror. Her hair wasn't quite right; she fluffed it a little more and put some of the peppermint lipstick on her mouth. When she went back to the cabin she said, "Okay, guys. The baby's bottles are ready. Give her peas with her cereal tonight and see if she'll eat some of those apricots. If she doesn't eat them all, Billy, you eat them. We can't keep them without a refrigerator."

"Yuk. Baby food."

Jenny smiled at him and picked up her purse. Mike got up from the table and kissed her. Jenny was startled. She felt the heat of a blush rise from her neck. "Your lipstick tastes good," Mike said. "Drive careful."

"I invited Tony for dinner tomorrow," Jenny said.

"Great," Mike said, "I'll challenge the old bastard to some poker."

▽　▽

Saturday night at Mom's went smoothly. They weren't as busy as usual, Mom Bradley said, but there was a high school football game in town, and a crowd of young people came in later. Richard didn't show up, so Mom Bradley watched the front when business slowed down, and Jenny caught up on all the dirty dishes before two o'clock. As she swung past the bar with a tray full of dirty plates, Jenny was stopped by a middle-aged man with bleary eyes.

"Wanna have some fun when you get off work, Blondie?"

The tray was heavy; Jenny shook her head and said, "My husband wouldn't like that," and went into the kitchen. As she ran the dishes through the dishwasher she thought about the men who came into the bar. They looked at her a lot, but Jenny wasn't sure they really saw her. They saw some private idea about women. She didn't like the skimpy uniform any better than she had before, but tonight she'd been too busy to be aware of it. It didn't have anything to do with her. She considered the man who had spoken to her. He doesn't even know what fun is anymore, she thought.

Mom Bradley touched her arm. "It's two o'clock, Jenny, and that's the last tray. You're a whiz on the dishwasher."

Jenny smiled. "I like it. I can hide in the noise and listen to myself think."

Mike was asleep when Jenny got home. She checked the children and crawled in beside him. She slept late on Sunday morning and woke feeling grateful to Mike for watching Billy and Corey.

Tony arrived just in time for dinner, and after they ate he said, "Let's go look at that ore again, Mike."

Jenny said, "Can I come, too? I never did look at the ore. I was too busy mucking at first, and then I was too tired."

"Me too, me too," Billy said, hopping up and down. "I want to see the tunnel."

"All right," Mike said, "but I'll have to start the generator and get some hard hats." He stood up from the table. Corey was awake in her crib, but not fussing. Jenny had put a red plastic spoon on a string above the crib. Corey looked at it as it swung slightly.

Tony watched the spoon a moment, too, and then said, "This old cabin's not exactly airtight. You better strike it rich before winter."

"Long before," Mike said as he went out the door. "Long before."

"I hope so," Jenny said. "I don't look forward to driving that road in the snow."

Tony went out to his truck and came back with a stainless steel kettle with no lid and an old camp cooler with a broken handle. "Thought you could bring ice up from Mom's and at least keep milk cold for the kids."

"You're sweet to bring us stuff," Jenny said, and kissed the brown cheek.

Mike stuck his head in the door. "If you two are done smooching, the mine tour is ready."

Corey was asleep, so Jenny took Billy's hand and they followed the men into the mine. Tony was just a step ahead of them, wearing a yellow hard hat.

"How come there are trees up there?" Billy asked, looking at the ceiling.

Tony turned around. "Those are stulls, Billy. They hold the rock up."

Billy's eyes widened. Jenny could see the whites flash in the dim light of the overhead bulb. Mike looked back. "I've got to cut a bunch of those damn stulls, too, while I'm cutting wood. I think I'll stack 'em in the tunnel—keep 'em out of the weather."

"Thought you were going to strike it rich before winter," Tony said. Mike had turned back to the tunnel. He walked along the rail without answering.

Jenny stopped to show Billy the long needles of stone. "I can never remember which is which," she said to Tony.

"When the mites go up, the tites come down," he said. "The ones that hang from the top are stalactites; the ones that come up from the bottom are stalagmites."

"Sta-lac-tites," Jenny said to Billy, pointing to the dripping rock above. She looked down, but underneath the hanging needle there was only a wet spot. The stalagmites that had begun to form had been walked away.

"We better catch up with Daddy," Billy said.

But Mike had stopped just a few feet ahead to wait. "Can't give a mine tour without tourists," he said.

"I'm no tourist," Jenny said. "I'm a mucker."

"Me, too," said Billy.

Mike and Tony laughed, the sound echoing oddly in the tunnel. Billy gripped Jenny's hand as they went around the corner and the daylight from the opening was lost to them. "It's dark, Mama, and it sounds scary."

Before Jenny could speak, Mike said, "That's right, Bill. You remember that about mines. They're scary if you don't watch what you're doing."

"Yep," Tony said, "a mountain's got a thousand ways to kill you. You don't want to make any mistakes."

Men are so stupid, thought Jenny. They don't have to scare him to death to teach him something. She tried to ease Billy's grip on her fingers, but the boy clung tightly. "Come on, honey," she said, "let's go see the sparkly ore."

The vein of ore *did* sparkle as the metals in the rock caught the light. "That's just the iron pyrite teasing you a little," Tony said, running his fingers along the six-inch width of the vein. "But this is good ore. The quartz is hard to drill, but it holds together better, and sometimes you find free gold."

"Free?" Jenny said.

"Yeah, gold and nothing else. Doesn't need crushing or separating. Just take it out of the rock pure and clean." The old man ran his hand across the face of the rock again. "I wish I had good lungs. I'd drill this out today." He turned toward Mike. "When you gonna shoot another round?"

"Don't know," Mike said. "I've got a lot to do."

Jenny wanted to stay in the tunnel a moment. Even though the men were talking, she had begun to feel the peaceful feeling, now mixed with a kind of excitement as she gazed at the ore. She ran her hand over the sparkling vein. It felt different from the rock on the other side. She smiled at her own foolishness. It probably feels that way because I know there's gold in it.

Billy pulled on her arm. "They're going. They're going."

Jenny turned reluctantly. "I like the tunnel. The darkness makes me feel peaceful and safe."

"I don't like it, Mama."

Jenny followed the men out of the mine. When they reached the daylight, Billy let go of her hand, dropped his hard hat, and ran up the hill toward Rosie.

As they walked toward the cabin to check on Corey, Jenny said to Tony, "Do you think I could learn to drill and shoot?"

CHAPTER

22

▲▲▲▲▲▲

"Now, Jenny. You're just a little bit of a girl. You don't want to fight a drill."

"But that vein of ore is exciting, Tony. Does it look like that every time you shoot?"

Mike laughed and answered before Tony could. "Hell, no. The vein might open out to a foot wide or pinch down and disappear."

"And," said Tony, "you never know till you shoot."

"That might be as much fun as finding treasure on the dump," Jenny said.

"You stick to the dump," Tony said. "A mine's no place for a woman." The men headed toward the shop, and Jenny went into the cabin.

She put Corey on the big bed while she washed the dishes, and the baby ended up at the edge every few moments. Jenny watched and moved her back, laughing. The dishpan sat on the kitchen table; occasionally Jenny added hot water from the kettle on the stove. "This dishwasher is pretty primitive," she said to Corey as she dumped the water on the rosebush by the front door and hung the dishpan, which doubled as a wash pan, on its nail on the shelf where the water bucket was kept. She spread the dish towel across the side of the crib to dry.

Corey was at the edge of the bed again. Jenny sat down on the bed and pulled the baby into her lap; then she lay back and held the baby up above her face. She brought her slowly down and kissed her, snuggling her close to her shoulder. The baby made sucking motions. "Sorry, Corey, I'm all dried up." Corey looked up when Jenny spoke. As Jenny gazed down into the solemn face she thought of the first time she'd seen her daughter, and then of the truck ride to the hospital. David Garvey must think I'm a complete fool. He's never seen me act normally.

Billy came into the cabin. "I'm hungry, and Rosie's hungry.

"Let's go give Rosie an apple and bring her down for her oats," Jenny said, handing Billy two apples. She carried Corey up the hill. Except for a few purple blossoms, the flowers were gone. The grass was a mixture of pleasant colors: orange and tan, yellow and gray and green.

"Isn't it nice on the mountain, Mama?"

Jenny looked around. The hill sloped sharply upward behind the cabin. The evergreens went right up the steep slope, bony roots clinging to the soil, their textured branches woven into a rough hill-covering. In Simpson Gulch the aspens shimmered along the banks of the stream. "It's wonderful," she said. "I wish I could stay home and play with you."

"I wish you would be home to put me to bed."

Jenny placed her free arm around Billy and they walked up to the burro. Rosie lowered her head as Billy came near. Billy leaned his forehead against her muzzle, his hands behind his back.

"Do you want an apple?" he said in a low gruff voice.

Rosie answered with a huffing little snort; she stuck her nose around behind Billy and took the apple from his hand.

"Your whiskers tickle," Billy said, giggling. He turned to Jenny. "She says, 'Henh, henh, henh.' That means yes."

Jenny unhooked the picket rope. Rosie turned her head sideways and looked at Jenny with one eye. Before Jenny could reach for the halter, the donkey tossed her mane, shook all over, and took off for the creek. Billy ran after her even as Jenny yelled, "Don't chase her, Billy."

Mike and Tony came out of the shop. Jenny pointed toward the creek. Rosie had her head down to the water. Billy stood on the bridge, bent at the waist.

Mike turned and went back into the shop. He came out with the oats can and started toward the creek, but before he'd passed the cabin, Billy came up the hill, dripping wet, holding Rosie's halter with one hand and waving with the other.

"I got her. I got her," he yelled.

Mike backed slowly toward the shop yard with the oats can as Rosie and Billy came over the top of the dump. Tony stood by Jenny and watched as Mike shut the burro in the corral and gave her some oats. Jenny looked at Tony; his smiling face made her feel good.

"When you smile, your whole face helps out," she said. Tony just grinned more widely.

Mike carried Billy over to them on his shoulder. "Let's go play some poker," he said to Tony.

"Will you teach me to play?" asked Jenny.

"Poker's a man's game," Mike said. "Besides, me and Tony are gonna run into town and play with a coupla guys we know."

Jenny looked at Mike, then bit her lip and turned away. The men took both pickups and went down the hill.

▽ ▽

Jenny sat on the floor in the open doorway with the baby and Billy until the sun started down behind the darkening pines at the crest of the mountain to the west.

When it was dark she lit the lantern and built a new fire in the stove. She heated water, bathed both children, and put them in clean nightclothes. She tucked Billy in with a kiss and took Corey on her lap in the rocking chair, rocking and singing until both children were asleep.

It was only eight thirty. Jenny went out to the corral and slipped in through the gate. She put her arms around Rosie's neck and rested her cheek on the burro's bumpy head. "Are you lonesome, little jenny?" she asked. The burro flicked her ear. It tickled Jenny's cheek. Jenny raised her head toward the dark mountain. A bird called from the depth of the black trees; then the night was silent. Looking at the hill behind the cabin, Jenny began to sway in rhythm with her breathing. The solid little donkey stood still as Jenny leaned into her and away again. After a time, Jenny stopped and scratched the burro around her ears.

"There's some kind of music in this mountain," she said. "No matter how mad I am, or who hurts me, I get peaceful here."

She went back into the cabin, picked up the Old Testament, and pulled the rocking chair close to the lantern. Sitting down, she turned to Genesis, began to read chapter one, and was surprised to discover that the Bible was written like a story. The words made pictures, and Jenny enjoyed watching God create the earth.

In chapter two she read about God's making a wife for Adam. I don't feel that I am bone of Mike's bone and flesh of Mike's flesh, Jenny thought. I don't know what I am, but I'm *not* just a part of Mike.

She read chapter three. Was this the God Richard didn't believe in? He told them not to eat from the tree. Jenny was exasperated with the man for blaming the woman, and then she was exasperated with the woman for blaming the serpent. Billy was more honest than that.

"In sorrow shalt thou bring forth your children." I wasn't sorry I was having Billy and Corey, Jenny thought. Then she read that God had said, "Your husband shall rule over thee."

She put the book down and said out loud. "That's not fair. Adam ate the fruit too." She rocked gently, thinking about the story. If I tell Billy to do something and he doesn't mind me, I punish him, but I love him anyway, and I still take care of him. I understand that part of this God. And I understand Eve. She wanted to know things. The only one I don't understand is Adam. What was his reason for eating the apple? He didn't do it to be wise. How stupid he was to disobey the Lord because the woman told him to.

Jenny got up from the rocking chair and set the book back on the shelf. She looked at Mike's stolen clock. It was nearly midnight. She raised her arms above her head and stretched and yawned. As she went outside for more wood she saw the pickup lights coming around the last curve. She laid an armload of wood in the woodbox and waited for Mike at the door.

As he came in he picked her up and swung her around. "I tripled your tip money tonight," he said, setting her down and digging in his pockets. He gave her a handful of dimes, nickels, and quarters. "Here, you can put the small stuff in your dish."

He whistled while he undressed, and when she joined him in bed, he kissed her hard and ran his tongue around inside her mouth. He tasted of beer and garlic.

Mike's boisterous mood didn't match Jenny's, but she didn't pull away. When he was inside her, she thought, Flesh of one flesh. But she could feel Mike's flesh moving roughly across her own. He climaxed before she could and withdrew *his* flesh limply, leaving *her* flesh tense.

When Mike was snoring beside her, Jenny whispered into the dark. "You, God, if you're up there; what do you think about *this?*"

"Wake up, Jenny."

"I am awake. What do you want?"

"Get up and fix breakfast and come help me on the mountain."

Jenny rolled over and looked at Mike, lying beside her. "Doing what?"

"Cutting big trees for wood. Billy and I dragged in most of the downed wood already."

"I've never cut down a tree. How can I help?"

"I'll show you when we get up there."

Jenny sat up on the edge of the bed. "I guess we'd better get started then. I have to work today."

Mike put his hand on her shoulder. "I hate for you to go down there to Mom's."

Jenny said, "It won't be forever. When you get the mine going, if we get some ore, maybe I can quit."

"When . . . if . . . maybe. Jesus." Mike said.

Jenny got up and put on her jeans. The children were still asleep. Though it was nearly seven the cabin was dim. "What do you think winter will be like up here?" she asked as she built up the fire.

Mike said, "Not too bad. We're facing south. We'll get more sun than we did below the dump."

The water bucket was empty. Jenny said, "I can't make coffee without water."

Mike grunted and sat up. He dressed, took the bucket, and went out. Jenny mixed pancakes and fried them in the skillet. She didn't have a bottle of syrup. When Mike came in with the water bucket, she stirred sugar and water together and set it at the back of the stove. By the time it was bubbling, the children were awake.

"We'll have to take Corey up the hill with us," Mike said. "It's going to take a while to cut those trees."

"I wish I had something to carry her in," Jenny said.

Mike ate his pancakes quickly and stood. "Come on, Billy, let's get Rosie ready."

After Jenny dressed Corey, she made the bed, then prepared peanut butter sandwiches. Dipping water into the large kettle Tony had brought from the dump on Sunday, she added onions, potatoes, cabbage, carrots, and a can of tomatoes and set the pot at the back of the stove. She covered it with the skillet. "I'll be glad when I get a paycheck," she said to Corey. "We need some meat."

Mike called from outside. She opened the door and saw Mike and Billy, both grinning widely, with Rosie between them. Across Rosie's back was a strange-looking rig: two rock bags tied together, the straps resting on Rosie's back and a bag hanging down on each side. One of the bags was full: the chain saw and a hatchet stuck out of it. Mike set down the gas can he was carrying and went to the empty sack. "Here," he said, "bring the baby to me."

Jenny wrapped Corey in the lavender terry-cloth robe and stepped outside. Mike slid the baby into the rock sack. Jenny watched anxiously as Corey seemed to disappear into the khaki bag, but when Mike stepped back, her head and shoulders extended from the carrier, and she was waving her arms about. Mike tucked the end of the robe under the straps on the burro's back. Billy came to Corey and said, "Don't be scared, baby. Rosie's nice."

Jenny wrapped the sandwiches and two jars of baby food in a dish towel and tied knots in the ends. She tied that bundle to the straps on Rosie's back and stuck a bottle in beside Corey.

"You ready?" Mike asked.

"Just a minute," Jenny said. She went back for the gloves Mom Bradley had bought her and stood for a moment looking around the cabin. It looked nice—a little crowded, maybe, but the blanket on the bed was cheery and the afghan in the crib was beautiful. The pot was beginning to give off the good smell of cooking onions. By the time the fire went out, the vegetables would be done. Jenny closed the door behind her and smiled at Mike. "I always feel good when I'm about to learn something new," she said.

Billy led Rosie; the baby swung against the burro's fat side as they moved slowly up the hill. Mike kept one hand near the chain saw. Jenny stayed close to Corey.

"We'll just cut beetle-killed trees," Mike said as they stopped on the steep slope to catch their breath. "Damn real estate people have cut so many good trees, we'd better try to save what few are left on the mountain."

When they reached the stand of beetle-kill Mike took the tools from the burro's back, and Jenny settled the baby in a circle of bushes, pushing branches under the robe and around her. "Now you stay put," she said. "No traveling."

When she joined Mike and Billy, the boy said, "Mama, you cut the tree on the side you want to fall down first."

Jenny laughed and looked at Mike. "Yeah," he said. "Billy's right. Decide which way you want the tree to fall and notch it on the side toward the fall." He jerked the starter rope on the chain saw. The motor started, sputtered, and quit. Mike pulled an odd-shaped button at the back of the saw.

"What's that?"

"The choke." He pulled the starter rope again. The chain saw took off with a buzzing roar. Jenny hated the nerve-racking sound.

Mike set the saw at an angle on the downhill side of a tall tree with reddish-brown, brittle needles. He cut into the tree, pulled the saw out, and, starting above the first cut, completed the notch. Then he eased off on the saw and knocked the wedge of wood from the tree.

"Now come around on this side," he said, "and push on the tree so it doesn't bind up my saw." He turned. "Billy, you go stand by Corey, and when the tree starts to fall, you yell, 'Timber!'"

Billy grinned and did as he was told. Jenny looked at Mike. "You're good with him."

Mike said, "He's a pretty smart little kid, and he isn't always whining about something. Jesus, I hate a kid who whines."

"Why did you scare him about the mine?"

"Because he ought to be scared of the mine."

"I want him to respect it," Jenny said, "but I don't want him to be afraid."

"Respect starts with fear," Mike said shortly. "Let's get this tree down."

As Mike ran the saw near the base Jenny pushed on the tree. When the trunk had been nearly cut through, the tree seemed to come alive in her hands. It moved slowly at first, but she could feel the tree get heavier as it leaned toward the weakened spot, and then it began to bend, like a tall man making an awkward bow. Mike pulled the chain saw away and stepped back. Jenny kept pushing until the tree let go of its stump and crashed onto the downhill slope. Billy jumped up and down and yelled, "Timber! Timber!"

Mike cut the tree in four sections with the saw. "Get the hatchet," he said, "and start chopping the branches off. I'll start another tree." He watched as Jenny brought the hatchet down on a dry branch. It broke, leaving a foot-long spike. "Hit it closer to the trunk," Mike said. "Those spurs catch like hell when we're dragging logs."

Jenny tightened her hand on the hatchet handle and tried to aim truer. She was finally beginning to get the feel of the hatchet when Mike said, "I'm ready for you to push again."

They worked all morning. Jenny's back and arms grew tired from chopping branches. Around noon she said, "Let's eat our sandwiches and rest. I have to wait tables tonight."

"Okay," Mike said, "but we've got to do this every day this week and maybe part of next."

Jenny sighed, licking peanut butter off her fingers. "I've got to go to the Laundromat again tomorrow too."

They went down the mountain at two thirty. When they got home, carrying the tools and the children on the burro, the soup was still warm. After they all had a cup Jenny put Billy down for a nap, and he was asleep in a minute. Corey fell asleep before she finished her bottle. "I'm going to lie down a minute," Jenny said.

"Me, too," Mike said, grinning. He pulled Jenny down on the bed, and unzipping her jeans, he put his hand inside her panties and began to caress her. Jenny lay back and closed her eyes.

▽ ▽

By two o'clock the next morning Jenny was almost too exhausted to drive. She had had a run of truck drivers for dinner and a large bar crowd all night. Her arms and shoulders were tight and sore. Her feet ached; she had a blister on one heel. Richard was in a foul mood. He washed dishes and drank beer, and when he acknowledged her at all he growled.

After the dinner rush in the kitchen Mom Bradley lost herself in the smoke haze behind the bar, filling Jenny's orders, tending bar, and flirting with a big man in a heavy plaid jacket and brimmed hat. At about eleven thirty Mom came into the kitchen.

"Can you handle things for a while?" she asked.

Jenny said, "Sure. I guess so."

"Richard, you help out at the bar," Mom Bradley said, and went out. Jenny caught the swinging door with one hand and watched as Mom Bradley joined the big man in the plaid jacket, and they went out of the café together. Richard came up behind Jenny.

"My mother, the county whore," he said.

Jenny stepped away from him and went to wait on tables, glad to be busy. When Mom Bradley didn't come back, Jenny cleaned up the bar and the tables and filled the sugars, salt shakers, and napkin holders. "Will you take care of the money?" she asked.

"Yeah," Richard said. "Go on home. Take what's left of your innocence and your tired pretty face and go home to your babies."

Jenny had just gone out the front door when Tully Stocker's truck rolled past the café and headed down the dump road. Jenny stepped back and waited a minute before hurrying to the truck. She unlocked it nervously and climbed up into it. Her hands trembled on the steering wheel as she backed the pickup out and headed toward Dolby.

▽ ▽

The rest of the week went by in a blur. Jenny was tired when Mike woke her in the mornings. She pushed on trees and hacked branches and fixed meals and made beds and drove to town and did the laundry and went to work. She put a smile on with her uniform. By the end of her first full week she felt as if she'd been a waitress forever.

She still enjoyed the families who came for the $1.99 spaghetti special, and the dinner hour was usually pleasant. But she could only get through the drinking hours by shutting off her mind, ignoring the too friendly hands that lingered on her waist and moving away from the bolder ones that rested on her leg while she took an order. She concentrated on the tips that would pay for formula for Corey, oranges for Billy, and oats for Rosie, and she made it through to Friday night, when Mom Bradley wrote her out a check and then cashed it for her. Jenny had counted fifty-six hours. The check should have been for one hundred sixty-eight dollars, but Mom Bradley pointed to the deductions. "Taxes—Social Security. Uncle Sam takes his, the governor takes his, and then you get yours."

Jenny put the money in her purse, feeling a sinking sensation in her stomach. The truck needed gas. Groceries would take the rest of her pay. She'd have to give most of her tips to Mike for the truck payment and insurance. Tomorrow, she decided, I'm going to start saving some of my tips back before I count them with Mike. He always takes extra. What if one of the children got sick?

▽ ▽

The next week passed the same way. Now Jenny was helping Mike to cut green trees. "For stulls," he said, but as far as she could tell he hadn't gone into the mine since the Sunday Tony had come to dinner.

As the third week of September went by and the night air grew colder on the mountain, Jenny began to wonder if Mike would get any ore out before winter.

On Saturday night when Jenny came home she found Tony asleep on the bed. Mike was not there. Tony's truck was gone, too; Mike must have taken it to town.

She sat down in the rocking chair and dozed until she started to get cold. Then she wrapped her robe around her and lay down on Billy's bed.

Mike came home at about four thirty Sunday morning. He stumbled on the doorstep and cursed in a low voice. Jenny kept her eyes closed.

Tony woke up and said, "Have a good time?"

"Not very," Mike said. "Damn cards were cold as a witch's tit."

Tony laughed and said, "I guess I'll get on down the mountain."

"You do that," Mike said. "Thanks for sitting the kids."

Jenny lay silently, listening. Mike was doing something that sounded strange. She opened her eyes slightly. Mike put his coat and hat back on and left the cabin quietly, carrying his gun.

CHAPTER
24

▲▲▲▲▲▲

Jenny listened for the truck, but it didn't start up. She rose and slipped quietly out the door. The moon was white in the early morning sky. The ground was cold on her bare feet; she half hopped around the east end of the cabin.

Rosie snuffled sleepily when Jenny opened the corral gate. Mike was not in the shed. She shut the door again and fastened it. Turning, she caught a movement on the hill to the north. She leaned on the corral fence, watching intently. That dark figure was surely Mike moving steadily up the mountain. Jenny looked for a moment longer and then glanced up at the sky.

"You, God," she said. "Look at that dumb Adam you gave me. He's going to shoot a deer out of season, and he's going to get put in jail. I hope you know where we'll get the money to pay his fine."

Jenny's feet were stinging from the rough ground and the cold. There's nothing I can do about Mike. I might as well get some sleep before the kids wake up. Jenny went in to bed.

The next thing she was aware of was a loud banging at the door. She looked at the clock. Nine thirty! How come the children hadn't wakened her? Billy was sitting up, rubbing his eyes, but Corey was sound asleep. Tony must have kept them up awfully late. The banging at the door was repeated. Jenny reached for her robe and called out, "Who's there?"

"Quentin Lacey."

"Just a moment." Jenny tied the robe around her, went to the door, and opened it. Quentin Lacey stood outside dressed in a tan suit with a tan vest and a pale green tie. Without an invitation, he stepped into the room and looked around.

"I was looking for your husband."

"He's not here at the moment."

"Oh." The man glanced around the room again.

I wonder if he thinks I hid him under the bed, Jenny thought. "Do you need something?" she asked.

"Yes." The man suddenly focused his eyes on hers. He was only three or four inches taller than she was. "I'm sorry," he said. "We haven't met officially." He put out his hand. "I'm Quentin Lacey."

Jenny looked at the smooth hand. He's got a good manicurist, she thought, returning the man's loose, clammy handshake with a hard squeeze. Quentin Lacey looked startled and withdrew his hand.

That's for crowding me on the road, Jenny said to herself, a bit startled at her own action. Aloud she said only, "I'm Jenny Williams. What do you need?"

"I need a jack," said the man. "I've got a flat tire, and I seem to have misplaced my jack."

Corey woke up and began to cry. "If you'll wait until I care for the baby, I'll help you."

Jenny diapered Corey and gave her a bottle. When the baby had taken all she wanted Jenny put her back into the crib. After poking the coals in the stove and starting up the fire, she turned to her visitor. "Where is your car?"

"About half a mile above here, on the Simpson Gulch road."

"Aren't you out of your territory? I thought Craggy Claims was on the other road."

"We've got a new development started," the little man with the mustache said, "just above your husband's claim."

"That's kind of dangerous in mining country, isn't it?" Jenny was surprised at the hostility she felt toward the real estate man.

"Oh, this won't always be mining country," Quentin Lacey said pleasantly, but he licked his lips under his mustache as he said it.

"Well, we better get you on your way," Jenny said. "Billy, I'm going to help this man with his car. Watch Corey and talk to her if she cries. I'll be back and fix your breakfast."

"Okay, Mama," Billy said.

Jenny turned and said, "If you'll step outside, I'll dress and drive you up to your car." She wasn't going to let this sharp-eyed little weasel spot Mike hunting up there if she could help it. When he shut the door behind him, Jenny dressed quickly; then she joined him outside.

She started the pickup and watched with a half smile as Quentin Lacey pulled himself up into the passenger seat.

"You ought to come and look at Craggy Claims," he said when he was settled.

"I don't like your houses very much," she said as she put the truck in gear and released the brakes.

"Why not?" The man turned his head as if surprised.

"They don't fit in. They scar the mountain."

"They're a good deal less primitive than your cabin."

"But not nearly as pretty," Jenny said.

"Our houses have electricity, plumbing, and cable TV," the man said, hanging on to the door as Jenny clattered across the bridge and pulled a hard right onto the Simpson Gulch road.

"I've seen TV down at Mom's Bar," Jenny said. "I don't think I'm missing much. I wouldn't want my kids to watch it. Most of the time somebody is hitting somebody."

The real estate man continued to look at her. Good, thought Jenny, he's not looking at the mountain.

"I'm sorry you don't think Craggy Claims is as distinctive as we do, Mrs. Williams. We want to stay on friendly terms with our neighbors."

"There's your car," Jenny said. She pulled in behind the red Datsun. It was headed uphill but sagged on the right side where the front tire had gone flat. "Are there houses up there already?"

"No, I'm just going up to meet a couple who may buy the first lot. If they do, they'll want to build before winter."

Jenny's throat tightened. "There are other people up there now?" she said.

"They should be. I gave them directions."

Jenny got out of the truck and reached into the toolbox at the back of the cab. Mike had shown her how to change a tire before she drove into town the first time. She pulled out the jack and tire iron and held them out to Quentin Lacey. He hesitated, looked at the greasy jack, and down at his sharply creased tan trousers.

Jenny laughed. "You're not wearing the right clothes for changing a tire. Why don't you let me do it?" The man did not protest as Jenny took the jack and tire iron to the front of the car. She turned her head as she knelt. "You could put a big rock behind each of those rear wheels."

After the real estate man had blocked the wheels, Jenny took off the hubcap, loosened the lug nuts on the wheel, and then jacked up the right front end of the car. She took the nuts off and slipped the tire from the bolts. The small Datsun tire was a lot easier to lift than the truck tire. Mike had insisted that she learn to handle the truck tire in case she ever needed to.

She rolled the tire around to the trunk. Quentin Lacey opened the trunk and Jenny lifted out the spare and leaned it against the bumper. She put the flat tire inside.

After she put the tire on the wheel and screwed the lug nuts on, she let the jack down. She tightened the nuts and replaced the hubcap. Then she picked up the jack and the tire iron and turned toward the pickup.

Quentin Lacey had taken out his wallet. When Jenny had put the tools in the toolbox, he came to her side and held out two one-dollar bills. Jenny just looked at the man. Mike would call him a cheap little bastard.

She said, "I can't take your money."

Quentin Lacey blinked his eyes. He reached out and put his hand on her arm just above her elbow. "Come on, honey. Take it. You can use it for your kids."

Jenny moved away from his touch. "I've got to get back to my kids," she said, climbing up into the pickup.

"Thanks a lot," the real estate man said.

"You're welcome," Jenny said and backed slowly down the hill until she came to a turnaround.

▽　▽

While she got breakfast Jenny worried about Mike's being seen by the people on the hill. After breakfast she walked with Billy to the creek for a bucket of water and looked around at the bright fall day. She thought, There's no sense tearing up my stomach over Mike. He's going to do whatever it is he's doing anyhow.

Billy said, "Aren't those yellow leaves pretty, Mama? They jiggle in the sun."

Jenny said, "Let's put our lunch and our baby on Rosie's back and go for a walk along the water." Billy clapped his hands and jumped up and down on the bridge.

As Jenny went into the shop to get the rock-sack saddlebags, she said, "If we had a red wagon, Rosie could take us all for a ride."

"I could sit on top of the straps, Mama," Billy said as Jenny brought the burro out of the corral.

"Okay, we'll try it. You put the sandwiches and oranges and Rosie's apples in that saddlebag while I put Corey in this one, and then I'll lift you up on top." When Billy was on the burro, Jenny tied a diaper around the straps and handed him the loose ends to hold onto.

Then she led the burro slowly down the road to the bridge and along the Simpson Gulch road in the direction of Dolby. The aspens along the creek were in full fall color: gold, then unexpectedly red. Once, when Jenny dropped the reins and came back to check on Corey, Billy reached out and hugged her head. "I like us," he said.

Jenny realized suddenly that Billy had not asked about Mike. Poor little kid. He was probably as confused as she was. She put both arms around him, and leaning against the burro's round rough side she hugged Billy tightly. "I like us too."

"Are you always going to go to work, Mama?"

"No, Billy. Not always. When Daddy gets some ore out of the mine maybe I can stay home."

Billy was silent. Then he said, "But Daddy's not digging in the tunnel. He took his gun and went away."

So Billy had been awake. Jenny sighed. It seemed she was always having to explain Mike's actions to Billy.

"Daddy will be back," she said firmly. Taking Rosie's halter, she led the burro toward a grassy opening by the creek and said, "Let's eat. I'm starved."

"I'm starved too," Billy said. He slid off the burro's back into the soft grass, tumbled forward, and sat up giggling. Jenny tied the burro's reins loosely around a small aspen. Rosie dropped her head and began cropping grass.

Jenny held Corey in her lap and gave her a bottle while Billy threw sticks into the water. Then, while Corey lay on Jenny's robe, Billy and Jenny ate peanut butter sandwiches and shared an orange.

"Look," Jenny said. "This orange peel is a little boat." She stuck a twig with a leaf at one end into the peeling and set the little sailboat in the water. Billy ran along the creek and watched until the boat disappeared under a tangle of bushes that hung low over the water. Then he made a boat out of a piece of bark.

When Billy tired of making boats, he and Jenny took off their shoes and sat side by side on the bank, dipping their feet in the cold water.

"Ooh! It squiggles my toes," Billy said.

"Let's make a dam," Jenny said. They put a branch in the water near the bank and piled rocks and sand over it and around it. Soon the water began to pool behind the branch. Billy lay down on his stomach to watch their lake build. Jenny went back to sit with Corey.

"Your six-month birthday is day after tomorrow," she said to the baby. She lay down on the robe beside her and looked at the sky. It was far away, high above her, and a clear, clean blue, except where the shredded remains of a jet trail hung like abandoned cotton stuffing. A breeze slid lightly through the aspens. Mom's Bar seemed far away and the house below the dump even farther. Jenny thought about the four weeks since Labor Day and said to Corey, "We're not doing so bad, no matter what that dumb Quentin Lacey thinks. We have a quiet house on a pretty mountain, food to eat, and Rosie to ride. I don't mind looking in the mirror anymore, and I can make money. I've made almost nine hundred dollars. Of course, that's before all those taxes." Jenny rolled over on her stomach and tickled Corey lightly under her chin.

"My mama used to tell me never to wait tables for a living, but I think she might be proud of me." Jenny ran her finger along Corey's lower gum, rubbing the tooth bump there. "But *you* won't have to be a waitress, Corey. You're going to go to school."

When the breeze began to feel chilly Jenny put the children back on the burro and went up the road to the Spanish Mary. They ate bread and milk and raisins for supper, and after Jenny bathed the children and put them to bed, she lugged another bucket of water from the creek and took a bath herself, using the washbasin for one foot at a time.

$$\triangledown \quad \triangledown$$

When Billy and Corey had fallen asleep Jenny began to worry about Mike again. To get her mind off of him, she finally dressed in her jeans, took the flashlight and a hard hat, and went out to the mine.

She propped the door open and stepped into the tunnel. Moving slowly along the track, she shone the flashlight on the rock above her head. Here near the opening of the tunnel there wasn't any sign of the sparkling rock she'd seen in the vein. How did the miners know? She looked at the walls again and then turned and looked toward the mouth of the tunnel. They must have followed some vein in here; only they blasted it all away and made this tunnel as they dug in after the ore. She moved slowly along, stopping to see the way the logs Tony called "stulls" were braced. The logs weren't big. A lot depended on the rock overhead. She looked for cracks and found a few small ones, but nothing that looked dangerous. Though the tunnel smelled damp, the air was fresh, and only a faint scent of powder remained. The walls were multicolored: one moment the beam of her light touched on a rich rust red; the next spot was gray; the next, a dark brown, almost black. She slid the beam of light slowly along the ceiling until she found the little dripping pencils of stone.

"Sta-lac-tites," she said aloud. "When the mites go up, the tites come down." Reaching up, she touched the drop of water that quivered on the tip of one stone column and then put her finger in her mouth. It tasted metallic and earthy, a nice taste.

She looked at each of the stulls as she went by. Near the end of the tunnel the rock at the top—no, Mike called that the back—the rock at the back looked freshly disturbed, as if several big plates had fallen away. She hadn't noticed that when they were in here before. She directed the light to the floor. Nothing there. It must have been mucked out.

She moved forward to the vein and studied it under the light. Running her fingers along it, she noticed again the different texture. *If that's just iron pyrite, how do they know there's any gold in it? I wish I could walk around in that lady geologist's mind for a little while.* Above the vein the ordinary rock ran up to the back. She looked at it for a long time, finally deciding, *That's got to come out before the vein can come out. I hope it doesn't all get mixed up together.*

She looked at the face of the rock and shivered a little with excitement. *If I could drill and blast, I'd be the first person besides God to see what's in there. I wish Tony would take me seriously.* Sighing, she turned away. *What I really wish is that Mike would start drilling and blasting.*

Jenny leaned against the rock and shut off the flashlight. The darkness flowed in around her. She rested in it. Her heart seemed to slow down and beat at a dreamy, peaceful rate. She listened to the sounds of the water dripping slowly, building stalactites one drop at a time. She yawned. *I'd better go back and check on the children,* she thought. Just at that moment all the lights came on in the tunnel.

Jenny's heart jumped and began to pound in her throat; the flashlight fell from her hands. She took a deep breath and squeezed her hands tightly together. It had to be Mike. She wanted to move forward, but she couldn't make herself take the first step. Dear God, don't let it be the game warden or the sheriff. She bent down and picked up the flashlight. The lens was smeared with muck.

Someone was walking in the tunnel. Jenny took a step away from the breast of the tunnel. Please let it be Mike.

"Jenny!" The loud voice echoed in the tunnel, and then Mike came around the curve. "For God's sake, Jenny. Are you crazy? What in the hell are you doing in this mine in the dark?"

Jenny was so angry and so relieved that she raised and lowered the flashlight twice before she could speak. "*I'm* crazy? *I'm* not the one who took a gun and went hunting two weeks before hunting season on a mountain swarming with real estate developers." Jenny's voice rose as she moved forward. "You're lucky you're not in jail for murder, let alone poaching. You could have killed someone." She stalked straight toward Mike, fear pouring into her anger. "Don't you *ever* do anything the way everyone else does it?"

She didn't stop walking or stop yelling until she was standing right in front of Mike, looking up at him. He reached out and put his hands on her shoulders and said, "We don't have time to fight, Jenny. I shot a goddamn big buck. We have to take Rosie up the hill and get it before morning."

"You're out of your mind," she said.

"No, I'm not. We can do it. If you lead Rosie, I can balance the carcass on her back."

"Have you forgotten that we've got two kids in that cabin?"

"They're sound asleep. They never wake up this time of night. We've got to chance it, Jenny. It means meat for all winter."

Jenny was silent for a moment. The kids needed meat, but did she dare leave them alone? "How long will it take?"

"An hour at the most."

If she didn't help Mike he might get caught in the daylight. The two of them could be finished before dawn, and surely the game warden wouldn't be roaming around in the dark. "All right," Jenny said finally, "if the deer is already dead, we might as well have the meat. I just hope Billy doesn't wake up. You really scared him, leaving with the gun like that."

She went in, checked the children, and added wood to the fire. She set a plate of crackers and a glass of milk on the table along with a bottle for Corey. She got her coat, and after wiping the mud from the lens of her flashlight she took the last two apples from the cold box, glanced at her children again, and went out the door, locking it behind her.

Mike had a coil of rope over one arm, along with an empty burlap sack. He got the other flashlight from the truck. Jenny took Rosie's reins and they started up the hill.

"I lost a little money last night," Mike said as they walked along, "so I thought I'd make it up by getting some meat."

Jenny didn't dare ask how much.

Mike went on, "But I hunted the whole damn day and didn't see a thing. I was a couple of hills away at dusk. I had just decided to turn back when this big old boy walked out across a meadow, proud as you please. Two-point buck. And he posed right there between me and the sun." Mike's voice rose a little. "A goddamn pretty sight, too." He cleared his throat. "That twenty-two ain't no big game rifle. I knew I had to get him in the head or the heart."

Rosie tossed her head and jumped sideways as a bush rose up, darker than the night. Jenny pulled the burro closer to her side.

"I hunkered down," Mike said, "steadied my elbow on my knee, and took aim. By God, I got him with one shot, right behind the eye." Jenny shuddered. "I bled him and gutted him right there."

"Did you see Quentin Lacey up there?" Jenny asked.

"No. What in hell would *he* be doing up there?"

"They're starting another development above our claim."

"Son of a bitch. How did you happen to see him?"

"He wanted to borrow the jack. I drove him up there and ended up changing his tire."

"You *what?*"

"He had an appointment, and his clothes were all clean. I thought I'd help him out. Besides, it kept him from looking around at the mountain. I didn't know where you were with that gun."

"Did he pay you?"

"He offered me two dollars."

"Cheap little bastard."

Jenny smiled in the darkness. "I didn't take it."

They walked steadily up the hill. Mike flicked the flashlight on occasionally, but the moon was rising and a haze of light dusted the mountainside. The crisp air made Jenny's nostrils tingle. If it hadn't been for her anxiety about the children, she might have enjoyed the walk.

They reached the crest of the hill and dropped into the shadowy valley on the other side, using their flashlights until they climbed back up into the moonlight. As they reached the top of the second hill, an owl hooted in the trees, and Rosie shied sideways again. Jenny pulled steadily on the halter and the burro finally calmed down.

"Wish to hell we had a bridle for her," Mike said. "She's not going to like the smell of that buck."

The deer was hanging in a tree at the edge of a large meadow nestled in the saddle between the hill they'd just climbed and the one to the west.

"See those great horns?" Mike said, flashing the light on the buck's head. Jenny swallowed and looked at the deer. One of the buck's eyes was covered with blood from the wound. The other, distended and glassy, caught the flashlight's gleam, making the shattered creature seem to have a light in its eye.

Rosie snorted and reared when Jenny tried to bring her close to the deer. The animal hung by its rear legs, its sides gaping open to reveal the hollow red belly. The front legs hung nearly to the ground.

Mike said, "Take her away until I get a rope on those hind legs. Then put your coat over her head and bring her back."

Jenny slipped out of her coat and put the coat around Rosie's neck. She gave Rosie one of the apples, and while she chewed Jenny brought the coat slowly over her head. "There, there, baby. It's all right." She kept her hand under the coat, scratching Rosie's ears.

When Mike called, she held the other apple just in front of Rosie's nose and slowly pulled the donkey to the tree. She gave Rosie the apple and scratched her ears and neck hard while Mike lowered the deer to the burro's back. He slipped the burlap bag across her shoulders and brought the carcass down so the belly side lay on the burlap, the head and front legs on Mike's side of the burro, the rear legs hanging over the other side.

When the burro felt the full weight of the deer on her shoulders, she quivered, but Jenny rubbed her ears and neck harder. Then she slowly pulled the coat back so Rosie could see to move forward. "Come on, baby. Let's go." Jenny tugged on the halter, and the little burro threw her shoulders into the load and moved forward.

They moved very slowly. We'll never make it back in an hour, Jenny thought. The antlers caught on the bushes even with Mike holding the deer's head up and pushing branches aside.

"Why don't we leave the horns behind," Jenny said.

"Not on your life," Mike said. "That's the best damn trophy I ever shot."

Jenny didn't say anything else to Mike. She just walked along, shielding the deer from Rosie's sight with her body. Holding the halter strap along Rosie's cheek, she talked softly to the burro. "We're at the top of the second hill now, honey. Just one more downhill to manage and then you can go back to your oats and hay."

Jenny shivered, but she didn't want to chance spooking Rosie by removing the coat wrapped around the burro's head.

They stopped before starting down the hill through the trees toward the cabin. Mike slipped out of his coat and handed it to Jenny. When they came into the clearing the sky was beginning to lighten in the east. Mike waited with Rosie while Jenny checked the cabin. The children were sleeping soundly; the crackers and milk and the baby's bottle stood just where she had left them. Jenny leaned against the doorframe with relief.

They tried to take the deer into the mine tunnel, but draped on Rosie, it was too big to get through the door. They finally angled the deer enough for Rosie to go along the track with it. Inside, Mike turned into the short tunnel where the water splashed from the spring.

"I'll rig up a dry place to hang it," he said. "It needs to cure for a couple of weeks."

They slid the heavy body and the burlap off of Rosie's shoulders. Jenny led the burro back to the corral and rubbed her all over with another oat sack. She took the water bucket down to the creek; it seemed terribly heavy on the return trip. After setting it in the corral and giving Rosie more hay and oats, Jenny went slowly to the house. She had just undressed and crawled into bed when Mike came in. He got in beside her.

"Did you get the deer hung up?"

"Yeah, for now. I'll do it better tomorrow. Jesus, I'm beat."

"Me, too, and I have to wait tables in a few hours."

▽   ▽

Mike got up with the children and let Jenny sleep until almost eleven, but she was still tired when he woke her, and by the time she had fixed their lunch and started dinner, she had a dull headache.

Billy was excited about the deer in the tunnel. Mike had taken him back to show him the horns.

"It's a big dead deer, Mama."

"I know, honey." She was grateful that Mike had cleaned it somewhere else. At least Billy was spared the sight of the blood and guts.

Mike couldn't resist telling the story of how he had killed the deer. While Jenny was combing her hair and cleaning her fingernails, Mike told Billy of the hunt and the kill with all the details. "After the horns have had time to cure, we'll mount a fine trophy," he said.

Billy took a new interest in the gun. "Could I shoot it?" he asked.

Jenny could tell Mike was pleased. "Sure, son," he said. "As soon as you can hold it steady I'll teach you to use the rifle."

Jenny looked at them. Billy was changing; he seemed more tuned in to Mike's world now. She sighed and looked out the window. Babies turned into boys; boys turned into men. But it made her lonesome to see Billy so interested in a gun. Turning to the crib, Jenny picked Corey up and hugged her close, sniffing the sweet baby smell.

CHAPTER

26

▲▲▲▲▲▲

Working the dinner hour at Mom's on Monday night, Jenny's legs ached, there was a pain in her lower back, and her head throbbed steadily. She tried to keep smiling, but there were more rambunctious children at the café than usual. She mopped up spilled Coke and wiped milk from the blue vinyl seat in the front booth. By nine o'clock she was trembling with fatigue, and she still hadn't taken her dinner break. She stumbled against Richard as she took a tray of dirty dishes to the machine.

"Here, give me those," he said. "You go sit down on my stool."

"I can't. Every table in the place is full." She went back through the double doors and hurried to the tables in the dining area. As she passed one a hand grabbed her wrist. She jerked to a stop and looked down into the bleary eyes of Tully Stocker. Her stomach knotted and her heart beat quickly; she pulled her arm sharply out of Tully's grasp and wrote the orders at the next table with a trembling hand. She avoided Tully's table on her way back to the bar, but he called out after her, "Nosy bitch. Where'd you take my wife?"

All evening long Tully Stocker cursed Jenny as she moved in and out of the area. When she took orders for refills at his table, he jabbed her with a stirring straw. "Bitch, bitch, bitch," he said with each jab.

"Lay off, Tully," one of his companions said.

But Tully was there until closing time, getting drunker and drunker and continuing to direct a stream of vile names her way. Jenny set her jaw and kept working.

By two o'clock she was totally exhausted. When the last bar customer left, Jenny sat down in the first booth and dropped her head onto her arms.

Mom Bradley paused beside her and put her hand on Jenny's shoulder. "Jenny, you've got to ignore drunk talk. You can't let it get to you." She laughed shortly. "Hell, sometimes a drunk will call me a fat slob or a whole lot worse. I just pass it off."

"But Tully scares me," Jenny said.

"You can't let him know that. Any bastard who beats up women is a coward. He enjoys scaring you. Are you going to let him make you a victim of his meanness?"

The word made Jenny look up. "I *was* his victim tonight."

"But you don't have to be. Stand up to him. Look him straight in the eye. Laugh at him."

Mom Bradley turned to Richard. "I told Ed I'd come by for a while. You make sure Jenny gets to her truck okay." Richard locked the door behind his mother.

Jenny got up slowly and started toward the double doors, but her mind began to whirl. She clung dizzily to the cash register, the wind roaring in her head.

"My God," she heard Richard say. The next thing she knew, he had grasped her chin and was putting a glass to her lips. He forced her to swallow. The whiskey burned her throat. She coughed and gagged; the tears rolled down her face. She shivered violently.

"Come sit down." Richard led her back to the booth. "You damn near passed out on me," he said. "That bastard really upset you."

Jenny's mind still whirled with confusing images, but she murmured, "It wasn't Tully. It's what your mother said."

"My mother?"

"She said, 'Don't be a victim.'" Jenny looked up at Richard, feeling terrified. He went to the bar, refilled the shot glass, and brought it to Jenny.

Jenny took the glass and sipped a little of the whiskey. Richard sat down across from her. "Jenny, do you want to tell me about it?"

"Richard," Jenny said. She stopped, swallowed, and started again. "Richard, *my* mother said 'Don't be a victim.'"

Richard said quietly, "Begin at the beginning."

Jenny curled both hands around the glass and looked into the amber liquid.

"My father was a coal miner in the mountains on the other side of the divide, but his lungs got bad and he had to quit, so he ran the ski lift at Wolf Hill. My mother met him there when she came out from the East to ski. They fell in love, and Mama married him without her parents' approval. They were so angry at her they tried to have it annulled, but she was old enough and they couldn't."

Richard said, "What did they do to her?"

"When she wouldn't leave him, they refused to send her back to college. They would have nothing to do with my father. They told Mother never to come begging from them."

"So what did your parents do?"

Jenny looked up. "During the winter they helped at the ski resort. Summers, they wandered, looking for work. When Daddy was well enough, he did maintenance work. Mama waited tables. And then they had me, so they settled in a little town."

"Were they happy?" Richard's calm voice steadied Jenny as the memories tumbled through her mind.

"I remember being happy. My father was a quiet man. He sat on the steps in the evening with me while Mama read to us. We never had television, but Mama had books. Mama loved books."

Jenny's voice broke. Richard reached out and put his hand on hers, waited a moment, and then said, "What happened to them, Jenny?"

Jenny pulled her hand away from Richard's and took another sip of whiskey.

"Daddy died of pneumonia when I was eight. Mama went to work six nights a week as a waitress. When I lost my father, I lost part of my mother, too. Mama was sad and tired all the time." Jenny shifted in the booth. "I went to school. After school, I studied at the café, or took care of the house."

"What did you do for fun?"

"I don't know. I read some of Mama's books or went outside and walked and looked at things. Mama was with me on Sundays. She cooked nice dinners; we set the table pretty."

Jenny stopped and stared into her glass again, drawing circles on the table with her index finger.

Richard said, "Tell me more about your mother."

Jenny took a breath and said, "When I was thirteen, my mother was raped."

"Oh my God," Richard said. "You don't have to tell me, Jenny."

"If I stop now, Richard, I'll never get it told." She met his eyes, then looked away. "My mother was raped one night on her way home from work. Raped and dumped in the weeds." Jenny looked down at her uniform, picking at a string on the hem. "The newspaper report said, 'The victim's daughter found her the next morning and began to scream for help. When the ambulance arrived the victim was unconscious; the victim's daughter had to be pulled away.'"

"Oh, God," Richard said again. "Did she die?"

"She might as well have. When she got out of the hospital she tried to go back to work, but she was afraid and ashamed."

"Ashamed?"

"She began to drink when she was at home. When she got drunk, she would cry and say, 'I can't even die and go to Bill. The victim is too dirty.'" Jenny looked up at Richard. His eyes held hers steadily.

She blinked and said, "She didn't read books anymore—just that newspaper story. She'd read it out loud and say to me, 'Never be a victim.'"

Jenny was silent until Richard asked, "How old were you when your mother died?"

"I was fifteen."

"What did you do?"

"The county did everything. They took Mama away, and they took Mama's things away, and they took me away."

Richard asked, "Do you think of yourself as a victim?"

Jenny folded her hands together and looked at her fingernails. "I thought I had run away in time. But then Karen came and made me see things in a different way." Jenny lapsed into silence again.

Richard got up and went out to the kitchen, coming back in a few moments with a cheese sandwich on a plate. "The grill's cold, but you need something to eat."

Jenny picked up the sandwich and took a bite. She swallowed. "I hate Tully Stocker, but maybe he did me a favor tonight. All these years I couldn't think about Mama without the fog, and I couldn't talk about finding Mama at all."

She finished the sandwich and stood up. "I've got to get home."

Richard walked her to her truck, and she drove up Simpson Gulch more tired than she'd ever been in her life.

CHAPTER
27

▲▲▲▲▲▲

After Mike hung the deer on a pole secured with railroad spikes at the top of the short tunnel, Jenny expected him to begin work in the mine, but he didn't go into the tunnel again that week. During the day he sat in the kitchen drinking coffee and talking to her or to Billy. Many evenings on her way to work Jenny met Tony on the Simpson Gulch road, but she didn't know whether he was coming to visit or to baby-sit. Mike was always home when she got there.

On Sunday Jenny said, "I saw a flyer advertising a Walt Disney picture. Let's take the children and go to a show." Though she had been afraid that Mike would want to go to town alone, he seemed to like the idea of a movie. They took money from the tips dish and went into Dolby. It was a silly movie about a very smart dog. Billy loved it. Corey slept through most of it, but Mike and Jenny laughed along with Billy. Jenny relaxed in the darkness, glad to be away from the café. She had wanted to thank Richard for letting her talk about her mother, and now that her mind was clearing she would have liked to talk more. But he had been drunk the next day, and the day after that he hadn't come to work at all. I don't understand him any better than I understand Mike, she thought, and turned her attention back to the movie screen.

The next morning she said to Mike, "Are you going to start drilling soon? This is already the second week of October."

Mike looked up from his breakfast and frowned slightly. "No," he said, "I've been thinking that before the ground freezes I'd better build a bin to store the ore, with a chute for loading."

"You never mentioned an ore bin before."

"Any miner will tell you you need one."

"I can't keep working at Mom's forever."

"Shit," Mike said, seeming angrier than necessary. "I told you mining was hard work, but you insisted on going ahead with it."

Jenny felt confused. "I thought you *wanted* to mine the Spanish Mary."

"I do, and I'm going to, but Jesus, Jenny, it doesn't all happen overnight. Let me get things set up right before you start to nag."

Jenny was silent. She played with the children for a while and then left for town with the laundry. While the clothes were drying she went to Natalie's Beauty Shop. Mrs. Swanson smiled when Jenny came in.

"How much would you charge just to wash and dry my hair?" Jenny asked. "I can't seem to dry it so it looks right."

"Three fifty."

Jenny stood still for a moment and then said, "Can you take me right away? I left my stuff in the Laundromat, and I have to be to work at five thirty."

"Sure. Do you want a manicure too?"

Jenny started to say, "No, I can't afford it," but she glanced down at her hands and sighed. Mom Bradley always made some comment if her nails looked ragged. "How much is a manicure?" she asked.

"Eight dollars."

Jenny glanced around the peaceful shop and caught the eye of a kind-faced woman who smiled at her. Jenny smiled back, thinking, Mike spends more than that on a carton of cigarettes. Natalie was waiting for her answer.

"Yes," Jenny said, "Mom Bradley insists I keep my hands nice." She grinned at the hairdresser. "You and Alice are going to spoil me."

▽ ▽

The dinner hour was peaceful. Jenny smiled at all her customers and by nine fifteen she had made enough tips to pay for her shampoo and manicure.

"You've got a good location here on the highway," she said to Mom Bradley during a lull. "It doesn't seem like Dolby could provide you with enough customers by itself."

"The truck drivers pass the word," Mom said.

Jenny went back to work, and when she came through the swinging door, both hands filled with plates, she saw that Bigfoot—David Garvey—had taken a table in the dining area. Thankful for her pretty hair and nice hands, she took a glass of water and a place setting to his table. He looked up and smiled.

"Hello," he said. "Are you still helping out?"

"No, I'm working here now." She took a breath to quiet her pulse. "I'm sorry I acted like such an idiot the last time you were here."

"I shouldn't have laughed," he said.

Jenny didn't know what else to say. She just looked into the blue eyes and stood still, aware of herself, aware of him.

"Is your husband still mining?" he asked.

"Yes," she said. "We live up at the mine now."

Someone called, "Miss."

She smiled at the truck driver and said, "I'll be back to take your order, Mr. Garvey."

"Bigfoot," he said, and a little light glinted in the blue eyes.

Jenny laughed and said, "I'll be back in a minute." She waited on the other table and took the order to the kitchen.

Mom Bradley said, "What happened to you?"

"What do you mean?"

"You look like someone lit a candle inside you."

Jenny ladled soup into a bowl and picked up a salad. "I had my hair done today." She pushed through the doors and served the soup and salad. Then she went back to Bigfoot. "I want to thank you again for my rocking chair. I never feel like Humpty Dumpty in it."

He smiled and said, "How's the baby? By the way, is it a boy or a girl?"

"Oh, it's a girl. Her name is Corinne Mary Williams." Jenny smiled. "I probably should have named her Bigfoot."

The truck driver laughed. Jenny took his order and turned toward the kitchen. Richard was standing by the door, a bottle of beer in his hand. "It looks good on you," he said, "but you better not let Mike see you look like that."

"What looks good on me?"

"True love."

"Oh, Richard, you're crazy. Get out of the way. I have to turn in this order."

When she served his dinner Bigfoot said, "Can you sit down and have a cup of coffee?" Jenny glanced around the room. It had calmed down after the regular dinner hour, and the bar crowd wasn't large. She poured a cup of coffee and sat across from the truck driver.

"Do you like it up at the mine?"

"I love the mountain and the mine," Jenny said. "They offer me something . . . something new. A new way of thinking about my life."

"Are you bringing out much ore?"

"Not yet. Mike is building an ore bin and chute right now, but he'll start drilling again soon." She wished she felt as certain of that as she sounded.

"How is Billy?"

"Oh, he loves the mountain, too, and Rosie."

"I thought the baby's name was Corinne."

Jenny laughed. "We call the baby Corey. Rosie is a little gray burro. Bless her heart, she puts up with a lot from us. She pulls the ore car and carries the kids. All she asks for is oats twice a day and an apple now and then."

"And what do you ask for, Jenny?"

Jenny was startled by his serious tone. She looked up and met Bigfoot's blue eyes. Their intensity held her. He waited for her reply. She tried to think how to answer him and then she said, "I want to know things."

"What things?" he asked, waiting again for her reply.

"Oh, there's so *much* I don't know. I think I'd have to start back with high school. Richard once said I could get a GED, but I don't know where to begin. I don't have the right books." She smiled, not wanting to sound like she was complaining. "So I learn what's around me. I've learned how to wait tables. And the other day, I changed a tire for a man." She told the truck driver about Quentin Lacey's tan suit.

Bigfoot sat back and laughed out loud. This time Jenny didn't run away. She liked his big booming laugh; it made her laugh too. The bar was beginning to fill up. "Can I get you some dessert?" she asked, rising from table.

"No, I'm quite well satisfied," he said. "Besides, I've got to get back on the road." He rose and went to the cash register with her. As she gave him his change he smiled and said, "Thank you for keeping me company, Jenny."

Jenny smiled at him. "I enjoyed it." He turned to leave, and Jenny began to collect bar orders at the booths in front. When she went to clear Bigfoot's table she found that he had gone back to leave her a five-dollar bill. He shouldn't have done that, Jenny thought. And then she saw the note beneath it: "Buy a book." Jenny put the five-dollar bill in her pocket with a new sensation of joy.

▽   ▽

Jenny carried the five-dollar bill in her pocket during the day and put it in the toe of her shoe each night. She helped Mike cheerfully with the work on the bin each morning, holding the upright poles as he guided them into the holes he'd dug on the mine dump. She made Billy laugh and played silly word games with him. She rubbed Corey's gums and rocked her.

The days were getting chillier. They kept the stove burning longer in the mornings and started it up sooner at night.

Jenny couldn't decide what book to buy. She looked on the rack in the grocery store, but saw only the type of books Richard had scorned. She couldn't spend Bigfoot's money on crap. Finally, after a week had passed, she spoke to Mrs. Marsh about it. The geologist often came in for dinner with her family. "Is there a book about rocks and mines?"

"Oh, yes. There are many of them."

"Could I buy a book about mining or mountains for five dollars?"

Mrs. Marsh said, "Possibly, if you went to the secondhand bookstore in Mitchell."

"Oh. I don't think I can get away to do that."

"I'll look for a book for you, Jenny. Next time I'm there." Jenny offered her the five-dollar bill, but Mrs. Marsh shook her head. "Wait until I find a book."

Jenny turned to find Richard leaning on the bar. When she went into the kitchen, he followed. "Since when do you *buy* books?"

Jenny smiled and said, "Since Bigfoot gave me a five-dollar tip and *said* to buy a book."

She expected Richard to share her pleasure, but he stalked back to the dishwasher and began throwing silverware into the tray. She watched him for a few minutes, but he never looked her way. She finally turned toward the swinging doors, feeling she'd done something wrong but not knowing what it was.

When she entered the dining area Tully Stocker was at a table in the back. As soon as he saw her he began to call her names.

Jenny walked over to his table. She put her hand in her pocket, touching the five-dollar bill as she looked Tully Stocker in the eye. He continued to mutter, but as Jenny continued to stare at him Tully lapsed into silence. Jenny still stared, and finally he dropped his eyes. Jenny went back to work. She never noticed when Tully left, but he wasn't there at closing time.

And neither was Richard. Jenny washed dishes until nearly three thirty and left for home tired and depressed despite her triumph over Tully. She was almost to the Spanish Mary when she realized that she hadn't changed out of her uniform.

CHAPTER
28

▲▲▲▲▲▲

"Where in the hell have you been?" Mike was sitting on the bed in his underwear, his sockless feet stuck into his unlaced shoes. "I got up to take a piss and found out you weren't home yet."

Jenny looked around. There were several empty beer bottles on the kitchen table, and one of the crates lay on its side. Billy slept on his mattress, curled into himself. Corey lay on her stomach, her bottom in the air.

"Come outside," she said, "so we don't wake the children."

Mike got up and followed Jenny outside. She pulled the door closed. Mike's breath was foul with the smell of stale beer. She stepped back a little. "I had to do all Richard's dishes," she said, "and I had another run-in with Tully Stocker."

Mike growled, "That bastard."

Jenny said, "But I won this one."

"The hell you say." Mike's voice was less grumpy. He shivered. "Let's get in the truck, and you can tell me about it." He opened Jenny's door, and as she stepped up to get in the truck her coat swung open.

Mike grabbed her arm and pulled her back out of the truck. He pushed her coat aside and stared at her body. "Good God, is that all you've been wearing to work?" His eyes narrowed, and his mouth tightened across his teeth.

"It's the uniform, Mike. You knew that," Jenny said, and pulled her wrist out of Mike's grasp.

"It's not a waitress uniform. It's a goddamn stripper's costume." Mike stepped toward Jenny and put his hand on the top of her breast. She trembled, but stood still. "How many other sonsabitches just reach out and cop a feel?"

"Mike!"

"What was really going on tonight? Where were you?"

"Nothing's going on, Mike. I was working."

"Well, I won't have you working in that dress, showing your tits and your ass both. I must be the county's biggest joke. You're not going back there."

"I *am* going back. We need the money."

Jenny rubbed her hand across her eyes and started toward the cabin, but Mike grabbed her arm again, "I said you're going to quit that goddamn job."

Jenny pulled free and whirled around. "Mike, I am dead tired, and I am not going to stay up all night arguing about this. I'm going to go on working because we don't have anything else. It's all invested here. The sooner you start drilling, the sooner we'll get to the point where I *can* quit waiting tables." Before Mike could reply, she went on. "If you really give a damn about this family, and you're not just bullshitting me about this mine, then prove it. Start drilling." Jenny's voice rose. "That's what we're here for. Start drilling."

Mike's face had gone white. He backed away from Jenny and leaned his head against the pickup cab, one hand shielding his face, the other gripping the doorframe.

Jenny stepped toward him, hesitated, and took another step.

"Mike?" she said. "What's wrong?" When he didn't answer, she went to his side and pulled his hand away from his face. He turned toward her; his eyes were hollow and shadowed.

Jenny reached up and touched his face. "Tell me," she said.

"Jenny, I can't drill."

Jenny stood still and looked at him. Finally, she said, "Maybe we should go get some coffee."

"No," Mike said. "I don't want Billy to hear me."

"Then let's get in the truck."

Mike climbed in the passenger's side of the pickup, and Jenny got under the wheel and started the engine. When the heater warmed up, she turned the fan on low and said, "I don't understand what you're saying, Mike. I know you've drilled in the tunnel before."

"But I can't now, Jenny. I can't work in there with that drill."

"Why not?" Jenny said flatly.

Mike looked out the window and replied in a low voice, "Because I'm afraid." The rising sun glazed the east ridge of the hills. Jenny waited, and Mike went on. "The last time I drilled in there, a slab of rock fell down from the back."

"Oh," Jenny said quietly. "I thought I saw a place where rock had fallen. Was it close to you?"

"No, it missed me by four or five feet. But I wish it had gotten me. You'd be better off."

"Don't say that," Jenny said.

"You would. You and Corey and Billy. How can I face my own son and tell him I'm afraid—too afraid to drill us out of the hole we're in?"

"Have you tried?"

"God, yes, I've tried. I started to take that damn drill in there today, but by the time I was halfway to the breast I was shaking. Jesus, you can't deal with machines and dynamite if you've got the shakes."

"You didn't seem to mind the mucking we did."

"Mucking doesn't rattle the whole goddamn mountain. Besides, you were with me."

"So," Jenny said, "you want to give it all up."

"No, I don't want to, but I can't make myself run that damn drill."

"Maybe we should quit. You could go back to construction."

"Jenny." Mike sounded like he was in a hollow tree. "There's something else I haven't told you."

Jenny's stomach tightened and a sharp spasm went down her side. I'm too tired, she thought. I can't listen to any more. But Mike didn't wait for a reply.

He said, "I can't get a construction job, either. I've been blackballed in this state."

Jenny's stomach curled around itself again. She looked at Mike and saw Billy staring out of his eyes. Her husband seemed totally lost, more fearfully wounded than the deer he had shot. She had to help him.

Jenny reached across and took his hand. "Mike, nothing lasts forever. We're okay here for now. We've got plenty of meat. We'll figure something out." He didn't respond to her touch, but he didn't pull his hand away. "It hasn't been very long since the rockfall. You'll forget it in time."

"Yeah," Mike said, "about the time Billy has grown up and taken off, disgusted with his old man."

"You're good with Billy," Jenny said. "He's already learned a lot from you since you've been with him every day."

"I wanted to show him how to work the mine."

"You will," Jenny said. "But even if you don't, Billy doesn't care. As long as you talk to him and love him, Billy doesn't care."

Mike looked at Jenny. "It's not that easy. I can't be his mother. I'm his father. It's not the same."

Jenny knew he was right. She said, "Mike, we've never talked like this before. It makes me feel close to you. Maybe we can figure out a way to run the mine together."

Mike's hand tightened on hers. "You remind me of Rosie," he said.

"I thought you said she was a nuisance."

"She is, sometimes, but when you need her, she humps her back and puts everything she's got into the job."

Jenny leaned against Mike's shoulder, sudden tears in her eyes.

"Jesus," he said, "I forgot that you've been up all night. Come on. You better get some sleep."

Mike got out of the truck and helped Jenny down. He put his arm around her shoulders as they walked to the cabin. When they stepped inside, Corey was crying. Jenny started toward the crib, but Mike said, "Let me take care of her. You go on to bed." Jenny slipped out of the uniform and, tossing it on the foot of the bed, crawled under the covers.

▽   ▽

When she woke it was late afternoon. She could hear Mike and Billy talking outside. Corey wasn't in the crib. Jenny peeked out the window. Mike and Billy were walking toward the creek. Billy had Rosie's water bucket; Mike carried the cabin bucket. From Mike's back Corey in her rock-sack saddlebag waved her arms in the air and reached for the leaves on a low-hanging branch.

Jenny started to dress but couldn't find her uniform on the bed. Puzzled, she looked around and saw it on a hanger by the shelves. Mike must have hung it up. Jenny washed with water from the teakettle and then dressed and made the bed. The cabin was quiet. Sun rays slanted through the window and across the red stripe on the Navajo blanket. Jenny stood still for a moment, watching the band of fire where the sun's gold mixed with the red. Dust motes danced in the orange light above the spread. Jenny moved softly about the cabin, making macaroni and cheese and setting the table.

When Mike and the children came back with the water, Mike said, "Did you get enough sleep?"

"Yes. I feel a lot better. Thanks for keeping the kids happy." She took Corey out of the sack and sat down in the rocking chair to give her a bottle. Corey's cheeks were rosy, and her eyes sparkled. "You like to go for rides on Daddy's back, don't you?"

Mike turned with a grin. "Yeah. That little ole girl is a good sport."

I don't want to leave this cabin, Jenny thought. We're turning into a real family here.

▽   ▽

When Jenny arrived at Mom Bradley's, Richard was alone in the café, and sober. "Mom went up to town a couple of hours ago to do some business and get the mail."

Jenny checked the napkins, sugars, and salt shakers. "It's a surprise not to have any customers," she said, sitting on a barstool.

Richard walked over and looked out the front door window. "Yeah," he said. "We've been so damn busy this week, we haven't had one decent conversation."

Jenny was startled. Was he going to ignore everything she'd told him about her mother? But she said lightly, "Well, we haven't had any indecent conversations, either."

Richard turned around. "Dear God—that's a joke! Jenny made a joke." He went over to her, and she looked up with a smile. Abruptly, he bent and kissed her on the mouth. Then he turned away and went out the front door. Stunned by Richard's action, Jenny sat on the barstool until the door swung open. A couple and two children came into the café.

Just as Jenny finished taking their dinner orders, Mom Bradley came in from the back. She had a package in her hand. "Somebody sent you something," she said setting the package on the bar. "Where's Richard going? I met him on the highway just this side of Dolby, pushing that Caddy like he had a bee up his ass."

"I don't know," Jenny said, "but I need two hamburgers and a couple of chicken-fried steaks." As Mom turned toward the kitchen Jenny asked, "Is that package really for me, or were you kidding?"

"It's for you, care of me."

Jenny served salad and soup to her customers and then went behind the bar. The package was big and heavy, with a return address in Tulsa, Oklahoma. Jenny quickly reached for a steak knife to cut the wrapping tape.

Inside the box was a state GED manual and several books. Startled, Jenny picked up the manual and opened it. A note was paper-clipped to the inside front page: "A starting place for a girl who wants to know."

Jenny put the manual down as Mom Bradley came to the serving window. "What's in the box, Jenny?"

"It looks like a whole high school education," Jenny said.

"That's an expensive present," Mom Bradley said. "Who sent it?"

"Bigfoot."

"Well, it's a good thing he can't see your face right now. He'd know he wasted his money."

"That's the problem," said Jenny. "I already owe him more than I can ever repay. I can't take this. It puts me too much in his debt."

"For a little gal, you've got a helluva lot of pride. Why don't you just take the gift and say thank you real nice next time he comes through."

"I'll have to pay for it," Jenny said. "When you don't have anything but your pride, you can't afford to lose it."

Mom Bradley snorted. "Oh, for Chrissake," she said, turning back toward the kitchen.

Jenny picked up the manual again and reread the note. As more customers arrived she put the box of books under the bar. What I need to know right now isn't in those high school books, she thought as the dinner hour sped up and she began her clockwise rounds of the dining room.

At about seven o'clock Tony came in for dinner. As he was finishing his dessert, Jenny sat down at his table. "Tony," she said. "I need a big favor."

"Sure, Jenny. What can I do for you?" His eyes sparkled, and his craggy grin gave her courage.

"I want you to teach me how to run the drill."

Tony's smile faded. "That's no job for you," he said. "You're too little."

"I may be little, but I'm no weakling. I washed clothes by hand for years before I got this job. I carry heavy trays here; up at the mine I chop trees and load wood, and I'm helping to build the ore bin. Mike said I was a good mucker."

Tony forked up the last bite of pie. "Well, you just keep on mucking and let Mike do the drilling."

"Mike won't be drilling for a while."

Tony set his fork down and looked sharply at Jenny. "I *thought* I saw sign of a rockfall. Is Mike spooked?"

"Mike is very spooked. Please, Tony. You've got to teach me to run the drill."

Jenny rose as a customer waved his empty coffee cup at her. When she glanced back, Tony was writing something on a napkin. As soon as she had a chance, she went back to his table and sat down. Tony pushed the napkin her way. She picked it up and looked at the crude drawing. "What is it?" she asked.

Tony said, "Mike has been mining the poor-boy method. He's collected his tools from this junkyard and that mine dump and cobbled them together into a ragged operation. None of the parts quite go with the other parts. Have you seen the drilling equipment?"

"So far it's just a pile of stuff in Mike's shop."

Tony pointed to the sketch on the napkin. "Well, that's an old-fashioned column post, and that's what Mike mounts his drill on. It sits down on the bottom timber, here," Tony's gnarled finger tapped the bottom of the sketch. "These here are the shoes that the column-tightening screws fit in."

The sketch of the column post seemed very complicated. Feeling slightly confused, Jenny listened intently, trying to hold every word in her mind.

"The old screws have square nuts on 'em. You're going to need a spud wrench to get 'em tight and then loose again. I loaned Mike one; he's probably still got it." Tony looked up from the sketch. "Do you suppose I could have another cup of coffee?"

Jenny refilled his cup and waited on a customer at the cash register. Then she went back to Tony. "Okay, so I set the column post in those shoes and turn the tightening screws with a spud wrench."

"Jenny, do you know how heavy this thing is? It's made of three-inch iron."

"Well, you're not much bigger than I am, and you've put it up, haven't you?"

Tony nodded, taking a long sip from his coffee cup. "All right," he said, "you set that post in the shoes and tighten the screws till you've raised the top of the post near to the back. Then you jam the roof-blocking timber in at the top, wedge it against the back, wedge it good."

Jenny told herself, The back is the top of the tunnel—the inside of the whale's spine. She smiled at the thought and then said to Tony, "The post has to stay firm. I get that. So after I wedge the roof-blocking timber against the back, what's next?" She looked up as Mom Bradley came out from the kitchen and leaned on the bar. Mom looked around the room and then opened a bottle of beer.

"Next you got to put the crossbar on the column post," Tony said.

"What does it do?"

Tony stopped and said abruptly, "This is too much for you to learn."

"No, it isn't," Jenny said. "Tell me about the crossbar."

"The crossbar runs at right angles to the column post. You clamp it on with these U-bolts." Tony pointed to his sketch. "And tighten the clamps with these here nuts. Then you put the safety collar under the clamps and tighten *it*." Tony glanced at Jenny; she nodded, and he went on. "Now, this thing on top of the crossbar is the saddle. The drill rides in the saddle."

"Ah, we're getting to the drill," Jenny said.

"You better figure out some way to lift all this stuff without busting your back," Tony said.

Mom Bradley said, "If Richard doesn't show up, Jenny, you'll have to do some dishes."

"Okay, Mom. In a minute." She turned back to Tony's sketch. "And then what?"

"You set that drill in the saddle and aim it at the breast of the tunnel. But before you get going, you'll have to hook up an air hose and a water hose on the tail end." He said, "You got something else I can draw on?" Jenny tore a couple of sheets from her order pad and gave them to Tony.

"I'd better go run a batch of dishes. Mom Bradley gets kind of cranky when she drinks. I don't want to upset her."

As Jenny went through the swinging doors Richard came into the kitchen through the back. He grinned at Jenny and said, "You mad at me?"

Jenny thought of his quick kiss. "No, I'm not mad at you." She started stacking dishes in the wood and metal tray that slid through the dishwasher. Richard came to stand beside her, scraping plates and handing them to her.

"Bigfoot sent me the stuff for a GED—manual, books, and everything."

"Good for him."

"I can't keep it, Richard."

"Why not?"

"I can't afford to pay for it, and I owe him too much already."

"Bullshit. He wants you to have it. You need it. I wish I'd thought of it."

"If I decide not to give it back, will you help me with the work?" Jenny glanced at Richard. He gave her a quick sweet smile.

"I'd like that, Jenny. At least I can help with the history and literature. Maybe not as much with the algebra. I'm not so good at math."

"Do you need math to understand about the earth?"

Richard walked around Jenny and pushed the heavily loaded tray into the dishwasher. "Well, I think you'd need math," he said, "and chemistry and geology, maybe physics too."

"Oh," Jenny said, "all that?" She turned. "Can you catch up now? I'm trying to learn something from Tony."

Another man was sitting with Tony when Jenny went back to his table. "This is Lloyd Daley," Tony said. "He's a state mine inspector."

Jenny's heart beat a little faster. Had he heard about the rockfall in the Spanish Mary? "I'm glad to meet you," she said. "Are you in Dolby on business?"

"Just routine checks, ma'am," the inspector said. "Checking for safety and proper procedure." He got up from the table and touched his hand to his cap. "Nice to meet you, ma'am." Jenny smiled at him.

As the mine inspector went out, Tony said, "You better be careful when he comes around, Jenny."

"He seems like a nice man."

"He may be a nice man, but he's a helluva strict inspector. Don't you ever let him catch you working in that tunnel alone."

"Mike will be around. I won't be alone. I guess we've got the braces—the stulls—in right and spaced right. You helped Mike with them, didn't you?"

"Yeah, the timbering in your tunnel is okay. That rockfall was just a freak."

"Tell me about the drilling now."

Tony handed her the sheets from her order pad. He had drawn a series of small dots in a pattern. "Well, you got that column post set up eighteen inches from the breast," he said, "and the drill mounted on it. Now you've got to learn how to drill them holes."

Jenny looked at the drilling pattern. "Are these holes for the dynamite?"

"That's right."

"Which one do I drill first?"

Tony pointed to the center hole and two side holes at the top of the sketch. "You'll drill the crown and arch holes first."

"What makes the power for the drill?"

"The compressor and you. You'll have an air hose hooked onto the drill. The air pressure runs the drill, but you'll have to crank the steel in."

"The steel?"

"The rods with the bits on the end. You'll see 'em in Mike's shop."

Jenny sighed. There were so many pieces of strange equipment in Mike's shop. "I'll have to learn to use it all," she said. "We really need to get that ore out of the mine."

"You'll have to go at it in two steps," Tony said. "You'll want your cut holes in the overhang—the rock above the vein. You'll shoot that first and muck it out before you shoot the vein."

"But I have to drill the whole pattern first, don't I?"

Tony smiled at her. "That's right. You'll drill it all, while your column post is set up."

"Which ones are the cut holes?"

Tony pointed to two little circles in the middle of the pattern he had drawn. "We're using a V-cut. You drill these two holes longer than the others. Angle them in toward each other, but don't connect them at the point of the V. They'll be the first to go—they have the shortest fuse."

Suddenly Jenny felt totally lost. Tony was trying to make it sound simple, but all the technical words were overwhelming.

"If I bribed you with a thick venison steak," she said, "would you come up and supervise while I try to learn this stuff firsthand?"

"Venison?" Tony said, glancing around him. In a softer voice he said, "You got venison?"

"It's hanging," Jenny said.

Tony grinned. "You chop me up some of that meat and make me a big old batch of spaghetti sauce on Sunday, and I'll teach you everything I know about drilling."

"It's a deal," Jenny said.

Tony rose, "I've got a game now."

"Leave the pictures of the drill holes. Do they all have names?"

"Yeah. I'll introduce you tomorrow."

Jenny took the sketches behind the bar and put them inside the GED manual. There were three bar customers, but nobody was in the dining room. She wiped off the table, cleaned all the trays, and filled the sugars and salt shakers. Mom Bradley was talking with the big man she'd left the bar with before.

Jenny wandered into the kitchen. Richard was sitting on his stool drinking a bottle of Coors. Jenny swung herself up on the empty counter by the dishwasher. "Who is that big man your mother's talking to?"

Richard scowled. "His name's Ed O'Brien. He works for the county road department."

"Why don't you like him?"

"The son of a bitch comes sniffing around here every week or so. He's got a wife at home—a sick wife at that."

"Maybe his sick wife doesn't mind if he goes somewhere else."

"Well I mind. I don't want him around my mother."

"She seems to like him."

"Yeah, she acts like a bitch in heat when he shows up." Richard tipped his head back for a long swallow.

Jenny said, "Why do men make different rules for women than the ones they have for themselves?"

"What do you mean?"

"Well, I bet you aren't living without women."

Richard flushed. "That's different."

"Why is it different?"

"It's just different."

"Come on, Richard. If you have a right to go out with girls, your mother has a right to go out with a man."

"Just don't try it yourself, Jenny, when Billy's grown up."

"Well, I have Mike, but if I didn't have Mike, I think Billy would understand."

"Don't count on it." Richard stood up and went out to the bar. Jenny swung her feet against the cupboard and thought about drilling and men and Billy and Richard. When Richard came back carrying three bottles of beer, she said, "My mind is full of such a jumble of things, I feel more ignorant than I did below the dump."

"Why did you marry Mike?" Richard asked.

Jenny looked at him. "Well, that's a funny question to ask me. I wasn't talking about Mike."

"You don't talk about him very much."

"Should I?"

"If you loved him, you'd just naturally talk about him. I don't think you love him. So why did you marry him?"

Jenny said, "He's good with the kids."

Richard laughed. "You didn't know that five years ago, that he'd be good with the kids. That's no answer."

Jenny slid down from the counter and wandered over to the swinging doors. She looked out. The café was empty. Mom Bradley and Ed O'Brien were gone. She turned back toward Richard.

"He had a job and a trailer. He wanted me to marry him."

"You don't have a damn thing in common. You don't use one tenth of your brain when you're around him." Richard twisted savagely at the top of a bottle. "Did you think how that would turn out?"

"It doesn't make any difference, Richard. I'm married to Mike," Jenny said, "and he's not as dumb as you say."

Richard chugalugged. "Want a beer?" he said.

"No, Richard. And I wish you'd slow down. It's a long time until two o'clock, and you're the only one around here to talk to tonight."

For answer, Richard tipped his head and swallowed long. Jenny went back through the swinging doors. She lifted the box of books from behind the bar and went to the blue vinyl booth. Taking the manual out, she spent a moment studying Tony's sketch of the column post. Then she opened the fat GED manual and began to read. She heard Richard come out to the bar again but she didn't look up.

She read the first two chapters of the manual, going slowly and stopping often to think. The section with the diagnostic examination was scary. I'm going to have to study a lot. I hope Richard really will help me.

At one thirty she put the books back under the bar. When she went into the kitchen for her regular clothes, she saw Richard sitting on the floor in the corner between the cabinets and the stove. She went to him and put her hand on his shoulder. "Richard, I'm going home now," she said. "You'd better lock up and count the money."

Richard looked up with dull eyes. "You comin' back, Jenny?"

"Tomorrow's payday. You'd better believe I'm coming back."

Richard squinted at her. "You can take old Jenny's body home to Mikey-Mike," he said, his voice slurring, "but you have to leave Jenny's mind here with me." Suddenly he slumped against the cabinet.

"Richard?"

He responded with a deep drunken snore. Jenny gritted her teeth and exhaled in aggravation. She stepped around Richard and checked the back door lock. Then she turned off the grill and the light and went out the swinging doors. She changed quickly and left by the front door, locking it behind her.

As she drove through Dolby and along Virgo Creek toward the mountain, Jenny thought about Richard's claim to her mind and shuddered. If I ever get my mind the way I want it, it won't belong to anyone but me, she decided. She considered the rest of their conversation that evening. Poor Richard. Despite his drunken rambling, he sometimes gets right to the point.

Do I love Mike? Well, I don't know what love is supposed to feel like. He's the father of my kids, and he's good with them, and that makes a difference, no matter what Richard thinks.

The drive had become a special time; Jenny enjoyed being alone. I'm glad I finally told someone about Mama, even if Richard doesn't seem to remember. Maybe I'll be able to think about her now, think clearly. If I'm going to get my GED I'd better start remembering the things she taught me. But then maybe I'd better just pay attention to the stuff Tony's teaching me for now. She passed the Craggy Claims turnoff and smiled, picturing Quentin Lacey. That little man wouldn't believe me if I told him I had far more interesting things to do than watch TV.

▽ ▽

Richard didn't show up Friday, so Jenny was busy with orders and dishes. The bar was still crowded after the dinner rush was over. Jenny served drinks, smiling mechanically, scarcely aware of the occasional hand that brushed her arm or leg. She was trying to memorize everything Tony had told her. If she could set up, drill, and shoot one day, Mike could muck out the next. They could get a system going and start filling the ore bin.

"Hey, Jenny are you with us? I ordered bourbon and Seven."

Jenny smiled at the man. "Of course you did. That Manhattan belongs to Larry." She set the drinks in the right places and stood for a moment, smiling around the table. The man who had spoken before said, "You look damn pretty tonight, Jenny."

She felt herself flush. It always pleased her when they said she was pretty. "Thank you," she said and turned back to the bar.

Mom Bradley was watching her. She smiled at Jenny and said, "You're good at keeping customers happy. I've decided you're worth more money—especially since you double as dishwasher about half the time." She pulled her blouse down over her belly and smoothed it. "I don't know what in the hell's the matter with Richard these days. He gets a bug in his ear, drops everything, and takes off."

At closing time the kitchen was full of dirty dishes. Jenny worked until three thirty again, hoping that Mike was asleep.

Mom Bradley wrote out Jenny's check. Jenny's pulse leapt as she saw that Mom had given her a raise of twenty-five cents an hour. The kids could have some warmer clothes. She might even be able to afford real boots. She didn't want to wear her old four-buckle overshoes to work.

Mom said, "You've worked damn hard, and it's late, Jenny. Why don't you take Saturday off. I'll catch Richard and make him work in your place."

"I can sleep in. That'll be a treat," Jenny said.

But the children woke her early, and Jenny decided not to waste her extra day off in bed. She gave Mike the rest of the money for the October payment on the truck loan and the insurance.

"Here's the grocery money and my list, too. I don't feel like going into town again." She didn't tell him that she wanted a chance to look at his shop. "Tony's coming up for dinner tomorrow," she said. "I promised him venison spaghetti sauce. I'd better get it started."

She walked out to the truck with Mike, out of Billy's earshot. "Tony's been teaching me a little bit about drilling."

Mike flushed. "You told him about me."

"He already knew. He saw signs of the rockfall."

"What makes you think you can run that drill?"

"I don't know. I can try. I want to try."

"Damn," said Mike. "I don't like it."

"What else can we do?" Jenny asked.

Mike shrugged and got in the truck. Jenny didn't ask when he'd be back. He was always late on the days he took the money to town.

After lunch, while Corey and Billy napped, Jenny went to the corral. Rosie made a friendly little *huff-huff* and came over to snuffle her nose in Jenny's hand.

"Sorry, Rosie. *Nobody* gets apples until Mike gets home with the groceries. You ate up all the apples this week." She held out a partially chewed cracker that Corey had been cutting teeth on. Rosie drew back her rubbery upper lip, but she took the cracker and ate it.

After scratching the burro's ear for a moment Jenny went into the shop. Tony's sketch had been quite accurate. She spotted the column post at once, leaning against the wall near the door. She put her hands around the post at a height just above her head, and putting her whole body into it, she pulled the post to a standing position. It was heavy. And it was dirty. The metal, rough with rust and dried mud, felt scaly against her fingers. Darn, she thought. My gloves are in the truck.

Jenny looked up the post. It stretched nearly two feet above her head. She looked at the door, and slowly lowering the heavy post in her hands while walking her hands toward the top, she finally gripped the post at the end and dragged it to the doorway, where she let it fall and stood a moment to catch her breath.

She found the top timber—Tony called it the roof-blocking timber—and the bottom timber with the screw shoes on its upper side, and then she turned to look for a spud wrench. Tony hadn't sketched that, but it had to fit the tightening screws. Jenny sorted through a bunch of wrenches that were piled on one corner of the workbench behind a tire jack and a heap of chain. She tried jaws on screws until she came to a big wrench with a tapered head and a square jaw that went easily onto the square heads of the tightening screws.

"I bet this is a spud wrench," she said to Rosie, who had poked her head through the door. Jenny considered the burro. "If I could get that harness on you, you could drag the post into the tunnel for me."

She put Rosie's halter on and tied her to the fence before lifting the heavy chains and leather from the nail in the shop. She brought the big leather collar, too, but when she got to the burro, she didn't know what to put on first, and though she knew that the chains and the butt stick went to the rear, she didn't know where to hook the other parts of the harness. She caressed Rosie's fuzzy back and laid the harness out on top of it.

"What are you doing, Mama?"

Jenny turned as Billy climbed up on the fence and dropped down inside the corral. "Hi, honey," she said. "Is Corey still sleeping?"

"Yup," he said, and asked again, "Whatcha doing?"

"I want to harness Rosie, but I don't know how."

"I know how. I helped Daddy when we cut the wood." Billy came closer and said, "You have to put the collar on first."

Step by step, Billy showed Jenny how to harness the burro. When the harness looked complete Jenny said, "You're a smart kid," and kissed him, adding, "I don't suppose you can start the generator?"

"Daddy didn't show me about the generator yet."

"Well, we'll have to take the flashlight then," she said. "You get your hard hat."

I'd better check for loose rock, she thought, remembering Lloyd Daley. The mine inspector wouldn't consider Billy proper help in the mine, and she wasn't supposed to go in there without help, but she wanted to set the column post up before Mike got back. If Mike saw her struggling with its weight he'd never let her learn to drill. At least Billy could hold the light.

Jenny backed Rosie up to the column post and hooked the chain around the bottom of it. She tied the top and bottom timbers and the spud wrench to the post. Slipping Mike's tape measure into her pocket, she led Rosie through the gate after Billy opened it.

Out on the mine dump she said, "Put your hard hat on and hold Rosie a minute while I check on Corey." The baby was still asleep. Jenny left the cabin, put on her own hard hat, and led Rosie to the portal of the mine.

Rosie and Billy clunked along the railroad track. Jenny checked the stulls as they passed and kept the light moving on the ceiling and walls.

They reached the face of the tunnel and Rosie stopped. Jenny gave Billy the flashlight while she unhooked the burro, turned her around, and walked a few paces back toward the mouth. When Jenny dropped the reins the burro hung her head and slumped forward a little. "Have a good snooze, Rosie," Jenny said.

She went back to the face. Billy was flipping the beam of light back and forth across the sparkling vein of ore. Jenny watched for a moment and then said, "Billy, I want you to move over here where it's safe and shine the light at the bottom."

Billy moved to where Jenny pointed. She pulled the metal tape from the spring-loaded reel, checked the measure to be sure she had it locked at eighteen inches and then untied the bottom timber from the post. She set the bottom timber eighteen inches from the face, put the spud wrench and the roof-blocking timber within reach, and dragged the post to the bottom timber and lined up the screws and the holes.

Squatting behind the post, she put her hands around it and slowly began to stand up. She could feel the muscles in her shoulders and stomach pull tight. Her knees made little crickling noises as she rose and straightened them. She rested the heavy post on her shoulder a moment and then began to push it upward; her arms trembled as she pushed the post into an upright position.

"Shine the light on those round things at the bottom. Tony calls them shoes."

Billy giggled. "I didn't know posts had feet."

Jenny didn't answer. She wrapped her arms around the post, trying to hold it steady with her body as she lifted it slightly and attempted to put the tightening screws into the shoes on the bottom timber. As the screws slid past the shoes instead of going up, she said, "Damn," under her breath. Extending one hand down the pole, she guided the screws while the rest of the pole wobbled above her.

Finally the screws went into the shoes. Jenny reached around for the spud wrench and bent to tighten them. The wrench slipped and banged her shin. She rubbed her leg, and when the pain eased, she fitted the wrench to the nut again and slowly turned the screw that jacked up the right side of the column post. The screw on the left side took longer.

"My left hand is dumb," she said to Billy, turning the other column-tightening screw slowly until the top of the post was near the back. Then she reached for the roof-blocking timber and stood up, one hand holding the post.

"Is your right hand smart?" Billy asked.

"Yes, my right hand knows how to write my name. My left hand can't do that."

"Will you teach *my* right hand to write?"

"Sure, honey, whenever you want." Jenny reached up to push the top timber into the space between the post and the back. The space was tight, and she couldn't push the timber in with her hand. "Why didn't I bring a hammer?"

"Shall I get you a hammer, Mama?"

"No, baby. It's too big. I need wedges, too. Besides, it's time to check Corey."

When Jenny let go of the post it leaned inward. She rested it against the breast of the tunnel and stood for a moment looking at the vein of ore. "I hope this sparkly rock is as rich as it looks," she said, taking the light from Billy and leading him to Rosie. She put him on the burro and guided them out of the tunnel.

When they reached daylight, Billy said, "You're all dirty, Mama." Jenny looked down. The rusty post had coated her clothes. She dusted off the best she could and went to the cabin. Corey was still asleep. Jenny took a handful of crackers back out to Billy, who was holding Rosie's reins. He gave one to Rosie.

Jenny stepped into the shop. She picked up a flat-nosed hammer and several wooden wedges. Glancing around, she saw a hard hat with a light on it. She exchanged her hat for the one on the bench, untangled the wires that went from the battery pack to the hat, and slipped the clip on the pack over her belt.

Jenny's headlamp lit their way. Jenny stopped about halfway into the tunnel and gave Billy the flashlight and Rosie's reins. She didn't want him too near when she was hammering on the top timber. "You keep Rosie company until I get the post up, Billy."

"Okay," he said, taking the flashlight and shining it on Rosie's face and then up and down the track.

Back at the breast of the tunnel Jenny wallowed the post upward again and looked down, trying to make sure that the screws had stayed in the shoes. But she couldn't bend her neck at an angle that would light the screws with the headlamp. She finally bent and checked the screws by feel.

When she held the roof-blocking timber at the top of the pole and aimed her headlamp at it, she could see fairly well. She lifted the heavy hammer and hit the timber as hard as she could. It moved a little way in between the post and the back. She rested and listened. There was no sound of cracking rock, no sound at all except the murmur of Billy's voice as he talked to Rosie, and the faraway trickle of water. She hit the timber again, and it moved again. Taking the hammer in both hands, she gave the timber a solid whack. It slid into place on top of the pole. Jenny picked up the wedges, thinking of what Tony had said about the column post: "It has to be tight. When you get that doggone machine on there, and it starts pushing in, if you let that thing get out of line you got trouble. You gotta get that post tight."

She drove the wedges in solid and then put the hammer down and tugged on the post, putting her whole body weight into it. The post was firmly lodged.

"Well, I've got that part of it up."

She led Rosie and Billy out of the tunnel. Using Tony's sketch, she found the crossbar and dragged it from the shop. She tied the crossbar to the chain at the back of the harness, listened for sounds of Corey, and then hoisted Billy onto Rosie's back and led the burro back into the tunnel.

The crossbar was easier to install. She assembled it near the bottom of the post, slid it upward and, balancing it on her shoulder, tightened the nuts on the U-bolts. Next she slid the safety collar up underneath the crossbar and tightened that.

Then she stood back and enjoyed the sight of the column post with its crossbar extended, waiting for the drill. I can do it, she thought. Now I know I can do it. She shut off her headlamp and stood still. The darkness curved around her. Standing there, she saw her mother's table clearly in her mind. The sun shone through the blue glass vase and made a puddle of shimmering blue on the white tablecloth. I'm proud of myself today, Mama. She flicked the light on again, gathered her tools, and went down the tunnel to pick up Rosie's reins.

When they reached the tunnel mouth, Billy slid off of Rosie and ran ahead calling, "Mama, somebody's here. There's a car by the cabin."

"Oh, God," said Jenny. "You, God. Don't let it be that mine inspector."

CHAPTER
31

▲▲▲▲▲▲

As Jenny led Rosie out onto the mine dump, a woman opened the door of the car by the cabin and got out. She came toward them, frowning slightly.

"Is that you, Jenny?" she said.

"Karen!"

Jenny dropped Rosie's reins and ran toward Karen, but stopped just in front of her and looked down at her rust-covered clothes. She laughed and took off her hard hat.

"I can't hug you in these clothes."

Karen smiled and said, "What on earth are you doing in that hole?"

"That's not a hole," Jenny said. "That's the Spanish Mary, and I'm getting ready to drill."

Corey was crying. Jenny said, "If you'll go in and comfort the baby for me, Karen, I'll put Rosie in the corral and join you in a minute. Oh, I'm so glad to see you." She turned to reach for Rosie's reins. "Billy, will you go get some water? First get half a bucket for Rosie and then bring me half a bucket to wash in."

"I can lift a whole bucket, Mama."

"Well, you just bring half a bucket anyway."

Jenny put her tools in the shop and unharnessed Rosie. What can I offer her to eat? she thought frantically. There's coffee. I can make that right away. Dinner will have to be some of the spaghetti sauce I made for Tony for tomorrow. There are a few crackers left; there's a handful of walnuts and raisins. I can make a salad out of canned pears, nuts, and raisins.

Billy came up the mine dump with the water bucket. His teeth were chattering. Jenny took the bucket from him and filled the burro's pail.

"You better go in, honey. You're too cold."

"I want to be with you. Karen makes me lonesome."

Jenny knelt and hugged the little boy. "Thank you for all your help today, Billy. I couldn't have put the column post up if you hadn't taught me how to harness Rosie, and if you hadn't held the light."

Billy smiled into her eyes. "I like the mine when it's you and me, Mama."

"You're a good helper. Now you'll have to be a good host. Karen is company, and Daddy's not here to say welcome." She dusted a red smudge from his jacket and kissed him again. "Why don't you go and show Karen the cabin, and I'll get some more water."

Billy went slowly toward the cabin. Jenny picked up the bucket and started toward the creek. A few flakes of snow floated past her nose. Snow! How could I have been so stupid as to let us get this low on groceries? What if we got snowed in? I'm a complete fool to risk letting the kids go hungry. Corey can't eat the spaghetti sauce. Jenny dipped the bucket in the creek; the water was icy. No wonder Billy was cold. I'd better start thinking more about my kids.

Jenny took the bucket to the cabin, built up the fire, set the wash pan on the stove to heat, and started a pot of coffee. Karen was sitting in the rocking chair with Corey. Billy sat stiffly on the edge of the big bed.

Karen said, "This is a nice little cabin. I was surprised to find it so warm."

Jenny unbuttoned her shirt and slipped out of it. "It's a lot better than that old house, and we don't pay rent." She set the wash pan on the stand and moved the coffeepot toward the front of the stove. She washed her face and arms and combed her hair.

"I like your hair," Karen said.

"I have it done in town."

"You do!" Karen stopped rocking. "What does Mike think about that?"

Jenny laughed. "Let me get some supper started, and I'll explain everything. It's lucky that I have the day off."

"Oh," Karen said, standing to put Corey in the crib. "I have a present for you. I was so surprised to see you come out of that tunnel, I forgot. I'll go get it."

Jenny slipped into her robe as Karen went out the door. Billy got off the bed. Karen backed into the cabin a moment later with a bulky package in her arms. Setting it down in the middle of the floor, she said, "Open it. I'm dying for you to see it."

Jenny knelt and untied the yellow ribbon. The pretty paper tore as she pulled it away, but she forgot the wrapping as soon as she saw the red wagon.

"Oh, Karen." Jenny rose and hugged her, tears starting in her eyes.

"I owe you much more than that," Karen said. "You saved my life."

"You aren't going back to Tully?" Jenny looked at her friend anxiously. "He said you would."

"Don't worry," Karen said. "I'll never go back. When you put me on that bus, you sent me to the right place."

Billy had climbed into the wagon and was making truck noises. Jenny said, "The coffee should be ready. Let's have some dinner, and then we'll put the children to bed and talk. Can you stay awhile?"

"I can do anything I want to do," Karen said. She seemed relaxed, softer.

"I'm beginning to think I can too," Jenny said, pouring two cups of coffee. "Today I put up a column post in the mine. A week ago, I didn't even know what a column post was."

She opened the canned pears and added the nuts and raisins. She set the salad on the table and spooned spaghetti sauce and a few chunks of meat into three bowls. She put the last crackers onto a plate and poured the remaining milk into Billy's glass.

"I wish Mike were here," she said. "He's gone to town for groceries, and I don't have any spaghetti to go with the meat sauce."

Jenny felt nervous, remembering the expensive food Karen had always served her.

"Better the sauce without the spaghetti than the spaghetti without the sauce," Karen said, pulling the crate she sat on closer to the table. Billy came reluctantly away from the red wagon. He climbed on his stool. Poking his fingers into the sauce, he pulled out a chunk of meat and sucked it noisily.

"Billy, eat with your fork," Jenny said. Billy picked up his fork and ran it through the sauce and then licked it. Some of the red liquid smeared his chin. "Billy," Jenny said, "use your spoon."

"You said to use my fork."

Jenny glanced at Billy. The pouting little face was nothing like the one he'd turned to her after they'd harnessed Rosie. Jenny held back her annoyed response and said, "You decide how to eat the sauce," and pulled her own crate toward the table.

While they ate she told Karen about her job at Mom's Bar, without giving any reason for Mike's leaving the construction company. Karen said, "So Mike finally decided to work the mine full time."

Jenny left it at that. "I like the mine too," she said. "Tony's going to teach me how to drill."

Billy looked up, and Jenny said, "Mike said I can learn if I want to." Billy went back to stirring his cracker around and around in his sauce. Jenny wished he would hurry. She and Karen couldn't have a real talk with the boy listening to every word. She rose and took Corey from her crib, where she'd been batting at the plastic spoons and spools. "Come on, baby, you'd better have some of Mama's pears."

Karen said to Billy, "Tell me about the burro. What's his name?"

Billy said, "Rosie's not a boy; she's a girl."

"Oh," said Karen. She looked over at Jenny, who smiled, though the back of her neck tightened with tension.

"Billy," she said, "do you have to be so exasperatingly male?"

Karen laughed. Billy looked confused, and Jenny felt instantly ashamed. "I'm sorry, honey," she said. "But will you please hurry a little, so I can have time to visit with Karen. She came a long way to bring us that red wagon."

Billy picked the last meat chunk out of his bowl with his fingers, tipped up the bowl and drank the sauce. He wiped the back of his hand across his mouth.

Jenny gritted her teeth and stood up. She held Corey out toward Karen. "Can you feed her the rest of those mashed pears?"

"Sure," Karen said. The baby studied Karen solemnly before opening her mouth and sucking the pears from the spoon.

Jenny said, "Billy, I was so excited about having company, I forgot to give Rosie her oats. Come and help me." She took Billy's hand and stepped outside. It was snowing.

"Ooh. Snow," Billy said, reaching his hands toward the flakes.

"We'd better bring in more wood too," Jenny said.

Billy carried hay to Rosie while Jenny got the oats. Then he carried kindling into the cabin while Jenny brought in heavier chunks. By the time the woodbox was piled high there was a light blanket of snow on the ground. Karen looked out the door and said, "Maybe I should go on down the hill."

Jenny shut the door firmly and said, "Oh, Karen, please spend the night. Mike won't be back until late, maybe not until tomorrow. We haven't had a chance to really talk.

Karen glanced at Billy. The little boy suddenly seemed to remember Jenny's earlier words. "Welcome, Karen," he said. "You're welcome."

The two women laughed. Jenny hugged Billy and helped him get ready for bed. Corey was soon ready, too, and then Karen and Jenny did the dishes together, chatting about Mom Bradley and Richard. When the dishes were done and the children asleep, Jenny said, "Why don't you sit in the rocking chair." She took the Navajo blanket from the bed and, sitting down on the floor, wrapped the blanket around her and leaned back against the bed. "Did someone from Hope House meet your bus?" she asked.

"Yes," said Karen. "The house director met the bus, looked over the passengers, and picked me out at once." She laughed shortly. "I know now that it wasn't hard to guess which one I was. God, I saw plenty of first-timers while I was at Hope House: all subdued, ashamed to be there. Not one of them will ever look you in the face."

"How long did you stay there?"

"I lived there full time for a month. Then they helped me get a job and I rented a room, but I went to the House almost every night for meetings."

"Meetings?"

"To talk with other women—women just like me. The meetings were the only things that kept me going. Can you believe that after the first week I started thinking about all the good times with Tully, and I started to feel ashamed about running out on him? I even talked about coming back."

"Karen, you wouldn't have." Jenny sat up straight, remembering the night she'd put Karen on the bus.

"Oh yes I would. I was that sick."

"Why didn't you, then?"

"When I talked about it at the meeting, someone asked me to describe the situation that made me leave, and after I'd told them the whole story, one of them said, 'And what about Jenny?'"

Karen stopped rocking and looked at Jenny. "And that's the first time I really thought about how brave you were to get me out of there." She shook her head slowly from side to side. "I knew I couldn't go back. I couldn't make it all for nothing—all that you had done."

Jenny pulled the blanket closer around her and said, "I'm glad you didn't come back. I don't think I could have done any of the things that I've done since, if you had. I needed for you to be free." She smiled. "Nobody knows where you went. I've never told a soul, not even Mike."

"What about Mike, Jenny? Why are you really on this mine dump?"

Jenny glanced toward Billy's bed. The little boy's eyes were closed, and he was breathing deeply and regularly.

"Mike lost his job and couldn't get another. He wants to take the ore out of the mine. It's good ore. It could give us a start."

"And you're waiting tables." Karen leaned back in the chair. "Do you love Mike, Jenny?"

Jenny got up and opened the stove door. She poked at the coals with a piece of wood, then shoved it into the fire with another piece and closed the door.

"Richard asked me that," she said, returning to sit cross-legged on the bed. "It's not that simple. Mike and I haven't been bad for each other, but Richard says I only use ten percent of my mind when I'm with Mike."

Karen made a sound. "God, if Richard could only see himself."

"He's right in a way, Karen. There are a lot of things I never talk to Mike about. But I don't know if that's normal or not. I just sort of assumed that a woman usually goes about her daily chores with a familiar mask that keeps the children feeling secure and doesn't upset the man too much; a mask that hides all the questions she's gathering in her mind."

"And Mike doesn't have a clue?"

Jenny grasped her toes with her hands and rocked back and forth. "He's too busy thinking about his own problems." She rubbed her right hand up and down the sore place on her shin, where she'd banged it with the wrench. "We're okay together. He's great with the kids, and we've had some nice moments." She paused, then said, "I only wish we could be more honest with each other."

Karen got up from the chair and walked around the small space in front of the bed. "I don't know if it's possible, Jenny. Tully promised me a thousand times that things would be different."

"Mike doesn't promise anything, and I don't think he tells me outright lies. He just doesn't tell me anything at all about some parts of his life." Jenny thought fleetingly of the grocery money she'd sent with Mike. She was sure he was playing cards tonight.

"Do you know an honest man?" Karen asked.

Jenny laughed. "Well, Tony's too old-fashioned to be honest with a woman. And Richard . . . Heavens. There are so many sides to Richard. If he were honest on one side, he'd be lying about himself on two others." She stretched one leg out on the bed. "But I do think I know one honest man."

"Who?" Karen sat down on the foot of the bed.

"The truck driver who gave me that chair. The other truckers call him Bigfoot, but his name is David Garvey. I see him sometimes. . . ." Jenny hesitated and then went on. "When he looks at me, I have the feeling that I can trust everything he says."

Karen said, "It sounds as if you really like this guy. Does Mike know about it?"

"He's just a relief driver who comes through on Eighty-six and eats at Mom's sometimes. He doesn't even have a regular run. If I told Mike, he'd be jealous for no reason."

Karen said, "Jenny, I've been to six meetings a week for four months talking about stuff like this, and there's one thing I've learned: you can survive if other people aren't honest with you, but you're done for if you're lying to yourself."

Jenny felt the warmth rise in her face. After a moment of silence she said, "I feel different about David, but I don't know how to describe it. He makes me feel that things are possible."

"Even if you stay with Mike?"

Jenny nodded. "Even then. Nothing can stop my learning if I want to. I've even got the GED books at the café." Jenny suddenly knew that she was going to keep David Garvey's gift.

"That's great." Karen put her hand over Jenny's. "You still give me courage, and I'm going to need it. Tomorrow the sheriff and I are going to get my stuff from the trailer and serve divorce papers on Tully."

Jenny thought of Tully Stocker and the misery he'd caused her at Mom's Bar. "I'm glad, Karen." She clasped her friend's hand. "What will you do then?"

"I'm going to go back home and see if I can help my mother get out of her abusive situation. She might not be able to make the break, but I've got to try."

They were silent. The fire crackled in the stove, and the Coleman lantern hissed. The wind had risen; it whirled around the corners of the cabin. Jenny held Karen's hand in hers until the closeness of the moment was almost more than she could bear. Then she laughed and said, "And you came all the way up here to bring me a red wagon."

CHAPTER

32

▲▲▲▲▲▲

Mike had not returned by the time Karen was ready to leave on Sunday morning. There were three inches of snow on the ground, but the snow had stopped falling, and the sun sparkled on the snow-trimmed evergreens near the dump.

Karen kissed Corey and gave Billy a pat on the head. Then she turned to Jenny. They hugged each other close and Karen kissed her cheek.

After Karen's car crept slowly down the winding snow-covered road and out of sight, Jenny said, "Well, we're going to need some more meat for Tony's spaghetti sauce. Shall we use our little red wagon?"

Jenny smiled as she remembered her anxiety about Mike's killing the deer. She never thought of that deer as an animal now. It was The Meat; she mentally capitalized the words. She realized that she had learned something new, and she thought, Richard would be proud of me. Last week I made a joke, and now I'm having a philosophical thought: your perception of cruelty changes when your kids are hungry.

She dressed the children warmly and set them in the wagon. She fastened a hard hat on Billy and set another on Corey's head. "Hold her hat," Jenny said. Checking the tunnel for loose rock, she pulled the wagon slowly inside, the wheels bumping from tie to tie. She hacked off a large piece of meat from the hanging carcass and put it into the skillet she'd brought.

Billy said, "Can I pull the wagon?" When Jenny nodded, he took the wagon tongue and tugged the wagon into motion. "I'm Rosie," Billy said as he trotted out of the tunnel. The wagon started to bounce and Corey's hat tipped over her eyes, so Jenny picked Corey up and let Billy haul the meat to the house.

After they had eaten their funny breakfast, as Billy called it, of spaghetti sauce and fruit, Jenny chopped up the chunk of meat and began to simmer it in the rest of the sauce.

Jenny had hoped Mike would get home with the groceries before Tony came, but when Tony drove up on the mine dump and got out, the first thing he did was to reach for several sacks of groceries in the rear of his pickup.

"Mike sent these," he said, carrying them into the house. With Billy standing close, all ears, Jenny didn't want to ask when Mike was coming home. She checked the groceries. Mike hadn't filled her list completely. Damn. She should have gone to town herself. But there was milk and cereal for the baby, and Jenny felt the anxiety that had crimped her stomach all morning ease slightly. She fixed a bottle for Corey, who took it in her hands and sucked greedily.

"Don't blame you one bit," Jenny said, rocking Corey gently.

"That spaghetti sauce smells good," Tony said. "When do we eat?"

"Right after I drill the first hole," Jenny said, grinning at him and trying to put away her worry about Mike.

When she was full Corey settled contentedly into her crib. Jenny and Tony went to the shop, with Billy at their heels. "I already set the column post," Jenny said.

"The hell you did!" Tony turned to look at her.

"You'd better check it."

"We can take the drill when we go," he said, reaching for a piece of equipment that looked to Jenny like a snub-nosed fish.

"Tell me about the drill while we're out here in the light," she said.

"All right." Tony pointed to the round part at the bottom. "You set that thing that looks like an upside-down saucer into the saddle on the crossbar and clamp it down." He touched the end of the

· 182 ·

larger cylinder, which had a hole in the center. "Aim this end toward the rock."

Looking around, he picked up a steel bar. "The drill steel goes in here," he said, shoving one end of the bar into the hole in the cylinder and pulling the clamp down over the lip. Attached to the other end of the steel bar was a clove-shaped piece. "This is the bit, the cutting edge," he said.

"With the steel in place the drill looks like a gun," Jenny said, resting her hand on the long bar.

"You'll probably feel like you're holding on to a machine gun when this thing gets some air."

Tony pointed to the rear of the drill. "You clamp the air hose on here, and the water hose here."

Jenny said, "This is easier now that I can see the equipment."

Tony touched the edge of the track underneath the drill. "The drill moves forward on this track. That screw goes all the way through and keeps the drill up close, crowding the steel. And"— Tony put his hand on a handle at the back of the drill—"you're cranking the steel in farther all the time."

"How do I keep from getting tangled up with the air and water hoses?"

"You'll have two long tails, but you get used to 'em. You'll work it out, once you've got the drill set up."

"Okay," said Jenny. "Let me check the baby, and then we'll go into the tunnel."

"Right," Tony said. "I'll oil the drill and start the generator so we'll have some light."

Jenny stirred the spaghetti sauce and looked down at her sleeping daughter. "You be a good baby and sleep for just a while," she said, "and I'll come back and tell you all about drilling."

Tony and Billy had loaded the drill into the red wagon. Billy pulled on the handle, but the wagon moved slowly until Jenny bent and pushed it along inside the tracks to the breast of the tunnel.

Tony inspected the column post and then turned and gave Jenny a long look. "I think you're cut out to be a miner," he said, "even if you are just a little bit of a girl."

Jenny felt warmed by the praise—and she needed the spurt of energy it gave her when she bent to pick up the drill. The mass of steel seemed for a moment beyond her strength. She squatted beside the wagon and gripped the drill with both hands, feeling the muscles in her upper arms and chest pull taut as she slowly stood up. Tony reached out a hand, but Jenny shook her head, saying, "No, if I can't do this, I need to know."

Slowly and carefully, she raised the drill toward the crossbar, the muscles in her shoulders and back tightening, her thighs beginning to quiver as the heavy drill came up level with her waist. Jenny gritted her teeth and pushed the saucer onto the saddle on the crossbar. Holding the drill with her left hand, she clamped it tight to the saddle. Then she leaned against the cold rock wall until the trembling in her arms stopped.

"I'm glad I've been hauling all those trays of dirty dishes," she said.

"That's the worst of the lifting," Tony said. "All we have to do now is raise it closer to the back so you can start with the crown hole." Tony raised the crossbar and drill. "Now Billy and I will bring the hoses in."

Billy and Tony left the tunnel. Jenny slid down the wall and sat in the dirt on the floor of the tunnel. How many times would she lift that drill before they got the ore out? She looked up at the vein and felt the same excitement she'd felt the first time she saw it. What if there was one of those pockets of free gold just behind the surface?

I do believe the gambling bug has bit me, Jenny thought. I can hardly wait to blow this rock to pieces.

She could hear Tony and Billy coming down the track. She scrambled up and went to meet them. "Is Corey still asleep?"

"Sound asleep."

Jenny grabbed hold of the bulky air hose and pulled it toward the drill. "Will I always have to take these clear out of the tunnel?"

"Cut holes throw like the devil." Tony said. "One rock punctures a hose, and you can't drill till it's fixed. And you won't want the hoses on the track when Rosie hauls ore. It's safer if you put the hoses clear out of the tunnel while you shoot and muck out." Tony pulled the other hose toward the face.

Jenny said, "I'm trying to be safe in this mine. I don't feel scared, but I feel very respectful."

"Good for you," Tony said. "You'd better teach that to the boy, too." He lifted the air hose to the connecting valve on the drill and fixed it in place. Then he connected the water hose. "This thing won't work without some water pressure," he said. "Let's drag that pressure tank in here and fill her up."

"There's sure a lot to do before you start drilling," Jenny said. She followed Tony out of the tunnel and went into the cabin.

When she came back Tony and Billy were waiting with Rosie, who was harnessed to a tank that looked like an old hot-water heater. They dragged the tank into the tunnel. Tony ran a line from the water trough in the other tunnel to the pressure tank. The immersible pump in the trough near the falling water started right up when Tony turned on the switch and opened a couple of valves. He filled the tank, shut off the pump, and hooked the free end of the water line from the drill to a line coming from the tank.

"Now we're ready to crank up the compressor and bring some steel down here."

The compressor took longer to start. It was cold in the shop. Tony opened the air vents first and then tried the starter. It turned over slowly. Tony choked it a little and tried again. The engine took hold and began a loud banging that eased a little and steadied its rhythm as the air warmed up and Tony closed the valves and backed off the choke, explaining each step to Jenny as he worked.

When the compressor was running steadily, Tony said, "I think you're going to need a powder box to stand on. At least, for the crown and arch holes and those top relievers." He dumped a hodgepodge of tools from a box under the workbench. "This'll do." He handed the box to Jenny and picked up several lengths of drill steel.

"Your cut holes will be five feet deep, the others four. You'll start short and change the steel as you get deeper." Jenny reached for the steel with her other hand.

"Don't you have gloves?" Tony said sharply.

"They're in the truck."

"Here," he said, stripping his gloves from his hands, "use mine."

She put the gloves on, appreciating the warmth Tony had left in them. She picked up the bars and the box again, and they went into the mine.

Tony swung the drill away from the breast. He took a black crayon from his pocket and began to make circles on the rock. Jenny recognized the pattern he had drawn on her order pad. When Tony finished drawing, he put a two-foot steel into the drill and latched it. He loosened the drill and slid it toward the column post, centering the bit on the crown hole he had drawn. He reached for Jenny's box and set it below the drill.

"The steel is just touching the crown," he said. "Get on that box and stand behind the drill. Steady it with your left hand and crank the steel in with your right."

Jenny stepped forward. "Here's your controls for the air and water," Tony said, touching two levers. "I'll have to move the electric wires and the light. Are you ready to use your headlamp?"

Jenny looked around. "I'm ready."

"Okay. Pull those goggles down over your eyes. After Billy and I leave the tunnel, you start her up, and keep that steel right into the face."

Jenny nodded, stepped up on the powder box, and watched while Billy and Tony went down the track. The compressor idled down, filling the tunnel with a pleasant, earnest humming sound.

Jenny pulled her goggles down and aimed her light at the end of the steel. The bit rested against the crown hole. She took a deep breath to ease the sudden pounding of her heart and turned on the air and water.

The drill came to life in her hands. As air powered the drill, the steel began to bite into the rock, throwing sparks and bits of stone. Jenny started to turn the crank, frantically at first, and then more steadily. Finally she settled into a rhythmic motion that seemed to keep the steel turning at a reasonable rate.

The noise was deafening. The tunnel roared about her; the water splattered against the rock and a fine dirty spray filled the air. She could see it in the small circle of light—gritty-looking sparkles moving away into the darkness.

There wasn't time to think about anything else. The vital machine under her hands required her full attention. Her ears adjusted to the roar and her hands stopped trembling. She steadily cranked the steel, turning, turning, turning, as the air pounded the bar into the rock.

When the drill nosed up to the rock, Jenny shut off the air and water levers. The drill went still in her hands, though the roar still echoed in her ears. She jerked the drill back along the track, cranking the steel in reverse until it came free of the rock.

When some of the mist cleared she stood on tiptoe to peer into the crown hole.

"Not bad, Jenny, though you could cut your air a little and use it to crank the steel back."

"I didn't hear you come in, Tony. How did you know I had stopped drilling?"

"I could tell by the sound of the compressor."

"You're not supposed to be breathing this stuff."

"No, but I want to help you with the latch on the steel." Tony swung the crossbar back and pried up on the clamp that latched the steel into the drill. "Son of a gun don't want to let go," he muttered. After he finally loosened the latch, he pulled out the two-foot steel, inserted a four-foot steel, and repositioned the bit inside the hole Jenny had drilled.

"How long is it supposed to take to drill a hole?" Jenny asked.

"Oh, you'll do a four-footer in half an hour when you get going."

"That's over four hours just for the overhang," Jenny said, figuring quickly. "I hope I can get that good. I'd like to shoot every other day."

Tony said, "Better just practice a bit more and quit for today. Your arms will be plenty sore." He nodded at Jenny and disappeared once more into the darkness.

Stepping back up on the box, Jenny flipped the levers and began cranking the handle. The steel went quickly into the two-foot hole she'd already drilled, and then with a jolt the bit dug into the rock. A sloppy fine grit coated her face; she could taste sulphur. Jenny had loved the silence in the tunnel and now she found the same refuge in the encompassing roar. She cranked the steel forward, her wrist and elbow and arm vibrating with the drill, until the snout of the drill came close to the rock again.

She wrestled with the bar latch. It took both hands and several minutes of struggle. Tony appeared again just as she conquered the clamp. "You ready to quit?"

"No," she said. "I'm just getting into it. Let me do one more hole."

Before he left the tunnel Tony helped her to reposition the drill in front of the arch hole on the right side of the face. Jenny swept the back with her headlamp. Everything looked solid. She turned eagerly to the drill.

She could feel the vibrations along her collarbone and down her spine. The water splashed against her jeans and into her boots. The spray from the drill wet her face, fogged her goggles, and swirled in the light. She leaned into the drill, into the noise, and kept turning the handle.

As the drill nosed up to the rock, she grabbed for the air lever, backed the drill away, pried up the stubborn latch, and removed the short bar. Her hands trembled as she struggled with the clamp again, but she finally locked the four-foot steel in place and repositioned the drill. When the drill reached the face one more time she shut off the air and water and stepped down.

The lights came on in the tunnel and Tony soon appeared. He pushed the drill back and peered at the hole. Jenny watched, suddenly aware that her boots were filled with cold water, her gloves cold and mucky. Tony turned. "You did a good job."

"How long did it take me to do two holes?"

"About two hours."

"Oh," Jenny said, feeling let down.

"It's the latch that's getting you," Tony said. "Come in and eat. Then I'll dig up something to help you with that clamp."

CHAPTER
33

▲▲▲▲▲▲

Jenny walked slowly out of the mine, her boots squishing, her ears still ringing. It was cold outside. She'd forgotten about the snow. Taking off her boots at the cabin door, she dumped the water out of them. Her clothes were dripping. She hated having to step onto her clean floors, but there was no way around it.

Billy said, "You're all soppy, Mama."

Jenny washed her hands and face gratefully in hot water. Then she stepped around the end of the crib, peeled away her shirt and jeans, put on her robe, and sat on a crate by the table. Tony spread her clothes over the woodbox and set her boots and gloves behind the stove. Jenny just watched, too tired even to say thank you. Tony put a plate of spaghetti covered with venison sauce in front of Jenny. She bent her face toward the steam.

"Up you go, Bill," Tony said, swinging the boy onto a crate in front of a second plate of spaghetti.

"How about Corey?" Jenny said, looking toward the crib, where Corey held on to the bars, staring through them like a little monkey. "Has she eaten?"

"Cereal and milk just before you came in."

"Oh, Tony, you're a saint."

Tony grinned and sat down with his plate heaped with spaghetti. He forked a huge chunk of venison out of the sauce. "A man'd do most anything for sauce like this."

Jenny smiled and began to eat. The spaghetti sauce tasted better than it had at breakfast. "Did you do something to this sauce?" she asked.

Tony's smile sparkled. "It's that drill that makes the sauce so good. The compressor used nearly a tank of gas. I reckon you were just about out of fuel too."

Jenny was beginning to feel better. "I should remember to check all the equipment," she said.

"Don't you think you've had enough for today?"

"No," Jenny said. "I won't try to drill the whole round, but I want to do the other arch hole and a couple of breast holes before I quit. I want to get faster."

"Oh, you'll get faster. It'll just come natural after we get you something to pry that latch with."

Jenny's clothes were only partially dry by the time she finished dinner, but she struggled back into them, putting on dry socks and warm boots and gloves.

She snuggled her face close to Corey's cheek for a moment. The baby smelled faintly of sour milk. "You get a bath right after I drill the next three holes," she said. "I'll need one, too, by then."

"We'll get that other arch hole," Tony said, "and then drop down and do 'em as they come. I move that crossbar up and down and across, and I swing the drill under when I get to the swimmers and lifters."

Jenny visualized Tony's chart and remembered that the holes he'd just mentioned were at the bottom.

▽   ▽

The other arch hole went easily. Tony had given her a bar to pry the clamp on the drill steel. Jenny finished in thirty-five minutes. She drilled the breast hole even faster. In twenty-five minutes she was ready to start the rib hole.

Jenny appreciated the chance to rest when Tony came in to help, but she worried about his lungs. "You need a mask or something in here," she said.

"Gets too wet and makes mud," Tony said.

Jenny felt awkward now, working closer to the rib. She couldn't keep the drill up tight. Her cranking arm was erratic. By the time she'd finished she was tired and discouraged.

"A whole hour. Twice as long as it should have taken me," she grumbled to Tony.

"Your boss will probably fire you," Tony said, "an old hand like you." He touched her arm. "It's quittin' time. You've had enough for today."

Outside the mine, Jenny said, "Why don't you go back in and cut yourself a venison steak?"

But Tony said, "I'll come in the morning and help you drill awhile. I'll get one then."

"What about your customers at the dump?"

"Nobody's going to come out there in the snow." Tony climbed in the truck, waved away her thank-you speech, and went down the road and over the bridge as a cold dusk settled on the mountain.

▽ ▽

Jenny had bathed and was just finishing up Billy and Corey when Mike finally drove onto the mine dump. Jenny went to the door, and Mike came in with a grocery sack. He set it on the table. Jenny was relieved to see the groceries. She wanted to ask where he'd been all night but she didn't want Billy to hear the answer, and she didn't want to start a fight with Mike. She just said, "Hi. I'm glad you brought the rest of the groceries."

Mike said, "I brought us some treats for a change." He took a six-pack of Coca-Cola and two large sacks of chips from the bag. Fishing around in the bottom, he retrieved two bowl-shaped plastic containers. "Dip," he said. "Here, Bill. Have some guacamole." Billy climbed up on the crate.

Junk food, Jenny thought, but Mike was smiling at her as he poured himself a glass of Coke. She sat down at the table and took a chip from the sack Billy had torn open.

"Mama drilled in your mine," Billy said.

Mike looked up at Jenny. "So you went ahead with it."

"Yes," Jenny said. "Tony helped me get set up." She waited. Mike

· 191 ·

drank a long swallow of Coke, stuck a chip into the guacamole and crunched it between his teeth.

Finally he said, "Well, did you get a hole drilled?"

Jenny said, "I drilled the crown hole, two arch holes, a breast hole, and a rib."

Mike's eyes widened slightly, and he said, "Come on now. How many of those did Tony do?"

Jenny's eyes prickled, but he wasn't going to make her cry. "You know Tony can't breathe that stuff," she said.

She set her glass down and went to the crib. Corey was almost asleep, but Jenny picked her up, wrapped the afghan around her, and sat down in David Garvey's rocking chair. She rocked slowly while Billy chattered to Mike about the generator and the pump and the hoses and the new red wagon.

"Red wagon?" Mike looked over at Jenny.

She nodded and said, "Karen brought it."

"Jesus, I hope she's not going to hang around. I saw that bastard Stocker on the street. He was drunk and mean and swearing he'd kill her."

Jenny shook her head slightly and tipped it toward Billy. Mike glanced at the boy and said, "Want some more Coke, kid?"

"No," Billy said. He climbed down from the crate and went to lie on his bed.

"Use the pot before you get under the covers, honey," Jenny said, rising from the rocking chair with Corey, who had fallen fast asleep, her fingers entwined in the crocheted pattern of the afghan.

When Billy was asleep, too, Jenny sat down at the kitchen table and looked at Mike. He had finished the guacamole dip.

"Tony's coming back in the morning," she said. "Aren't you glad I drilled five holes today?"

"What? Oh, hell yes, Jenny. Just drill and shoot and run the whole goddamn mine." Mike got up from the table and turned toward the bed. He unbuttoned his shirt, removed it, and tossed it on the foot of the bed. He unlaced his high-topped shoes and kicked them off.

Jenny watched, too close to tears to speak, too tired to clean off the table. Mike unzipped his pants and stepped out of them. Jerking the covers back, he climbed into bed. He turned on his side and pulled the covers up around his shoulders.

Jenny sat on the wooden milk crate and leaned her elbows on the table. She stared at the potato chip crumbs stuck in the bottom of the dip bowl and watched the reflection of the lantern light in Billy's empty Coke glass. The crate began to cut into her legs, but she didn't move. She just sat and stared at the mess on the table until Mike said, "Goddamn it, Jenny. Turn out the light and get in bed."

CHAPTER
34
▲▲▲▲▲▲▲

Corey was crying when Jenny woke up. Mike's side of the bed was empty and cold. The whole cabin was cold. She sat up slowly and moved her legs over the edge of the bed. Every muscle in her body was sore. Groaning with effort, she got up. She went to the crib, glancing toward Billy's mattress. Billy wasn't there either. His blankets were thrown back, his pillow and pajamas dumped on the floor.

Jenny picked Corey up and walked to the window. The truck was right outside. She turned around to get a diaper, and her eyes caught the gun rack Mike had built on the back wall. The rifle was gone. Mike must have taken Billy into the hills.

Bending stiffly over the crib, she changed the baby, carried her to the door, and opened it. The sky was blue; the sun sparkled on the snow. She shaded her eyes from the glare and stepped outside.

She looked down, startled to feel snow on her bare feet. Shaking her head, she stepped back into the cabin, settled Corey in the crib, put her sneakers and robe on, and went outside. She could see Mike and Billy's tracks going up the mountain. She went to the outhouse and hurried back. After building a fire she fixed a bottle for Corey and took the baby and the bottle back to bed.

While Corey sucked, Jenny said, "Oh, baby, what are we going to do now? Your daddy and Billy are out there with that gun." She snuggled Corey close and began to cry. "It's all so stupid and useless," she wailed. She cried until her nose ran, her upper lip swelled, and her eyes felt puffy. She cried until Corey began to cry, too, and then she wiped the arm of her robe across her nose and got up and walked around the room, rocking Corey back and forth in her arms and saying, "It's all right, honey, it's all right. Mama isn't going to fall apart on you."

When Corey quit crying Jenny fixed her some warm cereal and a cup of juice. Corey grabbed hold of the edge of the cup as Jenny put it to her mouth and wouldn't let go. Jenny laughed out loud. "Oh, you're a stubborn little lady—just like your mama."

Corey looked up and said, "Mama," quite plainly.

Jenny clapped her hands together and laughed again. "Oh, Corey, you said 'Mama.' Say it again. Say it again. Mama. Ma-ma."

But Corey just gurgled and paddled her arm in the air, tipping the cup of juice. Jenny lifted Corey from her lap and swung her up to her face; she nuzzled the baby's neck and kissed both cheeks and rubbed noses with her. Staring straight into Corey's eyes, Jenny said, "We're going to get that ore, and we're going to get you some clothes and a nice place to live and a good school. Oh, Corey, I want so much. I'm going to get *me* some sweet-smelling perfume and a bathtub with three hundred gallons of hot water."

Corey blinked. Jenny laughed and put the baby in the crib. By the time Tony arrived at nine Jenny had cleaned up the mess of potato chips and Coke on the table, made the beds, and hacked off some venison for stew. She studied the carcass for a moment. Mike had mentioned once that he'd have to cut up the meat and store it in a colder place soon. It looked all right.

She dressed in some of Mike's jeans, pinning them to a clean shirt from her box. Then she got her own gloves from the truck.

Tony came in with a bundle in his arms. "Here," he said, "they call these tin pants, and they're a lot more waterproof than what you wore yesterday."

Jenny took the strange-looking brown canvas trousers and pulled them on over her jeans. She buckled her boots tightly around the legs of the tin pants and turned to Tony. He looked at her quietly for a moment and then said, "Are you ready to finish the ribs and breast holes and get on with the cut holes?"

"I'm ready," Jenny said, though every muscle in her body ached and her head throbbed from crying.

"Mike and the boy go up the hill?" Tony asked. Jenny nodded but didn't say anything.

They worked from ten until three thirty, stopping only for a short lunch break. Tony watched the baby while Jenny drilled the other rib and the breast hole. Then he showed her how to angle the drill for the V-cut and brought in the six-foot steel she needed to get a five-foot hole. When the compressor coughed and died Tony restarted it. Jenny kept drilling.

When she stopped at three thirty, her arms were trembling, and her ears roared whether the drill was running or not. The canvas pants seemed like heavy weights as she dragged herself toward the mouth of the tunnel. But she had drilled the other rib and breast hole and both cut holes. Tony had checked her angles, and he said they were good. She and Tony had dropped the bar two thirds of the way down the column post into position for the relievers, and she had drilled one of them.

Tony cut himself a big venison steak and went on down the mountain. Jenny washed her hair and bathed in hot water after hauling two buckets of cold creek water and heating it on the stove. She soaked her hands clean and tried to smooth her nails. She fed Corey and then lay down with her on the bed.

She woke to the smells and sounds of frying meat. She opened her eyes. Corey was no longer beside her. Mike was standing at the stove. Billy saw her move and ran to the bed.

"Daddy shot a rabbit, and I shot the gun, and it kicked me. The rabbit has fuzzy fur, and we're gonna eat him for dinner."

"Pipe down, kid," Mike said, but he didn't sound rough. Billy ran over and jumped up and down on his bed.

Jenny sat up gingerly. To her surprise, her muscles were not as sore as they had been that morning. She put on her good jeans and the blouse that Karen had given her. She didn't offer to help with dinner, and Mike didn't say anything when she sat down in the rocking chair and began to comb her hair.

Before Jenny left for Mom's Bar, Mike went out and checked the oil in the truck, but he never mentioned the drilling and she scarcely spoke to him. She kissed the children and started down the snowy road, feeling lost in Mike's silence.

The café was busy in spurts. Jenny smiled automatically as she waited on tables, ignoring the crude remarks. Her body ached with fatigue. Richard was late, and Mom Bradley was cross.

Just after Richard had finally arrived and started on the dishes, David Garvey came in and sat at a table on the south side. A crowd of local teenagers came in at the same time, and Jenny didn't have much time to talk. The truck driver lingered over his coffee, and when the café cleared Jenny went to his table to refill his cup. He shook his head.

"Is something wrong, Jenny?" he asked. "Are Corey and Billy all right?"

She shook her head no, then nodded it yes, but she suddenly could not speak because of the lump in her throat.

"Do you want to talk about it?"

Jenny swallowed and said, "Yes." She looked around. "But not in here."

David Garvey rose and put some money on the table. "We can sit in my truck."

Jenny didn't even look back. She went through the door he opened and let him lift her into the truck, which was idling in the parking lot.

When they were up in the high cab with the doors closed, he turned on the dome light and said, "Tell me, Jenny."

His blue eyes held such a look of concern that she almost burst into tears, but she bit her lip until the tears subsided. She began to tell him about the drilling. As she described what she had learned and named the holes she'd drilled, her sense of accomplishment returned.

He smiled as he asked questions, and she talked about the sounds in the mine and her peaceful feelings as she drilled. At the end of her story he said, "You've really done something, Jenny. Why aren't you happy?"

Jenny looked away and said in a low voice, "I wanted Mike to be glad."

David Garvey was silent for a moment. Then he said, "We males are proud bastards, Jenny. We don't like to admit that there's anything we can't do."

"I didn't say Mike couldn't drill."

"No, you didn't. But maybe Mike can't stand to have you turn out to be so good at two jobs when he doesn't even have one right now."

"I'm just trying to help us. Why can't he be grateful?"

Bigfoot put his hand on the steering wheel. "Jenny, he'll probably come around to seeing that it's all you could do, but he's never going to be grateful. If you're going to drill in that mine, or do anything else, you're going to have to do it for yourself and not for anybody else."

Jenny looked at her hands; then she raised her head and looked at the truck driver. His eyes seemed to have silver slivers of light in the deep blue. Jenny's heart began to pound in her throat, and she thought of what Karen had said about honesty.

Suddenly she was ill at ease. "I owe you so much," she said. "I'll never be able to pay you back for the chair and the GED course." She slid across the seat and opened her door. But before she could climb out, his hand closed on her wrist. He pulled her back across the seat and into his arms. Jenny felt a stinging wave of disappointment sweep over her as she thought, Not you too. And then she found herself wedged tightly against the steering wheel as David let go of her wrist and reached to lift her face.

He kissed her hard on her mouth, and then his lips softened a little, and he kissed her for a long time.

Jenny had no idea what to do; her mouth moved under his without her mind's direction, and her body seemed to be filled with fireflies.

Suddenly David let her go. Opening his door and sliding out of the truck, he turned and held out his arms. Jenny let him help her down. Then she ran toward the café.

Richard was standing behind the bar when she jerked the front door open. He looked up and started to speak, but Jenny rushed past him into the kitchen. He followed her and said, "My God, Jenny—" but she interrupted.

"Don't say one word, Richard. Don't say one damn word."

CHAPTER
35

▲▲▲▲▲▲

Jenny was glad when after the basketball game the café got suddenly crowded. Being busy helped her not to think about Bigfoot. She heard his truck leave the lot, but she didn't even look up. Tony came in at about ten thirty and Jenny brought him a beer.

"Do you want to drill the rest of those holes tomorrow?" He asked.

Jenny said, "No, I've got to do laundry and stock up on food tomorrow. Let's drill Wednesday." She paused, taking a breath. "And I'd like to learn to load and shoot right away. Will you draw me some more pictures?"

Tony laughed. "Sure I will. No point in your learning to drill unless you learn to shoot."

At about one thirty the crowd thinned out. Instead of helping Richard with the dishes, Jenny took a cup of coffee and the GED materials to a table in the back part of the dining area. She opened the literature workbook, but she couldn't get into the story. The characters were strangers who had nothing to do with her. She doodled at the top of the notebook page, then ran a line through the figures and tried again to read. But her mind kept returning to David Garvey, and each time she thought of him the same emotions somersaulted through her stomach.

She was frighteningly angry. Why did he have to turn out to be just like all other men? Grabbing at her body—taking what he wanted without asking. Why couldn't he have been different?

But then she heard Karen's voice in her mind: "Be honest with yourself, Jenny." She remembered the way her body had felt when David kissed her and hated herself for the hot feeling that went clear down between her legs. She shivered as she thought of Mike. Mike would be wild with anger if he found out that Bigfoot had kissed her.

She wrote *anger-shame* at the top of the notebook and then drew a heavy line through it. She moved the pen back and forth, blocking out the words. Then she wrote another word: *sorrow*. If David hadn't kissed me, I could still talk to him. Tears came into her eyes as she realized how much she had counted on his being different.

But once more Jenny's stomach quivered as she remembered Bigfoot's mouth on hers. She put her head in her hands for a moment and then raised her eyes and forced herself to begin.

She had read the story and was looking at the study questions at the end of it when Richard sat down across from her.

"How's it going, Jenny?" He was sober.

"I can't seem to find what they want me to in this story. Listen to this: 'By his question in the last paragraph, the author is seeking to invoke in the reader the feeling of: one, despair; two, indignation; three, sadness; four, nostalgia; five, wonder.' Do you think the man who wrote it was really trying to do any of that? Wasn't he just telling a story?"

Richard laughed. "Oh ho, Jenny. I can see which side of this game you're on. There are creators and consumers and never the twain shall meet, except to exchange their money and their contempt."

"Which am I?"

"You're a creator. And literary critics are consumers. Right away you're defending the fellow who wrote that story, thinking all along that he knew what he was doing."

"Well, didn't he?"

"The critics obviously think they know more about it than he did."

"Well that makes me mad. I can read what he wrote, but I can't answer all that other stuff."

"Well you'd better learn to fake it, Jenny, because you'll never get your diploma unless you can shovel that bullshit right back to the professors who wrote those questions."

Jenny smiled and said, "*You* can sure get a lot of talk out of one little paragraph." She was silent a moment, and then she asked, "Why do you call me a creator?"

Richard said, "Because you never ask anyone's permission to do what you do."

"Whose permission? You mean I should ask Mike?"

"No, that's not what I'm talking about. Take television, for instance. You never watch television. A woman of your age, education, and economic status is supposed to be watching television."

"But, Richard, I don't have time—and besides, television is boring. My own thoughts are more interesting."

"Now, there. That's just what I'm talking about. If you're going to go around thinking your own thoughts, you won't be watching the commercials and developing a healthy desire to buy."

"But the people who wrote these questions aren't selling anything."

"Don't kid yourself for a minute, Jenny. Literary critics—and most professors are just third-rate literary critics—literary critics are selling you all these complications to keep you on the string. They're just like preachers. How would preachers and professors make a living if they let you start believing that you could think for yourself or read a novel or a Bible and understand what it *really* says?"

Jenny laughed.

"Don't laugh, girl. My God, you don't know how dangerous a radical you are."

Jenny laughed again and reached out impulsively to touch Richard's hand. "You're a good influence on me," she said. "You're pessimistic about everything in the whole world, yet you make me laugh."

Richard covered her hand with his other hand. "I wish I could keep the world away from you, Jenny."

Jenny withdrew her hand and said, "Richard, every day I find more things that I don't know about the world. I used to wander around that dump feeling pretty content. Now I have more money than I did before, and I've learned to do a couple of things, but I'm not at all content."

"You're coming alive."

"Well, it's painful." Tears started in her eyes, and she looked away. She hadn't known she was going to say that.

But Richard did not invade her privacy. He said only, "Is there anything I can do to help?"

Jenny looked back at him. "Yes, there is, Richard. You could stay sober and teach me all this stuff so I can get my GED before the end of the year. I'm afraid if I don't do it now—if our situation changes and I don't have it—I'll get stuck in some bar for the rest of my life."

"Do you hate it here that much, Jenny?"

Jenny felt the wetness in her eyes again. I'm a crybaby tonight, she thought. Damn that David Garvey.

"I hate being on display," she said. "I hate hearing the things men say about women. I like to look nice—but for myself, not for every drunk who thinks I'm yearning for his filthy fingers and reaches out . . ." As Jenny said the words she realized that most of all she was speaking about David. She hated remembering how he had dragged her across the seat.

"Jenny," Richard said. "Where are you?"

"What?"

"You stopped in the middle of a sentence."

"I'm sorry, Richard. What were we talking about?"

"You asked if I could stay sober long enough to be a teacher." His tone was bitter.

"Oh! I didn't mean to insult you," Jenny said. "It's just that you're different when you drink. You scare me a little."

Richard looked down at the table, and his hand flipped the pages of the workbook. When he raised his eyes again they were dark with pain, but he smiled. "I'll do it, Jenny. You'll get your GED for Christmas."

▽ ▽

On Tuesday morning while she was washing the breakfast dishes, Jenny said, "Let's go into town, Mike. I realized when it snowed on Sunday that I've been really dumb about buying groceries. This far from town we need backup supplies."

"You got any money?"

"Yes. Mom's Bar was crawling with generous customers last night, and I have a little in my dish. I want to get some extra gloves and some warmer boots for Billy. And do the laundry."

"What do you need me for?"

Jenny turned from the dishpan and wiped her hands on her jeans. She went to the table and put her hand on Mike's shoulder. "You're my husband. We had fun when we went to town together the last time. I just want to be with you."

"While we spend your money."

"Oh, for Pete's sake, Mike. Why does it make any difference whose money it is? I've spent money you made for the past five years. Please come to town with me."

"No, you go. And take Corey. Billy and me are going rabbit hunting again."

▽ ▽

Jenny bought dried milk and dried fruit, twenty pounds of flour, five pounds of shortening, a box of salt, ten pounds of sugar, several large jars of peanut butter, and a huge tin box of crackers. She bought instant orange juice, a case of canned green beans, and another of canned peas. She picked up a two-pound sack of pinto beans and two pounds of macaroni. She considered her shopping cart, where Corey sat banging on the handle and singing a gurgling song. Jenny had just decided to add ten pounds of apples and a case of canned tomatoes and some tuna fish to her groceries when someone said, "Hello, Jenny."

She turned to find Mrs. Marsh offering her pointer finger to Corey. "What a cute baby. How old is she?"

"She's going on seven months. She was born in April."

"Jenny, I've been wanting to get over to Mom's to see you. I found a book you might like."

David's five dollars. Jenny felt a moment of sadness. That had been such a wonderful clean moment of joy when she had read his note: *Buy a book*.

She smiled at Mrs. Marsh. "I can hardly wait to see it. What book is it?"

"It's called *Mining Rights*. It gives you some history of mining rules, tells about annual assessment work on a filed claim, and it's got a good glossary of mining terms."

"It sounds marvelous."

"I'll bring it in next time we come for the spaghetti special." The geologist chucked Corey under the chin once more and wheeled her cart down the aisle. I'd like to go to Mitchell and look at books, Jenny thought. She watched the geologist until she turned the corner.

▽   ▽

After getting oats and hay for Rosie, Jenny stopped by the hardware store for work gloves. She couldn't find boots that were Billy's size at the dry goods store, so she bought him several pairs of thick socks. Then she went to the drugstore.

"What would we need if we got snowed in?" Jenny asked the druggist. "We're seventeen miles out, and we have two young children."

"You ought to have Tylenol, teething lotion, maybe some cough syrup. Are the children often ill?"

"No, we've been lucky."

"You should have a thermometer in your first-aid box."

Jenny said, "I don't have a first-aid box."

The druggist set a blue and white plastic box in front of her. "How about a vaporizer?" he said. "It's invaluable in case of croup."

Jenny smiled a thin smile. "I don't have anyplace to plug it in," she said. "I need a book, though. Do you have some sort of instruction book?" The rows of bottles and the bright boxes with the names of all the possible winter illnesses in loud colors made her nervous.

The druggist picked a thick paperback from a shelf of pamphlets and books: *First Aid and Home Remedies for Common Ailments*. Jenny took all the items to the cashier.

By the cash register was a sign that read DAILY JOURNAL—HALF PRICE. Jenny picked up one of the thick books. The blank pages were dated with the current year's dates.

"It should be one third the price," she said to the cashier. "The year is two thirds over."

"All right," the woman said unexpectedly. "You can have it for one third the price."

Jenny didn't know what to do but buy the journal. She also bought a candy bar for Billy and one for Mike and started back to the mine.

▽ ▽

Mike and Billy were home with two rabbits. Mike had scraped and stretched the skins. He was cheerful as he helped her unload the groceries. "I think I'll tan those hides and make Corey a pair of boots for Christmas."

"What a neat idea," Jenny said. "It's almost November. I'll have to start saving for presents. Christmas should be fun in our log cabin." She put the last sack of groceries in the red wagon and Billy pulled it to the house.

Before she left for work, Jenny stored the canned goods on the shelves and underneath the crib and their bed. As she drove down the hill that afternoon she felt prosperous. The sky was cloudy again, but the truck had four-wheel drive, there was plenty of wood, plenty of meat, and now plenty of other food. She felt grateful to Mike. The cabin on the Spanish Mary was snug and safe.

▽　▽

Tony came early on Wednesday. Jenny fixed breakfast, then stacked the dishes and dressed in the tin pants and her boots, coat, and hard hat. Mike asked Tony about the county dump, which he had left open. "I put a box by the gate for the dump fees," Tony said. "Probably half the bastards will ignore it, but what the hell." Mike started the compressor and Tony followed Jenny into the tunnel.

"We'd better oil your machine," he said. Tony loosened the nut on the top of the drill, poured oil into the chamber beneath it, and retightened the nut. Then he left the tunnel. Jenny flicked on her headlamp, flipped the air and water levers and moved into the noise and spray, drilling steadily until she finished the other two relievers. Tony came back to show her how to swing the drill under the bar to reach the swimmers and lifters, and she drilled those.

Jenny wasn't aware of being hungry or tired when she finished the seventeenth hole. She pulled the drill steel out of the wall and stood back. When the haze cleared a little she ran the beam from her headlamp over the face. A shiver of excitement made its way up her neck and around her cheek to her mouth. She smiled and reached out a hand to touch the cut holes. "I did it. I drilled a round."

Tony inspected the drilling and followed Jenny to the cabin, where Mike had made coffee. Jenny washed and began to get ready for work. She made sandwiches for supper while Tony told Mike about a poker game he'd sat in on. Mike didn't mention the Spanish Mary, and Jenny was afraid to speak of the drilling.

Finally Tony said, "Well, we're ready to load those holes, Mike, and we're going to need some dynamite."

"What in the hell makes you think I can get dynamite?" Mike said, putting his sandwich down and glaring at Tony. Jenny could hardly swallow the peanut butter and bread in her mouth. She took a sip of coffee and waited for Tony's reply, but Tony just looked at Mike, his wrinkled face sober, his eyes serious.

Finally Mike looked away. "Okay. What the hell? I'll get you a round of powder."

CHAPTER
36

▲▲▲▲▲▲

Mike rose so abruptly that he knocked over the milk crate.

"Can I go with you, Daddy?" Billy said.

"No," Mike said. "Stay here."

Billy got down from the table and crossed to his mattress. Jenny took Corey from her crib. Tony had been silent since Mike left, but now he dug in his shirt pocket with two fingers and brought out a folded paper. He said, "We'll have to clean up in there, get the drill and column post out of the way and put down some muck plates. We shoulda put them plates back down sooner; you may have to muck out some of the stuff you drilled, to get 'em down." He unfolded the paper.

"I drew you a picture like you asked, but I'd rather show you how it's done right there in the tunnel. Why don't you get it cleared out tomorrow, and I'll help you load and shoot the nine holes in the overhang on Friday."

"Only the overhang?" Jenny asked.

"I told you," Tony said, "shooting the overhang separate saves a lot of sorting."

Jenny finished feeding Corey her vegetables and rose to take her to the crib and change her. Over her shoulder she said, "It takes so much time. I thought I could do it faster."

Tony frowned. "You can't get impatient, Jenny. You'll make mistakes. You want to get your head set just right for powder work. You got to move quickly, especially when you're lighting fuses, but you can't get sloppy." He tapped his fingers on the table. "Is the dynamite going to make you nervous?"

Jenny considered a moment and then said, "I don't think so, Tony. I know you have to do it in some kind of order and keep some kind of rhythm—but I'm used to that. Every job's got that."

"Right, rhythm's the word. You got to move smoothly." The old man continued to look at Jenny. He seemed to be studying her face. Finally he shook his head slightly and said, "Damn, but I never thought I'd be teaching a woman to load and shoot."

"I want to learn," Jenny said quickly.

"I know you do, young lady, and you're smart. You'll be a good miner. But"—he peered at her face again—"you sure you're not scared of the powder?"

Jenny said slowly, "I respect it. I don't want to do anything stupid and blow myself up. But I know I can do it right. I'm good with my hands." She looked down at her nails; they were chipped and rough again. She put her hands in her lap and said, "We've got to keep going, Tony. If I don't shoot what I've drilled, we'll never get any ore into that bin."

Tony nodded and pushed the paper across the table, but before Jenny could look at it, Mike came back into the cabin.

"All right," he said to Tony, "there's powder in the shop for one round, but I don't have any electric caps. You'll have to use what I got."

"Caps and fuses?"

"Yeah."

Tony was silent for a moment. Then he said, "Well, I've got forty years experience with the goddamn things. If I can't teach Jenny how to use 'em, nobody can."

Jenny said, "We'll get the tunnel cleaned out tomorrow."

She looked at Mike, who nodded and said gruffly, "Yeah. We'll clear out all that stuff."

"I'd better get down to Mom's," Jenny said.

▽   ▽

Despite his promise, Richard wasn't sober when Jenny got to the café. He and his mother were bickering as Jenny came into the kitchen. Mom Bradley looked tired, and Jenny felt sorry for her.

When Richard left the kitchen Mom Bradley said, "God, Jenny, I don't know what to do with him. He's my own kid, but I swear sometimes I'm tempted to have him committed someplace."

Jenny put her hand on Mom Bradley's arm. "You can't do it for him, Mom. He's got to do it for himself." She bit her lip, realizing she was speaking Bigfoot's words.

Mom Bradley smiled at her and said, "You're a comfort to me, Jenny. Half the time you're the only totally sane person around here."

Richard came through the swinging doors with a six-pack. He stopped next to Jenny and said, "You thought you trapped me, didn't you?"

"Trapped you?"

"Trapped me inside your glorious, shining, dazzling, shimmering bubble of hope. Hope for better things—new days—broad pathways to glory."

Jenny reached out her hand, but Richard jerked away from her touch. His eyes narrowed. "Seductress," he said in a shrill whisper. "Temptress."

Jenny dropped her hand. Richard put the six-pack under his arm. "Don't wait up, girls," he said as he went out the back door.

$$\triangledown \quad \triangledown$$

Jenny was busy all night doing her own work and Richard's too. Tully Stocker came in at around one thirty. He growled, "Gimme a beer," and then sat and nursed it. Once he murmured, "Nosy bitch," as she walked past, so she took a tray of dishes into the kitchen, leaving Mom Bradley to deal with Tully and the late bar customers. The dishwasher didn't seem so loud anymore compared to the drill, but she drifted into the shelter of its noise and finished the plates and glasses. When she came into the front at a little past two to change clothes, the bar was empty and it was snowing outside.

Jenny hurried toward the pickup. Her heart jumped and began to beat wildly at the sight of Tully Stocker's pickup, parked on the other side of hers. She hesitated, looking back at the bar, but the truck was closer than the door, and Mom Bradley had locked it anyway. She ran to the truck and unlocked it with trembling fingers. She slipped as she tried to climb up onto the high seat and banged her sore shin against the edge of the door. Blinking back tears, she scrambled into the truck, pulled the door closed, and locked it.

"Thank God," she breathed as the truck engine turned over. But as she looked ahead into the whirling snow that obscured the highway, she heard Tully Stocker's pickup engine start too. She backed out of the lot and plunged forward into the blizzard. In a moment she saw two wide hazy circles of light behind her in the storm. She drove as fast as she dared to on the slippery highway, but the circles of light were always behind her. She sped up as she passed through Dolby, and when she reached the Virgo Creek road she made an abrupt turn off the highway. The lights behind her seemed to jump and then slide sideways, but they didn't make the turn. Breathing more easily, Jenny followed the Virgo Creek road to the bridge and concentrated on taking the truck up the hill. The snow was blowing in wide spirals in front of her lights. It made her dizzy to look into the storm, so she looked to the side of the road and watched as the tree trunks edged past.

She finally reached the mine dump, needing badly to use the outhouse. When she came into the cabin, it was warm. The children were covered up with their blankets; a big chunk of log burned slowly in the stove. She crawled into the bed and moved close to Mike. He shifted slightly in his sleep and drew away from her. She couldn't blame him; her skin was icy. But as she scrunched down under the covers to try to make a warm spot of her own, she realized that Mike had not made love to her—had not even touched her—since she'd started drilling. The thought bothered her, but she was too tired to hold on to it.

▽   ▽

It had stopped snowing by morning. To Jenny's surprise, Mike went cheerfully into the tunnel with her. They took the drill and crossbar off the column post and carried them out of the mine. Mike loosened the column-tightening screws, and they took the column post back to the shop. After Mike cleared away some of the drilling debris, they put the iron muck plates down on the track close to the face. Mike never mentioned the drill holes.

When they were finished, Jenny wanted to ask how to use the blowpipe to clean the holes, but she said instead, "Tully Stocker started to follow me last night."

Mike turned quickly toward her. "That bastard. I ought to get you a gun to carry in the truck."

Jenny shivered. "I don't think I could use a gun, even against Tully Stocker."

"Well, keep the tire iron handy, then," Mike said.

Back in the cabin Jenny put some beans in water to soak, and before getting ready for work she read Corey's book to Billy. He had almost memorized it and wanted to "read" it back to her. Jenny picked up Corey from the crib and settled her between Billy's legs, behind his outstretched hands holding the book.

"Read it to your sister," Jenny said.

She sat on the mattress with them, listening as Billy said the words almost perfectly. Then she pointed to the word *boy* and said it out loud. Billy put his finger on the word and said, "Boy."

"Good," Jenny said. "When you can look at a word all by itself and know what it says, that's reading. Of course, you have to know what it means, too. What's a boy?"

Billy giggled. "I'm a boy."

"Well, then. That's a good word to know," Jenny said. "You think about it today, and tomorrow tell me another word you'd like to know."

Billy nodded and touched the word again. "Boy."

Corey flapped her hands against the book, and it fell. Jenny picked up the book and the baby. "Daddy can read you the book again later, Billy. I have to go to work."

Mike said, "Why don't you buy that kid a book with a real story? I'm tired of reading about the boy, the ball, the dog, the cat, and the hen."

Jenny looked at the price on the binding of the book: fifty-nine cents. She smiled at Mike. "That's a really good idea. Why didn't I buy a book for him before?"

Mike laughed. "You haven't got it clear in your head yet that books don't have to come from the dump."

Mike walked out to the truck with her, checked the door lock on the right side, and pulled the tire iron from behind the seat. "Here," he said. "Keep this on the seat beside you, and if that bastard even reaches toward the door, you break his goddamn fingers." He tossed the iron onto the seat and turned back toward the cabin.

Before going to Mom's, Jenny stopped at the drugstore and bought a Little Golden Book about a boy who found a lost pony. When she pulled up in front of the café, several young women came out the front door, laughing and calling to each other. As Jenny watched them, she wished one of them would speak to her, but then she turned her head, so that none of them would try. She stayed in the truck for a moment after the girls pulled onto the highway, thinking of Karen. But when Bigfoot's face came into her mind, she jumped down from the truck and slammed the door behind her. As she locked it, she muttered to herself, "I will *not* think about David Garvey."

CHAPTER

37

▲▲▲▲▲▲

In the tunnel on Saturday morning Tony connected the air hose to a pipe that had an elbow and a valve. Jenny put its nose into the holes she had drilled and blew them clean.

"We'll make up the fuses in the shop," Tony said, taking the blowpipe out of the tunnel.

As Jenny followed Tony into the corral, Rosie ambled over and nibbled on the back of Jenny's jeans. "Ouch," said Jenny. "Stop that, you little beast." She pulled the shop door partway closed.

"You need powder," Tony said, motioning toward a wooden box on the workbench, "and a loading stick and fuse and caps." He picked up a roll of thick black string coated with tarry-looking stuff. "This is your fuse stock; it's filled with black powder. You might as well make up all seventeen caps and fuses." He reached in his side pocket for a knife and a tape measure. "Here, make 'em seven foot apiece."

Jenny pulled the asphalt-covered fuse away from the roll. It was really more like wire than string. She measured carefully and cut a seven-foot piece with Tony's knife. She laid the fuse on the bench and cut another. When she had a bundle of fuses, she counted them again and looked at Tony.

"Caps next," he said, handing her a small yellow box. "And you'll want these crimping pliers."

"Funny-looking pliers," she said, studying the round-headed pliers with a hole in the jaws. She opened the box and took out one of the small silver-colored cylinders.

"Poke the fuse in the hollow end," Tony said.

Jenny picked up a strip of the fuse and pushed one end into the space in the cylinder.

"Crimp the cap around the fuse."

Jenny slipped the pliers over the cylinder and squeezed the metal down tight on the fuse. She held up the silver cap with its long black tail.

Tony nodded. "Do the others."

Jenny started on the fuses, laying each on the bench as she finished it. Tony left the shop; she heard him speak to Rosie as he went out the gate. She wondered if Mike was sulking around the house. No, she thought, trying to be fair, he's usually cheerful around the children. She had been right to stay with Mike. Billy watched him and copied everything he did; Corey gurgled when Mike picked her up. The kids needed their daddy. Jenny crimped the last cap. *I just wish he'd make love to me. If he'd even touch me, maybe I'd forget about David's kiss.*

Tony came back into the shop. He handed her a glass of milk and an apple. "Eat these. I don't want your hands to get shaky."

Jenny bit into the apple, and Tony took a stick of dynamite from the box Mike had brought to the shop. I wonder where he got it, Jenny thought. He must have it stored somewhere on the mountain. "Where do you keep dynamite when you're mining?" she asked Tony.

"In a magazine."

Jenny laughed, picturing the stick of dynamite tucked into a copy of *Reader's Digest*.

"A *powder* magazine," Tony said. "It's got to have thick reinforced walls, a solid door, and a good lock. You can't get a powder permit without an inspection of your magazine."

"Oh, dear," Jenny said. "We don't have a powder permit. What if that Mr. Daley comes around?"

"Don't worry about that till the time comes. I know all about those applications."

"You do?" Jenny was surprised.

"Yeah." The brown face was somber. "I can't breathe good in those tunnels anymore, but I keep up-to-date."

Jenny looked at the old Italian and said slowly, "I never thought about it before, but you're not really a dump keeper, are you? You own property, and you have valuable skills."

Tony grinned at her. "I've got a broken-down, unrented, one-room house, a junkyard, and fifteen acres of rocky ground. Yessir, I'm wealthy."

Jenny met his eyes and smiled too. "Richard says everything is relative. Compared to me, you're relatively wealthy and definitely smart." She tossed the apple core out the door.

Tony laughed and held out a stick of dynamite. "You want to get acquainted with this stuff?"

Jenny looked at the dynamite. It was about eight inches long, maybe an inch and a quarter in diameter, and it was wrapped in heavy brown waxed paper, the ends pushed in like the ends of the rolls of coins in the cash register at the café.

"We'll need five of these for each hole except the cut holes," Tony said. "They take six. But only *one* stick in each hole—the primer—carries a cap and fuse."

Tony picked up a small pointed wooden stick. "Make a hole in the powder with this punch." He pushed the punch into the end of the dynamite. "Now push that cap and fuse down into the hole in the powder."

Jenny pushed the cap into the hole.

"Bend the fuse around the bottom end and bring it up toward the other end." Jenny did as she was directed. "Now, you've got a primer. For nine holes, you need nine primers."

Jenny took the punch, and after poking eight more holes in eight more sticks of dynamite she inserted the caps and bent the fuses up. She felt calm and her hands were steady.

Tony counted out thirty-eight more sticks of dynamite into an empty wooden box. He took the primers from Jenny and placed them in the box. "Bring that loading stick," he said, nodding at a long piece of wood that looked like a broom handle with a flat end. "And don't bring nothin' made of metal."

They put their hard hats on and went into the tunnel with the box of dynamite. Jenny was pleased with her calmness. She welcomed the dark of the tunnel and walked carefully toward the face, curious and happy.

Tony ran his hand over the vein and said, "If we do this right, we'll leave that ore right out in the open, and we'll cut it out clean with the *next* round of powder."

He picked up a stick of dynamite and the loading stick. "We'll start with one of these for a cushion. I never like to push the primer, with the fuse and that loaded cap, up against hard rock." He started the dynamite into one of the cut holes and then said to Jenny, "Here, take the loading stick and push this all the way back."

Jenny scooted the dynamite gently along the inner surface of the hole until it would go no further. Tony placed the primer in the hole. "Okay, push the primer back, but don't bunch up the fuse. It's got to stay straight and hang out at the mouth." Jenny pushed the primer carefully into the hole. "Be sure it's up against the first one."

Jenny nodded when the primer was in place. "Okay," Tony said, "put in the next one and tamp it a little harder." Jenny pushed the dynamite firmly into the hole. "Now the fourth one. Tamp it good and tight."

Jenny gave the loading stick a final shove and turned to Tony, who handed her the last two sticks of powder. "Pour it on these. Load that hole tight."

Jenny put the fifth and sixth sticks in the cut hole, ramming the loading stick against each one.

"All right," said Tony. "That's the first hole." He pulled the fuse straight; it stuck out of the drill hole about two feet. "We'll load the other cut hole next and work our way up from there."

When the top nine holes were loaded and the fuses stuck out like bristly black whiskers, Tony said, "Now we'll time these things by cutting the fuses to the right length."

Jenny watched carefully as Tony measured eighteen inches from the far end of the fuse in the first cut hole and cut the fuse. He did the same thing with the fuse in the other cut hole. Then he took one of the eighteen-inch pieces he'd snipped off and cut another two inches off of it. Using the sixteen-inch length as a measure, he cut the fuses on the breast holes. Then he cut another two inches from his measure and timed the fuses in the rib holes. Turning, he handed the knife and the measure to Jenny.

"Cut it again and do the arch holes; then cut it once more and do the crown."

"You should have been a schoolteacher," Jenny said as she handed the knife back to Tony. "You make it easy to understand."

Tony grinned. "I can show it. I can't write it down. My eighth-grade teacher woulda laughed if she'd heard you."

"Well, anyway, Teach, what do we do next?"

"We're getting close to the time to light 'em up. The fuse burns a foot a minute, and the cut-hole fuses are the shortest: they'll go in five and a half minutes. It should take us less than four minutes to light all the fuses, and then we get out of here."

Jenny nodded, and Tony continued, "Don't run, but turn around and walk fast and careful out of the tunnel."

Jenny said, "Let me do it once—walk out, I mean. And I'll warn Mike to keep the kids inside."

When Jenny came back into the tunnel Tony picked up the end of one of the fuses. Bending it upward, he said, "I'm going to split the end of the fuse open so the powder will light easy. Be careful to keep it upright when you do this; you don't want to spill any powder." Tony split every fuse and brought the ends as close together as he could. Then he took up a short piece of leftover fuse and peeled back some of the covering.

"I'm making a spitter. I'll light it with a match and then use the spitter on the fuses." Tony looked up from the fuse. "When we get outside I want you to count the shots. You gotta know there's no duds left in here to blow you up."

"That's a cheery thought," Jenny said.

"There ain't many *old* careless powder men," Tony said. "Now. I'm going to start lighting fuses. I want you to watch how it's done, but when I say 'Go' you get out of here. I'll be right on your tail." He grinned. "'Scuse the words."

Jenny laughed. "I'm just another miner, Tony."

"Here we go," he said. He lit a match and held it to the spitter. When it caught, the spitter lit the tunnel with its fire. Tony ignited the cut-hole fuses first. Jenny watched as the black powder in the fuse flared with a smoky light. Tony moved the spitter quickly from fuse to fuse. When all the fuses were hissing, he stood still for a second or two, checking the entire job, and then he said, "Go."

Jenny turned and walked briskly toward the mouth of the tunnel. Just outside, Tony grabbed her arm and stopped her. Before she could speak, the first concussion reached them; the steel mine door quivered, rocks rattled down the slope, and the shovels inside the portal clattered against each other. An undulating wave of sound washed over them as they stood. The mountain in front of Jenny and the mine dump under her feet vibrated with shock. Smoke rolled from the portal.

She glanced at Tony, who had said "One" with the first explosion and continued as the explosions followed ten seconds apart until he had counted five. "Five," he said again. "That's it. Did you catch all five?"

Jenny was holding her fingers up. "One for the cut holes, two for the breast holes, three for the ribs, four for the arches, and five for the crown. I did. I did hear five. I think I almost *saw* them go."

Tony clapped her on the shoulder. "By damn, Jenny, you're a natural."

"I can hardly wait to shoot a round all by myself," she said.

"You've got a helluva mucking job ahead of you first," he said.

"I know," said Jenny, "but I'm gonna do it in a hurry. I'm dying to see that ore."

C H A P T E R

38

▲▲▲▲▲▲

But Sunday morning, when Jenny asked Mike to help her, he said, "No, by God. This is my day off, and I'm not mucking rock on my day off. Besides, while the ground's wet, and before it freezes, I want to build a fence around the cabin. Corey will be walking before the spring thaw. She wiggles all over the house now when I put her down. I can hardly keep her away from the door."

Jenny stirred her coffee and said nothing for a moment. She felt very strange, almost as if she were the father of the children, and Mike their mother. She worried about Corey, too, such a surprising little traveler she was. But Mike was the one who had to keep track of her most of the time.

Jenny smiled at last and said, "For a baby who just started crawling, she sure gets around."

Mike turned toward the crib, where Corey sat happily playing with the smooth wooden blocks that Mike had cut from a piece of aspen log and fine-sanded. "She's sneaky," he said. He looked at

Billy, who was finishing up his pancakes and syrup. "What do you say, son? You want to help me this morning?"

"Sure, Daddy."

"Think you can haul fence posts in that wagon?"

"If Rosie helps too." Billy picked up his plate and licked the syrup. Jenny wanted to protest, but Mike said nothing, and she somehow felt as if she didn't have the right.

Mike looked at Jenny and asked, "Can you baby-sit Corey for a while?"

A flush of anger prickled her scalp and forehead, but she couldn't tell if Mike was trying to hurt her feelings or not. He didn't even seem to be thinking about her.

"Well, of course," she said, forcing a little laugh. "Of course I can take care of my own baby."

Mike didn't answer. He was buttoning Billy's coat.

Even though it was the first of November, the day was warm. The snow had melted on the mine dump and the southern slope of the mountain. After Jenny filled the woodbox and emptied the ashes from the stove, she heated water for dishes. Outside, the steady *thunk-thunk* of the shovel punctuated the singsong of Billy's chatter. When the house was tidy, the dishes stacked in neat rows on the shelf, the floor swept and mopped, and the bright red and black blanket spread smoothly over the bed, Jenny put Corey's outdoor clothes on and went outside. She could see at once what a good addition the fence was going to be.

Mike had staked out an area from just behind the woodpile in the back clear to the edge of the grassy meadow in front of the cabin—a wonderful space for the children. He had left a gap for the gate on the side near the dump where the pickup was parked. Wooden fence posts were set into fresh holes and tamped down with mud along the outline of the new yard. Mike was just beginning to nail some long skinny poles to the uprights.

"Looks nice," Jenny said. "Do you want some help with the poles?"

"I guess Billy will do fine," Mike said.

Jenny turned away and buried her face against Corey's shoulder.

Mike was determined not to need her for anything. She walked over on the dump, where Rosie waited patiently, the chain from the butt stick on her harness attached to the handle of the red wagon. Rosie flicked one ear toward Jenny and looked at her sideways. The wagon carried a load of poles much longer than the wagon bed; they dragged on the ground for a good eight feet.

Jenny set Corey on top of the burro and held her there. Corey grabbed the hair on Rosie's neck and pulled it with her fingers, staring soberly at the coarse black strands.

"Don't let the baby get cold," Mike called. "I think she's cutting another tooth."

"She's all right," Jenny answered. "The sun is shining on her, and Rosie's back is warm." But after a moment or two, she took Corey into the house.

She played peekaboo and stack the blocks, and she read the book out loud. About midmorning, when Corey got sleepy, Jenny put her in her crib and covered her up.

She went outside and watched the fence builders silently, not offering to help again. He knows the baby better than I do, she thought. I was so engrossed in the drilling and shooting I wasn't even aware that my own baby was getting a new tooth. Maybe I should give up on the mine and let Mike go out and look for work.

Mike and Billy had most of the poles on the fence by the time they got hungry. They lunched quickly, went back to the yard, and finished all but the gate before supper.

After they had eaten again, Mike said to Jenny, "Okay, dish out my allowance and give me the truck payment. I'm going into town."

"How can you pay the loan payment on Sunday?"

"Oh, I sit in on a game with the guy from the bank. He takes it in on Monday.

"I didn't know bankers gambled."

Mike grinned. "Most don't. Just old Charlie, and he's got a face you can read like the baby's storybook."

"Will you be late?"

Mike glanced at her and seemed to see her for the first time that day. "No later than you are the rest of the week."

Tears stung Jenny's eyes. "That's not fair," she said. "You act like I go down there for the fun of it."

"I think you like it well enough," Mike said.

"Oh, Mike," Jenny said. "Let's not fight. It's lonesome enough on this mine dump when you go."

"Tell me about this dump," he said, glancing around the cabin. Jenny followed his eyes. In the uncertain light of the November dusk, the cabin looked crude and poor. She suddenly recalled Mike's laughing face as he'd joked with his friends on the night she'd walked up to Mom's, when he'd bought her a Scotch and soda. She got up and got the loan money. Billy was sitting on his bed with his truck, but Jenny could tell he was only pretending to play. The knuckles on the hand that held the toy were white with tension.

"Here," she said to Mike, trying to sound relaxed and friendly. "Have a good time." Mike rose and put on his jacket. Jenny walked over to him and said in a low voice, "Billy's upset. Please don't go away acting angry."

Mike glanced toward the mattress on the floor. Then he put his arm around Jenny and went with her toward Billy. He held his hand out to Billy. "Tell me good night, son. Your mama's going to read your book tonight."

"That's right," Jenny said. "I haven't heard that new story yet."

Billy took Mike's hand and stood up. He leaned against his parents. They each put a hand on one of his shoulders. Jenny rested in the touching. Even though Mike's affection for her was faked, it comforted her.

After he was gone, she washed the dishes and let Billy dry them and put them away. Then she said, "Let's play ring-around-the-rosy."

"Corey, too?"

"Sure. We'll sit her in the middle."

They went round and round the baby, holding hands and singing, and then laughing as Corey clapped her hands together. When Billy was dizzy from going around, they sat down on the floor and peeked through their fingers at the baby. Then they counted her fingers and toes and took off Billy's shoes and counted his toes and fingers.

"Now you, Mama," Billy said. So Jenny took off her shoes and let Billy count her toes. He got to ten and then said, "Eleven," and rolled around on the floor giggling wildly. Jenny picked Corey up and bounced her gently in her lap and smiled at Billy until he got the hiccups from giggling so hard.

"Let's have a cocoa party before bedtime," she said.

His hiccups ceasing abruptly, Billy scrambled up from the floor and got the cups from the shelf. Jenny made cocoa and toast for Billy and herself and warm milk for Corey.

After Corey was dressed for bed, Billy recited the storybook for his sister; then Jenny put Corey in the crib.

"Now what?" she said to Billy.

"You said you'd teach me to write my name."

"Yes, I did, didn't I?" Jenny looked around for something to write on and spied the journal she'd bought at the drugstore. She tore a page out of it and wrote Billy's name in careful print. She gave Billy the pencil and guided his hand as he wrote each letter.

"Now let me do it by myself," he said. She watched as he bent his head over the paper and slowly printed a large lopsided letter *B*.

"That's a wonderful start," Jenny said. "Let's put it up on the wall by your bed."

"How?"

"I'll go get the hammer and a nail from the shop."

It was sharply November outside. The night-blue sky was high, the stars remote and icy. She hurried through the gap where the gate would be and went to the shop. Rosie ambled across the pen and snuffled around Jenny's fingers. "Sorry, babe," she said. "I wasn't thinking about you." Rosie nibbled at Jenny's thigh. Jenny laughed and left the corral.

Billy held the paper while Jenny nailed it to the wall above his bed. "We'll have to save all your papers now that you're learning to write. I'll get you some drawing paper too."

Billy yawned. "Read me my book now, Mama." He was asleep before the boy in the story found the pony, but Jenny read the whole story out loud anyhow.

After that the cabin was very quiet. She stirred the fire and built it up until it made a crackling sound. She put the dishpan on to heat some water. She liked the businesslike little hisses the water made just before it boiled. She washed the cocoa dishes and put them away. She filled the pan again, and while her bath water heated, she undressed slowly near the stove. When she was naked, she looked down at her body. Her breasts were firm and round, with a little brown circle and a few blond hairs around each nipple. She ran her hands over her ribs and across her belly. I'm getting skinny, she thought, and moved her right hand to the soft blond-white hair on the rise between her legs. She remembered the wave of heat that had twisted through her body when David kissed her. She moved her hand away and quickly took her bath and put her nightgown on.

But she wasn't sleepy. She was usually hard at work this time of night. She looked at the books on the shelf. She had no taste for the Old Testament. The last thing she wanted to think about tonight was Adam and Eve and sin. She picked up the mining book Mrs. Marsh had bought for her, but she didn't want to think about mining either. She put it back and took the volume of Shakespeare's plays that Richard had given her. She opened it idly to a play called *Twelfth Night,* and her eyes fell on a line: "Excellent. It hangs like flax on a distaff, and I hope to see a housewife take thee between her legs and spin it off." Jenny felt herself blushing as she quickly closed the book and pushed it back onto the shelf.

She turned away from the books and saw the journal on the table. Sitting down, she picked up the pencil and opened the journal. She wrote, "My name is Jennifer Norton Williams." She sat still and read the line over twice. Then she wrote, "I am twenty-three years old, and I have a daughter and a son."

She stopped again and put the tip of the pencil against her front tooth. Then she wrote;

> My father died before I even knew enough to think
> about having a father. He was quiet and gentle. I
> think he loved me, but he never told me so. My
> mother loved me. Before she hated herself, my mother
> loved me. My mother wasn't to blame. It wasn't her
> fault that some man thought he had the right to reach

out and take her. Mom Bradley thinks men have a
right to a woman's body. She sells part of my body
every night.

Jenny was writing so quickly now the pencil's point was wearing
away.

Richard wants to own my mind, but even *he* thinks he
can have a part of my body. He kissed me.

She stopped writing for a moment, remembering how exposed her
mother had looked, sprawled in the grass, her dress torn, her legs
bare. She shivered and wrote, "It must have been a thousand times
worse for Mama." Jenny looked around the cabin. Her hand trembled slightly as she turned the page and began to write again.

Bigfoot kissed me, too—David kissed me. He grabbed
my wrist and pulled me across the seat. My side hurts
where I was squashed against the steering wheel. He
kissed me without asking. He kissed me without even
saying my name.

Tears rolled down Jenny's cheeks as she wrote the words. She closed
the journal and, still holding the pencil in her hand, put her head
down on her arms and cried, big sobs dredged up from deep inside
her chest, rocking her body on the wooden crate. The sobs made her
ribs ache and her throat burn. She finally took a deep shuddering
breath, and just then she heard the sound of a truck coming up the
hill.

Oh Lord, she thought, it's Mike. She grabbed up the journal and
put it out of sight behind the Old Testament and the Shakespeare
book. As she dipped some cold water from the bucket to wash her
face, another thought hit her: What if it's not Mike? She looked at
the clock; it was too early for him to be home. Going to the door,
she locked it as the truck came up on the dump. She turned out the
lantern and leaned against the door, her heart pounding as footsteps

came into the yard. Someone tried the door handle, and then Mike called out, "Jenny, let me in."

Jenny fumbled at the lock. When it gave way, she snatched the door open and fell against Mike. "I am so glad it's you. I was scared to death it was going to be Tully Stocker."

Mike held her tight to him for a moment. Then he stepped to the table, lit a match, and held it to the lantern. Turning, he said, "Hey, you've been crying." He grinned. "Well, you can smile now, babe. I've got great news! They're going to open up the Mitchell mill for small loads—twenty-five-ton minimums. I won't have to concentrate that damn ore myself, and we'll get our payoff a lot sooner."

Jenny tried to smile at Mike, but he had turned away and begun to undress, saying, "We'd better get to bed because tomorrow we've got to muck out that waste rock so you can drill and shoot the payload. Things are finally turning our way."

Mike crawled into bed; Jenny turned the light out and followed him, too unsettled to know what to say. But when Mike turned to her in bed and began to slide her nightgown up slowly, she jerked it over her head, threw it on the floor, and moved her body close to Mike's. As he reached for her, she grabbed his shoulders and dug her nails into his flesh. She kissed him wildly and bit his lip. She wrapped her legs around him, pulling him on top of her. As he entered her, she thrust herself up to him again and again until Mike groaned and fell away panting.

Then Jenny lay in the warm sticky mess, and the tears rolled silently down the side of her face and puddled in her ears and leaked along her neck and turned cold.

CHAPTER
39

▲▲▲▲▲▲

Jenny switched on her headlamp and stepped carefully from tie to tie between the tracks. In one hand she held Rosie's halter rope, and in the other, a shovel. Mike had gone to start the generator, but she couldn't wait to see the results of her first round. She sniffed the air as the daylight pinched off behind her; it was fresh, but different from before. Now added to the moist earthiness of it was the tang of black powder smoke and the faintly hot smell of newly broken rock.

The ore car rattled on the track, the scaling bar banging back and forth inside. Jenny's breath came quickly when she saw the immense pile of rock extending some twelve feet from the breast. She stopped walking; Rosie stopped, too, and the ore car ceased to grumble. Jenny passed her light over the rock pile. It was bigger than the one she'd helped Mike shovel out the first time. She ran her headlamp beam over the back and sides.

One spot on the back looked rough and loose. She turned around, slid past Rosie's fat woolly side, and got the scaling bar. Mike had told her how to use it. It was safe as long as she was behind the loose rock. She lifted the bar and prodded the rough patch along its edges. A chunk of rock slabbed off the back and fell on the pile. Jenny climbed up on the near edge of the pile and looked at the back again. It looked solid now, no cracks or rough patches. She leaned the bar against the rib and inspected the nearest stull and the wedges that held it tight to the back. The wedges still looked tight, but the stull had a gash in it from a piece of flying rock.

The lights went on in the tunnel, and Jenny switched off her headlamp and looked around, inspecting all the sides. She glanced again at the immense pile of rock and sighed. They had to muck all that out before she could see the exposed vein. She felt her mouth tighten. What if the ore thinned out or disappeared altogether? What if, as Tony had warned her could happen, the vein had changed direction, and she'd blown the payload into a billion pieces?

She could hear Mike and Billy in the tunnel.

"Haven't you got that rock mucked out yet?"

She turned. Mike was grinning at her from under his hard hat. He had a shovel in his hand.

She smiled back. "I can't decide whether I'm more excited or more scared to see what happened to the vein."

"No need to feel anything, yet, Jen. It goes where it goes." He said to Billy, "Okay, kid, can you unlatch Rosie and hook her onto the other end?" He watched as Billy tried to pull back the safety catch on the hook and then reached his own hand to help the boy. He moved over near Jenny to give the burro room to pass. Billy pulled on the rope and Rosie turned around and followed him, nuzzling him softly in the side.

Billy giggled, "She's trying to eat me up."

Mike said, "Go get her an apple and peek in your sister's crib while you're there."

Billy trotted along the track out of the tunnel. Mike and Jenny picked up their square-nosed shovels, and beginning at the bottom of the near edge of the pile they started to muck out the Spanish Mary again.

It took them fifteen minutes to fill the car. Jenny leaned on her shovel, resting before she helped to take the car out to the dump. "Why do you suppose they called this the Spanish Mary?"

Mike said, "Half the mines in this country are named after women. Those old-timers left home to follow the lure of the gold, but when they saw how much cold hard work they were in for they began to think more of the girls they left behind them."

"Were the Spaniards here?"

"There's part of an old Spanish *arastra* over on the other side of the hill."

"Arastra?"

"It's a big stone wheel their mules or oxen dragged around to crush the ore."

"I'd like to see it."

Mike leaned his shovel against the wall and came over to Jenny. He pulled her close and ran his hands over her buttocks and up her back. "When we're rich—when spring comes—we'll take a day off and go on a picnic with the kids."

Jenny leaned against him, grateful that their silence was broken. There was still another silence between them: the silence on Mike's part to the thoughts Jenny never voiced. But at least for now they were back on the level she'd learned to deal with. They talked about facts; they talked about the kids. They didn't argue, and Mike was touching her again. She was used to giving him money now, and he didn't get so angry each time he took it.

Mike ran his hand over her bottom again. "These old tin pants kinda hide your charms," he said. "I liked you better in the outfit you wore in bed." They heard Billy come into the tunnel.

"Daddy, Corey's awake."

Jenny started toward the mouth. Mike said, "Okay, Bill, Mama will go to her. You take Rosie's rope, and let's get this rock out to the dump."

When Jenny came back, they loaded four more cars and emptied them over the side of the mine dump before going in for a late lunch. Jenny noticed that Mike seemed nervous each time she left the mine ahead of him. When she had fried bacon and potatoes and opened a can of tomatoes, she sat down at the table with Billy and Mike. "I don't think you should work in the tunnel when I'm not here, Mike."

His face flushed. "Why not?" he said.

"It's not safe; it's against regulations. Besides, the kids need you."

"You're probably right," he said. "Okay, if there's any daylight left when we're done mucking, I'll put the gate on the fence."

"I'm afraid we're done now," Jenny said. "I was hoping we'd finish, but it's almost two. I have to be at Mom's at five, and I'm a mess."

"I'll bring up some water," Mike said, adding, "God, I hope that creek don't freeze over this winter."

▽ ▽

It wasn't until late Tuesday that they finally finished mucking out Jenny's first round. They dumped the last load and hurried back in to the face. Jenny switched on her headlamp and shone it into the deep hollow she'd made by blasting out the overhang. The light picked up the vein of sparkling ore. Jenny squealed with excitement.

Mike leaned in beside her and said, "Son of a bitch, it's four inches wider than before."

Jenny couldn't stop looking at the ore as it fanned out in the stone floor the blast had leveled. Finally she bent to inspect the rest of the holes she'd drilled. They would have to be cleaned out with the blowpipe, but otherwise they looked okay.

"Do you think we can be ready for Tony to help me load and shoot tomorrow?"

"No, probably not," Mike said. "We still have to clean out the tunnel and then do some timber work."

Jenny looked up at the back and sighed. "So many details before we get to the gold."

Mike grinned. "You're no tenderfoot now."

"I might as well plan to do the grocery shopping and get my hair done, then." She turned away from the face and pulled her gloves off. "And my nails." Even with the gloves on, her hands got rough.

"Yeah," Mike said, "get your hair done. I've gotten so I kinda like it."

Jenny smiled at the compliment. "One of these days," she said, "let's get up early and go to Mitchell. We need to check out the mill, and I want to find out where they give the GED test. And there's a bookstore that has some mining books."

"Well, if you load and shoot on Thursday, we might as well go into Mitchell on Friday while the smoke clears. We can start shoveling the ore on Saturday."

▽ ▽

Tony came up to the Spanish Mary on Thursday and supervised while Jenny cleaned out the remaining eight holes and loaded them.

"Since these holes are all the same depth, the fuses will all be the same length at the opening," she said.

"Right," said Tony.

"Which fuses shall I cut the shortest then?"

"Your relievers."

"Where do I start?"

"With the center, and you'd better give yourself five and a half minutes again. You're going to light them without help this time."

Jenny felt the nerves tighten all over her body, but she took a deep breath and began to cut the fuses.

When she had finished, Tony said, "Okay, now make your spitter. Bend a piece of that fuse and make plenty of notches so you'll have a fire for every fuse and some extra in case one blows out." Jenny made sixteen notches in the spitter. Tony handed her a match and stepped back.

Jenny lit the spitter and began with the center reliever. When the fuse in the last lifter was smoldering, she stepped back, looked at all eight fuses, and said, "Go."

They walked rapidly toward the mouth, and Tony turned with her as they reached daylight, and the first concussion rattled the steel-mesh door and rocked the shovels. Jenny began to count, and when the last rolling echo died away, she said to Tony, "They all went, didn't they?"

"Right," Tony said, adding as he had before, "It's a damn good thing you can hear those to count them. There's been guys killed because they missed one and went to banging around in there with a live hole."

Jenny shivered. Things could go wrong.

"Anyway," she said. "Today's shot went great, and tomorrow we're going to Mitchell to check out the mill."

But the next morning, just as they were loading the children into the truck, Quentin Lacey drove his red Datsun over the bridge, and close behind him was an official state vehicle. They parked on the dump in front of Mike's pickup.

Lloyd Daley got out of the state vehicle and stuck out his hand to Mike. "Hello, Williams," he said. "Quent Lacey says he's heard some blasting over this way, and he thinks it's about time I inspected your claim."

CHAPTER

40

▲▲▲▲▲▲

Jenny could feel the tension rise in Mike as he turned from shaking hands with the mine inspector to look at Quentin Lacey. The real estate man started to hold out his hand, but when it became obvious that Mike was not going to shake hands with him, he dropped it to his side. Mike walked a step or two forward and kicked the right front tire on the Datsun.

"I see you've got new tires, Lacey. Maybe my wife won't have to change any more flats for you." Quentin Lacey flushed and Mike continued. "It's kinda hard on these city cars to drive 'em around on mining land." He raised his glance from the tires and looked Quentin Lacey right in the eyes. "You do remember, don't you, Lacey, that the land around here is zoned Mining One."

Quentin Lacey shifted his weight slightly and glanced at the mine inspector. Lloyd Daley said mildly, "I reminded him of that not more than an hour ago, but he's still feeling nervous about that explosion he heard. Have you been shooting off any dynamite?"

Mike's face flushed a deeper red. Jenny stepped forward with a smile and held out her hand to the inspector. "Mr. Daley, I'm Jenny Williams. Tony DiAngelo introduced us down at Mom's Café one night." The man took her hand and smiled at her. He started to turn back to Mike, but Jenny said, "As a matter of fact, we have just finished drilling and shooting a round in the Spanish Mary. We'd be

· 230 ·

glad to have you come in and inspect the tunnel, but the smoke is still pretty heavy in there. So why don't you all come into the cabin for some coffee. We have an old mining regulations book, but I'd like to ask you some questions."

Jenny glanced at Mike. The angry flush was gone from his face. He gave her a quick smile and turned toward the cabin, saying, "Yeah, come on in. We've always got the coffeepot ready." He took Corey out of the truck; Billy scooted into the cabin ahead of them.

Jenny was glad she had tidied up the cabin before they had come outside. The bright morning sunshine slanted through the window and dipped into the water bucket to make yellow sparkles just under the surface. The men scraped their feet on the step and took off their caps as they entered. Mike stirred up the coals they had left to die and soon had a fire to heat the coffeepot Jenny filled.

Jenny took down the cups and spoons and set the sugar bowl in the middle of the table. Lloyd Daley and Quentin Lacey pulled the milk crates away from the table and sat down. Quentin Lacey looked uncomfortable; when he opened his mouth, Jenny said to Mr. Daley, "What do you look for when you inspect a small mine?"

Quentin Lacey closed his mouth again, and Mr. Daley said, "Well, mostly for loose rock, bad air, unstable timber. What we're trying to do is make a safe environment for the miners to work under. And we enforce the state laws. *Bulletin Twenty* is a state law book. It contains a bunch of laws—you know: do this and do this and do this. How to store your explosives and how to handle explosives.

Jenny smiled to keep from laughing. It was funny how easy it was to get this man talking.

"That's what we look for," he said. "And we also do some training for the new miners coming on. All of the inspectors for the state division of mines are old miners, and they have firsthand experience."

Jenny could tell he took his job seriously. She liked the man, his seriousness and the way he looked right at her when he talked.

"How often do you inspect a mine?" she asked after waiting a moment to see if Mike would say anything.

"It depends on a lot of things, but usually twice a year."

"That must mean there's a lot of you."

"There's only three gold-mine inspectors and two coal-mine inspectors in the state. Yeah, we're cut way down right now. Three years ago, the department had twenty-six people; now we're down to nine."

"And every day you go to some mine?"

"Normally, yeah. I work at the office part time. We also issue the explosive permits for all the mines in the state. They file an application with us. We follow it out and check their powder magazine. If it's acceptable when we make the inspection, we issue the explosive permit."

So there it was. There was the weapon Quentin Lacey could use against them. But he didn't know that; he didn't know yet that this fine honest inspector could be his best friend and shut down the mine in five minutes.

Jenny looked at Mike, but he turned suddenly to the stove to get the coffeepot. He filled the cups, and for a moment there was a small social bustle as the men stirred sugar into their coffee, clinking their spoons against their cups and setting them aside to drink.

Jenny waited, but Mike still didn't say anything. Trying to hide the sick feeling that rose in her throat, Jenny started to speak to the inspector again. Just then another pickup turned across the bridge and drove up onto the mine dump. Jenny felt like crying with relief as she saw Tony get down and come to the gate. She went to the door and opened it.

Tony came inside and said to Mike, "Well, I got the rest of the stuff we'll need in that tunnel." He stopped as if in surprise and said to the mine inspector. "What in the hell are you doing up here, Daley? I've been following you around for a week trying to get you to sign my application and come up and inspect my powder magazine." He held out his hand to the inspector.

Lloyd Daley half rose and reached across the table to shake Tony's hand. He said, "Hell, Tony. I didn't know you were drilling again."

Tony walked over to the shelf behind the stove for a cup. He poured himself a cup of coffee and came back to the table.

"Well, I'm not really drilling, Lloyd. I'm teaching the young lady to drill."

Lloyd Daley looked over at Jenny. "The hell you say. How's she doin'?"

Tony grinned his whole-face grin. "She's a natural, Lloyd. She takes to that drill like she was born to it, and her hand is rock steady when she's got hold of the spitter."

Tony turned to Mike and said, "Mike, why don't you take Lloyd up there and show him the powder magazine so we can get that permit signed." He looked back at the inspector. "I guess we shouldna shot that first round without it, but Jenny was anxious to see if she could do it."

"Well," the inspector said, "now that I know you're running the show, I guess I don't need to look at the magazine." He turned to Jenny and Mike. "I'll be back when the powder clears to check the tunnel."

"Sure," Mike said. "Come back tomorrow morning. We're going to muck her out then."

Daley laughed. "You wouldn't be thinking of handing me a shovel, would you?"

Mike laughed, too, and got up for the coffeepot again. "Anyone for a refill?"

"Not me," the inspector said. "I've got to get back down the hill." He said to Quentin Lacey, "I don't think you've got a thing to worry about, Lacey. Tony was likely drilling and shooting before you got out of grammar school back east." Then he said to Tony, "Come out and move your truck, and I'll take that application. You want the permit in your name?"

"No," Tony said. "Mike and Jenny filed the claim. Better put it in their name."

The men left the cabin. Jenny leaned weakly against the window and watched as Tony went to his truck and brought out a piece of paper. God bless him, she thought. I hope the ink is dry.

After the two visitors had left, Jenny went to Tony, put her arms around him, and kissed him on his scraggy startled grin.

"You are a lifesaver!" she said.

Tony grinned more widely. "Maybe so, maybe not. You know what Daley said to me when he took that application?"

"No," Mike said, "what did he say?"

"He said, 'Tony, you old bastard, I hope that ink is dry.'"

Jenny began to laugh. "Oh, I *like* that man," she cried. Mike and Tony laughed with her, and Billy joined in, bouncing up and down on his bed.

Finally Jenny said, "Well, it's too late to go to Mitchell, but you'd better stay for lunch, Tony, and tell us what else we're going to need to keep Mr. Daley happy."

Tony looked at Mike, "Would that magazine have passed inspection?"

"You can be goddamn sure that magazine would pass inspection. I built it a whole helluva lot tighter than this house is built." Mike's face was flushed and angry-looking again.

"That's what I figured," Tony said mildly and turned to Jenny. "You still got venison?"

Mike stood up. "I'll go hack off some steaks." Then he grinned. "You like 'em to taste of powder and smoke?"

Tony walked over to the crib and held a crooked brown finger out to Corey. "I was raised on powder and smoke," he said, adding, "but you'd better get that meat out of the tunnel pretty soon or it's going to rot on you."

"I'm building a cold box for it now," Mike said. "We can keep it out north of the house in that snowbank."

▽ ▽

After lunch, while Jenny did the dishes and the men sat at the table with their cigarettes, Mike said, "How did you happen to show up at just the right moment this morning?"

Tony said, "I saw that Lacey talking to Lloyd in Mom's, and when the two of them started off together, I just hightailed it back to my shop and dug up an old application blank." He laughed. "It had grease stains and coffee rings on it, but it's official now."

Jenny said, "The inspector seemed to be on our side. Why is that, do you suppose?"

"Small miners have it plenty tough," Tony said, "and he knows it. It frustrates the hell out of him to see these real estate developers pussyfoot around the rules."

Mike said, "We were thinking of going over to Mitchell to check out the mill, until he and Lacey showed up. You want to ride over there this afternoon?"

Jenny was already dressed to go to town, so she played with the children until it was time to go to work, feeling almost light-headed because the danger was past. Tomorrow they could bring out their first payload.

They all went down the hill together, Jenny in Mike's pickup, and Tony and Mike and the children in Tony's. When they reached the junction of the Virgo Creek road and the highway, Tony and Mike turned left toward Mitchell. Billy stood on his knees and waved out the back window of the cab. Jenny waved until the pickup was out of sight, and then she turned right and went through Dolby and on down the highway toward Mom's Bar and Café.

When she turned into the parking lot, her heart began to beat so fast that her ribs seemed to rattle under her skin. There were two big blue and silver semi rigs idling in front of the cafe, and both of them said TULSA TRUCKING COMPANY on the side of their doors.

CHAPTER

41

▲▲▲▲▲▲

Jenny pulled the pickup around the side of the café and shut the engine off, but she stayed behind the wheel. I don't want to see him today. I don't know how to act, what to say to him. She put her head on the wheel until her pulse slowed and she breathed easier. Finally she opened the truck door, slid to the ground, and went into the café by the back door.

The kitchen was warm and steamy from the dishwasher. She slipped quickly past Richard, took her uniform from the hook, and looked through the serving window. David Garvey sat in the front booth with his back toward the north end of the café. The other Tulsa driver sat across from him.

Pushing through the swinging door, Jenny went quietly toward the rest room. The café was about half full. Mom Bradley, who was waiting on a family at one of the tables, looked up and smiled. As Jenny changed, she thought, No matter what happens today, I'm not going to make a fool of myself. I'll be polite and businesslike.

Luckily, Mom Bradley had already served David Garvey and the other Tulsa driver, and Jenny could start immediately with the tables in the north end. She didn't approach David's booth until she had made a wide swing with the coffeepot to give refills. She stopped by the booth and said in a pleasant voice that, to her relief, did not quaver, "Would you like more coffee, Mr. Garvey?"

He looked up, and a light glanced across his blue eyes, but he flushed a little and looked toward the other driver. "How about it, Jake? You want a refill?"

The other driver held out his cup to Jenny. She filled it carefully, fighting the trembling in her body. David shook his head when she reached toward his cup.

"None for me, thank you. I've got to get going." He rose and followed Jenny to the cash register. She put the coffeepot on the hot plate, then turned to take his ticket and the twenty-dollar bill he handed her.

"How are your studies coming?" he asked in a friendly voice.

"Fine," Jenny said and gave him his change. Mom Bradley came through the swinging door with an armload of plates. "Thank you, Mr. Garvey," Jenny said and turned toward the kitchen.

David said, "Jenny," in a low voice and reached out his hand as if to touch her arm, but she kept going and pushed the swinging doors with more force than she intended.

Richard looked up. "Slow down, whirlwind. There's a long night ahead of us."

Jenny didn't want to talk to Richard either. She picked up the salad plates she needed and went back through the door. David Garvey was gone. Mom Bradley stood by the cash register. Jenny took the plates to a table near the window and returned to the register just as the other Tulsa Trucking driver handed Mom Bradley his check. She punched the cash register buttons and said, "I'm surprised to see both you Tulsa drivers at the same time. I thought Bigfoot was your relief driver."

The truck driver looked at Mom Bradley and smiled an odd smile. "You puttin' me on?" he asked.

"No," Mom said. "Why?"

"Bigfoot's no relief driver."

"Oh?" Mom Bradley said, while Jenny stood still to hear the conversation.

"Hell, no. He makes these runs to keep his hand in, but he doesn't have to drive for Tulsa Trucking."

"Why not?" Mom Bradley said, leaning slightly toward the man.

"He *owns* Tulsa Trucking Company."

"Well, I'll be damned," Mom Bradley said with a laugh. "He's been coming in here for eight months now, and this is the first I heard he owned the company." She turned to Jenny. "Did you know that?"

Jenny could hardly force her reply past the lump in her throat. "No, I didn't know." She shook her head and went toward the rest room. She entered the toilet booth and leaned against the wall, determined not to cry. He *owns* the company. What an idiot he must think I am, with my clumsy efforts at mining and my complaints because Mike doesn't appreciate me. And I bragged to Karen that he was an honest man. The gifts he gave me meant nothing at all. He probably gives gifts all over three states. He can afford to waste his money. Maybe he considered it charity—or maybe he expected me to pay him back some other way. She thought of his kiss, and a hot anger rose up in Jenny. She no longer felt like crying. She left the booth and washed her face, glancing in the mirror as she reached for a towel. Her face looked as rough and gray as a cement sidewalk. She rubbed her hands on her cheeks and bit her lips.

When she came out the other Tulsa driver was still chatting with

Mom Bradley. Jenny hurried into the kitchen and got her purse. She counted out all the money she had, about twenty-five dollars. She'd meant to look for a coat for Corey, but this was payday. She'd take the coat money out of her check. She hurried out to the counter again. "Do you have an envelope?" she asked Mom Bradley.

"There's a couple of dog-eared ones under the counter."

Jenny put the money in one of the envelopes. She tore a page from her order pad and wrote, "This is to repay you for the GED materials. Thank you very much. Jennifer N. Williams."

She put the note in the envelope, too, and as she raised it to lick the seal, she found Mom Bradley looking at her. The other driver was turning away, but Jenny said, "Jake?" and he looked back.

"Would you please give this to Mr. Garvey when you see him?"

"Sure, be glad to." He put the envelope in his shirt pocket and went out the door.

"Why did you do that, Jenny?" Mom Bradley said. "He doesn't need your money."

"That's why," Jenny said. "I don't need his charity."

Mom Bradley gave a loud, cross-sounding sigh. "Jenny, your pride is going to cause you a lot of heartache sooner or later. Couldn't you just keep that stuff as a gift and not let it upset you so much?"

"No." Jenny tried to keep the hurt out of her voice, but it was still too strong. "It didn't mean anything to him. Getting my diploma is one of the most important things in my life, and it didn't mean anything to him at all."

"You don't know that, Jenny. He always seemed to be interested in you."

"Why me?" Jenny said. "He's got a whole company to run."

Mom Bradley put her hand on Jenny's shoulder. "Jenny, I want you to get your diploma, too, but an education isn't everything. I worked my tail off to send Richard to the university, and what did his education do for him? You're an intelligent, loyal, hardworking, good-looking woman. Richard says you're smart enough to go to college, but don't sell yourself short because you don't have a formal education."

Jenny reached up and put her hand on Mom Bradley's hand. She swallowed and said, "Ever since I took Karen away from Tully's place, I've tried to stand on my own two feet and take care of me and my kids. But there's no way to really stop depending on other people if I can't get a good job, and I can't ever get a good job if I don't have a diploma." She swallowed again to keep the tears back.

A group of people came up to the register. Mom Bradley squeezed Jenny's shoulder and turned toward them. Jenny went to clear their tables.

Friday night business was brisk as always, but time seemed to drag by. Jenny felt as if she were wading through deep mud. She forced herself to smile at a customer only to find her mouth tight and dry when she got back to the kitchen. During her break she sat on Richard's stool in the kitchen and forced herself to read the history section in the GED workbook. Gradually she became absorbed in the information. Parts of it dealt with the beginnings of mining in the West.

A little thrill of excitement lightened her mood somewhat. Tomorrow she and Mike would muck out that beautiful ore. The ore meant money, but it now had a lure for Jenny that had nothing to do with paying the bills and sending the children to school. Even if we really hit it big, she thought, I wouldn't want to leave the mine. She pictured the tunnel and the mist that danced in the light from her headlamp when she drilled. Her nose prickled when she thought of the smell of the drill oil.

She rose and put her plate on the dishwasher tray, feeling slightly less miserable. She was able to joke with her customers again, and by closing time she had earned some of Corey's coat money back in tips. When she left the café at two o'clock it was snowing hard.

CHAPTER

42

▲▲▲▲▲▲

A mean wind knifed along Simpson Gulch, cutting through their coats and gloves when they were outside the tunnel. It was impossible to sort the ore.

"I was going to hand pick it and high-grade it a little," Mike said at lunch, "but if I don't get it into the bin, we're liable to lose more than we'd save by sorting it." He drained his coffee cup and stood up.

"Can we finish pretty soon?" Jenny asked. "I'd better leave early in this weather."

"We can try; a couple more carfuls should do it."

But the ore in the tunnel was not quite shoveled out by the time they quit. As Jenny was dressing for work, Mike brought a wagon-load of lumber into the cabin. Billy danced around the floor.

"I get to help with Daddy's secret," he said to Jenny.

Jenny looked at Mike. He shrugged and said, "It's too cold to take the kids to the shop, and it's too early for us all to go to bed, and I'm tired of reading those two story books, so I've decided to build some stuff we need." He set the wagon out of the way. "When the kids are asleep, I'll muck out the rest of the ore."

"No, Mike," Jenny said. "We agreed that it's too dangerous when you're up here alone. I'll help in the morning, and you can still take most of Sunday off."

▽ ▽

They had pancakes and syrup and cocoa for Sunday breakfast. "Daddy and me are building chairs," Billy said. "I'm the sandpaperer. I'm going to make my chair as smooth as your rocking chair."

Jenny smiled at her son and glanced at the rocking chair. She ought to give it back to David, but how would she explain to Mike? Besides, she didn't think she could part with it. The chair was the only pretty thing she owned.

"I want a blue glass vase," she said out loud, leaning down to buckle her overshoes around the tin pants.

Mike was bending over to lace his work boots. He looked up, caught her eyes, and frowned slightly. "Billy and me thought you'd want kitchen chairs."

"Oh, I do. I do want chairs." Jenny picked Billy up and hugged him, but he wriggled in her arms and scrambled down after her kiss.

"We're going to harness Rosie."

"Can Corey and I come watch?" Jenny asked, looking at the baby traveling around on Billy's bed.

"Sure," Mike said. "Wrap her up; she can come out for a while."

When Mike brought Rosie onto the dump in harness, Jenny said, "I'll finish mucking the ore, Mike."

"You don't mind?"

"No. I'd like to."

"Okay, if that's what you want. Shall I start the generator?"

"No, save the gas. I can use my headlamp."

"Take the other flashlight for backup."

"Do you want to talk to me while I shovel, Billy?"

Billy looked at Mike and then at Jenny. "I'm going to help Daddy work on my new chair."

▽　▽

It didn't take long to muck the ore. After she had scraped the last bit of sparkling rock from the muck plate and dumped it into the car, she walked forward to the breast. As she studied the vein, she began to feel excited about the next round of drilling. The first pay dirt was in the bin: they were really mining now.

Jenny put the shovel on top of the ore and went to Rosie. "Come on, you patient little beastie; let's go dump our dirt."

Just as she reached for Rosie's rope she heard a few grains of rock slide down the rib of the tunnel. She stopped as the rock sounds increased to the rushing of a real slide. From somewhere between her and the mouth of the tunnel came a haze of dust that captured the beam from her headlamp and blurred and diminished the light. Rosie stamped her front foot and snorted, flinging her head in an arc and canting her ears toward Jenny.

Jenny rubbed the hard hump between the burro's ears and murmured, "There, there, there, there."

When the sound of the sliding rock finally stopped, Jenny's first thought was, Thank God Billy didn't come into the tunnel.

Jenny let go of Rosie's reins and walked carefully forward, using both headlamp and flashlight. The fall wasn't bad. One or two large chunks and a cascade of yellow-gray clay had partially blocked the rails.

As she brought Rosie and the car forward and picked up the mucking shovel, her hands were trembling. She sat down on the ground at the side of the car and rested.

I've been damn careless. She could hear Tony saying, "There are a thousand ways the mountain can kill you. You have to respect it; you have to keep your eyes and ears open."

And your mind, thought Jenny. I should never have brought the children into the tunnel, even to cut meat, and I never will again. She got up, heaved the larger chunks into the car and then began shoveling the terrible gray clay on top of her precious ore.

It was only after she had the track clear that it occurred to her: A few more feet, and Rosie and I would have been right under that fall.

By the time she got the ore car turned around near the chute and had the chute gate open, Jenny felt older. Mining the Spanish Mary didn't seem nearly as possible as it had before. Her insides still trembled as she unharnessed Rosie, rubbed her down, and put her in the corral. She gave her oats and hay, broke the ice in the water bucket, and went to the cabin.

After she changed from her muddy boots and the tin pants, she went to where Mike was sanding a chair leg. She bent and kissed him on the cheek.

He raised his head, a startled look jumping across his eyes. But all he said was, "It's about time you finished mucking that little old pile of ore. I'm ready to head for town."

Jenny got his money from her purse and put it on the table without comment. The bottom half of a chair, a big wide-bottomed stool with stubby rounded legs, had taken the place of her milk crate at the table.

"This is going to be a nice chair," she said, with some surprise.

Mike said, "It will have a back on it in a couple of days."

"Try it, Mama." Billy jumped up and down. "Try it."

Jenny sat down on the smooth surface of the sanded plank seat. "This chair is just right," she said, smiling at Billy. "I'll have to buy us another book. You've never heard about Goldilocks and the three bears." To Mike she said, "I had that book when I was a little girl. I wonder who has it now."

He scowled. "Goddamn county. They didn't need to snatch everything you owned." He rose from the table and put his tools and the partly finished leg in a milk crate behind the stove. "I'll get some dinner in town," he said.

"Why don't you take us all to dinner and a movie," Jenny suggested. She bit her lip as Mike's face tightened.

"Jesus, Jenny. Don't you think I've done my fair share of baby-sitting this week?"

Jenny turned away to hide the sudden tears in her eyes. "You do take good care of the kids," she said.

"Then why do you have to pick a fight every time I leave for town on Sunday?"

There were a lot of reasons, and they boiled up in Jenny with a sour taste, but she didn't say anything except, "I'm sorry. I don't want to fight."

Mike slipped on his coat, and scooping the money from the table, he stuffed it into his pocket. He tousled Billy's hair and said to Jenny, "Maybe you'd better keep the door locked now when I'm not here. That damn Lacey's got strangers roaming all over these hills."

After Mike was gone, Jenny fed the children, dressed them warmly, and took them for a ride along Simpson Gulch on Rosie. Rosie's feet clattered on the ice-covered bridge. Jenny looked down at the burro's hooves. The pine tar treatment had helped to heal Rosie's feet, but Tony said she would need shoes if they planned to ride her around the rocky slopes near the mine next summer. Will we be here next summer? she wondered.

The children were tired after the ride in the cold air. By eight o'clock, they were both sound asleep.

Jennny went out to the corral to break the ice in Rosie's water bucket again. The sky had cleared and drawn high into blackness. The stars were no more than silver-headed tacks. She locked the shop door and went back to the cabin, shivering.

She tried to wash the dishes slowly, to fill time with the task, but her efficient hands went ahead at their own pace. When the dishes were on the shelf, the stove polished, and the fire stoked, Jenny took the journal from behind the other books and sat down at the table.

> *November 4.* The first ore is in the bin. Mike says
> maybe four tons. He doesn't know about the junk rock
> and clay I mixed with it.

Thinking of the rockfall, she stood and took down the mining book. After she had read about loose rock, she made a list of all the mining terms she recognized in the glossary. Then she wrote the heading for a new list: "Things to Buy When We Sell the Gold":

> Corey—a teddy bear, a ruffled dress, a high chair,
> books
> Billy—books, cars and trucks, a sled
> Mike—

She stopped and thought for a moment and then wrote, "a portable radio."

> Jenny—skirt and sweater, high-heeled shoes, paper,
> pencils, books, a box with a lid to put things in
> Rosie—a bushel of apples

She reread the list. Then she crossed out the title and wrote under it, "Christmas Presents." She looked at the items on the list. *I can't save enough money to buy all that.* She circled *teddy bear* after Corey's name. For Billy, she hesitated between the sled and the books and finally circled *sled.* Mike would enjoy the radio at night. *If only she could find one that didn't cost too much.* She studied the items by her own name for a long time. Finally, she crossed out everything but *books* and *a box with a lid.*

▽ ▽

Monday morning at breakfast Jenny said to Mike, "We need a plan."

Mike buttered a piece of bread and put it on Billy's plate. "A plan?"

"Some kind of schedule for working the mine, so that one of us is always with the children when they're awake. I don't think Billy ought to go into the tunnel anymore."

"Well, you're the goddamn driller. It's up to you."

Jenny glanced at him. If he was still angry about the drilling, it would be hard to discuss the mine. She changed the subject. "What do we have to do at the mill?"

"They'll assign us an ore bin," Mike said, "and assay our stuff periodically. We weigh in each time we haul a load down. When we get twenty-five tons, they'll process."

"When do they pay us?"

Mike snorted. "After all the processing is finished, and they've got their forty percent."

"Forty percent!"

"Be glad it's not more. The last mill that agreed to take small loads charged up-front money just to dump into the bin."

Jenny got up and put a pan full of water on the stove. She took Corey on her lap and fed her a soft egg.

Mike said, "So how is this plan of yours supposed to work?"

"Well, today we should get the ties and rail down, put the muck plates back, and set up the column post."

"But you won't have time to drill today," Mike said. His voice was cold again. Wasn't he ever going to forgive her for drilling when he was afraid to? But maybe it wasn't that. He'd been acting strange ever since he'd come home from town the night before.

"No, I can't drill today," Jenny said, "and unless I get faster, it will take me two days when I do get started. Changing the steel still takes me forever."

"Well, that's Tuesday and Wednesday," Mike said.

"On Thursday, I'll load and shoot the overhang."

"We won't be able to muck out until Saturday."

"I know it, but I can do the laundry and grocery shopping on Friday." Corey grabbed at the spoon. She'd eaten most of the egg. Jenny let her keep the spoon as she set her in the crib.

"So we muck out on Saturday," Mike said.

"And I shoot the ore on Sunday."

Mike's face darkened again. "I don't want to hang around here all day Sunday."

"It won't take me all day to load and shoot," Jenny said. "Besides, I'd like for Tony to be around on the days when I drill and shoot. Maybe he'd watch the kids."

Jenny ran her fingers through the dishwater. It was nearly warm enough. Mike got up and poured himself the last of the coffee.

"You're leaving something out of that fancy schedule."

"What's that?"

"Ore hauling. I can't haul more than a ton at a time in the pickup, if that much. I'll have to start getting that rock to the mill if we're ever going to have a payday."

Jenny wondered what he called the Fridays when she brought her money home. She picked up her empty cup and held it out. "Give me a swallow of that coffee." Mike poured part of his coffee into her cup. "How long will it take you to get the ore into Mitchell and get back here?"

"Oh, six or seven hours, if there's no holdup at the scales."

"Do you think you could go in and back before I leave for work?"

"I guess. If I pushed it."

Jenny passed her hand across her face. "I hope there's some time left for sleep in this schedule."

"Well, hell, didn't you think of that when you decided to become the powerhouse of this family?"

Jenny said, "That's dirty, Mike. I didn't have much choice, and I'm doing the best I can."

CHAPTER

43

▲▲▲▲▲▲

Mike stood up. "I'll get the generator started." He looked at Billy, who had finished his bread. "Coming, Bill?"

"Sure," Billy said. "Can I take Rosie an apple, Mama?"

"Yes. Rosie works hard. She deserves an apple."

Mike and Billy went out. Corey gabbled a few words, a couple of which sounded like *Mama* and *Dada*. Jenny poked her nose under the curve of the baby's cheek and said, "Nummy, nummy, nummy." Corey giggled.

"You sound like the teakettle when it starts to boil," Jenny said, dressing Corey in pants and a long-sleeved pullover. She set the baby on the floor. Corey headed for Billy's bed on all fours. She picked up his little truck. Jenny said, "Maybe I'd better buy you a truck instead of a teddy bear."

▽ ▽

Jenny took care of the children while Mike moved the muck plates, dug out the floor for new ties, and laid the joint rail. When Billy and Corey were both down for their naps and sound asleep, Jenny went into the tunnel.

"You want me to do the column post and the drill?" she asked.

"No," Mike said, and she could see the muscle jumping in his clenched jaw. "I'll set 'em up. How high you want that drill?"

"Up by the arch. I'll start with the crown hole again."

"You better bring back some extra gas for the compressor tonight."

"I'll have to leave early then. There's nothing open at two in the morning."

Mike reached out and put his hand on Jenny's breast. "You come straight home at two o'clock," he said, squeezing her nipple between two fingers. "I don't want you messing around town." He squeezed a little harder.

"I have to go back to the kids," Jenny said, starting to back away.

Mike put an arm around her shoulders and pulled her close. He ran his hand down between her legs. His fingers rubbed against her hard. Jenny struggled in his grasp, but Mike tightened his hold and raised his hand to unzip her jeans. His hand slipped inside her panties.

"The kids," Jenny said, trying to push herself away from him.

"They're asleep, aren't they?"

"They were."

"Well, this won't take long." He pulled her toward him again and pushed her jeans and panties down around her legs. He opened his own pants and pushed Jenny up against the side wall of the tunnel. "I've got some drilling of my own to do," he said in a rough voice as he pushed himself up inside of her. "You may act like it most of the time, but you're not the man in this family."

Jenny felt him swell inside of her as he backed her against the rough damp wall and thrust himself upward, fast and hard, over and over, until she could feel the bruising in her buttocks from the rocks.

"Stop, Mike, you're hurting me."

But if he heard her at all, he couldn't have stopped, because at that moment he came inside of her with a hot final thrust; a moan that was almost a snarl came through his gritted teeth. He stepped back from her and said, "There, goddamn it. Now you know there's a man up here in this tunnel, and those bastards down at Mom's don't need to get any ideas."

Jenny brushed the moist earth from her bottom, pulled up her panties and then her jeans, and ran from the tunnel.

The children still slept. As Jenny washed herself, her anger stuck like a hot stone in her windpipe. She dressed, grabbed her coat, and left the cabin. Jamming her fists into her pockets, she stalked along the fence line. The sonofabitch. She gulped the cold air and said it aloud, "The sonofabitch." She gritted her teeth. He's no better than Tully Stocker. She made the circle again. He may be my husband, but that doesn't give him the right.

She came up by the woodpile on the northwest side of the cabin. A log stood near the edge of the pile, a wedge half buried in it. Jenny picked up the ax and whammed the wedge with the blunt side of it. A piece split from the log. She kicked it aside and picked up the wedge. Ramming it into the log, she thought, he's not going to do that to me again. She raised the ax and brought it down full force onto the wedge; the log began to split, and she raised the ax once more. I may have to stay here, and I am damn well going to get my share of the ore, but—she brought the ax down fiercely— he's not going to take out his anger on me. The log split. Jenny picked up the pieces and threw them in the wagon. She rolled another chunk of log from the pile and hammered the wedge into it. She swung the ax in a wide arc and hit the wedge. My body belongs to me. The log split and the wedge fell against a rock, the steel ringing in the cold air. But how can he be so good with the kids one minute and then do that to me?

Jenny retrieved the wedge and stuck it into another section of log. She split the log and tossed the chunks in the wagon. I wonder what they do to him at those poker games. She set the edge of the ax into another log and looked around. She rubbed her bruised bottom.

Suddenly she was very tired. It's all so confusing and dirty. God, what is sex supposed to be for? It can't be right the way we're using it. She leaned against the rough log wall. I grab sex with Mike because I want David, and Mike slams me into a rock wall to prove he's a man. Jenny rubbed her hand across her forehead, feeling slightly nauseated. We're acting like trash. I'm glad Billy and Corey don't have to know.

Cold and empty, Jenny gathered up an armload of firewood and went into the cabin. When Mike came in a little later, he avoided her eyes as he washed his hands and face at the washstand. Jenny set the table quietly.

Before she left for work, Jenny said, "Will you please put the gas cans in the truck for me, Mike?" in as pleasant a voice as she could force past the lump that had stayed in her throat all afternoon.

Mike glanced at her, the first time he'd looked at her since she'd left the tunnel. "Sure," he said and went outside. Jenny kissed the children and put on her coat. When Mike came back into the cabin, she took a deep breath and said, "Mike, would you hug me before I leave?" Her heart hammered in her chest during the long moment before her husband stepped forward and put his arms around her. He leaned his cheek against the top of her head for a moment, and then he said, "What do you want for Christmas, Jenny?"

Startled, Jenny looked up into Mike's red face. He was trying to say he was sorry. She smiled, though she was close to tears. "I want a box with a lid on it," she said.

$$\triangledown \quad \triangledown$$

It was snowing again as Jenny wound around the curves on Simpson Road and headed for Dolby, grateful for the short time alone. I hope Mom Bradley's in a good mood and Richard is sober. All I want is a peaceful night filled with hard work.

The café was almost full. For the next three and a half hours Jenny was constantly on the move. Then suddenly the café was empty again. Mom Bradley came out to the bar, wiping her hands on her cook's apron. She glanced at the clock. "Whatever they're going to must start at nine o'clock."

Jenny said, "They were mostly strangers to me, but they were certainly good tippers." Unloading her uniform pocket, she dumped several handfuls of coins and bills into her purse. "Do you have one steak left back there? I'm starving."

"Sit down and rest, Jenny. Richard just ordered a T-bone. I'll put one on the grill for you."

Jenny dropped down on the cracked blue vinyl seat. Richard came from the kitchen, bringing two full setups with steak knives to the table and arranging them. Jenny glanced up. "Thanks."

Richard sat down. "Running up and down the canyon between here and the mine must keep you busy. Are you getting any time to read?"

Jenny shook her head. "I don't read as much as I used to, but I think more. My own life's as interesting as any book I ever read."

Richard said, "I can see it, Jenny. When you talk to Tony about the drilling, you glow like a woman in love." He grinned at her. "Is it Tony?"

Jenny laughed, feeling less tired. "He's a darling, for sure. But seriously, Richard, it's the mine—no, it's more than that; it's the mountain. The mine belongs to the mountain, and as Tony says, 'Mother Nature holds her treasures dear.'" Jenny nodded her head and continued. "You have to be alert in the mine. I've already made some dumb mistakes."

Jenny ran her finger gently along the serrated edge of the steak knife. "I have to learn to see more, to listen more intently, and to think . . ." She hesitated. "To think *broader*. I seem to think only of each little skill I'm learning and not enough about how one thing in the mountain affects everything else."

Mom Bradley came through the door with a plate in each hand. "Watch it," she said, "the plates are hot as hell."

Richard picked up his knife and fork. "I've been considering your GED along the same lines," he said. "Those workbooks are okay if you just want to learn enough to get a diploma, but they don't offer concepts broad enough for a mind as good as yours."

Jenny looked up from her steak in surprise. Maybe Richard was going to keep his promise to stay sober and teach her.

"For instance," Richard continued, "take this math—well, actually, it's just arithmetic. You're good at addition and subtraction and you know your multiplication tables, but do you understand our number system—the concept of the decimal system?"

"You mean ones, tens, and hundreds. We did those groupings in grade school."

"Yes, but more than that. Did you know it isn't the only possible system?"

Jenny cut the steak close to the bone. "No, I didn't know that. What other systems are there?"

"Well, there's the binary system, for one. Instead of being based on tens, it's based on twos."

"Is that better?"

"It's better if you're working with a computer. A computer understands power-on and power-off. There's no way to tell it anything else, so you need to translate the decimal system into the binary system before you can program a computer."

The front door opened, and a family came in and sat at a table. Jenny set their places and gave them menus. Her mind busy with the ideas Richard had presented, she served her customers quickly and returned to the front booth.

In every spare minute the rest of the evening Richard worked with Jenny. He started with the first math problem in the workbook and moved forward. As soon as Jenny did the problem and checked it, Richard began to ask her questions about it, difficult questions about the ideas the numbers represented. Sometimes Jenny's mind was totally blank.

"I don't know. I can't begin."

But Richard kept asking questions, and Jenny began to see the outlines of the larger structure behind the figures. By the time a large late bar crowd pushed open the doors and came in from the storm, Jenny felt like she'd been walking in a cold stinging wind herself. Her mind felt blasted clean and rubbed raw.

"I enjoyed that a lot," she said to Richard as she was getting ready to go home. Richard looked up from the tray of dishes he was loading and smiled at Jenny.

"You're a good student," he said, his eyes warm.

"It's not me," Jenny said. "You make those workbooks give up hidden treasure."

CHAPTER

44

▲▲▲▲▲▲

Jenny drove home through the storm, her purse bulging with tips, her mind bulging with ideas. She set the clock and woke Mike early. It was no longer snowing, but the sky was low and heavy.

"Tony's coming up. Can you go to Mitchell with a load in this weather?"

"Yeah, sure. I've got four-wheel drive if I need it, but the load will keep me on the road."

Jenny went with him to the lower end of the bin. Mike backed the pickup under the lip of the loading chute, climbed the ladder on the side of the bin, and took hold of the lever that controlled the ore gate. He let the ore slide into the pickup in small batches, getting down from time to time to check the load on the tires, which Jenny knew were recaps. The truck sat heavily on the tires by the time Mike closed the gate completely. Jenny felt anxious as she saw the tires sag.

"I'll put in a little more air in town," Mike said.

Jenny fixed his breakfast, gave him some of her tips for gas and for lunch, and just before he left, she stood on tiptoe next to the truck cab and kissed him on the cheek. He flushed a little and looked down at her with a crooked grin.

"What was that for?"

"Married people shouldn't have to have a reason," Jenny said, "but call it for luck if you want."

Mike grinned again. "If this ore's good enough, we won't need any luck." He ground the starter and pulled the loaded truck slowly away from the bin, around the bottom of the dump, and across the Simpson Creek bridge. Jenny watched until he was out of sight and then went in and cut up venison and vegetables for stew.

Billy knelt on the big double bed, looking out the window. Corey was trying to pull herself up on Jenny's new chair. Jenny ran her hand around the smooth rungs of the back Mike had added to the chair while she was at work.

"Did you help Daddy with the chair?"

"Yep," said Billy, turning from the window.

"It's a wonderful chair," she said, and Billy's look reminded her of the way Richard had looked when she praised his teaching. Before she had time to wonder if her GED teacher would really show up for the next lesson, her mining teacher drove up on the dump.

Tony and Jenny reviewed what she had learned about drilling. Jenny listened carefully and asked some new questions, trying to see the whole picture: why the holes had to be where they were and what the powder did.

"Why does the dynamite blow backwards?" she asked.

"Backwards?" Tony's brow wrinkled.

"It seems backwards to me to drill a hole in one way and have the rock come back out the same way. The dynamite has so much power. Why doesn't it blow *into* the rock?" The question sounded dumb to her as soon as she asked it, but Tony answered seriously.

"There's no place for the rock to go. Dynamite is loud, Jenny, and it's dangerous if you misuse it, but the power is in the mountain. When the dynamite meets that face rock, it backs up and follows the path of least resistance, taking a few tons of rock with it, but that's all."

Tony rose from the table. "Men have been trying to blow these mountains to pieces for nearly a hundred and forty years, and now the miners are mostly gone, but the mountains are still here. Every foot of tunnel was hard fought for." He grinned suddenly and said, "I'd better quit preachin' and go get that compressor started. Did you get the column post set up?"

"Mike's got everything ready, even the water tank. He and Rosie dragged it in there last night."

"You be careful. Don't try to do too much," Tony said after he checked out the drill.

"I'm learning to be careful, Tony, but I want to try for nine holes today."

Jenny went into the tunnel at nine o'clock and began to work. She had checked the back and ribs on her way in and noted with surprise, and a rush of affection, that Mike had put a stull across the place on the back where her rockfall had come from. She drilled five holes before she turned the air and water levers off. As the grit settled slowly toward the muck plates, and the mist cleared, Jenny started out of the tunnel.

Tony met her at the cabin door. "It's about time you quit for a while."

"What time is it?"

"Noon."

Jenny put her gloves in her hard hat and set it upside down like a wobbly kettle. She draped the mucky tin pants over the woodbox, where they warmed slowly, giving off a rich smell of drill oil and minerals.

"I fed the kids," Tony said. "You eat."

Jenny sat down at the table, glad to lean her arms against it, too weary for a moment to pick up the spoon that Tony had stuck into the bowl of venison stew he had set before her. Jenny wrinkled her nose; the steam rising from the stew carried the wild smell of venison. She thought of the T-bone steak she'd had the night before. "I'm not a true mountain woman," she said.

"How come you to say that?" Tony asked, sitting down across from her with his own bowl of stew.

"I can't get used to the taste of wild game."

Tony smiled. "Well, you've got Thanksgiving to look forward to. Mom Bradley's going to cook a big turkey and feed us a real holiday meal. She says she'll open late that day."

"Us? Who's us?"

"She stopped me outside her trailer this morning and said to tell you to bring Mike and the kids. I'm invited, and I suppose Richard will be there."

Jenny turned to Billy. "Isn't that neat? We're going to have a real Thanksgiving." Billy looked up and nodded but went right back to his toy. Jenny watched him a minute; he hadn't ever seen a big turkey dinner.

She took the spoon and ate the stew, then asked for another bowl, feeling guilty as she watched Tony get up from the table, bent from arthritis and breathing roughly.

"I should be waiting on you," she said.

"You've been working," he said.

Jenny smiled. "How do you know?" she said. "Maybe I slept the morning away in that cozy tunnel."

"That compressor tells me when you're working," Tony said. "While the little miss napped, Billy and I puttered around in the shop. You were drilling pretty steady."

Jenny felt cherished, knowing that he had been checking on her. She smiled at him. "I drilled the crown, the arches, a rib, and a breast hole, and I'm going back for the other four right now."

She got up from the table surprisingly refreshed and went back to the tunnel. When she finished the other holes and broke her concentration, it was like coming back from a long narrow journey into her mind. She blinked and looked around; then she ran her headlamp over the face. Nine new holes marked the rock, nine round dark holes. She grinned and said out loud, "Nine holes."

By the time Jenny was washed and dressed in clean jeans and a shirt, ready to head for Mom's, Mike's truck had rumbled over the bridge.

Tony and Mike came in together. Jenny poured coffee for the men, and Mike reported on his trip to Mitchell.

"Damn slow ride," he said. "Thirty miles an hour with that load. Snowed halfway, then cleared, but the road was icier than hell. Cars slid off to both sides." He leaned back, stretching his legs out in front of him.

"Saw one poor bastard clear off the bank. The sheriff stopped us there for about ten minutes. The driver didn't seem to be hurt, but when the wrecker dragged his fancy Saab up from the creek, I thought he was gonna bust out bawling."

Jenny said, "I'm sorry for the man, but I've got to leave for work, and I want to hear about our load. How did it weigh in? How much ore do we have at the mill?"

Mike said, "Hell. I only had three quarter ton on that truck. Those damn tires."

Jenny looked at the clock; she was late. "Are you going to haul ore tomorrow?"

"Yeah," Mike said, adding, "Will you fill up the truck? Loaded like that, it guzzles gas."

▽ ▽

Richard was at Mom's, sober and eager to get back to work on Jenny's studies. Every time business let up he joined her, pushing her through the math problems, questioning, explaining, demanding bigger ideas, better answers.

The familiar drive home through the snow was a relief. Her stomach, which had tightened with excitement and fear each time Richard had challenged her, slowly unknotted itself. Everyone was asleep. The lantern, turned low, made a small circle of light on the kitchen table. Tired as she was, Jenny took the journal from behind the other books. They needed to keep a record of the ore hauling, and she had decided to keep track of her drilling schedule, her studies, and her Christmas fund too.

> *November 6.* Mike hauled three quarter ton to our bin
> in Mitchell. I drilled the upper nine. Richard brought
> in some harder math books. $16.95 in the Christmas
> Fund.

She put the journal away, turned the lantern out, and crawled into bed.

Wednesday night she wrote:

> *November 7.* Another three quarter ton to Mitchell.
> The round is drilled, I shoot the overhang tomorrow.
> Richard wants me to figure out problems *before* he ex-

plains them. $26.50 in tips, but Mike needs $15 for gas again . . . only $11.50 to the CF.

Thursday morning after Mike left, Jenny spent as much time as she could with the children. She had brought some paper napkins from the café and she showed Billy how to cut out snowflakes. She hung his paper designs in the window from short pieces of thread. She played patty-cake and peekaboo with Corey. The games and laughter with the children relaxed her. She kept her mind away from the box of dynamite Mike had set on the shop bench.

"I want to do it all myself," she told Tony when he came into the cabin.

"Mike and I took the equipment down yesterday, and I blew out the holes," Tony said.

"Mike told me. I appreciate it, but should you be doing that?" She looked closely at the old miner. "I don't want you to get sick because of the Spanish Mary."

"Oh, that little bit of dirt isn't going to hurt me," he said, and changed the subject. "You go ahead and get them holes loaded, but I don't want you lighting the fuses unless I'm in there. We'll wait until nap time."

"Okay, Tony, I'll get everything ready."

She took the fuses, caps, dynamite, and tamping stick into the tunnel, checking the tunnel as she moved toward the breast. Nothing that could be damaged had been left behind, and the track and ties were clear for a quick, safe retreat.

She began to load the dynamite into the holes in the overhang. When she was finished, she cut the fuses; then she went back to the cabin for Tony.

Tony seemed a little stiff and slow as they walked into the tunnel, and Jenny worried suddenly about his ability to get out in time. When they stood in front of the breast and the nine holes with their black whiskers, Tony glanced at her face and said quietly, "Don't worry. I wouldn't go in if I weren't sure I could get out."

Jenny nodded at him and began to gather the fuses.

$\triangledown$ $\triangledown$

On Friday Mike and Jenny and the children went to Dolby. Jenny did the laundry, shopped for groceries, and had her hair done. She joined Mike and the children for a late lunch at Mom's. She paid for the lunch out of her Christmas fund, vowing to put the money back that night.

Mike said, "Why don't you drive us home, Jen? I'm tired of pushing this rig."

Jenny thought the beer on his breath and the state trooper's car in the parking lot probably had more to do with it, but she climbed up behind the wheel without comment.

After they unloaded the groceries and put Corey down for a late nap, Jenny convinced Billy that he should play quietly on his bed even if he was still too excited to sleep. Mike and Jenny sat down at the table.

"You look real pretty," Mike said. "Maybe I'll wait up for you tonight." He looked away from her face, though, and she knew that he was thinking about Monday. Jenny felt the heat rise in her face as she remembered Mike's actions in the tunnel, then she looked down at her nails as she also remembered the way David had pulled her across the seat of his truck.

She had tried not to think any more about Bigfoot, but despite her anger about his kiss, despite his dishonesty—she still felt it had been dishonest of him to let her think he was just a poor relief driver, to let her feel too special because of the rocking chair and the books— it was hard not to remember certain things. It seemed as if she had stored them in a separate section of her mind, and if she stepped inside there, she saw all the lovely souvenirs and could not help picking them up, one by one: his arms around her on that rocky slope the day Corey was born; their laughter in his big truck as she dangled her feet and fought the contractions with jokes; their few brief conversations. And his eyes, always his eyes. She refused to think of his kiss. It wasn't a lovely souvenir. It was a trouble in her mind.

"Jenny." Mike's voice made her start. She looked up. Mike was staring at her. She could see his Adam's apple move as he swallowed. His face turned red, and then he said, "Jenny, I'm sorry."

Jenny's eyes swam with tears. She reached out both hands, and Mike took them. She couldn't speak. She felt completely shamed by his apology, built and delivered with such pain while she was being unfaithful to him in her mind. She pulled one hand away to wipe her eyes.

Then she said, "Thank you, Mike. I would like for you to wait up for me." She rose, and as Mike pulled her close to him and put his face against her hair, she reached back into her mind and closed the door again on Bigfoot.

CHAPTER
45

▲▲▲▲▲▲▲

Saturday they mucked the overhang together, checking the children each time they dumped the ore car and planning the schedule for the next week as they shoveled. Sunday Mike took his spending money and went to town while Tony and Jenny shot the ore. Mike was home before midnight, and when they were in bed in the dark warm cabin, Mike took Jenny in his arms and kissed her. They made love, each gentle and careful.

After that the days developed a rhythm of their own, and Jenny's journal marked the mining, the hauling, the tips, and the growing Christmas fund.

When Mike wasn't in the cabin, Tony was. The children thrived on the attention. Jenny took joy in their constant laughter. Billy was learning numbers and letters and words. He could write his whole name now. When Jenny put beans on the table and let him count them, he wrote the numbers and then the simple addition problems that Jenny gave him.

One crisp sunny day Mike took Billy rabbit hunting and then fixed a fried rabbit dinner. It was a welcome change from the venison, which was dwindling, as the meat in the cold box behind the cabin grew drier and harder each day.

Mike went into town on Sundays and came home with beer on his breath and sometimes strangely agitated and eager for sex. He never forced Jenny, though, and she began to wait up for him on Sunday nights so that he would feel welcome.

Jenny studied the math problems Richard gave her. Mike didn't mind it when she brought the GED workbooks home. He even offered a tiny bit of praise: "You sure do keep at that stuff."

And Richard stayed sober to teach her. Night after night he spent the slack times in the café shaking her mind.

"I sometimes feel as though my mind is like that glass tube that makes different pictures every time you turn it," she said one evening. "I looked into one at the dime store."

The next day Richard brought her one of the tubes, but he wouldn't let her look into it until she could spell *kaleidoscope*.

Richard had made a schedule for her, too: math until Thanksgiving, science and social studies until Christmas, and English every day—grammar, spelling, reading, and reading again.

"What does it say? What does it mean? Does it always mean that?"

Jenny sometimes felt a rise of anger when Richard pushed too hard and urged her to do more difficult reading, think more complicated thoughts. She took refuge in the factual mining book and an old geology text he'd picked up somewhere. At last she was learning how her mountain began, how her ore got there, why the overhang was colored where the layers of earth changed content, what had tilted the layers upward. The more she read about the mountain, the happier she felt in the tunnel. And by November 17 there were six tons of ore in the bin at Mitchell.

Jenny stuck to both schedules. On the way to work her ears rang from the drilling in the Spanish Mary; on her way home her mind rang from the drilling Richard gave her in arithmetic, basic algebra, and beginning geometry.

▽ ▽

On Thanksgiving morning Jenny was as excited as Billy. "I'm so glad for a few hours off," she said as Mike started the truck down the Simpson Gulch road.

"I'm looking forward to the turkey and dressing," he said. He was silent for a moment; then he asked, "Did Mom tell you that her boyfriend's wife died?"

"No," Jenny said, "but she never tells me anything about Ed O'Brien. Everything I know I hear from Richard's bitter tongue. Who told you?"

"One of the fellows in the game Sunday night. Works with Ed."

The rich smell of roasting turkey greeted them as they entered the café. Mom Bradley had pushed several tables together, covered them with a long linen cloth, and set them ahead of time with cloth napkins and the best of the café's tableware.

When Jenny offered to help, Mom said, "Nossir. You sit down and have a glass of cranberry-juice cocktail. This is a holiday, and you're my guest." She looked around as the door opened, and Tony came in. "Speaking of guests," she said, including Tony in her smile, "I've invited Ed O'Brien to eat with us today." Mike and Jenny exchanged glances. Jenny wondered if Richard knew.

Mom's friend arrived just after Mom Bradley had set the huge golden-brown bird on the table. It was surrounded by various dishes: cranberry relish in one, buttered asparagus tips in another, pickles, jam, potatoes, yams, olives, hot rolls, gravy. Mom Bradley introduced Ed O'Brien around the table, and he smiled and nodded his head but said very little.

Richard's Cadillac slid up to the front of the café. When Richard saw Ed, he scowled and took his place at the table in silence, greeting no one.

"Did your mother ever cook like this?" Jenny asked Mike.

"No, she wasn't interested in cooking," Mike said, "but my grandma always cooked a big Thanksgiving dinner."

"Do I have a grandma?" Billy asked.

"I guess you do, son," Mike said. "Somewhere."

Jenny put a little taste of everything on Corey's plate. Corey picked her food up with her fingers and tasted it, spitting the yams out immediately but sucking on her fingers after she tried the pickle.

When Mom offered to cut more turkey after they'd already finished second helpings, they refused, but they said yes to pie and whipped cream. Except for Richard. As soon as he cleaned his plate of turkey and gravy, he cast one more black look at Ed O'Brien, pushed his chair back, and rose abruptly. Before anyone could speak, he had slammed out of the café. The Cadillac rocked as he spun it around and took off up the highway without stopping to check for traffic.

Richard's departure broke the pleasant mood that had grown around the table. Ed O'Brien was obviously embarrassed; Mom Bradley was just as obviously angry. Jenny said quietly to Mike, "You might as well plan on my being late tonight. He won't be back to wash dishes."

▽   ▽

Tony took Mike and the children back up toward Dolby and the mine; Jenny changed into her uniform and helped Mom Bradley clean up and get ready to open the café. Ed O'Brien had followed Mike and Tony out the door.

"Damn that son of mine," Mom Bradley said. "I'm sorry if he ruined your day."

"Nobody could ruin a dinner like that," Jenny said, but as the evening wore on and the café filled and the dishes piled up, Jenny thought she might scream at Richard herself the next time she saw him. She didn't leave for home until after three. According to the mining schedule she should muck the ore on Friday, but Mike let her sleep in and worked in the tunnel himself.

When Richard didn't show up on Friday Mom Bradley was angrier than ever. Jenny was exhausted from the double work load. She didn't have time to study, and her legs ached at work and cramped in bed after she got home.

Saturday Mom Bradley called the state patrol, but Richard's name wasn't on any accident reports. Saturday night was slow. Jenny caught up on all the dishes and then took her books from behind the bar. But studying without Richard there was dull. Jenny read the simple paragraphs on science in the workbook and wished Richard could explain the broader picture and push at the edges of her mind.

Mom Bradley was silent and worried. When Ed O'Brien came in she turned to Jenny. "Can you close up?" she asked.

Jenny nodded, but it made her nervous to see them drive away. Though the late bar crowd was small, one of them was Tully Stocker. He harassed her as usual, and Jenny began to worry that she'd end up alone with him. When the young men who had been her first trial in the bar came in, she was relieved. They were always friendly now. Jenny said quietly to them, "Will you stick around until Tully leaves?"

They glanced around the bar and nodded. When Tully finally got up to go, it was almost two o'clock. The young men followed him outside and stood in front of the café until Tully's truck went down the dump road. They turned and gave Jenny an all-clear sign and she waved her thanks, but she locked the door ten minutes early.

How does Mom Bradley stand it? she thought as she cleaned the last of the bar glasses and put the day's receipts into the safe. If Billy were missing, I don't know what I'd do. She drove home feeling grim, wondering what could have happened to Richard.

But they stayed on schedule at the Spanish Mary. Mike took a load of ore to Mitchell on Sunday and a second load on Monday, while Tony played games with the children and Jenny drilled another round.

CHAPTER

46

▲▲▲▲▲▲

Monday evening the Cadillac was in the parking lot sporting a newly crumpled fender; Richard was in the kitchen, gaunt but sober; and Mom Bradley bustled cheerfully in and out through the swinging doors.

A generous crowd arrived for dinner, and Jenny soon put a handful of coins and bills into the Christmas jar. When business slowed, Richard helped Jenny study basic science: why things work the way they do.

"It's pretty boring," Richard said, "but you need to know it."

"I don't think it's boring; what I think is boring are those literary people who spend their time talking about mood and meanings."

"Ah, Jenny, I despair of making an intellectual out of you." Jenny stuck her tongue out at Richard and got up to wait on a customer.

The week whirled by, and on Saturday night Jenny reported to her journal:

> Eleven tons in the bin at Mitchell. $68 in the Christmas jar. I know all about levers and fulcrums. Mike says I should buy books and clothes for Billy. He's building him a sled.

Jenny didn't write down that David Garvey had come in just before closing time on Saturday night but had only stayed long enough to drink the coffee Mom Bradley poured for him while Jenny retreated to the kitchen.

▽　▽

After Mike took the truck money and left for Dolby on Sunday, Billy said, "Are you lonesome, Mama?"

Jenny looked up in surprise. "No, honey, I'm not lonesome. Are you lonesome?"

"I hate the snow," Billy said. "When it comes all around the house, it feels like the tunnel."

Jenny studied her little boy. "I think you've got cabin fever."

"I don't feel sick."

Jenny laughed and said, "Tony told me about two old miners who tried to keep working their mine together one winter, but they couldn't stand being snowed in at their cabin. They got mad and threw potatoes at each other. Tony called their madness 'cabin fever.'"

Billy asked with a giggle, "Are you going to throw potatoes at me?"

"Nope," Jenny said. "I'm going to sing 'Jingle Bells.'"

"Me too," Billy said.

Jenny had been teaching Billy the Christmas songs she could remember. They sang until suppertime.

Jenny went to bed early but woke again at two, just as Mike roared the truck up onto the dump. As he came into the cabin, he stumbled against the washstand. "Sonofabitch," he mumbled. Jenny closed her eyes. When Mike came into bed, he stunk of beer and cigars. Jenny lay still, and he didn't reach for her. He turned on his side, coughed several times, sighed, and began to snore, but his sleep seemed troubled. He muttered and moved about. One time he cried out in a loud voice that woke Corey.

$$\triangledown \quad \triangledown$$

The weather was miserable all week, but the nearness of the holidays seemed to make everyone feel generous. Tips were good. Richard was sober.

Mike was silent and nervous, but he worked in the tunnel Monday and Tuesday and made his runs to Mitchell on Wednesday, Thursday, and Friday.

On Sunday Jenny mucked out the overhang. When she was done, sore and tired from shoveling, she bathed in the dishpan and wrote in her journal:

> Fifteen tons in the Mitchell bin. When we sell the
> gold, I'm going to buy a bathtub.

She shot the ore the next Monday, marveling at how calmly she could light the fuses now. Mike mucked it out on Wednesday and set up the column post again. But right after Jenny started drilling on Friday, the compressor broke down, and Mike didn't get it fixed until late Saturday.

When she got home from work early Sunday morning, Jenny wrote the discouraging entry:

Still only fifteen tons in the bin—ten to go before we
get any money.

But her heart beat a little faster as she wrote the next item:

The GED tests are December 20 and December 21.

▽   ▽

Jenny tried to choose the right moment to tell Mike about the
tests. Worried about his reaction, Jenny waited until just before he
was ready to go to town on Sunday afternoon.

"I have to go to Mitchell Thursday and Friday to take the tests
for my diploma. Richard's coming along to keep me from getting
nervous."

Mike's eyes focused on her briefly. "Oh?" he said. "You'd better
drive the truck then. I don't want you riding with that crazy
drunk." And then he said, "You got any extra money?"

"No," Jenny said, "I'm saving it to get Christmas gifts when I go
to Mitchell."

But Mike persisted. "You've always got a handful of change."

Jenny hesitated. She was trying to keep back enough for her hair
and nails, but she said, "I've got six dollars in my purse."

Mike crammed the six bills into his pocket and went down the
hill, honking at Tony, who was coming up. Jenny drilled nine holes
while Tony helped Billy build a snowman and fed the children their
lunch.

On Monday and Tuesday Mike took ore to Mitchell. "Seventeen
tons," Jenny wrote in her journal.

Richard tutored her for her exams during every spare moment at
the café. She had her nails and hair done on Wednesday with the
tips she earned Tuesday. Her best jeans and the blouse Karen had
given her were clean and ready for Thursday, but her coat looked
terrible. It was the same coat she'd slid down hill in on the day
Corey was born. But it was too cold to go without a coat, so she put
it on over her clothes after she got dressed on Thursday morning.

"Do I look all right?" she asked Mike.

"You look the same as usual," he said. "What's the big deal?"

"The test's a big deal to me."

"Well, it don't depend on looks; it depends on brains. You got brains."

"I'm going to take this old coat off and carry it into the school anyhow."

"Take it easy on the roads."

"Wish me luck, Mike."

"You think that diploma is going to make mining any easier?"

"Oh, Mike."

"All right. I wish you luck. You've worked hard enough to get that goddamn piece of paper. You deserve it."

Jenny kissed the children. "I'll bring you a surprise," she told Billy. Then she put her workbooks and purse into the truck. She stood for a moment by the truck door. "Will you guys be okay?"

"Sure," Mike said. "When it warms up, we'll go get a Christmas tree."

Jenny felt a pang. She didn't want to be left out of the Christmas tree trip. After a short silence she said, "If I have any money left over, I'll buy some decorations."

"Well," Mike said, giving her a boost into the truck, "don't go running off with one of them professors."

Jenny looked down in surprise. Was jealousy making him so nervous and grouchy? "Don't worry," she said. "I have to come home and hang my stocking where Santa can find it."

▽   ▽

She picked up Richard and her Christmas fund at Mom's. The jar had $110 in it. They drove back through Dolby. When they reached the Virgo Creek turnoff, she said, "I hope this truck will stay on the highway. It's used to taking the creek road."

"Except on Sundays," Richard said.

Jenny was too busy looking at the storefronts in the other half of Dolby to respond to that. "I never go to the bank, the lumberyard, the real estate office, or the mortuary," she said as they passed those businesses. "I never come over here for anything. I only go to Safeway, Ben Franklin, and Natalie's Beauty Shop."

"Where do you buy clothes?" Richard asked.

Jenny shrugged. "I can't afford clothes. I get a few for the kids at Ben Franklin."

They were on the outskirts of Dolby now. Plows had cleared the snow, but the sun had not reached the top of the peaks, and there was ice on the curves. Jenny tried to concentrate on her driving.

"It's about six now. We should get to Mitchell on time, shouldn't we?" she asked Richard.

"It's ninety miles," he said. "We ought to be there by eight thirty."

"I want to do some shopping after I take the first tests at the school."

"It's a university."

"I can't think about that; it scares me too much."

The icy highway slowed them down, and they had trouble finding a parking place. It was just nine o'clock when Richard delivered Jenny to the door of the testing room. She was the last one to take her seat and her hands trembled as she opened the test booklet.

▽ ▽

Jenny calmed down as she read the first question. The tests were so easy, she couldn't believe she was doing them right. She checked and rechecked her answers, and she was still the first one to leave the room.

Richard was right outside the door. "How'd it go?"

"I think it went okay. The tests seemed too easy."

Richard gave her a big grin. "You had a good teacher."

They started for the truck. "What do you want to do while I shop?" Jenny asked. "Shall I drop you somewhere?"

"I want to go shopping with you."

Jenny glanced at him. She wasn't sure she wanted him along. His tongue had unexpected barbs, and she wanted to enjoy spending what money she had. Still, she owed him so much.

"All right," she said.

To Jenny's surprise, Richard was a lot of help. He navigated for her and helped find a parking lot within walking distance of a shopping area near the university. Jenny stared at everything: the campus buildings in the distance, the large houses with wide shoveled walks and decorated trees in their windows, the students cramming bulging suitcases into already loaded cars as they got ready for Christmas break.

"Hold it," Richard said, grabbing Jenny's arm as she stepped off a curb.

"Sorry," Jenny said and waited for the light to change.

Richard slipped his arm through hers. "I don't want you to get run over before you get your GED," he said.

They went into a toy store. Jenny picked a fuzzy brown bear for Corey while Richard poked around the shelves.

"Look at this," he said, holding up a miniature stuffed burro.

"Oh, I've got to have that for Billy." The stuffed toys were expensive. She'd have to save money on some of the other gifts. "Do you know where that used book store is?"

"We can find out." Jenny watched as Richard questioned the store manager. He was a constant surprise to her. Away from the café, he seemed poised and sure of himself.

The bookstore was even more fun than the toy store. Jenny bought *Johnny Rides the Big Tractor, Sister Pig's Surprise, Three Nickels for Benjy,* a thick Mother Goose book, and for Corey, a cloth book with bright-colored pictures. She saw a wild animal book she thought Mike might look at and decided to buy it. And then she looked at books for herself and saw dozens she would have liked to read, but ended up not buying a single one. Her money was going too fast.

"I want to find a portable radio for Mike, and there are still the kids' clothes to pay for," she said to Richard.

They looked in several shops, but the children's clothes that would last the winter on the mountain were too expensive. "I hate to buy stuff that pulls apart when Billy climbs over the fence. Even Corey is rough on clothes now that she's crawling."

"Let's get some lunch," Richard said.

"Okay," Jenny said, turning away as tears came into her eyes. "I did want to give the kids some new clothes for Christmas."

They sat down with their trays in McDonald's. "I have an idea about the clothes," Richard said.

"What is it?"

"Wait and see."

Jenny's curiosity hurried her through lunch. On their way out Richard stepped into a telephone booth and looked in the yellow pages. "I thought so," he said. "Never saw a college town without one." He took Jenny's hand and pulled her along the street. She skipped to keep up with him, trying to pull her hand away from his.

"Stop that," he said. "You'll get lost or squashed if I don't hang on to you."

Jenny hurried after him, wondering at this new act. Finally, out of breath, she said, "Richard, slow down and stop dragging me."

He turned and grinned, slowing his step only slightly. "I am excited about introducing you to another of the world's wonders." He stopped abruptly in front of a small shop. The mannikin in the window wore a blue sweater and matching plaid skirt. Richard pulled Jenny into the shop. "You don't mind used books," he said. "How about used clothes?"

Jenny picked up the price tag on a boy's jacket. She looked at another and another and then turned to Richard. "I can hardly believe it."

"I'm surprised your mother didn't at least introduce you to a Goodwill store," Richard said.

Jenny was startled to hear him mention her mother. He had never once spoken of the night she had told him her mother's story. But it must have been only a casual comment; Richard stepped away to speak to the salesclerk. Jenny turned back to the children's racks and started to check hems and elbows and seams. Soon she had a blue down jacket, three longsleeved plaid pullovers, and three pairs of jeans in Billy's size. She chose two pairs of pants, two shirts, and a furry brown coat with a hood for Corey, as well as boots for both children.

Richard returned with the plaid skirt and the sweater from the store window. "Here," he said. "Go try these on."

Jenny turned toward the display. The mannikin was now naked. "Nelly's Nearly New has only one of each item," Richard said. "I hope these fit you."

Jenny looked at the price tag. "I need to get something for Mike, too, but I don't think he'd want to wear used clothes."

"Try these on," Richard said again.

Jenny put the pile of children's clothes into Richard's arms and took the skirt and sweater to the dressing room. The outfit was just the right size. The soft sweater showed the curve of her breasts, but it covered them up as the waitress uniform did not. The color made her eyes seem bluer. She turned from side to side.

"Well?" said Richard from outside the door. Jenny stepped out, and when Richard's eyes widened she could feel herself blushing. Richard was holding a tan coat. "Here, this camel's hair will complete madame's perfect winter wardrobe."

The coat was fine wool; the lining satiny smooth. Jenny tried it on; it fit perfectly. "I do need a coat," she said, looking at the price tag. "Oh, Richard." She turned to him in dismay. "I can't afford this. I only have one hundred ten dollars in my Christmas fund, and I have to buy gifts for Mike, too." She hugged the coat around her and turned to the mirror again. She looked as nice as any of the students she'd seen on the street. Even her waitress shoes didn't look bad with the coat.

Richard reached into his jeans pocket. "Here." He handed her a couple of twenty-dollar bills. "You'll make that much in tips between now and Christmas." Jenny hesitated, glanced toward the mirror one more time, and took the bills.

"I'll start paying you back tonight." Jenny handed her jeans, blouse, and old coat to the clerk. "I'll wear these."

Richard laughed. Jenny waited until the clerk went to wrap the other purchases along with her old clothes and then said, "What's so funny?"

"You are. You sounded positively regal."

"Regal?" Jenny didn't see how the word applied.

"We'd lose sweet Jenny entirely if she got a whole wardrobe."

"I'm too happy to listen to you, you literary critic," she scoffed. Richard laughed again, and Jenny laughed with him.

They went to a department store next and bought jeans and a sweater for Mike, and they found a small battery-powered radio. Jenny bought wrapping paper, a box of Christmas balls, and three boxes of tinsel: then she was broke. It was time to go back to Dolby.

"I've got to get back to Mom's and start earning some money to pay you off," Jenny said as they were heading out of Mitchell.

"Why don't you call the coat a Christmas present?"

Jenny glanced at Richard. "You know I won't."

▽ ▽

Jenny was busy Thursday night. The tip jar began to fill up again. In her spare time she wanted to study, but Richard wouldn't let her. He said she didn't need to; so she wrapped all the Christmas packages except her skirt and sweater and the coat. She decided to stop at Mom's in the morning and change into them again. She could wrap them later to put under the tree.

▽ ▽

On Friday morning Jenny was once again the first one to leave the examination. When she came out of the room Richard said, "You aced that one, too, didn't you?"

"It seemed easy," Jenny said. "Too easy. Maybe I did something wrong. Oh, Richard, do you think we could find out my score?"

Richard turned and went into the testing room. Jenny walked up and down the hall. When Richard came out he said, "She'll do it. They usually send them through the computer, but she said she'd check yours by hand right now, while the others are finishing their tests."

In a few minutes the instructor came to the door. "Are you Jenny Williams?"

Jenny nodded, but her throat seemed too full for speech.

"Congratulations! You gave me a big surprise. No one has ever gotten a hundred percent on any of the tests I've graded before."

Richard grabbed Jenny by the waist and whirled her around. The woman smiled and said, "Of course, the test will have to go through the computer." Jenny nodded again, but she still couldn't speak. "Are you considering applying to the university?" the instructor asked.

Jenny swallowed and said, "I have two small children. I don't know. I don't live in Mitchell."

The woman said, "The university has a few correspondence courses. If you'll give me your address . . ."

"It's on the test," Jenny said. "Care of Mom's Café in Dolby."

"I'll send you a brochure." The teacher turned back to the classroom, where the other people who'd taken the test were rising from their seats.

"This calls for a celebration," Richard said. He took Jenny's hand as they left the building, and they ran laughing down the campus sidewalks and along the street. The cold wind burned Jenny's cheeks; she was grateful for her warm coat and her pretty clothes. People probably think we're students, happy to be free for the holiday. Finally Richard slowed down and turned to smile at her. He squeezed her hand. Jenny smiled back at him. But she stopped and drew her hand away when Richard opened the door of the Dropouts Bar.

"No, Richard."

"Come on, Jenny. Just one drink to celebrate. We've worked damn hard."

Jenny felt her jaw set, but she went into the dark place. They sat on high stools at the mahogany bar. Richard ordered a double Manhattan and Jenny ordered a Coke. When they were served Richard raised his glass to her. "To my prize pupil," he said and downed the drink quickly. He signaled the bartender for another. Jenny drank her Coke quickly, too, and when Richard finished his second drink, she slid down from the stool.

"What's your hurry?" Richard said.

"I promised Mom I'd come in early today."

"Oh, come on. You deserve a little fun."

Richard put his hand on Jenny's arm, but she pulled away saying,

"This is not fun." She turned and walked out of the bar, not expecting Richard to follow, but he caught up with her as she went toward the pickup.

He hunkered down on the far side of the seat, silent while Jenny found her way out to the highway. Halfway to Dolby, he said, "You had fun yesterday, didn't you?"

Jenny thought of their shopping trip and turned to smile at him, "Yesterday was a wonderful day," she said.

Richard sat up and leaned toward her. "Listen, Jenny, we could have lots more wonderful days. Why don't you leave Mike and come live with me in Mitchell?"

Jenny said, "Richard, you're crazy."

"I'm serious," he said. "You could go to school. If I tutor you, you'll get your college degree in no time."

Jenny laughed. "What about my master's and my Ph.D. in geology?"

"Don't laugh at me, Jenny. By God, I mean it. You're wasted on that hill and on that hillbilly. Come live with me."

Jenny said quietly, "I wouldn't do that."

"Why not? You don't love him, and I'm a lot better for you than he is."

Jenny drove carefully around an icy curve before answering. "I want to be honest with you, Richard. I owe you that much. You're right: I'm not always sure how I feel about Mike." Jenny took a deep breath, wishing for words that would sound less cruel, and finding none. "But Richard, I don't love *you*. I'm grateful to you, but I'm not in love with you."

Richard slumped back down in the seat. Jenny turned the radio on and concentrated on the icy highway. What snow the sun had managed to melt during the afternoon was turning to black ice as the short day neared its end.

When they pulled up in front of Mom's Café, Richard sat up and said, "It's that truck driver, isn't it? You're in love with that truck driver."

"Richard, I swear you're drunk on two drinks. Don't ruin our marvelous day. I passed my GED tests. Can't you just be happy for me?"

Richard turned and looked at her, the red of the neon sign gleaming in his eyes. He ignored her words. "And when did you decide you loved him?" Richard said. "Right after you found out he owns the company?"

CHAPTER
47
▲▲▲▲▲▲

On Sunday morning Mike set the Christmas tree in a bucket of mine tailings. Jenny and Billy put the new glass balls on the tree, along with some aluminum-foil decorations Jenny had made.

"Our tree is big—big," Billy said, trying to reach his arms around the broad fir, which touched the ceiling and filled the whole space at the foot of Mike and Jenny's bed. "I choosed it in the woods."

"Chose it," Jenny said. She opened a box of tinsel and handed it to Billy. "Here, honey, hang them on the lower branches one at a time."

Mike sat down at the table. Jenny took Corey on her lap in the rocking chair. "Would you mind if we didn't go to Mom's for Christmas dinner?" she asked.

"I thought you'd want to go," Mike said.

"Mom's invited Ed again, and you know how Richard is."

"Oh, shit. Why'd she do that?"

"She said, 'Ed treats me good, and he's got no place to go.'" Jenny rocked back and forth and then added, "Richard's sure to be drunk."

"If Richard didn't have Ed as an excuse," Mike said, "he'd find another one."

Jenny changed the subject. "Do you think I can cook a turkey in that oven?"

"If we keep it fired up."

"I'll get a small turkey tomorrow, then," Jenny said, "and I'll ask Tony to come for dinner too."

"I'm done with the bottom branches," Billy said. Jenny smiled, looking at the wads of tinsel he had placed on the boughs. "Are you gonna do the top ones, Daddy?"

"No, let your mama do 'em. I'm going to town."

Jenny sighed and rose to put Corey in her crib. The morning had been so pleasant. She went to her purse.

"I need all the extra you can give me," Mike said.

"Are you going Christmas shopping?" she asked, trying to give him a real smile.

"Maybe," Mike said. "By the way," he added, "you stay out of the shop—and keep Billy out, too."

"I don't need anything out of there today. Maybe we should take tomorrow off, too, and not muck the ore. It's Christmas Eve day."

"Jesus, Jenny, we can't go on taking days off and still get that bin filled. If we don't keep at it, we'll never see any cash."

"I just gave you fifty dollars." Jenny immediately wished she could take back the words.

"You always gonna throw that up to me? Every goddamn week?"

"I'm sorry. It's just . . . you make my wages seem so little."

Mike laughed. "Mom Bradley does that, not me. If we're ever gonna get a new stake, it's going to come from me or the Spanish Mary."

Billy said, "When do I get to hang my stocking?"

"Tomorrow night, kid," Mike said.

"But Mama won't be here."

Jenny reached for Billy's hand. "You can hang your stocking just before I go to work."

▽   ▽

Jenny left early on Monday to get the turkey. It bothered her to spend so much of the grocery money for just one day. She hoped her Christmas Eve tips would finish paying Richard back for her coat.

She didn't want to owe him anything. But I'll always owe him for teaching me, she thought. On impulse, Jenny went to Ben Franklin and bought Richard a silver-colored mechanical pencil. When the clerk said, "We're engraving them for free," Jenny had Richard's name put on the pencil. The pencil cost four dollars. Jenny counted her money again and bought Tony a plaid wool scarf and Mom Bradley a yellow and orange silk scarf.

▽ ▽

"Are you and Richard on the outs?" Mom Bradley asked when Jenny told her they were going to have Christmas dinner at the cabin. Mom and Jenny were clearing tables; Richard was in the kitchen washing dishes.

"Not really," Jenny said.

"What'd he do? Make a pass at you?"

Jenny felt herself flush. "Not really," she said again.

"Damn dumb kid," Mom Bradley said.

"He's really pretty smart," Jenny said. "He's a good teacher."

By two o'clock Jenny had more than enough tips to repay Richard. When the door was locked, she got the two packages and her tip jar from under the counter. "Merry Christmas," she said to Mom Bradley and handed her one of the gifts.

Mom Bradley blushed. She hugged Jenny to her hard round belly; she smelled of cooking grease and beer. "You're sweet to think of me." She dipped down behind the bar and brought out a box. "I've got some things for your tree and a couple little doodads for the kids' stockings."

Jenny hugged her again. "I'm beginning to feel really Christmasy," she said. "Mike has surprises in the shop, and Billy could hardly wait to hang his stocking. Even Corey's got the spirit. She crawls over to the tree and touches the icicles to make them swing. When they stop, she touches them again."

Jenny took Richard's gift and the money through the swinging doors. But Richard wasn't there. The dishwasher was silent; the clean hot dishes were stacked on the shelves. On the counter near the dishwasher was a package with Jenny's name on it.

Jenny set the tip jar and Richard's gift on the counter. She picked up the square package and pulled the tissue paper from it. Richard had given her a brand new Merriam-Webster collegiate dictionary. Jenny opened the book. There was writing on the inside page. Tears blurred her eyes. She wiped her hand across them and read what Richard had written:

> Always keeps learning, Jenny
> There are always new things for knowing
> Always a new street for running
> Always a new wind blowing.

For a moment Jenny was back on the campus, filled with the thrill of passing her tests, flying down the sidewalk with Richard in the cold air.

She stood for a long time in the kitchen, holding the dictionary and thinking of Richard. The same old sour wind had swept him away again. Richard would be drunk for Christmas, and Mom and Ed would be alone. She stepped through the swinging doors. "I have an idea," she said. "Why don't you and Ed come up to the cabin with Tony tomorrow?"

Mom Bradley said, "What about Richard?"

Jenny said, "Richard's gone, Mom. We'll save him some turkey and dressing."

▽ ▽

The cabin smelled of roast turkey by the time Tony's truck came up Simpson Gulch. Billy had wakened them just after dawn, bringing his stocking into bed with them and spilling the contents onto the Navajo blanket. The early sun just barely let enough light into the cabin for them to see an orange, nuts, candy, three big pencils, and a little rainbow pad of paper—Jenny's part of the Santa Claus game she and Mike had played after she got home from Mom's early Christmas morning. Mike had added a small hammer and a screwdriver. Billy was so excited he bounced all over the bed. Then he got off and began pounding on the nails in the chair legs.

Corey woke up and began to cry. Jenny rose and went to the crib. As she turned with the baby in her arms she noticed that the Christmas tree had been moved forward. She said to Mike, "Did you move the tree?"

He grinned at her. "Yep."

"Why?"

Mike sat up on the edge of the bed, stretching and grinning. "Wait until after breakfast."

"After breakfast! Oh, Mike, you can't make me wait. I have to get the turkey on before I can make breakfast, and I have to get the kids going."

Mike looked very pleased with himself. "All right then, sit down and shut your eyes. Billy, put your hands on your mama's eyes so she can't peek."

Jenny sat down in the rocker with Corey in her lap. Billy climbed on the front runners of the chair, leaned across Corey, and put his hands across Jenny's eyes. Jenny heard the bucket which held the tree slide heavily across the floor, and then something else heavy, and then the bucket again. Mike said, "Okay, you can open your eyes."

Jenny blinked and lifted her eyes to Mike. He was grinning; a piece of tinsel was tangled in his hair. And on the floor in front of him was a cedar chest, its varnish shining even in the early morning light. A brass key stood in the keyhole on the lid.

"Oh," said Jenny, rising from the chair as Billy backed away and clapped his hands. She gave the baby to Mike and went down on her knees beside the chest. She ran her hand over the smooth surface, as satiny soft as her rocking chair. "Oh," she said again.

"Unlock it, unlock it," Billy said. Jenny turned the key and lifted the lid; the fragrance of cedar filled the room. The chest was made of cedar boards, each about six inches wide, so carefully joined together the joinings were tiny lines. The inside was smooth, but not varnished. The wonderful scent came from the rose-colored wood. Jenny looked up.

"Mike, it's beautiful. Did you really make it?"

Billy said, "Me and Daddy made it, Mama. We cutted down a tree, and Tony and us tooked it to a sawmill and a man made

· 280 ·

boards and, and . . ." Billy was out of breath and too excited to go on.

Jenny stood up and went to her husband. She put her arms around Mike and Corey and said, "It's the most beautiful box with a lid that I ever saw in my whole life." Mike put his free arm around her, and they leaned together in a silence so intense and sweet Jenny felt she might faint from its beauty.

And then they were all laughing. Mike set Corey on the floor and said, "I'll be back in a minute." He went out the door. In a moment or two he was back with Billy's sled, a sturdy wooden vehicle, sanded and varnished, with metal runners. He set it on the crowded floor and ran back to the shop again to bring a small wooden horse on rockers with a deerskin seat on its back, deerskin stirrups, and two dowels for handholds just below the ears. He set Corey on the horse and put her hands on the pegs. He rocked her back and forth.

"I want to take my sled out in the snow," Billy said.

Mike looked at Jenny. "Go ahead," she said. "I'll feed Corey." By the time Corey was in her crib, Mike and Billy were back inside.

"It's a marvlus sled, Mama," Billy said.

Jenny laughed and said, "We haven't given your daddy a present yet, and he gave us all these nice things." She bent to run her hand across her "marvlus" cedar chest.

The rest of the morning was happy chaos. The tiny cabin was soon full of wrapping paper and ribbon. Mike seemed happy with the radio and his new clothes. Billy had to sit down right away and read one of the books. Corey bounced and gurgled in her crib, holding the fuzzy bear by one ear. Jenny got the turkey into the oven, and then before fixing breakfast she rolled up the ribbon and folded the wrapping paper. She put everyone's new clothes inside the cedar chest. Mike turned the dial on the radio until he could hear some faint Christmas music.

"Needs a bigger antenna," he said, and went to the shop for a thin wire, which he attached to the small rabbit ears antenna on the radio; then he threaded it under the door and up the side of the cabin. The choir from the Mitchell Methodist Church serenaded them with Christmas music from the university station.

After breakfast Mike found a country-western station, and when Tony, Ed O'Brien, and Mom Bradley arrived for dinner the cabin was fragrant with turkey and cedar, a guitar rang rhythmically through the room, and Corey banged on the crib bars with a spoon, her kicking feet shod in the rabbit-fur boots Mike had made. Mike and Billy were riding down the slope west of the cabin on a sled run they'd created by tramping down the snow.

Jenny gave Tony his plaid scarf. He wrapped it around his neck and wore it all day. He had brought Tinkertoys and a book for Billy, and a doll and a book for Corey.

The six of them were crowded at the small table, but no one seemed to mind when an elbow passed too close. They ate turkey and dressing, gravy, and vegetables. Mom had brought pumpkin pie and a fruitcake for dessert.

After dinner, the men took Billy to the shop to feed Rosie and look at Mike's equipment. Billy carried two apples to the burro. Mom Bradley helped with the dishes and then she sat at the table with a cup of coffee while Jenny made up a plate for Richard.

"I wish Richard could be here and be happy with us," Jenny said.

Mom Bradley lit a cigarette. Shaking out the match, she drew deeply, let out a cloud of smoke, and sighed. "Richard carries unhappiness around in him like a thorn," she said. "He can't let it go, and he can't quit hurting, so he just festers."

▽ ▽

It was dark before Tony, Mom Bradley, and Ed O'Brien started home. "Thanks for coming," Mike said as their guests got up to leave. Jenny stood with him in the door and watched the taillight on Tony's pickup dip down as it crossed the bridge and rose up again on the other side. She put her arm around Mike as they turned from the door and leaned her head against his shoulder.

"It's been a wonderful Christmas," she said. "I feel like things are just going to get better and better."

Mike stepped away to help Billy untie his shoe. "God, I hope so, Jenny." His head was bent over the knot.

Jenny stood watching, uncertain how to reply. Then she sat down by the bed and ran her hand across the lid of the cedar chest. "It's so beautiful," she said.

Mike pulled Billy's shoe off and took hold of his pants legs. Billy's legs flopped loosely as they came out of the pants. Mike rolled Billy over onto his bed and covered him up. He tossed the pants toward the foot of the bed and stood up. Corey had been asleep for an hour. Billy was soon sound asleep, too, snoring slightly as he breathed in.

Mike sat down at the table. He had turned the radio off to save the batteries. He looked at Jenny.

She said, "Now I know how you passed the time while I was down at Mom's. You tanned the deer hide and the rabbit skin and made the sled and the horse and my wonderful cedar chest."

Mike ran his hand across his forehead and back through his hair. "I'd have gone stark raving mad without something to do. As it was, I started going to bed pretty soon after Billy."

"Billy gets cabin fever, too," Jenny said.

"Anyone in his right mind would. Don't you?"

Jenny looked around the little house. "No. The cabin is just peaceful for me. I like the mountain and working in the tunnel and studying after the kids are in bed on Sunday night."

"Well, your studying's all over now."

Jenny got up and went to the table. "I'm going to miss studying."

"You're only up here one night a week," Mike said. "And besides, you're going to be busy. We've got to start producing again."

Jenny stood still by him, not knowing what to say.

"If we fill that bin," Mike said, "then maybe we can get off this goddamn mountain, get down to someplace with electricity—and a bathroom to offer company, for Chrissake."

"Our company didn't mind," Jenny said, adding, "I thought the radio would help you pass your evenings."

Mike looked up at her. "Hey, babe, it's a good idea you had. Sure it'll help. Until we move back to town. When we get some real money coming in, I'm going to buy a TV." He ran his hand up across her breast. "In the meantime, you and me are both home for the evening. Maybe we can entertain each other."

Jenny felt as though the day had somehow slipped out of line. She tried to push it back to the moment when she'd first seen the cedar chest, but it was like trying to put a jigsaw-puzzle piece into the wrong space. She undressed slowly and got into bed, willing herself to shut off all thought, to be unaware of anything but Mike's hands on her body. She thought of his hands sanding the cedar chest and began to feel loving again.

Later, when they lay side by side, Mike said, "I heard that that Bigfoot—you know, the guy who gave you the rocking chair—I heard he owns the whole damn trucking company. Did you know that?"

Jenny felt herself flush in the darkness, and despite herself, a silvery thrill streaked through her chest.

"I heard that he does," she said, "but he never told me." She wondered if Mike had thought about the rocking chair all the time he'd worked on the cedar chest.

"He must be some big wheeler-dealer," Mike said.

"I don't know," Jenny said. "I don't know anything about him at all."

Mike turned on his side and soon began to snore. Jenny lay in the darkness, carefully weighing three kinds of pain, each with a name of its own: Mike and Richard and David Garvey.

CHAPTER

48

▲▲▲▲▲▲

After Christmas, their life slipped quickly back into its routine. Mike urged Jenny to drill faster. She tried, but she couldn't seem to speed up. She had settled into a rhythm that worked for her; it took two full mornings to drill a round.

Mike took ore into Mitchell on the twenty-seventh and twenty-eighth of December. The bin on the dump was getting low. "Nineteen tons in the bin at Mitchell," Jenny wrote in her journal. She shot the overhang on the twenty-eighth and mucked it on the thirtieth, which was a Sunday. Mike insisted on going to town.

"I thought you wanted us to get some more ore in the bin," she said.

"Jesus, Jenny, stop nagging me. I've got some important business to take care of. Just give me the goddamn loan money and get off my back. I'll send Tony up."

Jenny was worried enough to ask Tony, "Is something the matter with Mike that I don't know about?"

Tony shrugged his shoulders and looked embarrassed.

"I'm sorry," Jenny said. "You're a dear to come up and play with the kids. Billy thinks you and Rosie are his best friends."

$$\triangledown \quad \triangledown$$

New Year's Eve there was a wild party at Mom's Bar. Mom Bradley gave each customer a free hat and noisemakers. Everyone Jenny had ever seen in the bar showed up at some point during the evening. Jenny was called and teased and touched and grabbed until she was exhausted and close to tears. When the fire whistle in Dolby went off at midnight, the customers broke into a mass cheer, followed by whistling and stomping and kissing. Jenny found herself caught in a painful bear hug and looked up just as Tully Stocker bent and kissed her hard on the mouth. She jerked away and ran into the kitchen only to be caught and kissed by Richard, who was staggering drunk. She pushed him away and went out the back door to stand in the cold shadows at the rear of the café. Up toward Dolby, she could hear horns and bells. She breathed the cold air that slid off the snowy mountain and watched the moon, icy silver in a pearl gray sky, move slowly behind a dark cloud. When she had stopped trembling, she went back to work.

The mill was closed on New Year's Day, but Mike took the last ore from their bin to Mitchell on Thursday.

"Only three quarter ton," he said with disgust when he got back.

"That's only nineteen and three quarters. When are we gonna get some more ore?"

"I'll shoot the ore on Saturday," she said. "It'll be Monday before we can muck it out."

Mike took off early on Sunday and came home late. Jenny played with the children in the snow and bathed them and rocked them and read to them.

The brochure about correspondence courses had come from the university, but when Jenny showed it to Richard, he said, "It'll take you a hundred years to get through college that way, Jenny, and you still won't know anything when you're done." She took the brochure home and put it in her cedar chest. She didn't have time to study at work lately anyway. Richard was usually gone. She did her work and his too at least four nights a week.

But being busy wasn't nearly as bad as not being busy. Nights when the bar and café were empty and the work finished too soon, Jenny searched for ways to pass the time. She watched the news, but found the other TV shows boring or just plain stupid. One Friday night after they had watched "Dallas" together, she said to Mom Bradley, "Those people have everything they could possibly want, yet they just keep making each other miserable."

Mom Bradley laughed. "That's what cheers me up. Makes my life look pretty damn good."

Ed O'Brien was in every night to eat dinner with Mom Bradley. The days edged slowly into the third week in January. Mike took two more loads to Mitchell. "Twenty-one and three quarter tons," Jenny wrote in the book.

On the eighteenth of January, a Friday, the compressor broke down again. Mike tried to fix it, but he had to go to Mitchell for parts. Jenny gave him money from her emergency fund, but by the time he got the compressor going on Saturday it was too late for Jenny to drill.

Sunday he announced that he was hauling ore. "The guy at the mill said he'd weigh me in on Sunday if I got there before noon." He loaded the truck until it groaned. Tony had come up to help Jenny drill.

"Be careful, boy," he said. "You don't want to load that thing so heavy that you can't keep hold of the reins."

Mike said, "Not to worry. I'm getting the hang of this ore hauling."

He stopped in town on his way back from Mitchell and didn't come home until late. Monday morning he said, "You can write twenty-two and three quarter tons in that book of yours, Jenny."

She smiled at him from the stove. "Super," she said. "Just two and a quarter tons to go."

"We're going to make it before the first of February," Mike said.

"What's the price of gold these days?" Jenny asked.

"Been runnin' three hundred twelve to three hundred twenty dollars an ounce," Mike said, "but we won't know nothin' about money until they run our stuff. That's why I'm pushing so damn hard to get that bin filled."

"I can hardly keep up with you," Jenny said. "We won't muck ore again until Sunday."

"I'll get Tony up here and muck it late Saturday," Mike said. "I figure on hauling again Sunday."

Jenny met Tony on the Virgo Creek road as she went home from Mom's early Sunday morning. She blinked her lights in answer when he blinked his. I hope he's not as tired as I am, she thought.

The café had been almost unbearable. David Garvey had come just at dinnertime, when everyone else in Dolby had decided to come to Mom's for dinner, too. Mom Bradley was busy in the kitchen; Richard was tending bar and trying to keep up with the dishes.

Jenny waited on David Garvey, her hands trembling so much that the water in the glass bounced as she set it down. There were two other drivers with Bigfoot. He gave her a brief smile and ordered a chicken-fried-steak dinner. After that he was involved in the conversation at his booth and never seemed to look her way. Jenny put on a bright smile and a burst of energy and took care of every table with swift vicious efficiency. When David had gone, and she had found a generous tip by his plate, she went into the rest room and cried. She hated having to go back out to the café. Richard had been watching her all the time, and he always knew how to pick at a sore.

But Richard said only, "You'd better sit down and eat, Jenny, before you wear yourself out. You've been going like a runaway engine on a downhill track."

She took a breath and smiled. "You sound like you've been reading old folk sayings," she said.

Richard laughed. "You'll find that in folklore one oh one at the university."

Jenny sat down on the barstool and said, "I'm still thinking about ordering one of those courses. I need something to do with my mind while my hands wipe catsup off the tables."

Richard said softly, "Jenny, I'm sober now, and you've got to take me seriously." Jenny started to get up, but Richard put his hand on hers. Jenny looked down at their hands. "Jenny, I love you," Richard said. "I want you to move to Mitchell with me. You can bring the kids. I'll even marry you if you want that."

Jenny raised her eyes slowly. She noticed that the silver pencil she had given Richard was in his shirt pocket. She looked up at Richard's face. His eyes were clear and serious; he *was* sober. She looked at him for a long moment and then said as gently as she could, "Richard, I don't want to hurt you. You've helped me so much. I never realized until we quit studying how much fun we had while we were doing it." She pulled her hand from his and reached up to touch his face. "But please stop asking me to move to Mitchell. Things are the way they are. I'd like to go to college someday, but right now I've got to keep this job, and I've got to help Mike."

Richard's face was rigid under her fingers. She dropped her hand. She said, "I was wrong about one thing the other day. I do love you, Richard, but not in the way you want me to."

"That's enough to start on," Richard said.

"No, it's not," Jenny said, "and it never will be. I love you as if you were Billy—as if you were Corey—as if you were Rosie."

"Rosie! For God's sake, Jenny."

"Richard, they're the dearest creatures in my life, and you're dear to me too. But I'm not in love with you." She looked down again.

Richard grabbed hold of her chin and lifted her face. His eyes were wild, and his hand hurt her chin. "And you know the difference now, don't you, Jenny?"

Jenny jerked her head away and stepped back from him. "Richard, you never seem to get the point of what I'm saying. None of this makes any sense." He grabbed her wrist with a searing grip that made her furious. "Let go of me, Richard Bradley. What makes you think I'd leave Mike for you? Talk about out of the frying pan. *There's* an old saying for you." She pulled her arm from his grasp and went into the kitchen.

Mom Bradley was standing near the serving window. She said, "You and Richard seem to be putting on quite a show; the customers are fascinated." Jenny felt a hot flush rise to flood her face and neck. "Oh, Christ," Mom said. "You'd better get ready to wash dishes. There he goes."

Jenny had driven all the way up Simpson Gulch without noticing where she was going. She checked the children and crawled into bed, quietly hoping that Mike wouldn't wake up. She was not going to make love after this night's emotional hailstorm. I sometimes wish my feelings were still bundled up in a fog, the way they used to be, she thought as she pulled the covers around her.

▽   ▽

Mike was up early, loading the truck. Jenny watched as the truck tires sagged, and still Mike let the ore roll into the pickup bed. When he finally closed the hatch the truck tires looked pregnant. Mike grinned at Jenny. "Stop scowling at me. This is the payload, girl."

"It looks too heavy."

"No heavier than the last load I took."

"We can't afford new tires, Mike."

He came up to her. Putting his arm around her shoulders, he walked her up to the cabin. "Just give me my allowance and take care of your kids, honey." He reached down and pinched her right buttock. "And wait up for me tonight."

Jenny played with the children all morning. She pulled them on the sled around and around the yard, read all their old books and all their new books to them, sang songs, and built a wagon with Billy's Tinkertoys. After lunch, when the children took their naps, Jenny was glad that Tony and Mike had mucked the tunnel. She was overcome with sleepiness herself. She left the dishes on the table and crawled into bed.

It was dark and cold in the cabin when Billy woke her. "Mama, Corey's wet." Jenny got up and lit the lantern. As soon as she had changed the baby, she built up a fire and began to heat dishwater. She felt rested and cheerful.

"What shall we have for supper?" she said to Billy. "You choose."

"Pancakes," he said, "and stirry eggs."

"Pancakes it is," she said. "Special pancakes." She made pancakes in the shape of snowmen and puppies and kittens and even one with long burro's ears.

Billy dipped the burro pancake in his eggs and giggled when the ears turned yellow. Corey gurgled and banged her spoon on the plate. "Ma-ma-ma-ma-ma," she said.

"Say Billy," her brother said.

"Bee," she said, "Bee-bee-bee."

"Bill-y," he said, wiggling his tongue in front of Corey to show her how to make the *L.* Corey put her finger in the middle of his tongue.

The children stayed up late after their long nap. Jenny gave them baths and dressed them in clean nightclothes; she read to them again before tucking them in. It was past nine thirty when Billy finally fell asleep again. At eleven Jenny heard the truck on the bridge. Mike was early, as he'd promised to be.

Jenny smiled and went to the door. She opened it just in time to see the Sheriff's black and white Bronco drive up onto the dump.

CHAPTER

49

▲▲▲▲▲▲

Jenny's heart began to pound against her ribs. She watched the sheriff's deputy climb out of the Bronco and unlatch the gate. His face was familiar; he'd been in Mom's once or twice.

The deputy walked to the door and asked, "Are you Mrs. Williams?"

Jenny opened her mouth but she could not force a word out through the wad of fear in her throat. She nodded. The deputy removed his hat and gestured toward the cabin. "Could we talk where it's warmer, ma'am?"

Jenny looked over her shoulder and swallowed. "I don't want to wake the children," she said, but she moved back into the cabin, and the sheriff's deputy stepped inside. Jenny closed the door and turned to face the officer.

"I have some very bad news," he said. "Your husband, Mike Williams, was killed in a traffic accident on the Mitchell highway this morning."

Jenny stood totally still and looked at him. Finally she said, "Did he blow a tire?"

"No, ma'am. There was a collision. He lost control of the truck. The other driver was also killed."

"It happened this morning?" Jenny shook her head in disbelief. "Why did you wait so long to tell me?"

"We couldn't find out where you lived."

Jenny didn't know what else to say. Nothing came to her, and she couldn't force herself to concentrate on anything. She looked toward Billy's bed and then at the crib. The children slept deeply.

"Can I call someone for you, Mrs. Williams?" the deputy asked.

"There isn't anybody—only Tony or Mom Bradley."

"We can't find Mom Bradley."

"She's with Ed O'Brien," Jenny said, and then she focused sharply on the officer. "Why were you looking for Mom Bradley?"

"Because her son was the other driver."

"Richard?"

"Yes, ma'am. Richard Bradley."

"In a pink Cadillac?"

"Yes, ma'am." The officer hesitated and then said, "He was on the wrong side of the highway coming back from Mitchell."

"And he's dead, too? Mike, and Richard too?"

"Yes." The officer's face was very red, his mouth tight.

Jenny moved back a few steps and sat down at the table. She said, "Did Richard do it on purpose?"

The officer's eyebrows jumped upward, and he raised his hand and ran it through his hair before replying. "There's no way of knowing, but I don't think so. He hit the left front side of the pickup. Apparently the truck was heavily loaded; your husband just lost control of it and went over the bank. The Cadillac ricocheted against an inside wall, and then it went over the bank too."

Jenny glanced at the children again. "Richard was drunk, of course."

"Ma'am, who is Tony? Can I call him for you?"

Jenny looked at the deputy. "Tony? Oh. Tony DiAngelo."

"Where does he live?"

"Below the county dump."

"I'll radio back to the department. They'll tell him."

"No," Jenny said, "don't wake him up. He's old, and not well."

"But you shouldn't be alone tonight."

Jenny stood up, clenching both fists at her sides. "Where is my husband?"

"At McBride's Mortuary, near the bank in Dolby."

Jenny went to the window and looked out toward the dark mountain. The deputy waited a moment, then cleared his throat.

Jenny turned. "Please don't wake Tony tonight. There's nothing he can do. If you'll send him in the morning to stay with the children, I'll come down to Dolby in his truck."

"I don't like leaving you alone."

"I'll be all right. I have to take care of my children."

The deputy put his hat on and moved toward the door. "Who told you where to find me?" Jenny asked.

He stopped and turned toward her. "A fellow named Tully Stocker. Said you used to be neighbors."

Jenny nodded. She went to the door and opened it. "I'm sorry you had to come all the way up here."

"Yes, ma'am," the officer said. "I'm sorry too. I'll send Mr. Di-Angelo first thing in the morning."

"Thank you."

Jenny closed and locked the door behind the sheriff's deputy and stood with her hand on the knob long after the sound of the Bronco faded away in Simpson Gulch.

The children slept on. The fire died down, and Jenny began to shiver. She left the door and put a chunk of wood into the embers. Little blue flames leapt around the dry pine bark, dancing on top of the orange and yellow coals. It was pretty. She put the lid back on the stove.

She went to the crib and bent over the baby for a moment; she moved to Billy's mattress, knelt, and listened to him. Then she left the cabin and went to the tunnel. She pulled the door back and moved into the dark portal. When she had gone ten feet, she sat down on the railroad ties between the rails. Wrapping her arms across her chest, she leaned into the darkness and began to sway back and forth.

▽ ▽

Jenny was feeding cereal to Corey when Tony came in the cabin door Monday morning. The old man looked dreadful, his skin like dried leather. Jenny held out her free hand to him. He took it in both of his and stood silently.

"There's coffee," Jenny said.

"Hi, Tony," Billy said. "I'm making Rosie." He had put the Tinkertoys together in the shape of a horse.

"Hi, Billy," Tony said and then asked quietly of Jenny, "Does he know?"

Jenny shook her head. She said to Billy, "Tony's going to help you think of lots of things to make. I have to go to town for a while."

Tony poured a cup of coffee and sat down at the table. "Did you get any sleep?"

"No," Jenny said, and then, "Have you seen Mom Bradley?"

"The café's not open."

Jenny got up, pulled the curtain across the bed, and took off her jeans. She put on the blue plaid skirt and blue sweater and her shoes. She slid the curtain back and said to Tony, "I made peanut butter and honey sandwiches for you and Billy. Give Corey fruit and some baby beef and carrots."

"Okay," Tony said. "Don't worry. Just do what you have to." Jenny picked up the coat Richard had chosen for her.

▽   ▽

Natalie Swanson looked up and took a half step forward. "Jenny! I didn't expect to see *you* here this morning."

Jenny stood just inside the beauty shop door. "I shouldn't be here, but"—her voice broke a little—"but I have to see so many people. I thought I could do it all right if I looked better." She turned. "Maybe I should go."

But Natalie came forward. "You come straight over to this chair, Jenny, and I'll take you right away. Alice will do your nails too." She took Jenny's arm and led her to the beauty bar. Jenny sat down. Natalie's hands were gentle.

When Jenny was ready to leave the shop, she said, "Can I pay you tomorrow? I forgot that I didn't have enough money in my purse."

"Bless you, Jenny. Pay me whenever you want. I'd tell you to forget it, but I know you." She smiled at Jenny with a warm look that brought tears to Jenny's eyes.

"Thank you," she managed to say as she turned away. She went out and climbed into Tony's truck.

▽   ▽

McBride's Mortuary was also the county coroner's office. Mr. McBride hesitated when Jenny asked to see Mike's body. "The accident was very damaging, Mrs. Williams. Perhaps you'd rather not view the body."

"I want to see my husband," Jenny said steadily, "and then I will make arrangements for his burial."

Mr. McBride led her down a long hallway and turned into a large well-lit room. As they stepped inside, the door closed behind them. There were two tables in the room. On the tables were two covered bodies.

The funeral director went to the first table, but he did not remove the cloth from Mike's face. "You will see severe lacerations and contusions, Mrs. Williams," he said. "There is extreme swelling around the eyes and widespread areas of black and blue."

Jenny swallowed but said nothing, and Mr. McBride slowly pulled the sheet down, adding, "There has been a post mortem, and so the body is unclothed."

Only the hands looked like Mike, and even they had purplish marks. The mortician followed her glance. "The marks are from the IV the paramedics used."

"Was he alive then?"

"No, he died in the crash, but they're required to take all possible measures until the patient is pronounced dead."

The hands were too still. Jenny took a deep breath and turned to Mr. McBride. "Richard Bradley was my friend," she said. "I'd like to see him, too."

The mortician flushed. "Are you related to the Bradleys?"

"No," Jenny said, "but I want to see Richard." She looked straight at the funeral director, and he shrugged slightly and went to the other table.

"Mr. Bradley is not so badly bruised. He died of a ruptured spleen."

Richard was marked very little. His cheekbones stood out in the gaunt face. The eyes were closed; nothing familiar remained. Jenny turned away from the thin dead man and followed Mr. McBride to his office.

CHAPTER

50

▲▲▲▲▲▲

The funeral director said, "Will you be seated, Mrs. Williams?"

She sat down, and before Mr. McBride could speak again, Jenny said, "I would like you to tell me just what to expect—here and at the cemetery."

"Certainly, Mrs. Williams. We'll take it a step at a time and explain everything."

"Please," said Jenny, "don't try to be gentle. Just tell me what I need to know."

The funeral director flushed again. "It may be too painful for you."

Jenny looked at him a moment. "The facts will help me do what I have to do." She swallowed before asking, "How much does a funeral cost?"

"Well, that of course depends on a great many things."

"How much does a casket cost?" Jenny gripped her purse and kept her eyes on the man's face.

He stood up. "If you'll come this way, I will show you the selection, Mrs. Williams." Mr. McBride took Jenny into a long display room. Caskets gleamed under soft lights, their lids raised to show the empty satin pillows. "This is our most economical model," Mr. McBride said.

Jenny looked at the gray cloth-covered casket and took a step away. A charity casket. Her mother had been buried in a charity casket. "No," she said. "Not that one. Do you have a nicer one?"

"Yes, of course," said the mortician. "We have this silver-colored nonsealing casket with an eggshell interior." He moved to the display just next to the charity casket.

The silver metal was burnished to a soft glow; the inside was pleated. Jenny nodded slowly. "That one will be fine."

"Perhaps we could return to my office to discuss the arrangements."

Back in Mr. McBride's office, Jenny took a pencil and the back card of a café order pad from her purse. "Now tell me the costs, please," she said. "Just give me a list."

Jenny waited. The funeral director said, "We don't usually do it quite this way."

"Please," Jenny said again, holding her pencil above the pad.

"Very well," the man said. "The professional service and facility fees come to nine hundred ninety-five dollars."

Jenny's hand trembled as she wrote the figure on the paper. "Does that include the coffin?"

"No, ma'am. The casket is seven hundred fifty dollars."

Jenny wrote that figure, too, and looked up at the man.

"The coach is sixty-five dollars." He paused for a moment and then asked, "Will you need the limousine as well?"

"Yes," Jenny said. "Our truck was wrecked."

"The limousine will be fifty dollars." Mr. McBride looked at Jenny. "Will your minister take care of the service?"

Jenny said, "Do you have a minister to suggest?"

"Well, yes, we could arrange for a minister, and an organist, too, if you wish. Stipends for the two of them will be another seventy-five dollars, and the flowers for the casket, about eighty dollars."

"Is that all of it?" asked Jenny, adding the figures.

"For the mortuary service, but there will of course be charges at the cemetery."

"Can you tell me what they'll be?"

"Well, with the plot and the vault and the opening and closing of the grave, it will probably come to seven hundred dollars."

"Two thousand, seven hundred and fifteen dollars total, then," Jenny said, her mouth dry and her throat tight.

"Was your husband a veteran?"

"No," Jenny said.

"Do you have insurance, Mrs. Williams?"

"Yes."

"That's fine, then. And of course, there's the Social Security death benefit of two hundred twenty-five dollars."

Jenny looked at her shining nails and then back to the man. "When do you expect to be paid, Mr. McBride?"

"We ask for at least a third of the costs before the funeral and the balance in thirty days. We can call and verify your insurance if you like. Our service also includes helping with the Social Security forms."

Jenny put her pencil and pad away. "I think our insurance is carried through the bank, Mr. McBride, and I have to go there this afternoon anyway." She rose. "I'll come back later."

The funeral director stood up. "Mrs. Williams, don't you have a friend or relative who could help with these arrangements?"

Jenny shook her head. "My children are too small. They don't even know about their daddy yet." She shook her head again. "But I'm fine. Now that you've given me the facts, I'll be just fine. Thank you, Mr. McBride."

He opened the door for her, and she went into the carpeted lobby feeling dizzy. She walked slowly toward the front door and stepped out just as Mom Bradley and Ed O'Brien came up the walk.

▽ ▽

Mom Bradley's face was splotched with purple, and her nose was red. Jenny went to her. Mom Bradley said, "Oh, God, Jenny. I'm sorry."

"I'm sorry for you, too," Jenny said.

Mom Bradley began to cry. Ed O'Brien took her arm. She sniffed and swallowed and said in a choking voice, "I'm sorry Richard did it. Oh, Jesus, oh, Jesus, why did Richard have to be the one?" She swayed, and Jenny took her other arm. They helped her into the lobby, where she sat down on a blue velvet bench.

Jenny stood helplessly, watching Mom Bradley weep, until Ed O'Brien said, "I think she'd calm down easier if you was to go." Jenny nodded and backed away.

▽ ▽

She drove Tony's truck back to the drugstore and called the Social Security office in Mitchell from a pay phone. When the clerk in claims information answered, Jenny said, "Can you tell me how much money a woman with two small children will get if her husband dies?" She bit the inside of her cheek as she listened to the reply.

"Well, of course, it depends on his wages," the clerk said, "and several other factors."

"Could you just tell me the minimum?" Jenny said.

"Let's see. Yes, here it is. Two children? A widow and two children would receive nine hundred eighty-eight dollars a month."

"A widow." Jenny took the word into her mind with the figure the clerk had given her. "How much of that has to be paid out in taxes?" she asked.

"Why, none at all." The clerk sounded surprised.

"Thank you." Jenny hung up and drove to the sheriff's office. The uniformed woman behind the counter asked her to wait.

When a deputy appeared, Jenny said, "I'm Jenny Williams. Do you know where our truck is?"

"It's still at the accident site. You'll need to hire a wrecker."

"Where is the accident site?" Jenny asked. "How far out is it?"

The deputy studied Jenny. "Maybe I'd better run you up there. It's not department policy, but you shouldn't go alone."

▽   ▽

The truck was upside down at the bottom of the gully, its rear end in the creek. The cab was smashed nearly flat; all the glass was broken.

"It's totaled," the deputy said. "I hope you've got insurance."

"We do," said Jenny. She walked around to the rear of the truck and peered up into the bed. Of course the ore was gone. She looked up the hill; only a few silver chunks sparkled against the snow. She looked into the creek. There were ferny edges of ice along the bank. A few feet away, the fingertips of a bush were trapped in the solid ice that had formed over a side-washed pool. Farther out, the current swirled across a small pile of ore, easing the last of Mike's payload downstream, a little at a time.

The deputy took her arm. "Are you okay?" Jenny looked around. She didn't see Richard's Cadillac anywhere. "Say, I think we'd better get you a cup of coffee," the deputy said. "Have you had lunch?"

Jenny looked at him. "No," she said, "but I have to go to the bank."

"The bankers are all out to lunch," the deputy said. "You'd better eat, too."

"I didn't bring enough money."

The deputy took hold of her arm and began to pull her up the slope. "I never should have brought you out here," he said as he arrived at the top of the hill with Jenny stumbling along beside him, "but I'm going to break some more regulations and buy you a hamburger and a cup of coffee."

▽   ▽

The girl at the information desk at the bank took Jenny's name and rang for a bank officer. When a man in a blue suit came out, the girl said, "This is Mr. Kingsley, Mrs. Williams. He'll help you."

They went into the man's office, and Jenny sat in the chair he offered. She folded her hands in her lap and said, "Mr. Kingsley, the truck we financed through your bank was wrecked yesterday. There was an insurance policy, which we paid along with the payments." She took a breath. "I need to know if there will be enough left after the truck is paid off to take care of my husband's funeral."

The bank officer looked uncomfortable. He cleared his throat and said, "Mrs. Williams, your file has been on my desk for several days. And first of all, let me say that we did not handle the insurance. An independent agency here in Dolby wrote that policy." He hesitated and cleared his throat again before continuing. "I am sorry to have to tell you this, but your insurance policy was not in force at the time of your husband's accident."

Jenny stared at him. "It had to be. I sent money for the premiums every time I sent the loan payment."

"That may be," said Mr. Kingsley, "but I've already checked with your insurance agent. The policy lapsed in December. And the loan payments have not been made on the truck since November first. Your truck loan will be three months in arrears on the first of February, which is the day after tomorrow."

"There must be some mistake. Mike brought the money to town in December and January both. I know he had the money. I gave it to him."

Mr. Kingsley said quietly, "Mrs. Williams, how much do you know about your husband's gambling debts?"

CHAPTER
51
▲▲▲▲▲

A sharp pain jumped across Jenny's left temple. She blinked her eyes, raised one hand slightly, and then dropped it back onto her purse. She answered slowly. "I know that Mike played poker on Sunday nights. He never told me whether he won or lost." She looked at Mr. Kingsley for a moment and said, "Do they call you Charlie?"

The banker flushed. "No, but we have an employee—or rather, we *did* have an employee by that name who took part in several high-stakes poker games. When this was brought to the attention of the board of directors, they suggested that he resign."

"Mike said old Charlie took the mortgage payments into the bank on Mondays."

"Apparently he did do that, Mrs. Williams, for several months."

"How did the bank get involved in my husband's gambling debts?" Jenny was afraid to ask how much Mike owed.

Mr. Kingsley said, "The bank is not involved, but it seems to be common knowledge around here that your husband owed Charlie Speers six hundred seventy-five dollars at the time of his death."

"Six hundred seventy-five dollars!"

"He signed an IOU stating that he would pay by the first of February."

Jenny rose from her chair and walked over to the window. If Mike hadn't paid the truck loan for two months, then they still owed at least twenty-three hundred dollars on the truck; the funeral would take twenty-seven hundred, and the IOU . . . She turned back to the banker.

"Were you aware that shortly after we signed the loan papers on that truck, my husband lost his job?"

The banker frowned. "No. I knew nothing about your account until late last week."

Jenny came back and sat down, her mind running wildly over the figures in her head. She had to get some money, and this cold man was her only chance.

"Mr. Kingsley," she said, "since Labor Day I've had the only job in our family. I've been working six nights a week at Mom's Bar and Café while Mike stayed with our children." Jenny's voice trembled; she took a breath and paused for a moment. "Each day I have set aside money toward the loan and insurance payments. Mike brought the money to town, but I earned the money, and I saved it."

The banker was listening intently.

Jenny said, "During the days Tony DiAngelo and Mike and I worked the Spanish Mary, a claim on Simpson Gulch." Jenny kept looking right into the banker's face. She didn't want him to stop her before she was finished.

"The Mitchell mill has agreed to take twenty-five-ton lots of ore. Our samples assayed at nearly two ounces of gold per ton, and we have twenty-four tons in our bin at Mitchell." Jenny swallowed and went on. "Mike was hauling the payload into town on Sunday— yesterday." Yesterday she had only been worrying about the cost of new tires for the truck. A picture of Mike's swollen face came into her mind. She had to find a way to bury him. Right now she was angrier at him than she had ever been, but she had to find a way to bury him in that silver-colored coffin.

The banker said, "Our business could wait until later, Mrs. Williams. You've had a terrible shock. We could postpone all this until after the funeral."

Had he heard her at all? Jenny tried again, "Mr. Kingsley, what I've been trying to tell you is that I want to borrow money from your bank to pay for my husband's funeral."

The banker said, "If your husband has life insurance, we will of course be glad to advance money against the policy payoff."

Jenny clenched her teeth briefly, sat up straight, and said, "I know that banks need collateral. I just got my GED, and I studied all about collateral."

"Do you have any collateral Mrs. Williams?"

"I have twenty-four tons of ore in the bin at Mitchell; I have some ore in the bin on the Spanish Mary, and I have a good vein showing in the tunnel."

The banker had picked up a pen and was tapping it gently on his pad. "The bank cannot accept the ore as collateral," he said. "It has no value until the mill pays you."

Jenny ignored his comment and said, "I've also been told that I will receive Social Security benefits of at least nine hundred and eighty-eight dollars a month."

The banker stopped tapping the pen. Jenny rushed on. "While I worked at Mom's Bar, my take-home pay was five hundred and sixty-seven dollars a month, and I averaged about three hundred and fifty dollars a month in tips. Out of that money, I supported my family and still set aside three hundred eighty-six dollars for the loan and the insurance payment. Out of nine hundred and eighty-eight dollars, I could afford four hundred dollars a month."

The banker interrupted her. "Mrs. Williams, what do you want from this bank?"

Jenny took another big breath. "I want to borrow five thousand, six hundred and ninety dollars."

"For a funeral?" The banker looked shocked.

"No," Jenny said, "the funeral will only cost two thousand, seven hundred and fifteen dollars, but I still owe you twenty-three hundred on our truck, and I want the other six hundred and seventy-five dollars to pay my husband's gambling debt."

The banker studied her for a moment and then smiled. It was the first sign of warmth he had shown in the whole interview. "You are willing to pay for the truck? Of course, you're obligated by law, but I understand that the truck is a total loss."

Jenny was aggravated with this man. He didn't seem to comprehend very quickly. "No matter what happened to the truck," she said, "I signed that note. I owe you the money. I intend to pay it."

The banker looked at Jenny for another long moment. Then he pushed his chair back and opened the right-hand drawer of his desk.

"Would you be willing to have your Social Security check deposited directly into the bank and to sign a form allowing us to deduct the loan payment automatically?"

He was going to let her have the money! Jenny said, "Of course. I'll be glad to agree to that."

The banker said, "I'll help you to apply for the Social Security payments, and my secretary will type up the note for the loan. There will probably be a two-month delay in the government paperwork. We'll make the first payment on your loan due with the first deposit of your check." Frowning slightly, he said, "Do you have any money for expenses until your Social Security checks begin?"

"I have the February truck payment, and I think my husband had fifty dollars in his wallet. I suppose they'll give that back to me."

The banker said abruptly, "How old are you?"

"I'm twenty-three."

"Where are your people?"

"My parents are dead. I have no other relatives."

"What about your husband's family?"

"Only his mother is alive, and I don't know where she is."

The banker asked his secretary to come in. He gave instructions for typing the papers. When she left, he said to Jenny, "I'll give Al McBride a call and tell him to go ahead with the arrangements."

"He wanted one third of the money now."

"He'll waive that if I guarantee payment. We'll get these Social Security forms sent down from Mitchell right away. The papers should be ready to sign by Friday."

Jenny nodded and stood up. The banker walked her to the door. He put his hand on her upper arm and squeezed it gently while one finger rested against her breast. "You're a courageous young woman," he said, and his voice had a thicker tone, almost husky.

Jenny stiffened at his touch, but she did not pull away. She said, "Thank you, sir. I'll come in and sign the papers on Friday."

When she had climbed into Tony's truck once more, she put her head down on the wheel and said out loud, "I wish I'd slapped him."

▽ ▽

Billy didn't cry when she told him. He just looked at Jenny. She said, "Do you understand, Billy?"

He nodded and said, "Dead. Like the deer."

Jenny put her arms around him, and he buried his face against her stomach. There was no way to explain to Corey.

She took the children with her to the funeral on Thursday. Tony sat with the three of them in the half curtained family room. She held Corey close while a strange minister spoke over the closed coffin, which lay on the altar in the carpeted chapel. The words didn't have anything to do with Mike. The minister didn't say, "He made a sled and a rocking horse and a cedar chest." And the minister didn't say, "He left his wife six thousand dollars in debt."

When the speaker began to urge the congregation to look to their own lives, to tend now to the salvation of their souls because death was always near, Jenny stopped listening. She glanced down at Billy's head. A lock of hair stood up on the crown just like the one on Mike's head. She thought, Billy will be five on March thirtieth.

Jenny looked up as a small group of people passed by the coffin. She saw Mr. and Mrs. Marsh, Mom Bradley and Ed O'Brien, and a group of men she didn't know. There were more flowers in the chapel than she had expected.

They followed the coffin to a raw new hole on the hillside in the Dolby Cemetery and waited for a few more words from the minister. As Jenny turned to go back to the limousine, Ed O'Brien stepped to her side.

"Will you come by the café before you go up the hill? Mom wants to talk to you."

CHAPTER
52

▲▲▲▲▲▲

As they pulled up in front of Mom's, Jenny said to Tony, "I don't think I could have done this without you."

The old man looked tired, and there was a gray tinge to his face. "I liked the boy," he said. "I'll miss him." Jenny's eyes blurred. "What are you going to do now?" Tony asked.

Jenny brushed a hand across her eyes and said, "I have to stay on the mountain where the rent is free. I have to keep on working the Spanish Mary. Will you go partners with me?"

She looked down at the children sitting quietly between them. "I think they need you, Tony. You won't have to be in the tunnel. I wouldn't feel right if you went into the tunnel. But could you come up during the day and stay with the children?"

"You think you can work that claim alone?"

"I have to, Tony. I'm six thousand dollars in debt, and the ore is my only way out."

"You won't try to keep on at Mom's, will you?"

Jenny hesitated. "I hope she can find someone else. I make her uncomfortable." Jenny opened her door. "Anyhow, I can't leave the children alone at night."

Before they stepped into the café, she asked, "Do you know anything about Richard's funeral?"

Tony glanced down at Billy and said softly, "Richard was cremated yesterday. There won't be no service."

▽ ▽

Mom Bradley had prepared an array of cold cuts with bread and potato chips and a relish tray. She hurried in and out of the kitchen while Ed O'Brien quietly put two tables together, found a booster seat for Billy, and put Corey in a high chair.

Jenny felt strange sitting at the table. She wanted to get up and go change into her uniform. She wanted to go into the kitchen and find Richard in a cloud of steam by the dishwasher.

After they had eaten, and Mom had cleared the table, she sat down next to Ed and said, "Tony, why don't you take the children down there and show them how to play those pinball machines."

Billy had been unusually quiet all through the strange meal in the closed café, but he got off his booster seat and followed Tony, who carried the baby in his arms.

Mom Bradley cleared her throat, pulled her blouse down over her belly, and said, "Jenny, I know I can't ever make it up to you for what Richard did." Jenny started to speak, but Mom held up her hand. "Let me finish. I want to get it all said now. First of all, if you want work, you can stay on here." There was an odd tone in her voice.

Jenny said. "No, Mom. I will have to quit and be with my children."

Mom Bradley's face relaxed. "Well, that makes things easier. I was about to tell you that Ed and I are going to get married. If you don't need the job, I'm going to go ahead and put the café up for sale. We're going to take the trailer down to Arizona." Mom hesitated and then said, "Now, Jenny, I know how stubborn proud you can be, but I want to give you something."

Jenny waited without speaking. Mom Bradley went on. "I'm giving you a month's wages for cutting off your job so quick, and," she went on before Jenny could object, "I want you to have Richard's truck. Ed's got it fixed up so it runs pretty good. And one more thing." She reached into the lower pocket of her blouse and took out the silver pencil Jenny had given Richard for Christmas. "He'd want you to have this. He'd want you to remember how he helped you get your GED," Mom Bradley said, her voice breaking.

Jenny took the pencil and bit her lip to keep from crying. When she could speak, she said, "As if I could ever forget." She got up and went around the table to the fat woman and hugged her head. Mom Bradley leaned against Jenny's breast for a moment. Then she sniffed and sat up.

"I was hoping to start some kind of trust fund for Billy and Corey with Richard's insurance, but I found out yesterday he didn't have any insurance." She sniffed again. "Hell. He didn't even have a driver's license." She began to cry, and Ed O'Brien reached out a hand to her.

"Don't worry about us," Jenny said. "We've got some Social Security money coming to us." She took Mom Bradley's free hand. "I'm grateful for the truck. You don't owe me anything, but if you're sure you want to give up that truck, I can really use it."

Mom Bradley stopped crying and smiled at Jenny. "Why, bless your heart. For once your common sense is ahead of your pride." Jenny smiled back. She bent and kissed Mom Bradley's cheek and began to gather up the children's coats and gloves.

Ed O'Brien walked them to the door. "You made her feel better, Jenny, agreeing to take that truck. We'll bring it up soon as we get the title changed. You going to be all right?"

"I have to take care of my children," Jenny said, and added, "I'm glad Mom has you."

▽ ▽

On Friday Tony drove Jenny and the children to the bank. Jenny took Billy inside with her. She signed the papers that put her officially into debt for six thousand dollars plus interest. Jenny was appalled to see what the interest would add to the total bill by the time the debt was paid off. She held Billy's hand as they rose to leave, and the banker did not walk them to the door.

Back in the truck, Jenny said to Tony, "Let's take a couple of days off. I won't go back into the tunnel until Monday. And we have to draw up partnership papers."

Tony said, "Wait until you've got that last ton down to Mitchell. You and Mike did all that." He grinned at Jenny suddenly. "I had a good time. Best eating, best company I've had in years."

When he dropped them off at the Spanish Mary, Tony gave Jenny a long look. "You gonna be all right?" he asked.

▽ ▽

Jenny wrote in her journal after the children were in bed that night:

> Everyone asks if I'm going to be all right. What is all
> right? Mike's dead. Richard's dead. I feel chopped in
> half, but numb where the pain should be. My son
> looks at me with wounded eyes asking questions I
> can't answer. Richard taught me hundreds of words,
> works like <u>collateral</u>, words for the banker. But I have
> no words for Billy.

Jenny spent all of Saturday keeping the children busy, keeping herself too busy to think. Sunday afternoon Quentin Lacey drove up on the mine dump. Jenny went out to his car. He peered up from the window of the red Datsun. "Sure sorry to hear about your husband, Mrs. Williams."

Jenny said, "It's kind of you to drop by."

The real estate man cleared his throat. "I wanted to find out when you'll be leaving."

"Leaving?"

"Leaving the claim," Quentin Lacey said. "It was in your husband's name. It will revert to the Bureau of Land Management now."

Jenny felt an icy anger rise inside her. "I'm afraid you've got your facts wrong," she said. "This claim is also registered in my name at the BLM."

She was glad to see the surprise on the little vulture's face. He said, "You surely don't intend to mine this claim alone?"

"No, I don't. We both know that's against the mining safety regulations." Jenny said no more. The man didn't need to know all her business.

"But if you don't mine," the man persisted, "you'll lose the claim."

Why did all men assume she knew nothing? Jenny said, "If I do the assessment work, I can stay on my claim forever. As my husband told you, this land is zoned for mining."

She started to turn toward the cabin, but Quentin Lacey said, "Craggy Claims owns all the land around you, Mrs. Williams."

"How nice for Craggy Claims," Jenny said and went through the gate. Inside, she sat down at the table, her stomach quivering with her anger and a new fear. The real estate people were going to try to take the Spanish Mary away from her.

CHAPTER
53
▲▲▲▲▲▲

Billy said, "Did that man make you mad, Mama? Your face is all red."

"He certainly did." Jenny took the mining book from the shelf. "I think I'd better start reading about patent deeds."

Jenny studied the book until her stomach calmed down, and then she and Billy hauled firewood and water and fed Rosie.

After supper Jenny rocked the children and sang to them. They crowded her lap and the rocking chair, but Billy especially seemed to need closeness. He held Corey in his arms and leaned against his mother.

After Corey was asleep, Jenny knelt by Billy's mattress. The little boy's eyes were open.

"Can't you go to sleep, honey?"

"I'm waiting."

"What for Billy? What are you waiting for?"

"I'm waiting for Daddy to come home."

"Oh, honey," Jenny smoothed the hair from Billy's forehead. "Daddy's not coming home."

"I know," Billy said, "but I'm waiting anyhow." Jenny sat by the mattress with Billy's hand in hers until the wide eyes drooped and closed.

▽ ▽

It took Jenny almost two weeks to get one round drilled and shot, the overhang mucked out, and the ore mucked out and into the bin.

"I don't know what's the matter with me," she said to Tony. "I work so slowly; I can't seem to get into the rhythm."

"You shouldn't be working at all," Tony said. "You've had too much shock."

Jenny shook her head. "No, Tony. I need to work. The tunnel helps me."

▽ ▽

Mom Bradley and Ed O'Brien had brought Richard's truck to the Spanish Mary on Wednesday.

"I listed the café with Pitkin Realty," Mom had said. "We're going to go on down to Phoenix and get out of this cold."

Jenny had hugged her. "I'll miss you, Mom Bradley."

The older woman had smiled then. "You'll have to call me Mom O'Brien now."

Jenny had watched them go down Simpson Gulch with mixed feelings. Mom still seemed uncomfortable around her. When Jenny looked in the envelope that held the truck title, she found six hundred dollars in twenty-dollar bills. Her last salary as a waitress.

Richard's truck seemed to have demons of its own. After Jenny managed, with the help of a milk crate, to get up into the cab, she could get the engine started, but about half the time the transmission stuck in two gears, and she had to climb down again and crawl under the truck where Tony had shown her how to pry the shifting levers.

Tony said, "I don't think you ought to haul ore in that old truck. We'd better take mine."

Tony was coughing more often now, but when Jenny said, "Maybe *you* ought to follow Mom and Ed down to Phoenix," Tony said, "Now don't you nag me like my sister does. She lives just across the river from Yuma. She thinks the heat and dry air down there would do me good."

"You can't go," Jenny said. "You and I are the last of the people from below the dump."

"Tully Stocker's still down there," Tony said.

"I don't like to go by Mom's place now," Jenny said. "I wonder where everybody went when she closed up."

"The boozers can always find another spot," Tony said. "It's the truckers who probably miss Mom Bradley the most. She was a good cook."

The big blue and silver truck flashed through Jenny's mind. In the cedar chest, in the box Mr. McBride had given her after Mike's funeral, were four cards that had come with the flowers at the service. Jenny hadn't even opened the box until a week after the funeral. According to the cards, Natalie had sent a plant from everyone in the beauty shop; Mom Bradley and Ed had sent an arrangement. The Marshes had sent pink and white carnations. The fourth card held the mortician's note, "Red carnations." The formal message said, "With sympathy, David Garvey."

Jenny had not cried until she read David's card. The children had been sleeping; Tony had gone for the day. Jenny had finally felt up to facing the contents of the box. Mike's wallet was there: she couldn't look at it. She set it aside. There was a guest book, most of its pages blank. There were fifty thank-you cards with envelopes. Fifty! There were thirty-five copies of the little printed folder from the funeral service saying Mike's name and date of birth and date of death over and over again. She kept five of them and burned the rest. She looked at the flower cards last and came upon David's last of all. She didn't know how he found out about Mike, but the note in his handwriting brought his face and his blue eyes strongly into her mind. She began to cry.

She put her head down on the gold-covered guest book, and still holding David's card in her hand, she cried for Mike—for the way life had cheated him of his payload. She knew he hadn't meant to leave her in debt. The payload would have let him cover his tracks. But his death followed the pattern of his life, and all he had left behind were a few handmade things and a hollow-eyed little boy who looked up the mountain and waited. And a wife who hadn't loved him.

I think I was starting to love him. The thought made her cry harder and feel guiltier. I should have loved him. He helped me when I needed help. He took me in. She sounded as if she were arguing with Richard. She would probably argue with Richard in her mind for the rest of her life. Her mind felt hurt and hungry because of Richard.

You stupid, crazy, uncaring drunk. You had so much to give, and you soaked it in alcohol and threw it away, and you took so much away from me. But the words changed nothing at all. She missed Richard as much as she missed Mike. She finally stopped crying and stumbled to bed exhausted.

The next day she wrote thank-you notes for the flowers. When she went in with the children later for groceries, she took the notes to the post office. The postmistress said, "Do you want the mail from your box, Mrs. Williams?"

Dumb with surprise, Jenny nodded. She hadn't known that they had a box at the post office.

"Here you are," the postmistress said, handing her two envelopes. "And say, the box rent is due."

Still numb, Jenny paid the box rent and took the envelopes out to the truck. Both letters were from the bank, overdue notices on the old truck loan, one dated December, the other, January.

"What's that, Mama?" Billy asked.

"Paper for you to write on," Jenny said. "See, there's nothing written on the back."

$$\triangledown \quad \triangledown$$

When Jenny finished mucking out the ore they needed to replace the payload, they loaded it into Tony's truck. Jenny said, "Tell me what will happen at the mill. When can we expect to get paid for the ore?"

"They'll have to verify the weight and run the ore."

"I hope there's enough left over after the mill takes its cut to pay off the bank." Jenny smiled. "I'd like to give that Mr. Kingsley a real shock. He didn't mind at all tying up a widow's Social Security money for collateral."

"Bankers . . ." Tony said.

The trip to the mill was hard on Billy. Jenny tried to concentrate on business. The ore weighed out officially at just a little over twenty-five and a half tons. She sat Corey on the counter and signed the papers that got the milling process underway. She nodded when they told her she'd be notified when it was finished. But all the time, she was aware that Billy had last been here with Mike. He clung to Tony's hand, his face pale and pinched-looking.

As she looked at her little boy, Jenny wished they were back on the county dump hunting for treasures. He'll be ready for kindergarten next fall. I'll have to have a stake by then.

$$\triangledown \quad \triangledown$$

That thought gave Jenny new energy. When they got back to the mine, she began to work longer hours and to produce the way she had before.

One day at lunch, Tony said, "Have you seen Mike's powder magazine?"

"No," she said, "but I'm going to have to find it. I need more dynamite."

"Billy and I found it this morning. You wanna see it?"

"Of course I do."

With Corey in her arms, Jenny followed Tony and Billy up the hill behind Rosie's pen to the hollow in the hillside that indicated an old prospect hole. Nestled inside the hole was a tightly-built shed; the door had been padlocked, but the padlock was broken.

"I had to break it to get in," Tony said. "I brought another lock." He took the broken lock from the hasp and swung the door open. Jenny gasped.

After all of their drilling, the shed was still half full of powder boxes. The company had had good reason to fire her husband.

Jenny considered this new debt for a moment. I already paid this one, she thought. Maybe I didn't pay the company, but I've paid for this dynamite.

They took what she needed for the next round, and Tony put a heavy new lock on the door. He gave Jenny one key and kept the other.

▽　▽

Jenny drilled and loaded and shot and mucked out, with Rosie always there, waiting patiently and then heaving her shoulders forward and tightening up her small body to pull the ore car out of the tunnel.

As February slipped away and they came into March, the sun lingered, and the snow melted in the yard on the south side of the cabin. Tony took the children out to play most of each morning. Jenny sometimes watched for a moment. Corey was walking— lurching really—her fat bottom keeping her unbalanced. Mike had built this fence to protect Corey when she walked, but he had not been there to see her first steps. Jenny sighed and forced the thoughts away. There would be a thousand firsts that Mike would never see.

One day Billy said to Jenny, "I'm going to go rabbit hunting." He took a stick from the woodpile and went down to the far corner of the yard. That night after he was asleep, Jenny removed Mike's rifle and its rack from the cabin wall. She fastened them above the door inside the shop. She put the shells in their box on a shelf above the workbench and set a bucket of nails in front of them.

Each week when Jenny went to town to do the laundry and to pick up supplies, she checked the mailbox. But the letter from the mill wasn't there. She had her hair washed and her nails done. "Maybe I shouldn't spend the money," she said to Natalie, "but I get so grubby in that mine, I can't stand the way I look."

The hairdresser patted her shoulder and said, "You have to do something to keep your spirits up, honey." Jenny leaned her cheek for a moment against Natalie's hand and went home feeling less alone.

She continued to run the drill. In the tunnel, she could keep herself from thinking about Mike and Richard.

▽ ▽

On Sunday, the eleventh of March, the air was crisp—too cold outside for the children to be in the yard, but too nice to think of staying inside the cabin.

"Let's go to town and see a movie," Jenny said.

It made her feel good to hear Billy laugh at the cartoon characters in the movie, and for the first time she thought about getting a TV set. Mike had wanted one. Maybe Billy would find more things to laugh at.

As she drove back up Virgo Creek after the matinee, both children fell asleep. Just below the turnoff to the Spanish Mary on the Simpson Gulch road, Jenny jammed the brakes on, one hand reaching automatically toward the children who were strapped in.

Stretched across the road, totally blocking access to her turnoff, was a tight barbed-wire fence attached to steel posts. Jenny set the brake and turned off the motor. She got out to look at the fence, feeling confused and disoriented. The fence, with its mean bright barbs on the taut wires, had not been there that morning.

CHAPTER
54
▲▲▲▲▲▲

"What did you do?" Tony asked when Jenny told him about it Monday morning.

"At first I just stood there and felt like crying, but then, when I started thinking about how mean and petty it was, I got mad."

Jenny grinned at Tony. "The kids were sound asleep. I wasn't in any hurry. I got those big old wire cutters out of Mike's toolbox and I cut every single wire. You should have seen them writhe and curl. They hadn't been off the spool twenty-four hours." She laughed.

"When I looked at the fence posts, I knew Quentin Lacey had put up that fence. The posts weren't even tamped down. Billy would have known better. I just pulled them out and laid them in the ditch. Then I cut the wire in nice short strips and put them next to the posts. I took one strip of wire and wrapped it around the posts and the other wires. I looked around for one of those survey stakes Craggy Claims has all over the place, and I borrowed the red ribbon off of it. I tied a perky bow on the bundle of posts and wires."

Tony was laughing so hard he couldn't talk. Finally he took out his handkerchief, wiped his eyes, and blew his nose. "That ought to fix old Quent Lacey and Craggy Claims."

"At least they'll get the message that I know they can't legally block the road to my claim," Jenny said. She put on her tin pants and her overshoes. "I'm going to muck out the tunnel today, and then if I can get hold of Lloyd Daley I'm going to ask him to come up here and inspect the mine."

"Why take that chance?"

"Because if I don't, Quentin Lacey will pressure him into coming up here some time when I'm not prepared. What was that other safety equipment you said we needed?"

"They're called self-rescuers. You wear 'em on your belt in case you need to counteract carbon monoxide. They're good for about an hour, plenty of time to get out of a tunnel."

"Okay. We'll get those and a first-aid kit for the tunnel. That's going to be the cleanest, safest, best-looking mine in this district."

Jenny shoveled and hauled ore until every bit of pay dirt was in the bin. Then she made sure that all of the equipment was stored in the shop or safely confined in the tunnel.

Tuesday morning, Billy ran into the cabin. "Tony's down at the bridge, hollering. He's got two flat tires. There's sharp tacks all over the bridge. He wants a magnet."

Jenny found a big U-shaped magnet in the shop and hurried

down to help Tony. He was furious and muttered under his breath all the time they were dragging the magnet back and forth across the bridge.

They jacked up Tony's truck, put the spare on one side, and left it while Tony took the damaged tires to town in Richard's truck.

When Tony came back, he had the mine-safety equipment Jenny had mentioned, and Lloyd Daley was in the truck with him.

The mine inspector was very gentle with Jenny when he greeted her. After offering his sympathy about Mike's death, he said, "I hear somebody's trying to drive you off this claim. Don't you let 'em get to you, Mrs. Williams. Tony says you're a coolheaded, careful miner."

Jenny smiled and said, "Come into my tunnel and be honest with me, Mr. Daley. If there's anything unsafe in there, I want to know about it."

Tony started the generator; Mr. Daley and Jenny put on their hard hats and went into the mine. The inspector tested the stulls and picked at the ribs and back with a scaling bar. He looked at Jenny's equipment storage and sniffed the air. "You got good air in here," he said.

▽ ▽

Back outside, Mr. Daley said, "That tunnel looks better than any I've been in this year. You keep Tony here to help you when you work it and you've got nothing to worry about."

"Except Quentin Lacey," Jenny said.

"Well, I think Tony chewed on his ear awhile today. He may back off a bit."

Jenny invited the inspector to stay for lunch. Billy was drawn to the man. Mr. Daley took him on his knee and said, "I've got a grandson about your age."

After lunch Tony took Mr. Daley back to town. "Check the mail after you get your tires, will you?" Jenny said.

Billy was quiet after the men left. Jenny asked him to dry dishes. Corey was standing in front of her on a chair, flopping her hands in the dishwater.

· 318 ·

"Mama," Billy said. "I wish I had a grandfather." He touched his breastbone. "Mr. Daley made me feel good in here."

"Do you like to be around people, Billy?"

"I like going to town."

"I thought you liked the mountain."

"I do, and I like Rosie, but they make me lonesome for Daddy."

Jenny was quiet for a minute. She knew what he meant. Every place she looked, there was some reminder of Mike. She had given his clothes to Tony, but all of his tools and the things he'd built were still here. Would it be easier for them all if they moved to town?

She said to Billy, "You'll be five in two weeks. Next year, you can go to school."

Just then, Tony roared up onto the dump and came into the cabin, grinning broadly and waving a letter in his hand.

"It's from the mill."

Jenny's mouth went dry, and her hands trembled so, she could hardly open the envelope. "Oh, Tony!" She hugged the man tight. "Our ore only milled out to a little over one and a half ounces a ton, but we had twenty-five and a half tons, and our sixty percent comes to seven thousand, four hundred and eighty dollars and twenty-three cents. They've sent a check." She picked Billy up and danced around the room until she was dizzy.

Tony sat down at the table and smiled. Jenny said, "It's too late to go to the bank today, but will you stick around awhile? I've just got to go and drill some holes."

Tony seemed perfectly content to spend the evening listening to a high-school basketball game on the radio. Billy seemed happy just to hear the voices and the crowd noises.

▽　▽

As Jenny lined up the drill and got ready to begin a new arch hole, she was startled to discover that she was feeling a strong urge for sex. She got down from the box to consider her feelings.

I feel alive again. For the first time since Mike died, I'm not numb. Getting mad yesterday and getting excited today must have shocked my body. She leaned against the cold rock wall. Or maybe it's just the hope. Tomorrow I'll be out of debt. The next twenty-five tons are for me and the kids.

But the need for sex frightened her—her body seemed alien and untrustworthy. She thought of Mike's hands on her body, and before she could prevent it, she remembered David Garvey's mouth on hers, and a rush of heat went down her. She moved blindly toward the drill.

"I'll work it off," she said out loud and stepped back up on the box. She drove the drill steadily and pushed herself to change the steel faster. By the time she quit at about nine o'clock she had drilled two thirds of a round.

Tony looked up when she came into the cabin. "You trying to wear out that compressor?"

She smiled as she took off her gloves. "I may have finally stepped up to a new pace."

$$\triangledown \quad \triangledown$$

On Wednesday Jenny dressed in her matching skirt and sweater and wore her good coat. Tony watched the children in the truck while she went into the bank. She asked to see Mr. Kingsley.

The banker rose from his desk when she stepped into his office and said, "Is something the matter, Mrs. Williams?"

"No," said Jenny. She accepted the chair he offered and sat down. "I've come to pay off my loan."

The banker's eyelids flickered, but he said in a businesslike tone, "I'm surprised. You haven't had it very long."

When Jenny showed him the check, he suggested that she might wish instead to open a savings account.

"You ought to have an emergency fund," he said, "and, of course, you'd be earning interest."

"Not as much as I'm paying," Jenny said. She waited quietly while the banker asked his secretary to bring in Jenny's file. There was interest already due on the loan, but when the loan was paid off Jenny still had nearly thirteen hundred dollars.

"You aren't planning to close your checking account are you?" the banker asked.

"Not at this time," Jenny said. "I think it will be convenient to have my Social Security checks deposited directly to my account." She gathered up the canceled note and the deposit slip for the extra money.

The banker stood and walked with Jenny to the door of his office. He put his hand on her upper arm and let his fingers rest against her breast while he said, "I'm very happy for you, Mrs. Williams, that your ore proved out."

Jenny said, "Mr. Kingsley, please take your hand off my arm. I do not like to be touched by strangers."

The man dropped his hand, and his face turned bright red. Jenny lifted her head a little and left the bank feeling almost happy.

They went out to lunch, and Jenny said to Tony, "Since you won't take any of this money, let's go spend some of it. We'll get a battery-powered TV."

$$\triangledown \quad \triangledown$$

The TV worked fairly well after Tony ran an antenna wire partway up the hill. Jenny noticed that Tony was only a little less entranced with the TV than Billy, but Corey didn't pay much attention to it. She dressed Corey in warm clothes and took her along while she did the evening chores.

Jenny carried the water bucket in one hand and reached to her tiny daughter with the other, letting the baby walk until she was tired and then carrying her on one hip. As they moved slowly along, Jenny looked up at the mountain and then frowned. High up, at the very top, she could see the raw yellow color of a Craggy Claims house. When had they built up there?

Jenny returned to the cabin thinking, I've got the papers now to prove production. I better go see Mrs. Marsh. Maybe she knows a lawyer who can tell me how to get a patent deed.

CHAPTER

55

▲▲▲▲▲▲

Friday morning Jenny left Tony with the children while she drove into town. She stopped to talk to Mrs. Marsh and then drove to Mitchell to the office of the Bureau of Land Management.

On Monday, she loaded and shot the overhang. "If you feel up to it," Jenny said when she and Tony had counted the last shot, "we could haul ore twice this week, tomorrow and Friday, and still keep on schedule in the tunnel."

"Truck drivin's easier than baby-sitting that little girl," Tony said, his grin lightening the words. "She's always on the go."

They hauled ore on Tuesday, and Jenny mucked the overhang on Wednesday. As the pile dwindled, her "gambler's fever," as Tony called it, rose as high as ever. After she dumped the last load, she hurried back to the tunnel, her heart beating faster as she neared the face. What if it's gone? What if I'm stuck with twelve tons of dirt and nothing to get me to the payload?"

The excitement added to her pleasure when she saw the sparkling vein, wandering a little sideways, but on its same old course through the mountain. She shined her headlamp on the ore and ran her fingers across it.

On impulse, she decided to take her bath in the fall of mineral water in the short tunnel. She stripped and stood under the icy stream, shivering with the cold but welcoming the stinging spray that washed away the muck and left her skin tingling. She dried with her shirt, dressed again, except for the tin pants, shut off the generator, and went into the cabin.

"You haven't been working," Tony said. "You don't even look tired."

Jenny laughed. "I've been playing."

"You still got ore?"

"Faithful and true, my mountain has a heart of gold." She spread the tin pants behind the stove. "I'll shoot it tomorrow."

▽   ▽

They hauled ore on Friday. That night, Jenny wrote in her journal, "March 23. Two tons of ore in the bin in Mitchell."

Saturday she and the children went to town in Richard's balky truck for groceries and to look for mail. "I want a letter from the BLM," Jenny said to Billy.

"BLM," he said, trilling the *L* on his tongue. But there was nothing in the box.

When they got back to the mine, Jenny said, "You go get your red wagon and we'll bring the groceries in." She got out and took Corey into the house.

Billy ran in a moment later shouting, "Mama, the gate is busted. Rosie is gone."

Jenny ran to the pen and stood still. Someone had torn the gate from its hinges and thrown it on the ground. "Did Rosie kick the gate off, Mama?"

Jenny looked at the tool marks on the hinges and clenched her teeth. "No," she said, and went into the pen. The shop door was still closed and padlocked.

Jenny went to the cabin for the key. "You stay with Corey," she said to Billy. "Watch television. I'll see if I can find Rosie."

Sick at heart, she took a can of oats and went up the mountain and back again to the creek, rattling the can and calling the burro's name. Surely they wouldn't hurt a little old donkey. On her way up from a fruitless search along the creek, she thought of the dynamite magazine. Her breath quickened. "Please, God, don't let them have found the powder."

She hurried up the hill behind the pen. As she neared the prospect hole, her breath evened. The magazine was intact. As she started to turn back down the mountain, a familiar *huff-huff* came from the hole, and the little jenny stepped out from behind the powder shed, her ears pointed forward, her nose twitching toward the oats can. Jenny hugged Rosie and took her back to the pen.

The sight of the mangled hinges made her feel vulnerable. The harassment was getting too close. She fixed a temporary enclosure and went back to the cabin.

When the children took their naps, she lay down on the bed feeling desolate. If they'd just leave her alone, she could work the mine until she got a start. She wouldn't want to stay here forever. She didn't really know enough. What if the compressor quit for good? Or the drill stopped working?

But where else can I go? There are only eleven tons in the bin here; only two in Mitchell. And it's just like that man at the bank said: until the mill pays me, the ore has no value. I can't leave here with only a thousand dollars. Rent would eat that up in no time. She thought of the six thousand dollars she had just given to the bank, and a bitterness sharp as bile rose in her mind. Mike and Richard. She thought their names with anger and with sorrow, and at the same time she felt a hot return of sexual desire. "No," she said aloud.

She got up from the bed and went out into the chill March air. She ran through the gate and around the cabin and began to climb the hill, half running, sobbing with every breath. She finally stopped to rest, and looking up, she saw the windows of the ugly house at the crest. Feeling spied on and invaded, she turned and rushed back down the hill. She stumbled to the mine door and pulled it open. She moved into the tunnel until she was in total darkness. She leaned against the rib thinking wild thoughts: If I didn't have any responsibilities, if I didn't have any kids, I'd go to college and become a geologist and I'd buy me a whole mountain and hire a mechanic. And then I'd run the mine. I'd fill the bin with three hundred tons of ore. No small batches.

▽　▽

They hauled their third ton to Mitchell on Thursday. Friday they took the day off because it was Billy's fifth birthday, and he wanted to go to a movie.

The matinee didn't start until two, so they went to the park, where Billy dug his new birthday steam shovel into the sandpile, and Corey sat on the merry-go-round with a runny-nosed, solemn-eyed little boy while Jenny and the boy's mama took turns pushing.

The theater was next door to Pitkin Realty. Jenny paused to look at the picture of Mom's Bar and Café. The familiar little building in the photo made her feel homesick. My alma mater, she thought, wishing she could say it to Richard, who had taught her the Latin phrase. Jenny Norton Williams, graduate of Mom's Bar and Café. It hurt too much. She looked at the other photos, and a printed poster caught her eye. She called out, "Tony!", and he turned and came to where she stood. She pointed at the sign:

CRAGGY CLAIMS: Just $20,000 an acre for a glorious mountain view. Close to the major highway and the university town of Mitchell. Stores, banks, and conveniences in nearby Dolby. Will build to suit.

"Twenty thousand dollars!" Tony said. "That makes your claim worth a hundred thousand dollars just for the rocks and dirt."

"They can't put more than one house for every five acres," Jenny said.

"Don't count on it," Tony said. "If they ever get hold of the Spanish Mary they'll have the whole mountain sewed up. They'll never let another miner in there, and eventually they'll force a rezoning."

Jenny walked away from the realty window and joined the line of mothers with small children. Billy was chattering with the little boys as the line moved into the theater.

▽   ▽

By Monday, they all had coughs and runny noses. Tony came up to baby-sit, but his face was pale and he coughed constantly. Jenny stayed in the cabin. She gave everyone hot soup and cough syrup and Tylenol, even Tony. He didn't object when she said, "You'd better stay here tonight. You've got a fever." Jenny gave him the big bed, and she crawled in with Billy.

Late Tuesday afternoon Jenny took Tony to the emergency room at the hospital in Dolby. When she drove back on Wednesday Tony's sister was at the hospital.

"I'm sorry," Jenny said to the small dark-skinned woman who had introduced herself as Teresa Chase. "My children caught colds, and Tony got the bug from them."

Teresa looked at her oddly and said after a moment, "Mrs. Williams, my brother is dying of silicosis—from a lifetime of breathing rock dust."

▽　▽

When Jenny saw him later, Tony held out his hand. She clutched it, hating all the bottles and the awkward tube in his nose. "I'm going to have to skip out on you," he said. Jenny bent and kissed his cheek.

"Just get well," she said.

Tony said, "The doctor agrees with Teresa that I might fight this better at a lower altitude. Her stepson's coming out to drive us down to Yuma." He coughed and his voice was hoarse when he said, "I'm sorry I let you down. I hope you can hang on to the Spanish Mary."

CHAPTER

56

▲▲▲▲▲▲

J enny stayed out of the mine for three days. The children's colds cleared up rapidly. She played with Billy and his steam shovel in the sunny spot outside the front door, sang and read to the children, and did the chores and housework when there was something suitable for Billy on television.

Sunday night, after both children were asleep, knowing it was dangerous and against regulations, Jenny went into the tunnel and grimly mucked out the overhang. Monday night she shot the ore. Tuesday night she slept. Soon she had developed a regular routine. She rigged up a signal light on an extension cord, which she ran from the generator to the front gate and looped around the post before taking the bulb into the tunnel. She hung the bulb where she could see its glow, but far enough back so the flying rock wouldn't break it. She gave Billy a flashlight and showed him how to pull the plug from the cord.

"If you want me and I'm not in the cabin, if Corey cries, pull the plug, and I'll come right in."

She worked from around eight thirty, when the children were sound asleep, until one or two o'clock in the morning. During the day she napped when the children napped. Now she was seldom plagued by the sexual urges that had made her feel so miserable and guilty, especially when her thoughts were of David Garvey and not of Mike. The first time the signal light went off she dropped her shovel and ran. Billy was shining the flashlight toward the tunnel when she got to the gate.

"You came," he said.

She knelt and hugged him. "I said I would." She went back into the cabin with him and sat on his mattress.

"Mama," he said, "did Tony go with Daddy?"

Jenny's throat tightened, but she said lightly, "No, Tony went to Arizona to live by a big river in the sunshine."

"Everybody goes away from the mountain. Are we going to go away from the mountain?"

"Do you want to go away, Billy?"

"Will you come too?"

"Yes."

"Then I want to go and live in town and play in the park."

"Do you remember that ore bin in Mitchell?"

"Where Daddy took us to dump his dirt?"

"That's the one. When I dig enough dirt to fill that bin again, we can talk about moving to town."

"Can we take the cabin?"

"No, but we'll take the sled and the wagon and the rocking chair and Mama's cedar chest."

"And the chairs and the table and the crib and my mattress and Rosie," Billy said.

"If you say so," Jenny said, "but I have a lot of dirt to dig first."

"You go dig dirt, Mama. I'll unplug the light if Corey cries." Billy's voice sounded sleepy. Jenny stayed until he was deeply asleep again and went back to the tunnel feeling lonely.

If I leave, I may never get back to any mountain at all. The brochure about correspondence courses lay on the kitchen table, but she hadn't had time or energy to fill out the form.

$$\triangledown \quad \triangledown$$

By Tuesday, April 17, when Jenny took the children to town for groceries and mail, she had sixteen tons of ore in the bin on the Spanish Mary, but only the three tons she and Tony had hauled in the bin in Mitchell.

At the post office, they discovered that Tony had sent three picture postcards from Arizona. The other mail was a deposit slip from the bank for her first Social Security check and a long envelope from the BLM.

Billy loved the colored pictures of an Indian and the red rocks in the Grand Canyon, but best of all, he liked the picture of the big locomotive in Yuma, Arizona. He liked to say "Yuma, Arizona." Jenny helped him nail the colored pictures above his bed.

Then she showed him the letter from the government. "*I* like to say BLM," she said to Billy, trilling the *L*. "The BLM, the wonderful Bureau of Land Management has accepted the *old* official survey of the Spanish Mary and my *new* production records. The BLM is going to issue a patent deed to Jenny Norton Williams, now that the state has agreed that there was no estate to probate and I am not tied up in a legal tangle."

Billy wrinkled his face. "You don't look tied up and tangled."

Jenny picked him up by his armpits and swung him around and around. When they fell laughing on his mattress, Jenny said, "I am not tied up and tangled because Mrs. Marsh is a wonderful woman, and she has a smart lawyer, who is worth the money I gave him."

"Mama," Billy said. "I like it when you laugh."

That evening Jenny filled out the form for a correspondence course in college English and enclosed a check. On Wednesday night she mucked the ore. Thursday morning at breakfast she said to Billy, "I've got twenty tons of dirt in our bin."

"What's twenty tons?"

"Almost enough for a payload."

"A payload means money," Billy said. "Daddy told me that."

▽ ▽

Thursday night Jenny drilled a whole round. The mountain seemed softer. The drill bit deep and moved in fast. Friday night after the children were asleep, Jenny started the generator to give her lights in the shop and began to make up caps and fuses. She was reaching for the crimping pliers when a man spoke her name. She whirled around, dropping the fuse and the pliers. Tully Stocker stood in the doorway.

CHAPTER
57
▲▲▲▲▲▲

"What are you doing here?" Jenny said, her heart pounding inside her chest.

"I told you you would pay, bitch, and now you're going to." Tully Stocker's eyes were red, but not bleary, as she'd seen them when he was really drunk. "I know you're all alone up here," he said, "since that old Dago went to Arizona."

Jenny reached behind her and felt along the bench, but her hands closed on nothing. Before she could do anything else, Tully Stocker had lunged across the shop and grabbed her arm, twisting it behind her as he reached inside her jacket for the buttons on her shirt. She began to kick at him with her heavy boots, twisting her body from side to side. He tightened his grip on her arm and with a vicious jerk of his other hand, pulled away the front of her shirt. He grabbed at her bra and made a deep growling sound in his throat as her breast came free of the cloth. Jenny began to beat at his face with her hand, pushing him toward the door of the shop with her body. He stumbled against the powder box and loosened his grip. Jenny gave him a hard shove, and he went through the door, sprawling into Rosie's pen.

Jenny jumped up on the box and grabbed the rifle from its rack. Tully Stocker had climbed to his feet. He came toward her cursing, but he stopped. In the light from the shop she saw his eyes go wide and then focus on the barrel of the rifle, which she held steady, pointing it right at his chest. He took a step backward. Jenny took a step forward. The man raised one hand as if to shield himself and kept moving back. Jenny stepped forward again, and Tully Stocker disappeared into the darkness toward the back fence.

Jenny stepped out of the light herself just as Tully Stocker gave a terrified scream. She saw the dark shape of Rosie's head rise and then go down as her body whirled. Rosie kicked Tully Stocker with both hind feet. Jenny saw the shadows connect and heard the sound of bone against bone.

Tully Stocker cried out again and began to hobble toward the fence. He didn't even try for the gate. He began climbing the fence, and Jenny heard him hit the ground on the other side as she ducked back into the shop and reached for the box of rifle shells.

By the time the gun was loaded Tully Stocker had opened the door of his pickup, which was parked just below Richard's truck on the road toward the bridge. Jenny walked toward Richard's truck, and when she reached it, she rested the gun carefully on the side of the bed and leaned it against the cab, with the barrel pointed at the sky.

When she pulled the trigger the explosion sounded like a whole box of powder. The gun bucked out of her hands and lit in the back of the truck. Tully Stocker ground the starter on his truck and ground it again. When it took hold, Jenny heard him gun the engine. By the time he hit the bridge, Billy was at the yard gate.

Jenny closed her coat and buttoned it and then went to Billy.

"That was a noisy truck, Mama," he said. "It made a big bang and waked me up. Who was it?"

"Just someone who didn't know where he was going and got what he had coming."

Jenny took Billy back to bed. She didn't light the lantern. She had no idea what she looked like. Her arm ached where Tully Stocker had grabbed her. Her heart was still bouncing around in her chest. She sang to Billy in a voice that trembled at first, but then steadied and stayed on tune. When Billy was asleep, she checked Corey, thinking, Bless that little sleeper. Corey was breathing softly and regularly.

Jenny took the water bucket with her to the shop. She washed herself and looked at her wounds. Her upper right arm was bruised, there was a scratch just above her breast, and three fingernails were broken. She buttoned her coat and went out into the darkness to find Rosie. The burro seemed jumpy, but calmed as Jenny caressed her and praised her. After a while Jenny went back to the shop.

She held her hands out in front of her. They were steady. She looked around on the floor and found the crimping pliers and the cap and fuse. She made up enough fuses to shoot the overhang. She took the powder and fuses into the tunnel and came back and plugged in Billy's signal light. She hesitated at the cabin door. Should she lock it? That would frighten Billy. She finally decided to leave it unlocked. Tully Stocker would not return tonight. He was too much of a coward to face a loaded gun.

In the dark tunnel again, she took a deep breath, aimed her headlamp at the face, and began loading drill holes. By midnight she was ready to fire the round.

As she stood at the tunnel mouth counting shots, two things occurred to her: if the residents of Craggy Claims had heard the rifle they probably thought it was dynamite; and the residents of Craggy Claims were probably going to start complaining about these midnight rounds. She closed the tunnel door and went back to the shop. After taking two bullets from the ammunition box she hid it again behind the can of nails. She locked the door, retrieved the gun from the truck, and loaded it. Inside the cabin she put the gun down between her bed and the wall, put on her nightgown and her robe to cover her bruises, and went to bed.

$$\triangledown \quad \triangledown$$

She woke when she heard the sound of an engine and pulled the rifle up onto the bed. It was broad daylight, and the engine noise came from Quentin Lacey's red Datsun. She dressed quickly. Billy was just waking. She picked up the rifle and took it with her as she went out the door.

The real estate man's eyes flared slightly when he saw the gun, but he said, "Good morning, Mrs. Williams. How are you?"

"I'm just fine," Jenny lied. Her arm and her head both throbbed. The sunlight made the pain in her head feel even worse. She squinted, and it felt like a scowl. "What can I do for you?"

Quentin Lacey glanced toward the gun and said, "I've come to make you what we consider a generous offer. Craggy Claims will pay you five thousand dollars to give up your claim to the Spanish Mary."

"Five thousand dollars?" The pain in Jenny's head angled across her temple and pulsed like a drill in a cut hole. She was suddenly furious. Here was another damn coward who was trying to rape her.

She looked into the eyes of the small face framed by the Datsun window, and she spat the figure back at him. "Five thousand dollars! You intend to sell it for a hundred thousand, and you offer me five thousand."

"That's quite a bit for a filed claim," the man said.

"I don't have a filed claim to this land," Jenny said, enjoying the surprised look on Quentin Lacey's face before she added, "I have a patent deed."

"A patent deed!"

"A patent deed," Jenny said, "and it's for sale for fifty thousand dollars."

Quentin Lacey went pale. "That's a lot of money, Mrs. Williams."

"Not as much as a hundred thousand," Jenny said.

"I'll have to get back to you on this," the real estate man said.

"Get in touch with my lawyer, Charles J. Harris," Jenny said. Again she enjoyed the look of shock that crossed the face in front of her. Poor man, she thought, you don't know that Tully Stocker got here first.

▽   ▽

When the Datsun bounced over the Simpson Creek bridge, Jenny sat down on the ground by the gate and unloaded the gun. After putting the gun on the rack in the shop, she spotted a piece of blue material on the ground in the pen. She picked it up and recognized the back pocket of a man's trousers—the back pocket and the pants fabric behind it, slightly spotted with blood. For a minute she didn't know how it had gotten there, and then she realized that before Rosie had kicked Tully Stocker she had bitten his bottom.

Jenny began to laugh, but her laughter soon changed to hysterical crying. She leaned on the fence and sobbed, unable to stop even when Billy tugged at her sleeve. Billy began to cry, too, and when Jenny stumbled into the house, Corey was wet and crying in her crib.

Jenny cried while she changed the baby, trying to stop, but beginning anew with each breath. She finally grabbed a cloth and dunked it into the water bucket and then held it, sopping wet, against her face. The cold water made her take a deep breath, and her sobs subsided into hiccups and finally quit. She washed the children's faces and her own again and then fixed breakfast.

Billy watched her silently. After breakfast she took him into the rocking chair, and rocking slowly, she said, "Billy, mamas are just like everybody else. Sometimes when they feel bad, they have to cry, and when they feel real bad, they can't stop crying."

"Why do you feel bad, Mama?"

Jenny rocked quietly for a moment, and then she said, "Billy, just like you, I miss Daddy. Things happen that wouldn't happen if your daddy were here."

"You never said you missed Daddy."

Jenny was startled. Billy was right. She had never told him that she grieved for Mike too.

"Every time I look at the pretty cedar chest Daddy made, I think about him," Jenny said. "There will always be something that reminds me of your daddy, like this little piece of hair on top of your head. It looks just like the one on your daddy's head."

Billy reached up to touch the lock of hair. He smiled a little. "But Billy," Jenny said, "even if we miss Daddy, we have to try to go ahead and make a good life. It wouldn't be fair for you and Corey to be sad all the time. We have to make sure you have happy lives."

"It's not fair for *you* to be sad and cry," Billy said. "You should have a happy life."

Jenny hugged him close, for a moment too touched to speak. "I do have a happy life," she said. "I've always got you and Corey, and I've had some good friends. Richard helped me to study. Mom Bradley had my hair fixed and gave me a job. Tony taught me how to drill. And David Garvey gave you a ride in a big truck and gave me this rocking chair."

"Do I remember riding in a big truck?" Billy asked.

"I don't know, honey. Do you?"

Billy thought for a minute and said, "Yep. I remember riding in a big truck." Jenny smiled. Billy said, "Is the man in the red car your friend?"

Jenny laughed then. "Not exactly, Billy, but maybe he's going to help us to have a better life."

▽ ▽

Jenny took the children outside in the afternoon to see if they could find a spring flower. "After all," she said to Billy, "Corey will be a year old a week from tomorrow, and she was born in the spring." To her surprise, Billy actually found a fuzzy pasqueflower on the sunny side of the house.

Sunday night Jenny mucked the overhang, and Monday she shot the ore. When she went into town on Tuesday Natalie and Alice scolded her for her ragged nails and unkempt hair.

"I came in here to have you fix me up," Jenny said, sinking into the chair with a sigh of pleasure. Billy and Corey played on the floor nearby. After they left the beauty shop Jenny did the laundry and loaded up on burro feed and groceries.

When they stopped at the post office they found a letter from Jenny's lawyer. When the BLM issued her patent deed, Craggy Claims would pay her fifty thousand dollars for it. Numb with surprise, Jenny read the rest of the letter. There would be a generous down payment, but she didn't have to leave until she got her next check from the mill. Mr. Harris would arrange the rest of the payments over a period of time to ease her capital gains loss. Capital gains. She knew Richard had talked about that in the same math session when he'd made her learn to spell *collateral*. She couldn't remember. She shook her head and stared again at the letter. There was a paper for her to sign. Feeling light-headed, Jenny went back into the post office to use the pen.

When she had mailed the paper to Mr. Harris, Jenny went to Ben Franklin and bought herself a new shirt. She let Billy pick a book for Corey's birthday and she chose a windup music box in the shape of a clock and a cloth sack full of colored blocks. Corey jabbered and waved her arms around in the cart; the other shoppers smiled her way.

"Are we going to a movie on Corey's birthday?"

"No, Billy. I think we'll just bake her a little birthday cake and stay home."

On Wednesday night Jenny mucked the ore. The letter from her lawyer didn't seem real. She could count on the tunnel. She wasn't sure about anything else.

"I think I've got enough ore in the bin now," Jenny said to Billy on Thursday morning, "but I'm going to drill one more round, to be sure we'll have twenty-five tons."

She drilled on Thursday night and shot the overhang on Friday. Saturday, while the tunnel was airing out, Jenny cleaned the cabin and baked a birthday cake for Corey. Billy licked the frosting dish. They put new batteries in the TV and watched a show about animals in Africa.

"There's a lot to learn from TV," Jenny said. "I should have got us one sooner. You'll have to watch every good show and catch up by fall."

That night Jenny wrote in her journal:

> Approximately twenty-three tons in the bin on the Spanish Mary. Three tons in the bin in Mitchell. If I had a decent truck, I could get the money for the ore. If I had the money for the ore, I could get a decent truck. I hope the BLM doesn't take forever to get the rest of the paperwork done on that patent deed. Mr. Harris can't take Craggy Claims's wonderful money until he gives them the deed.

It made her feel empty to think of selling her mountain, and she sat for a long time, pencil in hand, just staring into space. But she slept well and woke early to sing "Happy Birthday" as she changed Corey in her crib. They all went out to feed Rosie, and just as Rosie took an apple from Corey's hand a blue and silver pickup came over the bridge and onto the Spanish Mary. David Garvey got out with his arms full of packages.

Jenny stood still, her hand on the fence. The spring sunshine was lemony silver on the budding aspens behind David's head. Her heart, which seemed to have stopped for a moment, began bouncing a pulse in her throat. Billy tugged on her hand. "Mama, we've got company."

Jenny moved slowly forward, holding on to Corey's hand and letting the little girl walk. Billy ran to the yard, climbed up on the gate, and stared at the man. Jenny stopped in front of Bigfoot, who smiled and said, "I hope I'm not too late for the birthday party."

Suddenly Billy jumped down and shouted, "Mama, I do remember. I rode in a big truck, and we went to a hospital to get Corey, and I galloped on his foot."

Jenny heard Mike's words: *Billy was bouncing on the biggest foot I ever saw.* She smiled down at Billy and then raised her eyes to David's face, pain and joy bright-edged and bitter in her mouth. She said, "You're just in time for breakfast."

David stepped into the cabin and put his packages down on the table. Jenny put Corey into the crib, where she promptly stood up and rattled the bars, looking at the big man as he sat down in the chair that Mike had built. Billy was on his knees on a chair, looking at the packages.

"Would you like a cup of coffee?" Jenny said as she put wood on the fire. It helped her to notice that David seemed as nervous as she felt. He glanced several times at the rocking chair but didn't mention it.

"Billy," Jenny said, "would you like to show Mr. Garvey where we get our water?" She handed the bucket to the boy, and the two males went out the door. Jenny picked up her daughter. She held the baby's soft cheek close to her own for a minute. Then she put Corey back in the crib and said to her, "He's the only person who came into the café that I never told you about."

▽　▽

During breakfast David talked to Billy and Corey and asked Jenny questions about mining. It was easy for Jenny to talk about the mountain. She told him how Tony had helped her, and she described the routine in the tunnel. She wanted to ask him about his work, but she felt uncomfortable about that.

He said, "Does Tony live in Dolby?"

"Tony went to Yuma, Arizona," Billy said.

"For his health," Jenny said. "I hated to see him go. I haven't done a day of legal mining since he left."

"Jenny," Bigfoot said, "have you been mining that tunnel alone?"

She nodded. "At night when the kids are asleep." She looked at him for a minute. "But I'm almost done. I have enough ore in the bin to meet the requirements at the mill, and I've sold the Spanish Mary." The words made Jenny understand completely that she had, indeed, signed a paper agreeing to sell the claim.

"What are you going to do?"

"I'm going to college," Jenny said. She smiled a little before adding, "If I can ever get that ore off the mountain." She told him about the gears on Richard's truck and then asked, "Do you know a local trucker? I can pay to hire a truck, but I don't know anyone."

David Garvey smiled. "Sure. I can set up something for you."

Jenny felt more comfortable. She wasn't asking for favors; this was a business arrangement. As she cleared away the dishes Jenny blessed the money in her checking account. So many things changed when you were able to say, "I can pay." Richard would tell me that I'm turning into a cynic, she thought, pouring hot water into the pan, and for the first time she realized that as long as she still had mental conversations with Richard, he would stay alive. Like the unruly lock of hair on Billy's head that was Mike's mark in the world, the unruly twist of Jenny's thoughts carried Richard forward.

David Garvey was entertaining Billy and Corey. When Jenny finished the dishes, she said, "Let's put the children on Rosie, and we'll show you the mountain."

As they walked slowly up the hill behind the cabin with the burro and the children between them, Jenny and Bigfoot talked or were silent, and either way, it felt sweet to Jenny. Nothing ended or began. She concentrated on the moment as if she were in the tunnel with her headlamp lighting one small circle on the face.

▽ ▽

The birthday party was fun. David had brought party hats and noisemakers. And with every package for Corey, there was one for Billy. There were two blue and silver trucks, with trailers hitched on behind and hinged cargo doors opening at the back of the trailers. There were books. And last of all were a folding chair with the back in the shape of a clown's head for Billy and a small glossy rocking chair for Corey. At the sight of the little rocker, Jenny's pulse quickened. She found it hard to look at David; he said rather abruptly, "I might as well take one load of that ore to Mitchell on my way through." He stood up.

Jenny said, "Let me put the children down for their naps and I'll help you load it." She was afraid that Billy would be too excited to sleep, but the long walk on the mountain had tired him out, and he finally drifted off.

Feeling relieved, then guilty, and then so nervous her hands trembled, Jenny went out to the bin, where David had already loaded the bed of his pickup with ore.

He came back up to the top of the dump, and they leaned their arms against the corral fence. After a silence David said, "Jenny, what happened? I don't know why you stopped speaking to me."

"Two things happened," Jenny said. She hesitated and then asked, "Why didn't you ever tell me you owned Tulsa Trucking; that you weren't just a relief driver?"

David turned and looked down at her. "At first, there wasn't much opportunity, Jenny. When we talked, we talked about you."

Jenny realized that this was true, and she felt the heat rise to her face. She looked down, but David continued. "And later, when I wanted to tell you, I realized that if I did, you wouldn't have stayed friends with me. You had so much damn pride."

Jenny lifted her head sharply. "When you don't have anything else, your pride is important. You don't know the difference skill and money make in the way you feel."

"Yes, I do," said David Garvey. "I started out with one old beat-up truck, worse-looking than that." He gestured toward Richard's pickup.

They stood for half an hour there by the fence. Rosie poked her nose through the bars and snuffled for an apple, but gave it up and went back to the bale of hay in her trough when they ignored her. Jenny asked David questions, first about Tulsa Trucking and then about his life. When their conversation finally slowed, Jenny said, "Would you like to see the tunnel?"

She checked on the children, started the generator, and got a hard hat for David from the shop. "We can't go all the way to the face," she said, "and I can't show you the vein, because I haven't mucked out the overhang."

David moved slowly along the rail, occasionally bumping his hard hat against the lower ceiling where the rib sloped down.

"There used to be more stalactites," Jenny said, "but the blasting loosened a lot of them."

He was interested in everything—the timbering, the ties and rails, and the statistics about the ore. They stopped at the muck pile, and Jenny said, "This is where I spend my nights."

"Jenny." David was not looking at the muck pile. "You said two things happened. What was the other one?"

Jenny glanced away, and then she met his eyes. "You kissed me." In the silence she could hear the waterfall at the far end of the tunnel and the generator rumbling in the shop.

Finally David said, "Was it so wrong to kiss you?"

Jenny said, "All my life, men have just reached out and taken hold of me, pinched off a little part here, patted another little part there. They never asked—they just took. Just like they took from my mother before me."

The silence was long again, and David did not break it. Jenny said, "I thought you were my friend. Why did you kiss me?"

Even in the wan light of the bulb above them, Jenny could see the feeling gathering in David's blue eyes. He said, "You were so hurt, and so little. Oh damn it, Jenny. I've wanted to kiss you ever since I pulled you off that thorn bush. And I've loved you since the moment you sat in my truck holding that enormous belly in your hands and joking despite the pain. Oh, God, Jenny, you did look like Humpty Dumpty." He smiled, a small wry smile that made his mouth crooked, but he did not reach out to her. Jenny knew he never would again unless she did something right now.

She raised her hand and took off her hard hat, setting it on the muck pile. "It would just fall off anyway," she said to David, "if you were to kiss me again."

He took one step forward and she took two, and he gathered her close to his hard, lean body and kissed her until she forgot about the tunnel and the mountain. When she remembered them again it was because the generator had stuttered and gone out, and she and Bigfoot were standing in the dark.

$$\triangledown \quad \triangledown$$

Sunday night, after David had driven across the Simpson Creek bridge and away from the Spanish Mary with a ton of Jenny's ore in his truck, after evening chores and supper, after the children were asleep, Jenny turned on the generator, plugged in the signal light, and went to muck the rock in the tunnel. She gave Rosie an apple when she turned her around and hooked her on the other end of the car.

"I've worked off a lot of unhappiness in this tunnel," she said to the burro. "Let's hope happiness is made of tougher stuff."

As she worked, she thought about Mike and Richard and David. Billy's memories of his daddy will fade, and I'll never know what pictures Corey keeps. David won't want to hear about the men in my past. She threw a shovelful of rock into the car. But they'll hang in my thoughts sometimes, like the mist in the pines on winter mornings and the scent of the cedar in the box with a lid that Mike made for me. She scooped up the last of the rock from the muck plate and tossed it into the car. "And Richard might call them my demons," she said to Rosie as she picked up the halter rope, "but I guess they're just old friends." She unharnessed the burro and fed her some oats, and then she went back into the tunnel with the familiar rise of excitement. Whether she planned to mine it or not, she wanted to see the vein.

▽   ▽

But there wasn't any vein. A small silver line marked the front part of the ledge. After that, as far back as her headlamp would shine, Jenny could see no sign of ore. The fine quartz gangue was gone as well. The rock in the hole was yellowish-gray.

Jenny shivered from the shock of loss. "Pinched out," she said aloud, feeling betrayed.

And then she remembered that Quentin Lacey and Craggy Claims had just agreed to pay her fifty thousand dollars to get her to leave the mine. Jenny began to laugh. She pounded her fist on the rib of the tunnel and whooped with laughter. "You old mountain, you crazy old mountain. They always said you held your treasures dear, but nobody ever told me you had a sense of humor."

Finally, Jenny wiped her eyes, looked around the tunnel one more time, and went out of the mine, locking the door behind her. She shut off the generator and stood still, waiting while silence and darkness returned to the Spanish Mary.